ATTACK FROM ABOVE!

Like most low-level fighter attacks, the troops near the target never heard the jet coming. One moment the only noise rustling through the 11th NS positions was the gurgling of the river running by; in the next, the air was filled with a horrible mechanical scream.

The Harrier flashed by their positions at top speed, the exhaust from the engine creating a steamy turbulence on the river's surface. It was by them before any of the soldiers could react, sweeping from side to side before it streaked underneath the bridge and up into an ass-end climb.

Coming back around, the Harrier slowed its speed down to 300 mph, flying at a louder, slightly higher altitude.

The NS troops were ready for it this time, and they took the only action afforded them: they blocked their ears. The 11th was not outfitted with any kind of anti-aircraft weapons and was absolutely defenseless from the air.

And that's exactly what the pilot in the Harrier wanted to know.

WINGMAN

RETURN FROM THE INFERNO
MACK MALONEY

ZEBRA BOOKS
KENSINGTON PUBLISHING CORP.

ZEBRA BOOKS

are published by

Kensington Publishing Corp.
475 Park Avenue South
New York, NY 10016

First printing: September, 1991

Printed in the United States of America

Prologue

The clattering of horses' hooves galloping at full charge cracked like thunder against the asphalt of the abandoned highway.

There were twenty horsemen in all. Ten riding at top speed in front of the rumbling tractor trailer truck; ten behind. There were also three battered HumVees in the strange caravan. All of them were at the rear of the column, their gunners firing .50 caliber heavy machine guns wildly at the army of pursuers less than a quarter mile behind.

Captain "Crunch" O'Malley was behind the wheel of the last HumVee in line. More accustomed to piloting his famous F-4X Super Phantom than this four-wheel monster without shock absorbers, O'Malley was doing all he could just to keep the truck steady on the cratered, unlit highway. It was the dead of night and the only illumination was coming from the frightening flare of Katyusha rockets exploding all around them, plus the larger explosions off to O'Malley's right which told him that the enemy was zeroing in on them with long-range 122 mm artillery.

"Goddamn, are we going to make it?" he yelled up at his gunner.

The gunner—a sergeant in the now defunct Pacific American militia—slapped another belt of ammunition into his big .50 and kept right on firing.

"Not if we don't reach the bridge damn quick!" he yelled back.

The bridge was a mile ahead of them. The lead men on horseback, remnants from the Pacific American militia's single cavalry unit, would reach it in a matter of minutes. Could they deploy

5

their explosive charges in enough time for the trailer truck, the HumVees and the rest of the horsemen to cross the span, and then destroy it before their well-equipped, ruthless enemies finally caught up with them?

O'Malley looked in his rearview mirror and knew it would be very, very close.

I wish the old Wingman was still around, he thought. *We could sure use him now. . . .*

If they were lucky at all, it was because their pursuers were driving armored personnel carriers and light-armored vehicles, making their top speed only slightly less than that of the overloaded trailer truck and the winded, but determined, cavalry horses.

More 122-mm shells came crashing down in front of them as the ragged, harried procession rounded a long bend on what used to be California State Highway 15.

By the flash of these explosions, "Crunch" could see the charge of enemy APCs and LAVs closing in on his tail.

Once again, a desperate thought crossed his mind. *What would Hawk do?*

Major Hashi Nushi Three was the commander of the hundred-man, fifteen-vehicle mechanized column pursuing the ragged Pacific American soldiers.

He was new to the California theater of action, having come in on the third invasion wave which had landed just two weeks before on the beaches of Ventura. At the time, Nushi had been upset at his commanders. He considered it an insult to be kept in one of the invasion ships for so long before finally being allowed to land and join the conquest. This was especially grating as his grand uncle, Hashi Nushi One, was the Imperial Commander of all the Asian Forces.

By the time his unit hit the beach, much of the fighting on the West Coast of America was over. The much weakened Pacific American Army, depleted by the wars in the eastern part of the country, proved to be little match for the invading armies of the Combined Greater East Asia Divine Warriors' Association. Indeed, much of the Pacific American Army surrendered lest the overwhelming Asian Forces make good on their promise to destroy one major city along the West Coast and immolate their populations in the process.

It was no idle threat. The Asian Forces had happily provided information to the Pacific American Army on two *Fire Bats* submarines which were on station in the Gulf of Santa Catalina. Each one carried a nuclear-tipped, ballistic missile in its launch chamber.

With the fight for California nearly over, Nushi was pleased to get the assignment to hunt down and liquidate the last remaining enemy armed force inside the newly claimed territory.

He knew very little about this ragtag band of soldiers, just that they numbered less than thirty, they were lightly armed, and were relying mostly on horses for transport. They'd been slowly moving eastward since the first days of the Asian Forces' invasion, committing various acts of sabotage along the way. This included destroying many of the main power stations around Los Angeles, which was now the site of the Asian Forces' main headquarters for the conquered portion of southwest America. Now it appeared as if the small enemy unit was making a break for the San Bernardino mountains to the east—and the unsettled, yet unconquered lands beyond.

Nushi's orders were to stop them and he'd been attempting that since early morning. But the enemy soldiers were doing strange things, not the least of which was driving the tractor-trailer truck. The large rig had been slowing them down all day. If they had stuck to the horses and their small combat vehicles they would have been in the mountains hours ago.

Nushi didn't know what was inside the truck—nor did he care much. He had little respect for the enemy or their stupid antics, therefore they were not worthy of his examination. Nushi just assumed that when he finally caught up with the elusive Americans the mystery of why they would sacrifice time and speed for the truck's cargo would be revealed.

The enemy was just a half mile ahead now, right around the bend in the highway. Nushi's LAV was in the lead, its gunner firing nonstop at the fleeing Americans, while his radio man was calling in the big 122-mm artillery rounds from a mobile firebase five miles to the south.

Nushi confidently ordered his second radio man to call back to the main headquarters to tell them that their quarry was in sight and would soon be destroyed.

Less than a minute later, Nushi's column roared around the bend in the highway to find the 150-foot bridge which spanned a wide dry gorge was still intact.

But not for long.

Suddenly three 122-mm shells flashed out of the sky and came crashing down dead center on the bridge. There was a huge explosion that was so sudden and violent that all of the drivers in Nushi's column instinctively slammed on their brakes.

Nushi was almost ejected from his turret by the screeching stop. Once he regained his balance, he peered through the smoke, dust, and flame to see that most of the bridge was gone.

He was stunned by this sudden turn of events. Kicking his driver on the back of his head, he indicated he wanted to move right up to the edge of the ruptured span. The rest of the column followed.

Beyond the separated bridge, the hills began. But where were the Pacific Americans? There was no way they had time to cross the span before his artillerymen had dropped it. So where were they?

He ordered his driver to stop completely as soon as they reached the edge of the wrecked and smoking bridge.

"Ssshh!" he hissed to his men.

Suddenly it was very quiet. There was no noise—no engines, no horses' hooves, no whispered voices.

Where could they be?

That was when he heard it.

The strain of a truck engine, not too far off. He turned his vehicle's powerful spotlight to his right and discovered a narrow service road which led down into the dry riverbed. Lifting the beam up slightly, he caught the reflection of the rear of the tractor-trailer truck about a quarter mile away.

He had them.

Cautiously, he directed his column down the service road and out onto the dry riverbed. All the while he kept the Americans captured in the searchlight. It was rather a pathetic scene. Many of the horsemen had dismounted and the gang of

8

Americans were desperately trying to push the squealing, skidding tractor trailer up the sharp incline of the far bank.

He laughed once and checked his watch. It was exactly midnight. Perfect, he thought. He would begin this glorious day by annihilating the last pocket of enemy resistance in the newly conquered land.

That was when the ground beneath his vehicle started shaking.

He turned left and right, trying frantically to find the source of the increasingly violent rumbling.

Suddenly one of his junior officers cried out, *"Tsunami!"*

Nushi spun around and saw to his horror an immense wall of water bearing down on them from the opposite end of the wash.

"The gods no!" Nushi screamed. The gigantic rush of water had appeared so suddenly, it didn't look real somehow.

But it was too late to escape, too late to scream anything else. Too late to do anything but await the deadly wave of rushing water.

In his last instant of life, the terrified Nushi knew he would spend eternity wondering from where did the tidal wave come.

The Pacific American column continued on into the night, reaching the rugged hills around Soda Lake by 4 AM.

Only then did they stop to rest.

The horses were brought down into a shallow ravine, where they were fed and lightly watered. The truck was backed into a rocky blind and quickly covered with desert camouflage netting as were the HumVees. A watch was posted and the rest of the men sacked out for what could only be a three-hour sleep until it was light and time to move again.

"Crunch" didn't even bother to bed down. He hadn't slept in days and didn't figure to start now. Instead he climbed the tallest hill and sat next to the young Pacific American soldier on watch and stared out toward the west.

He had no idea what had happened back at the dry river; no idea where the massive wave of water had come from. What he did know was it had saved their lives and vanquished their enemies. But strange as it was, "Crunch" realized it was only a very temporary victory. He'd been in too many wars to think of it as

9

anything else. The Asians would be after them again by sunrise, with their vicious combination of massive numbers and fanatical determination.

Sometimes it seemed that there was no stopping them.

"Crunch's" small band of cavalry and mismatched soldiers had taken out about six hundred of the enemy in the past few weeks and still they kept on coming at them. Like one long human wave, streaming over the Pacific, an endless line. *Invading his country.*

That was why "Crunch" couldn't sleep. No matter how bad it was awake, he couldn't bear to dream about it as well.

He and the others were heading east—to where? The Asian Forces controlled just about everything to the Nevada border and, at the rate of their conquest, they'd be over the Rockies within a month. Even if "Crunch" and the others made it across what used to be Kansas and into Missouri, then what? On the other side of the Mississippi waited an enemy that was even larger, even more barbaric than the Asian Forces.

These were the forces of the Fourth Reich—the other half of the combined Second Axis. When the vanguard of Norse invaders attacked the East Coast months before, little did anyone know that it was just a feint of what was to come. That was, the massive, coordinated two-prong invasion of the American continent by a new, enormous enemy: the Second Axis.

Like a bad nightmare from the early 1940s, the Second Axis combined the strengths of two massive mercenary armies. One was made up almost exclusively of renegade Asian military sects, the other nothing less than the rebirth of the fascist Germanic state. It was only after the Norse invaders were stopped in a titanic pinnacle battle on the eastern coast of Florida that the United American Armed Forces realized that the Norse invasion had been simply a way of deflecting the UAAF from what really lay out beyond the horizon. The UAAF was a clever, highly skilled group. They had won several wars and had finally succeeded in reuniting a fractured America. The Norse invasion was a bold ruse indeed to have tricked such a hearty alliance. No sooner had the Norse amphibious force been stopped when the power of the Fourth Reich showed itself, in the form of a massive air strike launched from somewhere out at sea, presumably from

10

an aircraft carrier.

In one bold stroke, the Fourth Reich fascists wiped out most of what was left of the United Americans' small but respected air force, and thus immobilized most of its ground forces. Already battered and bleeding from the bloodcurdling Norse onslaught, the East Coast was totally unprepared for the massive sea and air blitzkrieg carried out by the Fourth Reich. Just like the coordinated Asian invasion of the West Coast, much of the fighting was quick and brutal. The American armies on the East Coast surrendered in light of a threat to destroy a major city and incinerate hundreds of thousands of innocent civilians via a sublaunched nuclear weapon.

It had all happened so quickly. That was what bothered "Crunch" the most. They didn't even have a chance to fight. And in the process, he'd lost at least two of his best friends. One was Elvis, his longtime partner in the fighter-bomber unit for hire known as "The Ace Wrecking Company." Elvis was last seen taking off for a reconnaissance mission over an area west of Hawaii to check out rumors of a massive invasion force sailing eastward. The rumors were true: the invaders turned out to be the Asian Forces. Elvis was never heard from again.

His second friend lost was Hawk Hunter. *The Wingman.* The one person more than any other who had been responsible for pulling the shattered American nation together once again. After the air strike by the mysterious carrier force off Florida, Hunter had taken off in his Harrier jump jet with several weapons strapped underneath and headed out to find the floating airfield.

He never returned.

And now here was "Crunch," just about the last of the top officers of the United Americans still living and not in a POW camp, sitting on top of a barren hill. He was being chased by an enemy who wanted his country only because they were envious and not respectful of their own. And all he had left, really, was the contents of the dilapidated tractor-trailer truck.

It was a sad situation.

"How long do we have, sir?" the young soldier on watch suddenly asked him. He too was staring out to the west. "How long before they catch us?"

"Crunch" considered the frank, gloomy question for a moment.

"We've got the rest of our lives," he replied finally.

It wasn't until the next morning, when they gained the higher ground, that they saw the cause of the miraculous tidal wave had a very earthy explanation.

Off in the distance they could see the remains of a large irrigation dam which had burst, instantly flooding just about every dry riverbed in the area. By using long-range binoculars, they could see by the long streaks of black soot along its cracked sides that the dam had obviously been blown up, either by set explosives or a well-placed bomb.

But just who was responsible for destroying the dam and why was impossible for them to know.

Part One

A Man of Water

Chapter One

Black Rock, Indiana

Mike Fitzgerald yanked at his overly starched priest's collar and muttered a curse.

"Goddamn thing. Cutting off my windpipe, you are."

He was trudging down a very dusty road, the miserable summer's heat making his long, black wool priest's cassock seem twice as heavy and twice as hot.

"Next time you impersonate someone, check out the wardrobe first."

He'd been talking to himself a lot lately. Perhaps it was the first clue that this priestly charade was, in fact, driving him mad. Or maybe it was his body reacting to the fact that no whiskey had touched his lips in months. Or that he had not seen a grown woman in just as long, never mind touch one.

"A little of all three, I suppose."

His present location only made things worse. It was flat—flat as far as the eye could see. The only diversion in the landscape were some low hills to the south. Everything else was dry pastureland, withered cornstalks and acres of sallyweeds. It was a virtual hell for him, having grown up and thrived in noisy, boozy, wet, lusty urban landscapes.

About a mile down this straight, dusty, hot road was a place formerly known as Kathryn, Indiana. Located about twenty miles to the southeast of what used to be Lafayette, Indiana, the small typically Midwest American town had been renamed *Bundeswehr* Four. It was the capital of the Fourth Military District of the Fourth Reich Occupying Forces, an area that encompassed all territory north up to the city of New Chicago, south to the former city of Terre Haute, east to the old, virtually abandoned state capital of Indianapolis and west to old Illinois Route 57.

"Bummer Four," Fitzgerald spit out, as the string of gun towers surrounding the small city came into view. "Maybe another Dachau someday."

A short, sharp peel of a siren startled Fitz out of his sullen thoughts. He swung around to find a column of *Spahpanzer* armed recon vehicles and Panhard VBL Scout Cars tearing down the road.

He barely had time to jump out of the way as the first *Spahpanzer* roared by. The soldier sitting in the turret spit at him, but Fitz neatly dodged the expectoration.

"You need a bath, priest!" the soldier yelled at him, laughing.

It was all Fitz could do to restrain himself from letting rip a stream of select expletives. But such an act would immediately blow his cover as a man of the cloth, a profession that most of these neo-Nazi invaders curiously found nonthreatening.

He stood in the road ditch as the column roared by, many of the soldiers cursing at him in German and flashing universally understood obscene hand signals. Fitz retaliated by continuously making the sign of the cross as stoically as possible, while keeping his nasty curses under his breath.

The VBL scout car at the end of the column screeched to a stop in front of him. An officer stared out the open door, taking a full measure of Fitz's priest garb.

"What are you doing out here?" the officer asked him in a harsh, heavy German accent.

"Tending the flock, sir," Fitz replied in his best holyman's voice.

"Don't give me that!" the officer screamed. "Your bromides are not an excuse for being out of the perimeter!"

Fitz gently raised his hand to interrupt the officer.

"Excuse me, sir," he said, his voice fighting to stay calm. "I *was* tending the flock. The sheep, sir?"

The flustered officer turned to his driver and spat out a stream of German. The driver demurely replied that one of the priest's duties was to care for the herd of sheep and goats

16

that grazed in the pastureland several miles outside of town.

The officer's face went red in a second. He punched his driver on the shoulder, ordering him forward. As the driver put the scout car in gear, the officer turned back toward Fitz, spit at him and then roared off.

"Someday, you bastards," Fitz swore under his breath. "You'll all pay for this."

After walking for twenty more minutes, Fitz finally reached the edge of Bummer Four.

Here was *Bundeswehr*'s reason for being: the massive air field constructed by the Fourth Reich soldiers in less than two months using thousands of slave laborers. It was also a symbol of why the Nazi invasion of the American continent had been so complete and over so quickly.

Unlike many of the enemies Fitz and his United American allies had fought during the years since the end of World War III and the subsequent fractionalization of America, the Second Axis realized that the true secret to military dominance was the critical application of air power. Past foes of United America—primarily the long gone Soviet-backed Circle Army, the pre-natal Panama Canal Nazis of the Twisted Cross and the White Supremacist armies of the repugnant Knights of the Burning Cross—had all used air power to certain degrees. But just like the United Americans themselves, the quality of that aerial force was borderline Grade B in most cases.

Fighter planes, attack bombers, recon craft and other instruments of true air power were always in chronic short supply in America, due mostly to the rather irrational disarmament agreements forged after the Third World War. Even at its height, the post-World War III United American Air Corps numbered less than 200 fighter/attack planes and the vast majority of these were elderly machines like F-4 Phantoms, F-101 Voodoos, A-4 Skyhawks, F-104 Starfighters and F-106 Delta Darts. What's more, the aircraft flown by the various air pirate gangs which roamed rather freely across the post-war American skies were even more ancient: F-100 Super Sabres, F-89 Scorpions, even some Korean War vintage F-86 Sabre jets. The bottom line was that many of these airplanes were decades older than the men flying them.

But while the quality of most of the equipment on both sides was hardly state-of-the-art, it created a kind of balance of power. Simply put, if everyone was driving old stuff, then the playing field was even.

There was one exception though: the F-16XL once flown by Hawk Hunter. It was an airplane which far surpassed anything else flying at the time. But now it, like its famous pilot, were long gone.

While secretly gathering their forces in Europe for the huge transAtlantic attack on America. the Fourth Reich had stockpiled a modern air force larger than some belonging to major countries before World War III. They did this by two means. One, the timely acquisition of an entire carrier wing of pre-war aircraft, and two, the discovery of two hundred fighter aircraft that had been hidden away during the frenzy of disarmament which followed the cessation of hostilities of World War III. In two bold strokes, the Fourth Reich assembled an air force of the most modern aircraft ever made: US Navy F-14 Tomcats, F/A-18 Hornets and A-6 Intruders; European Tornados, Jaguars, Mirages and Viggens; Soviet Floggers, Fitters and even some rare Su-24 Fencers.

All of this, plus an impressive array of in-flight refueling aircraft, backup cargo and logistics airplanes and a large fleet of helicopters of all types, made the Fourth Reich the premier air power on the planet. They were so rich in airplanes that just a few weeks before they transferred more than 50 units to their Second Axis's allies, the Asian Forces presently occupying the American West Coast. Granted, most of the units were elderly United American types captured during the lightning invasion.

Now as Fitz walked past the huge, recently completed airfield, he counted by habit the number of aircraft parked out on the runway. The tally came to 43, mostly Tornados and Jaguars, with an odd Mirage or Viggen about, but no U.S. Navy craft. Still it was a formidable force sitting out on the freshly laid tarmac, not even counting the dozen or so airplanes that were always airborne and constantly patrolling above the *Bundeswehr* Four military district like murderous hawks looking for prey.

All in all, it was a sight that sickened him. Another reminder of just how firmly the country, that he and his friends and millions of people like them had fought so hard to preserve, was under the brutal Nazi heel.

"Maybe it's best that Hawk isn't alive to see this," he murmured sadly, resuming the ongoing conversation with himself. "And maybe I'm the fool for just hanging on."

It took another half hour for Fitz to reach his eventual destination, a little red schoolhouse on the far southern end of the city.

It looked like something out of a 1950s magazine pictorial, with its freshly painted white picket fence and tiny well-maintained flower garden intact. It was once a public elementary school. Now it was The Fourth Reich Reeducation Center #5781.

Fitz steamed every time he saw the meticulously hand-painted sign, imagining that the 5,780 other "reeducation centers" scattered across the divided, conquered country probably looked just as quaint. Just as perfect. Just as hideous.

"Propaganda swill holes," he mumbled, adjusting his clerical collar again. "I think I'd rather face a firing squad."

But his work here was important. He was certain of this. So it was necessary, for a few moments anyway, to buck up, take the deep breath, and prepare to act priestly.

He hurried up the white stone walk and through the front door where two heavily armed guards scrutinized his ID cards before letting him proceed. Walking down the long dark corridor, he reached the familiar green door and went in.

"Good morning, Father McKenzie!" came the chorus from the children in the classroom as soon as they saw him.

"Good morning, children," Fitz responded, giving them a quick and sloppy hand gesture that approximated the sign of the cross. "Is everyone well today?"

"Yes, we are . . ." came back the unified reply.

There were fifty-five of them in all—kids from four years old to seven. Orphans mostly, they were brought to #5781 shortly after the invasion to be "reeducated" in the ways of the European fascists. Four hours every morning, a constantly changing parade of Nazi political officers came to the school and filled the little heads with fascist garbage. The emphasis was on the life and times of Adolf Hitler, who was God Almighty for the Fourth Reich. For four hours in the afternoon, Fitz took over and taught them everything from English to math to science and spelling.

It was by the strangest quirk of fate that Fitz had become their teacher. After he'd bribed his way out of a POW holding center up near Decatur and assumed the only disguise available to him at the time (he had hidden in an abandoned church for two weeks), his wanderings took him into New Chicago. There, he had barely escaped a curbside execution by some Fourth Reich soldiers who mistook him for a rabbi. Dragged to the local military police station, he employed his considerable verbalizing skills to convince the harsh officers that he was not only a priest, but a Jesuit priest, an educator, a molder of men's minds.

"Rabbis we kill outright," the officer had told him. "Priests and ministers, we allow to work themselves to death."

Fitz was shipped to Bummer Four the next day and assigned a variety of duties. Tending the flock was one; teaching the kids was another.

He'd been at it for four months now, and couldn't help but grow fond of each one of his students. He also felt enormously sorry for them. The Nazis were experts at twisting minds—the younger the better. It was part of the grand scheme to prepare these youngsters as the first generation of New American fascists, homegrown human machines built and oiled by the Fourth Reich.

Of course, Fitz was doing everything in his power to derail that outcome. And the kids, though young and somewhat disenfranchised, were smart enough to be willing accomplices. He never pushed them on it, but he knew that they realized their morning propagandizing was a crock. The sure sign came during his first week as their teacher. Announcing that it was art period, he slyly instructed them to draw pictures of the "world's worst villain," just to see what would happen. Almost every kid produced ghastly renditions of Hitler. Some with knives sticking into his head; others with bullets being shot through his eyes; several with a hangman's noose around his neck. It was a violent reaction, for sure, especially for such young children. But it also spoke volumes about what they considered the truth.

From this spark, Fitz ran an everyday drawing period, always instructing them to draw the world's worst villain, or the man they hated the most. Invariably, they produced pictures of Hitler, or Bummer Four's top military governor, or their morning "reeducation" teachers. After each art period, Fitz would collect the drawings and destroy them, making sure never to miss one. If he did, and the authorities found one, then he had no doubts that they would execute the child responsible and him. Probably on the spot.

"What do you want to do first today?" Fitz asked the children after he settled behind his creaky desk.

"Drawing!" came the inevitable chorus.

Fitz smiled broadly. It was their little secret.

"OK," he said, "And what do you want to draw?"

"Villains!" came the reply, as the kids scrambled for their crayons and paper.

But just then, one of the older kids raised his hand.

"I'm sick of drawing villains," he said.

Fitz felt a sudden cold feeling swell in his stomach. What did this mean?

"What would you want to draw?" he asked the boy.

The kid thought for a moment and then replied. "I'd like to draw a hero. But I don't know any . . ."

"Do you know any heroes, Father?" another kid asked.

Fitz bit his lip. He had been anticipating such a moment. But should he take the next step? If he did, it would be a dangerous one, for both him and the children.

But he knew some things were worth the risk.

"OK," he said finally, getting up from behind the desk and taking a seat closer to the children. "Today, we'll talk about heroes."

"*Do* you know any?" one of the kids asked excitedly. "Have you met any in person?"

Fitz felt an embarrassing mist come to his eyes. "I've known a lot of heroes," he replied. "Great men who were always trying to keep this country free."

The kids were very excited by this time, though smart enough to keep their voices low in a conspiratorial way.

"Tell us about the greatest hero that you knew, Father," one of the youngest kids asked, nearly awestruck. "Tell us what he was like."

Fitz moved his chair even closer to the eager students.

"All right," he said slowly. "Let me tell you about a man named Hawk Hunter . . ."

Chapter Two

It was now midnight.

The air was still and hot around Fitzgerald's billet, the only relief coming from the slight, cool mist rising off the river nearby.

His shelter was a tiny wooden and tin shack located next to a small drawbridge which spanned the narrow, fast flowing Wabash River. Like his priest's collar, this dilapidated hut came with the job—it was another one of his many tasks to perform as the span's bridgekeeper. Whenever anyone with proper ID cards appeared on the far bank and wanted to cross, it was up to Fitz to lower the bridge. Of all his jobs, this one was by far the least taxing. The bridge was seldom used and was only open late at night or early in the morning while he was on duty. His traffic was made up mostly of Fourth Reich armored cars returning from long-range patrols, though on occasion, citizens would hail him from the far bank. Usually these people were on a pilgrimage to Bummer Four to pay their oppressive taxes.

It had been a long day. It had begun with his morning shepherding duties and then the hot afternoon at the school, and then the ten-mile walk back from Bummer Four to this place. Through it all he hadn't eaten anything and had sipped barely a glass of water. Just like everything precious, food and water were severely rationed to Americans living under the Nazi domination. Most people ate just once a day.

Fitz had just finished his only meal—watery soup and stale

crackers—when he heard an all too familiar sound coming his way. The distinctive sputtering of the VBL armed scout car's engine echoed off the tin roof of the small shack. By timing the engine pops, Fitz could tell the Fourth Reich vehicle was a half mile away and approaching fast.

Scattered on the table next to him were the scribblings of a very rudimentary sabotage plan he'd been working on for months. On top of the papers was a nearly depleted bottle of homemade wine. To be caught with either would mean certain death. He rolled the wine bottle under his bunk and then quickly stuffed the documents into a secret chamber inside his large, homemade crucifix. Hanging the cross over his damp, oily bunk, he tilted it slightly to give it a neglected look. Then he refastened his clerical collar.

A minute later, the small scout car screeched to a halt in front of his billet. The knock at the door came a few seconds later.

Fitz opened the creaky door to find two Fourth Reich officers and two of the hated *Nicht Soldats*—Night Soldiers—glaring in at him. The officers had their pistols out and ready. The NS were armed with rifles and large nightsticks.

"Come with us, priest," one of the officers snarled at him in barely recognizable English. "You have work to do."

Fitz pretended to check the time.

"It's so late, my friends," he replied. "The best work is done in the day."

The younger of the two officers reached in, grabbed Fitz's collar and dragged him out of the hut, pushing him into the pair of soldiers.

"Convince him," the officer said matter-of-factly.

With this, one of the NS men whipped the back of Fitz's legs with his baton.

Fitz instantly collapsed to his knees, whereupon both soldiers began striking him across his back, shoulders and kidneys. He tried to get up, but a boot heel knocked him flat to the ground. Suddenly there was a growling face next to his ear.

"You work when *we* tell you to work—do *you* understand?"

Fitz inhaled a mouthful of dirty sand. In all his experiences

23

against various foes, he'd never hated an enemy as much as these men. He vowed that it would be to their detriment that he was full-blooded Irish, and therefore an expert in holding grudges.

"I understand, my son," he spit out. "I'll be glad to go with you."

He was picked up by his battered legs and arms and thrown into the back of the VBL scout car. Soon they were speeding down the roadway toward Bummer Four.

The only sign of life inside the city's limits were the roving bands of mechanized NS who specialized in finding and summarily executing anyone breaking the strictly enforced dusk-to-dawn curfew.

Fitz could just barely see out of the scout car's rear window, but he could tell they were heading for the *Bundeswehr* Four Aerodrome. He could hear the constant, low rumbling of jet engines that always emanated from the airfield as the never ending aerial patrols took off and landed.

They roared through the Aerodrome's main gate, past the dozens of airplanes and out to its most isolated runway. The scout car came to a halt on a particularly dark edge of the base and Fitz exited the vehicle courtesy of an officer's boot. Once again falling to his knees, he found a shovel thrust into his hands.

"Am I to dig my own grave?" he asked the senior officer.

The man laughed cruelly. "Not yet, priest . . ."

The second officer yanked Fitz up by his clerical collar and directed his line of sight to three tall telephone poles driven into the ground about fifteen feet away. The one in the middle had a large wood beam tied across its top. A human body was nailed to the beam.

The man's arms and legs were broken, and the wounds where the nails had been driven into his hands and feet were grotesque and bloated. A string of barbed wire had been pulled tight around his neck and crotch. He looked like he'd been hanging there for at least several hours, maybe even a day.

Fitz made a quick sign of the cross, and not entirely to keep in character.

The four soldiers burst out laughing.

"Look familiar?" the senior officer asked him.

Fitz tried to say something, but couldn't.

The second officer kicked him hard on the back and then pulled out his pistol.

"Start digging," he ordered.

Thirty minutes later, Fitz had carved out a shallow grave.

The officers had departed briefly, returning with two slave laborers from the base. With Fitz's help, these men went about the grisly duty of removing the battered victim from the cross, using a ladder, ropes and crowbar. Not wanting to witness the gruesome task firsthand, the four soldiers had walked about fifty feet away where they spent the time smoking cigarettes and talking.

Once the limp body was down, Fitz steeled himself and studied the man's face. He was probably no more than thirty years old, with red hair, close cropped, and a hint of a beard. His hands were calloused and dirty—not with soil but with grease. He was wearing tattered and burnt blue coveralls.

"He was not a prisoner, was he?" Fitz whispered to the workmen.

"No, he wasn't," one of the workmen replied under his breath.

"Was he an American?" Fitz asked them.

"Yes, he worked here, on the base," the other man hastily whispered. "He was on the crew of the helicopter repair unit."

Fitz was surprised. "Why would they do this to such a valuable man?"

"He was a saboteur," came the hushed reply. "They caught him putting water into the gas for their helicopters. One of their big ones crashed up north last week. They traced the contaminated fuel back to him."

Fitz looked down at the man. His face was covered with dirt and dried blood.

"So he was a hero," he whispered, thinking back to his art class with the kids earlier. "Another hero . . ."

"They are in short supply these days," the first workman said.

They hushed as one of the Fourth Reich officers walked over.

"Are you not going to say a prayer, holyman?" he asked Fitz in thick, German accented English.

Fitz almost gagged. He'd buried more than a dozen people in the past few months. It was yet another one of his duties. But this was the first time he'd been asked to do a eulogy. In the past, the Nazi soldiers were loath to such religious necessities.

But now the workmen stopped and suddenly all eyes were on Fitz. He felt numb. A man was about to be laid to rest and a false priest was praying over him.

It was no way to leave this world.

"Take care of his soul, Lord," Fitz finally murmured, making up the prayer as he went along. "Take care of all our souls."

He looked at the victim's cracked and broken face; it was so dirty. Too dirty to be buried. Fitz took a canteen from one of the workers and pulled a rag from his pocket. Wetting the piece of cloth, he gingerly began to wipe the bloody grime from the man's face.

Suddenly the man's eyes opened.

The two workers yelped in unison and one fainted dead away. The Fourth Reich officer was frozen in place, hand grabbing his mouth, unable to move.

Fitz himself was absolutely stunned. It was as if the man had come back from the dead.

"Water . . ." the man gasped weakly. "Please give me water . . ."

Fitz quickly poured some water into his shaking hand and fed it into the man's caked and cracked lips.

"Am I dead?" the victim wheezed.

Fitz could only shake his head no.

Alerted by the workers' cries, the remaining soldiers had run over by this time.

"This man is still alive," Fitz informed them. His tone was one of disgust for the fascist troopers. They couldn't even kill a man correctly.

The four soldiers were wide-eyed and trembling at the strange turn of events.

"This is impossible!" one of the officers said. "I was here. I saw him die!"

"As did I," the other officer declared.

There was a long moment of silence as Fitz directed more canteen water into the man's mouth.

"What shall we do?" one officer asked the other in thick German.

The first officer was furious. Like all of the Fourth Reich soldiers, he was a slave to the curse of *Absolute Efficiency*. If something was not done right, it called for an investigation, to correct the imperfection. As such, expediency was not his virtue. The thought of simply putting a bullet into the man's brain never crossed his mind.

"Bring him to the hospital, of course!" he shouted at the others.

Instantly, three other soldiers pushed Fitz and the workmen aside. They lifted the seriously injured man into the back of the scout car. Then without another word, they climbed aboard and roared away toward the Aerodrome infirmary.

Chapter Three

The 747 jumbo jet circled the *Bundeswehr* Four Aerodrome once before coming in for a less than textbook landing.

For anyone remembering what the gigantic but graceful airliner looked like before World War III, the sight of this jumbo was an assault on the senses. Garishly painted in black and red, from the hundreds of square feet of flame decals on its wings right down to the enormous Flying Tiger-style, shark mouth painted on its nose, it managed to look both silly and demonic.

No sooner had the 747 set down when its two escort aircraft—a pair of ancient F-105 Thunderchiefs—landed behind it. They too were painted in almost obscenely showy colors: one was covered with black and Day-Glo orange checkerboard squares, the other was a swirl of X-rated tattoos. The Thuds rolled up next to the 747, and all three aircraft slowly taxied toward their appointed parking stations.

An edgy delegation of Fourth Reich officers was waiting for the trio of airplanes, surrounded by a company of heavily armed NS. They watched nervously as the jumbo jet screeched to a halt barely twenty feet in front of their review stand. Its huge, cartoonish mouth looming over them, as if to devour them whole.

The F-105 pilots popped their canopies and slowly disentangled themselves from their safety harnesses and life support systems. They emerged, both dressed in identical black leather flight suits, heavy flight boots and decal plastered helmets. Retrieving their AK-47 assault rifles from a special storage space underneath the F-105's seat, the pilots climbed down from the airplane and walked around in front of the jumbo jet.

Several NS men instinctively raised their own rifles as the armed flyers approached, but their officers waved them away.

"They're not stupid," the senior Fourth Reich officer crackled in German. "Let's make sure we're not either."

The two pilots yanked off their black helmets to reveal two long manes of gnarled, stringy hair, and scruffy beards to match.

"I'm Bone. He's Itchy," one of the pilots said by way of crude introduction. "First Squadron, Cherrybusters."

"Luft Seerauber," one of the Fourth Reich officers whispered to another who didn't speak English. "Air pirates."

"Do you have the cargo, my friend?" the senior Nazi officer, major, asked the air pirate named Bone.

"Do you have the blow, man?" Bone asked back.

The Fourth Reich officer turned and nodded to his second in command. This man in turn signaled the driver of a jeep waiting nearby. The vehicle lurched ahead, circled underneath the jumbo jet and came to a stop near the second F-105. The air pirates accompanied the Fourth Reich major around to the back of the jeep, where three suitcases had been placed.

The major snapped the buckles off the first of the suitcases and opened it. Inside was 75 pounds of pure cocaine.

Bone dipped his finger into the sea of white powder, tasted it and pronounced it good.

The second suitcase was opened. It contained 98 pounds of pure heroin. Bone picked up a pinch and put it into his right nostril. He sniffed, sneezed and then gave a thumbs-up signal.

The third suitcase was snapped open. Inside were ten football-size chunks of crack. For this test, the pirate named Itchy stepped forward. Using an enormous Bowie knife, he cut off a small piece, put it between his filthy teeth and gave it a crunch.

"Aces up," he assured Bone. "Fine as wine."

Bone immediately raised his hand over his head and

snapped his fingers. Instantly, the two large cargo doors installed on the 747's port side creaked open.

Inside were two hundred and eleven very frightened girls, ranging in age from young teens to early twenties. They were all wearing ill fitting T-shirts and baggy pants. Each one had their hands bound together.

"Well?" The air pirate Bone asked, turning back to the Fourth Reich major wearing a snide smile, "Can we do business?"

Chapter Four

Early the next morning

Fitz woke up to the sound of someone screaming.

He rolled out of his bunk, falling to the dirty floor. Beside him, gleaming in the dull light of dawn, was an empty bottle of bad wine. Next to that, scattered on the floor, were the notes of his fledgling sabotage plan.

He was horrified. It had happened again: he'd started working on the plan, got drunk, passed out, leaving himself foolishly exposed. If the NS had found his place in this condition, they would have shot him on the spot, or more likely, slowly, painfully crucified him.

"Help! *Please help us!*"

Fitz was suddenly going in three directions at once. He was gathering up the two dozen or so notes of his plan, stuffing the empty wine bottle under his bunk and grabbing his clerical collar—all at the same time. Outside he knew the Wabash River was up and raging—the fog and spray were all over his cracked and stained windows.

"Help us . . ."

He burst out of the door and saw two people—an old man and a young woman—floundering in swift moving waters near the opposite side of the river.

"Hang on!" he yelled to them, running to the small building which held the controls to the drawbridge. "Hang on!"

He punched the bridge release valve and was relieved that the thing worked on the first try for a change. Slowly the battered drawbridge clanked its way down, landing on the opposite side with a mechanical thud.

Armed with a thick coil of rope and two life preservers up and ready, Fitz was running across the rickety fifty-foot span even before it had secured itself on the other side. He tossed one of the life preservers into the water, nearly beaning the old guy in the process. The man was struggling to hold on to the young girl, but her slight frame made her particularly vulnerable to the rushing waters. The old man managed to grab the life preserver, but in doing so, lost his grip on the young girl. It was at this moment that Fitz knew that the rope and life rings wouldn't do it this time. Hungover and still groggy from the night before, he climbed up onto the bridge railing and plunged into the rapid chilly waters — clothes, collar, and all.

The two potential victims were about twenty feet from the shoreline at this point. Fitz hit the water with a mighty splash about ten feet further out. He allowed the cold, violent current to sweep him into both of them, hooking the old man with one arm, and getting a firm hold on the young girl with the other. Together, they all rode the current. Fitz kicked his feet madly in an attempt to gradually steer them all toward the safety of the bank.

But the water's current was stronger than all three of them.

Several times Fitz found himself underwater, being dragged along the river's rocky bottom, all the while trying like hell to hang on to the pair without drowning in the process. It quickly became a losing battle. He was gagging on mouthfuls of water and gasping for breath. The girl was screaming, the old man was gurgling and Fitz could feel the strength drain out of him as the mighty river violently tossed them about.

Is how it ends? he thought in his last flash of life. *A pilot all my life and I wind up drowning?*

Now his lungs were filling with water. He was sinking fast. Everything was quickly going to black.

He closed his eyes and felt the world crash in on him. . . .

The next thing he knew, he was carrying the two drowning people to shore.

More than a quarter of a mile away, a pair of NS sentries were watching the drama unfold from atop their watchtower.

"I don't believe this," one soldier said. "Did we really just see that?"

The other could hardly speak. "One second they were gone. But now . . ."

"Now, they're alive," the other soldier gasped. "But I don't know how."

"Was it a trick? Just for our benefit?"

"Impossible . . . yet."

The two guards felt a rising panic between them. Like most NS guardtower sentries, these two were forced to work—or at least stay awake—for eighteen hours at a time, six days a week. No surprise then that these men were drug abusers, amphetamine pep pills being their choice.

Were they now paying the price?

"We must we must report this," the second soldier said.

"How?" his partner asked. "What words could we possibly use?"

Shaken and confused, the two soldiers stared at each other and then back to where the incident had happened. They could see the man who'd jumped into the water helping the two near-drowned victims back across the bridge.

"It is the drugs," the first sentry declared. "We've used too many, too long . . ."

"Yes," the other replied, his voice shrill with numb fear. "It was an hallucination. A trick of the eyes."

Right then, they made a solemn pact. Never again would they discuss with anyone that they had seen a man walk on the water.

33

Chapter Five

The Reich Palast

The celebration had lasted all through the night and now into the early morning.

It had begun as a rather stately gathering. The Fourth Reich had carried a passion for such things with them from Europe, and so they never missed an opportunity to create a formal affair. The excuse this time: the air pirates—Itchy, Bone and the crew of twenty from the jumbo jet—were to be fêted at a welcoming dinner.

As soon as the initial business overtures were completed at the airport, the air pirates found themselves riding in a string of stretch limousines, roaring through the small quaint streets of Bummer Four. A full military escort of NS motorcycle troops and scout cars led the way, sirens screaming.

The short parade ended at the *Reich Palast*—loosely, the "Empire Palace"—which was the ceremonial seat of the *Bundeswehr* Four government. Huge, ornate, and imposing, the white concrete building was the first structure built by the Fourth Reich after establishing Bummer Four. Modeled after the late 1930s' *Reichstag*, the *Reich Palast* was by far the largest building within the thousands of square miles of the military district.

The ceremony was held inside the building's main dining room. A long white marble table had been set for the fifty participants, half being members of the Cherrybusters, the other half high officers of the Fourth Reich. At the head of the table was the perilously thin, ghostly pale man of sixty who was the supreme commander of the entire *Bundeswehr Four*, the one they called the *Erste Herrscher*, or First Governor. His face and mind bearing scars from a half dozen major wars, the First Governor was known far and wide as the most tyrannical of all conquered America's Fourth Reich military rulers. He frequently bragged about having no conscience, no shame, no fear. His life, he said, was of total service to the Fourth Reich. Nothing else mattered.

He read a long, rambling welcoming statement, one which arrogantly recapitulated his fairly substantial contribution in organizing and executing important elements of the Fourth Reich's secret invasion force. Then he lectured the air pirates on the benefits of living the fascist life. Finally he announced that he would soon be leaving for a trip. His destination was *Fuhrerstadt*, the city to the south that was once known as St. Louis and Football City, but that was now the capital city for all of Fourth Reich America. His purpose for the trip was to attend the wedding ceremony of the *Amerikafuhrer*, the top Nazi official in the occupied lands.

Once his speech was done, a lavish meal of broiled lamb, boiled cabbage and potatoes steamed in apple jelly was laid on. The wine flowed fast and furiously during the meal, and afterward, tankards of ale were brought on for the hosts and guests.

Crude and unschooled in the art of diplomacy, Bone and Itchy nevertheless knew a return gift was in order. They had a brief discussion and then Bone broke out one of the many two-pound bags of cocaine he'd just traded for. Tapping out two enormous lines of the nose candy, he offered his gold-plated coke spoon to the nearest Fourth Reich officer.

At first, the high-nose fascists were taken aback by the act. For many, the only benefit of cocaine was in its trade value. It was something only the lower forms of human life indvulged in.

But then the First Governor, drunk on wine and ale,

stepped up to Bone's place at the table, leaned over and took a long noisy sniff of cocaine.

"Fein als wein," he declared, signaling that snorting the drug was politically correct—at least on this night.

The two-pound bag was gone in less than an hour.

It was around midnight when the First Governor called for the young girls.

There were thirty of them in all, selected for their beauty, their innocence and their vulnerability from the load of more than two hundred brought in by the Cherrybusters. Just where the air pirates had captured them, none of the Nazis knew or cared. The only thing that mattered was that each girl had what the Nazis called *Erziehung eigenschaft*—"breeding quality." The purpose for buying the two hundred young women was to eventually match them with the perfect breeding males, impregnate them, and start the new American Aryan race.

Still, this did not preclude other uses for them.

The girls were ushered in by heavily armed NS sentries and separated into small groups, based on their age. The last bit of decorum left in the drunken First Governor demanded that the outrageous procession begin with the eighteen year olds. They were forced to walk up to the First Governor, lift their T-shirt or lower their pants, depending on his whim, and then stand mute and still while he fondled each with the grace of a man checking the skin of a sow. Once they passed this first hurdle, they were shoved down along the table, to be grabbed and groped by the other intoxicated guests. While this was going on, a second clutch of frightened girls, these below eighteen, was brought in.

The party evolved into an orgy just after the first rays of the sunrise filtered into the dining hall. It all began when Itchy passed a small canteen to the First Governor, indicating that he should sip from it. Inside was the mysterious, hallucinogenic drink known as *myx*. Originating with the Norse invaders who had unwittingly laid open the American East Coast for conquest by the Fourth Reich, the presence of the *myx* gave the gathering an almost mystical quality.

Only a few select members of the First Governor's inner circle were allowed a sip of the precious nectar, to the envy of those left out. Soon those who had imbibed became uncontrollable with lust. The lewd period of simply fondling the teenage girls quickly ended as the *myx* began to take effect on the dozen or so who had ingested it. Within seconds, they had set upon the young women and commenced to engage in every vile act imaginable; all to the utter astonishment and drunken delight of the rest of the guests.

Even the nefarious Bone and Itchy were amazed at the outburst of lewd behavior by the seemingly proper Fourth Reich officers.

"These guys are crazy," Itchy whispered to Bone as they watched the opiated, salacious display. "We better watch what we feed them next time."

Chapter Six

Fitz was praying.

It was the first time in years, but he was on his knees, reaching underneath his bed, and praying that there was just one more bottle of bad homemade wine hidden back there.

Sitting across the room from him were the two people he'd rescued from the murderous river. Shivering, wet, confused, they were staring at him — simply awestruck that they were still alive.

The truth was, Fitz had no idea what had happened out in the raging Wabash. One moment they were all drowning. The next, he was carrying them ashore. It had been as simple — and as frightening — as that.

"Who *are* you?" the young girl asked him for the tenth time.

"I'm nobody," Fitz replied, pulling out two empty wine bottles. "I'm just the person who runs the bridge."

"But you are a priest," the old man said.

"That makes no difference here," Fitz told them, finally giving up on the search for any vino under his bed.

He pulled three heavy army blankets out from underneath the bunk and passed two of them to the old man and the young girl. They quickly wrapped each other in the coarse covers and huddled as best they could to get warm.

"Where were you coming from?" Fitz asked them, wrapping a blanket around his own shivering body and then putting on a tea kettle to boil.

"We're lost," the old man croaked. "Neither of us can remember where the hell we've been. Where we're from. Or how the hell we got here. I thought we lived in the desert. But it's just been too crazy . . ."

Fitz took a closer look at the man. He was probably close to ninety years old or more. He was rail thin, with long gray hair pulled back into a ponytail. By contrast, the girl was no more than twenty-five or so. She was small, thin, with red hair, boasting a streak of blonde.

"Yeah, well, strange things have been happening all over," Fitz replied.

At that moment, his prayers were answered. He reached between his bunk mattress and spring and found a half filled field flask of wine.

He quickly retrieved some small cups and poured out three meager helpings. The old man sipped his cup while the young girl downed hers in one shot.

"More will be coming," the old man said. "You might save more souls than ours in the days ahead."

The water boiled and Fitz prepared three strong cups of tea. But just as he turned to serve them to the soaking pair, he heard an engine backfire. He looked oat the window and saw an NS scout car appear on the far side of the bridge.

"Damn," he whispered under his breath, spilling some boiling water on his hand.

He turned to the old man and girl.

"If they catch you, they might shoot you," he told them. "I'm going outside to try to stop them. Stay here. Don't move."

He ran out the door and down to the control house. He'd returned the bridge to its up position after the incident in the river. Now he pushed the bridge release valve to lower it again. But as was the usual case, nothing happened. He slapped it again. But still, nothing.

The driver of the patrol car blared his siren. Fitz could hear angry screaming coming toward him from the opposite side of the river. He hit the release valve again and was immensely relieved to hear the resultant clank of the bridge mechanism finally clutching into place. Slowly, the span began to lower.

Fitz tried to shake the excess water out of his hair as the patrol car rumbled across the creaky span. He was hoping the vehicle would drive right on past.

It didn't.

"Been baptizing again, priest?" the officer yelled down at him from the gun turret as the vehicle screeched to a halt.

"No, just bathing, sir," Fitz yelled back over the unmuffled engine noise. "Clean body. Clean soul."

"Raise that bridge," the officer ordered him. It was obvious that he was in some kind of hurry. "And until further notice do not let anyone across who isn't a member of our armed forces. Do you understand?"

"No one?"

"*No one!*" the officer screamed down at him. "Or I'll shoot you myself."

With that the patrol car roared off.

"No one?" Fitz was left to ask.

He returned to the shack, scratching his head, yet thankful the NS had not decided to search his place, just to harass him.

But when he got inside, he found that it didn't matter.

The old man and the young girl were gone.

The Reich Palast

The First Governor opened his eyes and saw the empty canteen of *myx* on the pillow next to him.

He felt a tear roll down his sleepy face; he loved the *myx* so. To see it gone was truly heartbreaking.

He looked at his feet and found one of the young girls curled up there. She was either asleep or unconscious. Her X-rated black lace bra and garter belt outfit at least a size too big for her teenage body.

A turn to the left found the second girl—a brunette, possibly a year older than the blonde girl at his feet, but certainly no more than that. She was naked, and a slight stain of *myx* was evident on her breasts. The First Governor immediately reached over and sucked it off her skin.

The room was dark and it smelled of liquor, smoked cocaine,

40

and body sweat. He had no idea what time it was, nor did he care. He remembered drinking the *myx,* watching the incredible orgy in the main dining hall, and then dragging the two young girls back to his luxurious bedchamber. There they drank some more of the hallucinogenic mixture and he had his way with them.

Now he supposed it was midmorning, but again he couldn't really tell. As usual, the curtains were pulled tight across the massive bedroom windows, and they never allowed even a single point of sun into the chamber. That was the way he liked it: *dark*.

He licked some more of the *myx* stain from the brunette's tiny breasts and then lay back to enjoy whatever reaction even this miniscule amount had in store for him.

He closed his eyes. . .

Suddenly there was a dark figure standing over him. It was a man. He was dressed all in black, and wearing a black hood over what might have been a helmet, complete with an opaque visor.

The First Governor shivered once. This was not what he was expecting. The figure before him was exuding power, strength, control. All three frightened the Fourth Reich high commander.

"What . . . what are you?" he whispered, frightened, to the strange form in black. "Are you a dream?"

"I am the ghost of Finn MacCool," the apparition hissed, his voice sounding oddly mechanical. "Have you ever heard of me?"

The First Governor immediately wet the bed. "I'm . . . I'm not sure . . ."

The ghost moved closer to the stricken officer.

"Is it worth your life to remember?" it said.

"Finn MacCool . . . was . . . an old . . . Celtic . . . warrior," the First Governor stammered, somehow remembering his student university studies in mythology from forty years ago. "The divine leader of the Fianna and the soldiers of destiny. Am I correct?"

The spirit didn't respond. A long silence seemed to indicate that the First Governor was correct.

41

"What . . . what do you want?" the First Governor finally blurted out.

"I want you to say your prayers," was the reply. The eerie, static voice was driving a wedge right through the petrified Nazi's psyche.

"You've been sent . . . to kill me?"

"I am here to save you," came the words that sounded like steam.

The First Governor let out a long, relieved breath. Strangely he could see it leave his mouth in the form of a blue mist.

"How . . . how can I be saved?" he asked the frightful figure.

The black ghost loomed even closer to him. Now it was almost as if it was hovering over the huge bed.

"You must find a man of water," it said.

Chapter Seven

The Bundeswehr Four Aerodrome

Both Itchy and Bone were used to flying with hangovers.

It had to do with their aircraft's oxygen supply. Nothing cured the morning-afters like a few gulps of the Big O. So the first thing both of them did after climbing into their respective F-105s was to lock in their oxygen hose and then start breathing deep. Instantly their heads began to clear and their stomachs began to settle.

They never expected to party so hard with the Fourth Reich soldiers. Before leaving their main base up near what used to be called New Chicago, their squadron commander had told them that the Fourth Reich soldiers were, in his words, "prissy little girls." Nothing that Bone and Itchy saw the night before really dispelled that notion too much. It was just that these New Nazis really hung the rag out when it came to boozing and nose candy and fricking young girls.

And as far as giving them some *myx* free of charge, well, that was a mistake Itchy vowed never to make again.

But all in all, the business trip had gone well. The Cherrybusters had their pounds of cocaine, smack, and crack. The Fourth Reich had their load of young beauties. For the air pirates, the dope meant they'd be able to get some hard currency, which in turn meant they'd be able to buy more airplanes, which in turn meant they would be one step closer to reestablishing some of their former dominance in the skies over North America.

43

With obstacles like the United Americans—and especially the late Hawk Hunter—out of the way, as well as the nod from the Fourth Reich, the air pirates were free to expand their operations up into Free Canada as well as down into Mexico and Central America.

In a word, their future looked "bright."

Itchy and Bone rolled their garish F-105s to the end of the Aerodrome's main runway and waited for the gigantic 747 jumbo jet to take off. The huge airliner made the best of the Aerodrome's three-mile-long main runway, lifting off a little shakily after a 12,000 foot roll and slowly banking toward the north.

Bone and Itchy went next, their antique Thunderchiefs ripping through the midmorning hot air and lifting off in a particularly ragged, one-two fashion. Once airborne, they quickly kicked in their afterburners and caught up with the jumbo, taking defensive positions slightly above and behind the flying behemoth.

It promised to be a short flight from *Bundeswehr* Four to New Chicago, an hour at the most.

The skies were clear, the weather perfect for flying. Although both Thunderchiefs were equipped with AIM-9 Sidewinder air-to-air missiles, neither pilot expected to fire any. For them, the skies above Fourth Reich America were virtually enemy free.

The jumbo reached 25,000 feet, and would stay there only a few minutes before starting its descent toward New Chicago's main airport. Itchy actually found his mind wandering back to the night before; the tidal wave of booze, drugs, broads and debauchery. He imagined similar scenes happening all over the eastern part of the country as the Fourth Reich tightened its vise grip over the population. Why, he wondered, had people bothered all those years with things like morals? Ethics? Laws? *Decency was a drag, man.* A dead-end street. Whether you live your life good or bad, you still die. So what's the point?

He felt a pleasant chill go through him. There was definitely a new order settling down across the continent, one which held promise for people like him. But it would be survival of the fittest and he would have to reach out and grab whatever he could. That was okay—he'd been doing that for most of his life anyway.

He made a routine flight check call over to Bone, who was barely paying attention himself.

"This is a fucking milk run," Bone called back over. "Don't bug me with this flight status crap."

Deflated, Itchy knew his pain in the ass wingman was right. Kick back, he told himself. Just fly the fucking mission, land, eat some steak, score some *myx* and then find something young and cute to deflower. Enjoy this new life in Second Axis America.

An instant later, they got the Mayday call from the jumbo.

Thirty-two men in an NS convoy witnessed the incident.

The seven-vehicle column had just unloaded a supply of barbed wire and electrical shock equipment to a civilian concentration camp forty miles south of New Chicago and was heading north again when they spotted the jumbo jet and its two escort fighters passing overhead.

As many would later testify, the big 747 appeared to be smoking from its left-side wing. One of the F-105s—later identified as Bone—pulled up close to the stricken airliner, almost as an attempt to get a closer look at the cause of the smoke. Meanwhile the second F-105, the one piloted by Itchy, began firing its weapons wildly in the general direction of the two other airplanes, almost as if he thought they were being attacked.

As the convoy of Atlantic soldiers watched in horror, the 747's left wing suddenly burst into flame. The big airliner began to veer over, clipping the close-in fighter in the process, causing it to explode almost immediately.

The convoy had drawn to a halt by this time and all of its members saw the jumbo slowly flip over on its back and plummet, slamming into a field about four miles away. The shock wave created by the frightening crash was enough to perforate the eardrums of some of the transport troops, causing them to bleed profusely. Those that were able, rushed to the crash site, but realized quickly there were no survivors.

The last anyone saw of Itchy's F-105, it was streaking off to the east; its weapons firing, as if chasing some phantom aircraft.

Chapter Eight

The small shack shuddered as the pair of Tornadoes streaked overhead, their engines screaming as they turned on final landing approach.

Inside the shack, Fitz was drunk again. He was sitting on the floor, two bottles of recently secured homemade wine beside him on this young, brutally hot night. The roar of the Wabash River now returning as the background noise for his solitary inebriation.

He knew he was drinking too much—but what did it matter? Just about everything he'd ever considered valuable was gone. *Long gone.* His country. His businesses. His women. His comrades in arms.

His friend. . . .

Yes, even the nagging suspicion that somehow everything would be okay if only Hawk Hunter was still alive was slowly draining out of him. Hawk was gone. He was dead. He had to face it. And gone with him were General Jones, the Cobra Brothers, Ben Wa, JT Toomey, Catfish Johnson, Elvis. All of the brave men who had fought so hard, sacrificed so much to keep America free, were now little more than cosmic dust. The only irony was that he was the last one left. During all those years of fighting he was convinced that he would have been one of the first to go.

Life was cruel, he thought, finishing the last of the second bottle of wine, and wiping his brow with a damp rag. And the universal joke was that few good intentions go unpunished. They had tried though. They had given it their best effort.

They had made history. But what good was that, if there was no one to tell the story to?

He crawled up on his bunk, stared out at the brilliant sunset and heard the words of a long-ago poem drift across his mind:

> *Other spirits having flown,*
> *I too will fly to the west some day.*

I hope it's damned soon, he thought.

He located the third of his wine bottles, uncorked and took an unhealthy gulp. He hoped this one would put him to sleep. With everything else in his life lost, sleep is what he craved the most. He did a slow boozy scan of the shack. Even in his drunken state he made sure that he'd left no evidence of his stillborn sabotage plan lying around the hut. Not that it would make much difference. The fire was gone from his heart, extinguished by the overwhelming, invincible brutality of the Fourth Reich and too many bottles of bad wine. He was now a prisoner. A shepherd. A gravedigger. A teacher. A bridge tender. A lifeguard. *A slave. A drunk.*

He had little opportunity then to be a saboteur.

He took a longer slug of wine and caught a glimpse of himself in the cracked mirror across the room. He was startled by his puffy eyes, his thinning hair, his sagging belly. His once, tough as nails fireplug physique was nowhere in evidence. Flab, age, and indifference were quickly taking their toll.

"My God," he whispered, studying the stranger in the mirror. "I'm beginning to *look* like a priest!"

He rolled back over on his bunk, took three slobbering gulps of wine and closed his eyes. All he could see were the faces of the young girl and the old man he'd somehow pulled from the river. His overtaxed mind was now telling him the strange incident had been due to an alcoholic blackout, hardly a comforting thought.

He took another long swig of wine and wiped the excess that ran down his cheek.

Sleep, he prayed. His words hanging in the brutally humid night air, *Please put me to sleep. . . .*

47

Whether he ever actually drifted off, he didn't know.

He was stretched out on the bunk, bathed in sweat; the bottle leaking wine at his side when a cry pierced his eardrums.

"Help!"

He was up in an instant. Was it a dream? Was he thinking back to the strange rescue earlier in the day?

"Help!"

He rolled off the bunk and scampered to the front door. It was the dead of night. He must have gone to sleep! Now he was wide awake. On the far bank he could just barely see the outline of a man, up to his waist in the water, trying to ford the rapid current and losing the battle.

Fitz was out of the hut in a shot. He knew there'd be no replay of his miraculous rescue the day before.

"Stop!" he yelled to the man. "I will lower the bridge!"

Somehow the man heard him over the roar of the Wabash and managed to haul himself back up onto the shore. Fitz was in the bridge control house by this time, punching the controls, swearing at them to work properly.

It took a few tries, but finally the ancient gears meshed and the rusting, creaking bridge descended.

He ran across the span and down to the far bank, where he found the man sprawled, coughing up a combination of river water and blood. It was obvious that the man was injured even before he tried to cross the river the hard way.

Fitz yanked him up as gently as possible, and then slinging him over his shoulder, carried him back across the bridge and into his shack.

He helped the man down onto his bunk, studying him as he did so. His upper body, neck and face, were covered with small cuts and abrasions, like he'd been hit with dozens of tacks. His arms and legs were in even worse condition.

"What happened to you?" Fitz asked him, wrapping him in the blanket and passing him the wine bottle. "Where have you come from?"

The man took a deep breath and a long swig of wine.

"I can just barely remember," he gasped. "I have been walking for days, down from what used to be Gary, Indiana."

He took another long drink of wine.

"I must tell you," he began again. "It happened two, no, three days ago. It was early in the morning. I'd worked until midnight at the steel mill and I'd just come home to go to sleep.

"My quarters were across the main square from what used to be the city hall. It was converted into the local headquarters for the NS garrison. The day before there was a small demonstration in front of this building. The people—it was about twelve old women and some young kids—were asking the NS for more food. We'd had very little to eat in the past few months. Everyone was going without.

"This little demonstration—you couldn't even call it a protest—lasted no more than ten minutes. Some soldiers simply came out and shooed them away.

"That night, as I was coming home from working at the mill, I saw the NS moving out of the city hall. They were taking everything with them—weapons, computers, even the desks. I didn't think anything of it. I thought they were moving to better quarters.

"Anyway, I'm sure it was right after sunrise, when I was awakened by this noise. It was so strange, so eerie. Like a loud, echoing whistle. I actually got up and looked out my window.

"That's when it happened."

The man took another long gulp of wine and wiped his weary brow.

"It hit about a quarter mile away, right on the other side of the square. First there was this tremendous roar and then an explosion. An *incredible explosion*. I was thrown against the wall and halfway through it. The entire building came down around me. Why my skull wasn't crushed, I'll never know.

"Somehow I stayed conscious and I was able to dig myself out of the rubble. What I saw I couldn't believe at first. Where the wide avenue and the square used to be was now a gigantic crater. It must have been a quarter mile around. Probably one hundred fifty feet deep—or even more. It was already filling with water. And bodies.

"Everyone else in my building was killed. Just about everyone

49

in the surrounding buildings was killed too. It was horrible. The flame. The smoke. The screams. The clothes shredded right off me. I was naked, cut, burned. But I was alive. Somehow. To the day I die, it will haunt me. Why me? Why was I spared?"

"Do you have any idea what it was?" Fitz asked him. "Did an airplane drop a bomb?"

"No," the man replied. "I'm sure it wasn't that. I looked. I could see no airplanes. I heard no engines.

"I pulled myself up and out and then another explosion hit. About a mile away. It was tremendous. Then there was another a minute later. And another after that. I counted twenty-three in all over two hours. I was hiding under rubble, praying that whatever was happening would stop. Now I know why the NS were pulling out. The first explosion was exactly where the old women had held their little demonstration the day before."

"If they weren't bombs dropped by airplanes, what were they?" Fitz asked.

"It was something more terrifying . . ."

"Such as?"

"Have you ever heard of the *Schrecklichkeit Kanone?*"

Fitz's post-inebriated brain strained to make the correct German to English translation.

" 'Frightfulness gun'?"

"A good description," the injured man replied. "We've been hearing rumors about this. Huge guns set up on high ground. Cannons whose barrels are as long as a ten-story building is high. They were said to be able to fire a shell weighing seven hundred pounds more than one hundred miles."

"Surely such a weapon would have little military value," Fitz said. The rational side of his brain telling him that this kind of gun would be very impractical to use, operate and service, especially by the terminally practical Fourth Reich soldiers.

"Exactly," the man replied. "They are used simply for terror. For 'frightfulness.' I'm convinced that is what they used against my city. I am also convinced that I'm the only one left."

With this, the man broke down; a gush of tears and emotion flowing out of him.

"For the first time ever, I am really all alone," he cried through the anguish.

Fitz ran a hand through his own thinning scalp.

"I know how you feel," he said.

He took his last clean blanket and walked down to the river, soaked it, and then returned. The wounded man was asleep by this time, so Fitz gently laid the wet blanket on top of him, hoping it would keep him cool during the mercilessly hot night.

When the man awoke in the morning, he would find that all his wounds had been healed.

Chapter Nine

Bundeswehr Four

Ober-Colonel Karl Lisz had reason to worry.

He was holding a printed message from the First Governor himself. It was a notice for all of the commanders of *Bundeswehr* Four to attend a high-level emergency staff meeting to be held in less than a half hour.

Attendance was absolutely mandatory.

The message gave no reason for the meeting; that was why Lisz was worried. The First Governor was an extremely busy man. His schedule was planned out weeks, if not months, in advance. Every official minute of every day was filled, with very little room for contingencies. It was a typical timetable for such an efficient and methodical Fourth Reich high official.

Calling high-level gatherings on such short notice was not the man's style. Not unless something was wrong.

Drastically wrong.

Lisz could only grimly speculate just what that might be. As head of the district's border soldiers, he was among the most high-profile officers inside *Bundeswehr* Four. His soldiers, human barrel scrapings when compared to the rest of the Fourth Reich army, were known for their efficient brutality in dealing with the dozens of refugees (derisively known as *sputniks*) that wandered into *Bundeswehr* Four every day.

That was, after all, their one and only job. But because of their necessary crude behavior, his men sometimes overstepped their bounds. When they did, Lisz was usually the first to hear about it.

He called for his car and then glumly climbed into his formal uniform. He was already beginning to tremble. He'd seen staff officers brutally executed on the spot at such hastily called meetings with the First Governor, sometimes for petty offenses such as requisitioning more fuel or food than allowed. The First Governor was a great believer in punishment by example. One way to stop fuel pilferage was to shoot the officer whose man had taken a gallon more than he should have. It was a frightful, yet highly efficient way of ending fuel theft.

Lisz had just buttoned his stiff uniform collar when the call came that his car was waiting. He was visibly shaking now. He needed something to calm down. He was out of valium. And being only nine in the morning, it was much too early for a drink of brandy. What could he do?

It came to him just as he was affixing his hat to his balding head. He'd attended the raucous dinner reception for the air pirates two nights before. Although he wasn't high enough on the staff ladder to have been invited to partake in the drinking of the *myx,* he had managed to steal a glass which contained a dozen or so precious drops of the powerful nectar.

Perhaps a dab on his tongue would be enough to settle him down.

He quickly opened his wall safe and retrieved the martini glass holding the drop of *myx.* He took first one, then two, then a half dozen drops; ritualistically placing each one under his tongue and letting it absorb into his system.

By the time he closed the wall safe back up, he felt like he was walking on air.

A minute later he climbed into the back of his stretch bulletproof Mercedes and commanded the driver to proceed to the *Reich Palast* immediately. The short journey through the streets of the town provided Lisz with a myriad of pleasant, *myx*-induced sensations. Every man he saw—be they a slave or NS—looked weak, ugly and nonthreatening. Every woman he saw, from schoolgirls to mature women, looked delectable, sensual, easily dominated. The few drops of *myx* had set his hormones raging. He vowed that if he got out of the staff meeting alive, he would reward himself with the gift of a young girl that night.

The limo arrived in front of the *Reich Palast* to find a small traffic jam of staff cars waiting outside. It was apparent right away that the First Governor had ordered the entire command structure of *Bundeswehr* Four to the meeting. Even the sky above the huge structure was crowded. Helicopters bearing officers from the outlying districts were lined up for landing at one of the three helipads near the *Reich Palast*. And, as always, the air was filled with the sound of jet aircraft taking off and landing at the nearby Aerodrome.

Lisz got out of his car and joined the somber procession up the marble stairs and into the *Reichstag*-like building. He could almost feel the trepidation of the other officers. They likewise knew what could happen at one of these meetings.

The First Governor was already there when they filed into the vast meeting hall—a highly unusual occurrence. Most times, he was ushered in only after the staff had assembled, and then to a bombastic overture of trumpets and drums. But now, the sixty-year-old man was already at his seat at the head of the massive meeting table, his uniform jacket discarded, his sleeves rolled up, documents scattered all around him, a swarm of underling officers elbowing each other in an effort to attend to his every need.

Lisz couldn't believe it; none of the Fourth Reich officers could. They had never seen their supreme commander so *informal*.

The rest of the usual formalities attendant to such a meeting were also missing. The First Governor was actually smiling. He seemed anxious for everyone to take their seats so he could begin.

"Please sit down," he boomed out with unlikely exuberance. "Please take any seat. Any seat will do."

Finally the ninety-two officers of the command staff were seated, their eyes and ears at peak reception for what surely would be a highly unusual session.

The First Governor stood at the end of the table and seeing that everything was in order, cleared his throat and began.

"We are entering a new era, my friends," he enthused in an uncharacteristically vibrant voice. "This is Day One. A new life awaits us all . . ."

A few brave souls dared to look to their fellow officers to see if they were just as puzzled. "New era?" "Day One?" "New life?" What the hell did that all mean?

"Take no notes, gentlemen," the First Governor went on. "What I have to say to you should go right into your ears and directly to your brains. It should not be slowed down or misinterpreted by your act of writing."

Instantly every man inside the room dropped his pen onto the table.

Lisz stole a look around the room. It was, to a man, filled with puzzled expressions. The officer to his right was the chief medical officer for *Bundeswehr* Four. He tapped Lisz and slyly passed him a note. Lisz read its two words: "Acute *myx* poisoning."

Lisz felt a shudder go through him; the effects of his own minuscule dose of *myx* were still reverberating throughout his body. It was easy then to agree with the doctor's covert diagnosis. Ingesting large amounts of the mind-altering liquor could loop anyone—including the First Governor.

The First Governor cleared his throat and began again. "What I have to tell you—or rather to ask of you—should be spread far and wide. To your soldiers. To your own staff officers. To the people here under our guard. To any refugees who might stumble into our territory. It is a message that should be blanketed throughout our domain. Carried to its farthest reaches. My quest will become your quest."

The First Governor paused for a moment and studied the

ninety-two officers. Then he smiled broadly once again. "To begin, gentlemen," he said, "we must find 'a man of water.' "

Chapter Ten

The air pirate named Itchy was one second away from death.

He was lying flat out in an open field, the remains of his tattered parachute wrapped around him, no less than sixteen assorted machine guns pointed at his head. He'd landed there after punching out of his fuel empty F-105 which he had run bone-dry chasing what he thought was the airplane that had iced the jumbo and his comrade, Bone.

"Don't shoot . . ." he said once again, staring up at the gun barrels. "I have heroin. Pure gold scag. I have crack. Good stuff. I can even get you some *myx*. The real stuff. Not the fake stuff. I'll give it all to you. Just don't shoot."

It was Itchy's fortune that the sixteen soldiers hovering over him had no interest in these drugs. He'd mistaken them for a band of outlaws, but it was an understandable error. They were dressed like bandits: each was wearing a black nondescript uniform. Their weapons—M-16s and AK-47s mostly—were of the type favored by many outlaw gangs roving the northern tier of the American continent. Even their general appearance—long hair and days-old beards—fit the bill.

But the sixteen men were not outlaws. Quite the opposite. They were members of the elite Football City Special Forces, specifically the Ranger Corps. They'd seen Itchy eject from his Thud and had him surrounded before he even touched the ground.

"This is a complication," one of the Rangers said now, as

Itchy squirmed on the damp ground. "What are we going to do with him?"

"He's already seen us," came the reply. "So we'll have to take him with us."

Itchy wasn't sure what the men were talking about, but it didn't really matter. All that was important to him at that point was that the men apparently weren't going to kill him outright.

"Okay, 'sleep him,' " one of the soldiers said.

"How long?"

"Give him three hours, for now."

With that, one of the men knelt beside Itchy and injected him in the right arm. Itchy blacked out two seconds later.

The next eighteen hours were ones of total confusion for Itchy.

He would wake up every three hours or so only to be injected back into unconsciousness again. In the few brief moments that he was awake, he saw things that made little sense, either separately or collectively.

In his first awakening, he found himself being trundled along in the back of a truck with the same sixteen grimfaced men. It was just sunset and the destination was unknown. He noticed before he went under that, besides the rifles the men carried, they were also equipped with several laser devices, the purpose of which he did not know.

When he came to the second time, it was the dead of night and the truck had stopped. In the minute before the soldiers injected him again, he managed a peek out of the back of the vehicle and saw that it was parked in an old highway rest area. One that looked out over a well-lit city about six miles away.

Waking up a third time, he found that the men had deployed their laser devices and were working over them feverishly. In the background he could hear tremendous explosions, the chattering of AA guns and the peel of air raid sirens. Still groggy, he leaned further out of the back of the truck to see that the city was now in flames and under heavy air attack.

In the thirty seconds he had before the soldiers realized he was conscious and stuck him again, he was able to determine that the men were using laser sighting devices—probably PAVE/PENNY—to target smart bombs falling on the city with ear-splitting regularity.

His fourth conscious period came close to dawn. The truck was just moving out from its targeting perch and heading back down the abandoned highway.

The soldiers quickly injected him again and when he lay back down he could see the sky through the flap in the back of the truck. It was filled with smoke, but there were brilliant patches of light blue and red, the prelude to a clear warm summer's day.

Just as he was going under for the fifth time, Itchy thought he saw a very strange sight. It looked like hundreds of *W*'s written in contrails across the sky.

But later on, he assumed that it was just a dream.

It was midmorning when Itchy woke up for the sixth time.

He was back in the same field where the men had taken him prisoner. They were off the truck. It was nowhere to be seen. Instead a large CH-47 Chinook was on hand. The soldiers were loading their gear into it as another dozen or so new troops maintained a tight defensive ring around the LZ.

Itchy was kept awake while an intense discussion about his fate carried on between the man who appeared to be the leader of the sixteen soldiers and the pilots of the big troop helicopter. Through stuffed ears, Itchy was able to hear the gist of the debate, which was that the Chinook was overloaded and underfueled and even one more person on board could make the difference weightwise as to how successful the flight would be.

It was very apparent that no one involved wanted to spend much time on the question. This made Itchy itchy. If he was simply excess weight to them, then a bullet to his brain would quickly solve the problem. Yet that option never really came up.

One of the pilots blew a whistle and immediately the troops began climbing aboard the helicopter. The man in charge of the sixteen soldiers walked over to Itchy and untied his hands and feet. Then he tossed the rope at Itchy's head.

"As long as you live," the man told him, "you'll never have a day as lucky as this one."

With that, he climbed aboard the chopper, closing the door behind him. Then in a great burst of power and engine wash, the Chinook took off, and went straight up until it was out of sight.

Chapter Eleven

The two Fourth Reich soldiers who manned Outpost #6406 began the day with a meal of powdered eggs and stale coffee—and no drugs.

The Wabash River was running particularly rough this morning, too rough for the men to take their usual morning bath. Instead they gathered some of the brisk water in cans and took turns dumping them over each other's head, the "in the field" equivalent of taking a cold shower.

The outpost—a thirty-five-foot high tower which sat on a slight bend in the Wabash—was equipped with state-of-the-art video equipment, infrared sights, NightScope devices and even thermo-detection gear. Its weaponry included two .50-caliber heavy machine guns, a small rocket launcher, an SA-7 portable SAM system and a small arsenal of light weapons. The outpost had spy drone launch capability and three ways of instant communication back to the main NS HQ in *Bundeswehr Four*.

The job was simply to keep an eye on things. A half mile to the south there was a large tract of farmland which was worked by two hundred slave laborers. Directly to their east was a small truck repair facility, also worked by slave labor. Next door to that was a small jail which held people marked for execution. Outpost #6406 provided surveillance and early warning threat detection for all three of these facilities. By keeping constant tabs on the many slave laborers in the area, they helped cut down the escape rate, which was fairly small to begin with.

They were also charged with looking for any refugees who might be inside the *Bundeswehr* Four military district illegally. Such a crime usually meant execution. From their vantage point, they were able to watch several roads leading down from the north, roads that the *sputniks* were likely to travel. This was the most active part of their mission. They averaged spotting six refugees a week, many of whom were simply tracked down and locked up in the jail next to the truck repair facility to await their turn before a firing squad or years of backbreaking labor in the fields.

Directly to the north of the station, a mile and a quarter up the Wabash, was the small rusting bridge. This too was supposed to be under the watchful eyes of Outpost #6406, but neither man had turned his scope in that direction for days, not since the strange incident in the river with the priest and the two drowning people.

Their lives began to change the moment the Mercedes staff car pulled up in front of the outpost tower. The two soldiers were horrified. They recognized the car right away as belonging to Colonel Lisz, their overall commander. His sudden appearance could only mean a surprise inspection, something Lisz was not known for in the past.

The two soldiers barely had enough time to fasten up their uniforms before Lisz and an entourage of six bodyguards rode the small elevator up to the watchtower and walked in.

There was a barrage of heel clicking and crisp salutes, with Lisz making the two soldiers stand at attention for about ten seconds longer than was needed.

"I am here at the personal request of the First Governor himself," Lisz began, his usually booming, Teutonic voice appreciably subdued and hesitant. "He has asked me—as well as every officer on his staff—to visit every outpost under their command. To talk to soldiers, such as yourselves, about a subject which has become very, very important to him."

The two soldiers looked at each other with twin expressions of puzzlement. What the hell was Lisz talking about?

"It has come to the First Governor's attention," Lisz began again. "That there may be a man within our territory who: perhaps unknowingly, has displayed certain . . . powers."

62

"What kind of 'powers,' Colonel?" one of the outpost soldiers asked.

Lisz was growing more uncomfortable by the second.

"Let us just say, 'unusual powers,'" he replied, the tone of his voice sounding embarrassed at such a silly notion. "Things that are out of the ordinary . . ."

The two border guards now eyed each other with considerable consternation.

"Well? Should I assume you've witnessed nothing of the sort?" Lisz asked them. "I've reviewed your reports for the past month and saw nothing in them that would indicate . . ."

Both soldiers were trembling slightly by this time. Both were eyeing Lisz's particularly fierce looking bodyguards.

Finally one soldier bucked up and cleared his throat.

"*Herr* Colonel," he said, stuttering. "May we speak to you alone?"

Colonel Franz Hantz was the chief medical officer for *Bundeswehr* Four.

His typical day would begin by making the rounds at the main infirmary which was located on the edge of the Aerodrome. This large, well-equipped facility was for the care of Fourth Reich personnel exclusively. It boasted a large staff, state-of-the-art medical technology and the latest in procedures and diagnostic care. Hantz would usually spend three hours at the hospital, reviewing the most important cases, even assisting in critical operations. It was, in many ways, the castle of his kingdom.

A second hospital—smaller, poorly staffed and poorly maintained—was located on the far edge of town, near the all but abandoned railroad station. It was used for little more than a storage facility for ailing civilians and the occasional sickly *sputnik*. The patients there received the bare minimum of care—food, water and antiseptics—and little else. Few operations were performed and when they were, the surgeons were usually undertrained medics or even unqualified nurses.

The second-class hospital had an even darker side however. Since its opening, there had been dark rumors that Dachau type human experiments were performed there, under the tacit agreement of the *Bundeswehr* Four leadership. Though meticulous records were kept on all patients entering the facility, there was virtually no accounting for what happened to them once they were admitted.

So it was an extremely rare occasion when Colonel Hantz, the physician, would visit the place. And never in the past had he stooped so low as to actually walk through the patient wards.

But things had changed drastically inside Bummer Four. And so on this morning, Colonel Hantz was indeed walking the floors, speaking with the sick, the injured, the dying, a demeaning task that could only be forced upon him by the First Governor.

Most of the four hundred or so second-class patients were ailing from lack of care of routine maladies—ulcers, appendicitis, swollen tonsils, cataracts. Some had sustained injuries in typical household or roadway accidents. Others were simply wasting away from incurable diseases.

But there was a small psychiatric ward, and it was here on his last stop of the hurried, distasteful tour, that Doctor Hantz met the *sputnik* from Gary, Indiana.

The man's story, according to the ward nurse, was typical in many respects. He claimed to be from the large industrial city to the north and that he'd witnessed a horrifying artillery attack several weeks before. A routine check by Hantz with *Bundeswehr* Four's military intelligence section confirmed that a section of Gary had been the target of a "fright" shelling earlier in the month. The man then made his way south, stumbling inside the *Bundeswehr* Four military district and making his way up to the crosspoint of Wabash River.

That was when a strange thing happened.

"I had to ford the river," the man told Hantz from his bed. "I was certain that troops were chasing me and I had to get away, or drown trying. I was injured though, and weak from my long walk. So I cried for help, near the place where the drawbridge is located.

"A man came out of the bridge tender's hut and lowered the bridge. He was a priest. He carried me across and

64

brought me to his quarters. He gave me wine and a blanket—a blanket which he had dipped into the waters of the river.

"It was a very hot evening and the wet blanket cooled me considerably. I fell asleep and enjoyed my longest slumber in months, despite my many injuries.

"But when I awoke . . ."

At that point, the man's voice trailed off. Hantz resented the break in the testimony.

"What happened?" he demanded of the man, glancing to make sure his restraining belts were secured to the bottom of the bed. "You awoke and found what?"

The man tried to fight off a bout of tears, but lost the battle.

"I awoke . . ." he said in a halting, raspy voice, "to find that I'd been healed."

Chapter Twelve

The Reich Palast

The two enormous oak doors opened slowly to reveal the opulent living quarters of the First Governor.

Two heavily armed *Nicht Soldats* stood in the doorway, their powerful CETME G3-J rifles up and ready as always. Between the soldiers stood two teenage girls. Both were dressed scantily. One was wearing the tightest of bikinis. It looked small against her young, well-developed body. The other was clad only in a T-shirt and high heels, an unlikely combination that nevertheless showed off her alluring, if petite, figure.

The two girls had been selected from the vast pool of "talent," that was always available to the First Governor and the top officers of his high command. They'd been sufficiently liquored up and each had been given a codeine tablet for passivity. Exactly what awaited them depended solely on what the First Governor's substantially deviant imagination was conjuring up at the moment.

The soldiers nudged the two girls forward, escorting them across the vast room and toward the pillow filled corner which was known as the First Governor's so-called "recreation area."

The Fourth Reich high commander was sitting on his thronelike chair poring over a ream of paper as the girls and their escorts approached. Lost in the sea of documents was the Daily Situation Report, a written summary of the previous day's activities within *Bundeswehr* Four. It carried three main items—one was a preliminary report which indicated that the crashed air pirate jumbo jet was probably shot down by unknown forces. Another reported an air strike by forces unknown on the city of Cleveland, which was now a major manufacturing center for parts and ammunition for the Fourth Reich's gigantic terror gun, the *Schrecklichkeit Kanones*.

The third item was a report on a so-called special prisoner who escaped from one of the work farms over the night. The man, who had been sentenced to death by crucifixion only to have his execution botched, had been recovering on a work farm to the north. He'd somehow managed to sneak out of the heavily guarded camp and was now the subject of a massive search. He'd left behind a note indicating that his purpose of escape was not a flight to freedom. Rather, he wanted a private audience with the First Governor.

Despite the potential implications of all three reports, the First Governor had barely given them a cursory glance.

He was too busy drawing pictures.

A small, moleish man, dressed in the uniform of a Fourth Reich propaganda officer, was uncomfortably perched on a huge satin pillow below and to the left of the large chair. He was surrounded with a myriad of artist's supplies—crayons, rulers, French curves, several large erasers—as well as a sea of crumpled pieces of paper.

"Excuse us, sir," one of the *Nicht Soldats* said with a sharp salute. "I believe you requested these visitors?"

The First Governor barely looked up.

"Can either of you two men draw?" he asked, his voice unnaturally restrained and struggling in English. "With pen or ink?"

The soldiers looked at each other briefly and both gave nonmilitary shrugs.

"No, sir," came the crisp reply to the odd question. "You are in need of an artist?"

"I *have* an artist," the First Governor declared, nodding toward the moleish man; his voice regaining some of its former voracity. "I *need* someone who can draw."

There was a confused silence as the mole man shifted even more uneasily in his pillow seat, scattering some of his artist's crayons in the process. It was obvious that the First Governor had desired his illustrative talents for a specific purpose but that the man was missing the mark. Perhaps dangerously so. The tension was only sharpened by the roar of two Fourth Reich Jaguars taking off from the Aerodrome's auxiliary runway, barely a half mile from the *Reich Palast*.

Once the roar died down, the uneasy silence returned to the huge room. It was broken finally by an unlikely source.

"I can draw," the young girl in the T-shirt and high heels said, her voice sounding very unsure and barely above a whisper.

The First Governor looked up for the first time and examined both girls. Then he turned to the propaganda officer.

"Please supply her with a pen and paper," he told the man in German. "And then everyone else is dismissed."

The officer did as told, and then joined the pair of NS men and the relieved bikini-clad young girl as they briskly exited the room.

"If I tell you a vision, can you draw it for me?" the First Governor asked the young girl, his heavily accented German sounding nearly incomprehensible.

She nodded bravely if uncertainly. "I can try."

The First Governor smiled and gently stroked her light brown hair.

"Sit," he said, gently prodding her to her knees right in front of him. "Let us see how good you are."

As the young girl took pen and paper in hand, the First Governor leaned back in his regal chair, closed his eyes, and wet his lips.

"The other night, I saw a ghost. . . ." he began.

Twenty minutes later, the young girl was putting the finishing touches on her drawing.

"Let me see it," the First Governor ordered her, his impatience getting the best of him.

She slowly turned the piece of paper over and held it out before her.

The First Governor was at once delighted. It was all there. The apparition of Finn MacCool, almost hovering above his bed. The midnight dark clothes. The strange black helmet beneath the hood.

"Perfect!" the First Governor declared, taking the drawing from the girl with the care and sensitivity of someone handling a Van Gogh. "You have captured it completely."

The young girl smiled.

"You are now my official illustrator," the First Governor told her, never taking his eyes off the eerily accurate drawing. "You will live here with me, and you will draw what I see in my dreams."

The young girl didn't know what to say.

"What is your name?" he asked her.

"Seventy-three," she replied.

"I mean your real name," he said, for the first time taking his eyes off the drawing. "Your given name . . ."

The girl shrugged sadly. "I don't remember."

The First Governor squinted slightly. An unlikely bolt of compassion ran through him. He actually felt sorry that the young girl could not even remember her name.

"From now on you are Brigit," he declared, looking down at her as a grandfather might his first granddaughter. "And from now on, you have nothing to worry about."

Outside the *Reich Palast*, at the small concrete building that served as the main guard post for the palatial seat of the occupying government, a man boldly approached two sentries. He was shirtless, thin, and wearing only tattered socks on his feet. He had red hair and a bare hint of a beard. His face was dirty, with long tracks in the grime made by a recent onslaught of tears.

"I must talk with the First Governor," the man told the grimfaced soldiers.

Already in bad temper due to the searing heat and their heavy wool uniforms, the NS guards simply ignored him.

"I must see him," the strange man insisted. "Now."

"Leave, *sputnik,* or we will shoot you," one of the guards barked at him in thick, German tortured English.

"If you do not let me see him, it will be you who are shot," the man insisted.

The soldiers lowered their G3 barrels and pointed them directly at the man's heart. They'd summarily executed others for less.

"Even if you shoot me," the man began, somewhat cryptically, "I will still live."

"We shall see," one of the guards interrupted, his finger wrapping tightly around the rifle's trigger.

"I have met the man of water," the strange man went on.

The words froze both soldiers. They knew the First Governor was on an almost religious quest to find a "man of water." Everyone inside Bummer Four did. Indeed, the day before, their entire guard company had spent 18 hours walking from house to house inside the city, asking citizens if they'd seen or heard about a man in their midst who might be able to perform some rather incredible feats. With each question, they were either answered with blank, confused stares and just a slow shaking of the head. (The real story, the citizens whispered when the guards were gone, was that the First Governor was quickly going mad.)

Now this strange man was claiming he might hold a key to the First Governor's frantic, bizarre search.

"What proof do you have?" one of the NS demanded.

The man stared at both of them for a moment. Off in the distance, two Mirage fighters were coming in for a noisy landing. One at a time, the man turned the palms of his hands up and displayed them for the soldiers. Each one had a huge scar in its center, scabbed over but obviously healing quickly. The man then kicked off his battered socks and revealed similar wounds on his feet.

"Who are you?" the other soldier asked him.

The man smiled broadly.

"Who do I look like?" he replied.

Chapter Thirteen

At the bridge

The Wabash River was flowing easily in the midafternoon summer sun.

Fitzgerald looked up from his position on the near bank to see two of his young students dive into the small pool of calm water close to the shade of the bridge.

"Look out for them now!" he called out to the two oldest students, both of whom were eleven years old. They were his lieutenants in supervising this rare outing for his schoolkids. "We don't want them to be swept away."

Although there was little actual danger of that, the two older kids waded into the shallow water of the natural pool and stationed themselves between the younger kids and the deeper Wabash. His mother hen instinct thus sated, Fitz lay back down on his blanket and took another sip of wine.

He'd been planning this outing for two weeks, knowing it would be a cure for restlessness among his twenty little charges. He'd told the NS officer in charge of reeducation within Bummer Four that the purpose of the field trip was to collect samples of "wild vegetables," with which to start a garden in back of the schoolhouse. Someday, he told the officer, the garden might provide vegetables for each kid, an attempt at resource-saving efficiency that nearly brought a tear to the fascist officer's eye.

That fact that Fitzgerald didn't even know if there was such a thing as wild vegetables had no bearing. The NS officer not only approved the trip, he allowed Fitz the use of an old beat-up military truck to transport the twenty young students.

So now here they were, jumping and splashing in the cool Wabash just like kids had done for generations.

Fitz didn't want them to see him imbibing so he had skillfully disguised his wine bottle to look like a simple water container. He took another long slug and then closed his eyes. The woman down the road who sold him his homemade wine had done an especially good job this time. Though she could have strained it better, its alcohol content was about double her normal wares, something Fitz was too polite to complain about.

In the midst of the gathering wine buzz, he searched for a tidbit of relaxation somewhere in the back of his mind. But there was none to be found. Even on this perfect summer day, with his extended family of youngsters enjoying themselves immensely and another two wine bottles back in his hut, Fitz could not find one iota of peace. Instead, his thoughts were filled with the unexplainable incidents of the past few days. The two people in the river. The wounded *sputnik* from Gary. The man hanged on the cross.

How could these things possibly be happening to him? Could there be only one answer?

Could he be going mad?

They heard them before they saw them.

It was just a low, dull tone at first; somewhere, way off in the distance, behind the trees, back toward Bummer Four.

But the noise steadily grew. expanding into the mechanical timbres. Soon it was so loud, it was competing with the trickling of the Wabash and the rush of the wind through the nearby trees.

The kids heard it all at once, and right away they were concerned. Fitz stood up, and from his perch atop the riverbank, circled around in all directions, trying to see anything that might be associated with the growing noise.

"Look!" someone yelled. "Up there!"

The twenty kids and Fitz all looked toward the southeast to see the sky filled with menacing black dots. As they watched, the dots began growing bigger, and the noise got louder. By this time, the kids were running out of the water, their concern growing by the second. Now, running up the bank, they huddled around Fitz, shivering slightly in the sudden cool breeze, wondering what was happening.

Fitz watched with increasing trepidation as the aerial dots turned into helicopters. At least ten of them, all heading their way. The screech of their engines was now loud enough that the youngest of the young kids were crying. Fitz tried to gather them all closer to him, praying—*literally praying*—that the chopper force would simply pass right over them, on its way to some far-off, undetermined site.

But soon enough, Fitz knew they were heading right for the bridge.

Thirty seconds of their ear-splitting roar and the first of the two choppers was circling high above them. These were the OH-58Ds, a scout and command aircraft. The next chevron consisted of seven UH-60 Blackhawks, traditionally gunships and troop carrying copters. Bringing up the rear, even more ominously was a UH-1 Huey medivac copter.

"All this?" Fitz asked himself grimly. "Just to arrest me?"

Two of the Blackhawks swooped low overhead and then swung around, kicking up a windstorm the strength of a small tornado. They were landing, and it was easy to see that their bays were filled with heavily armed *Nicht Soldats*. One set down next to Fitz's shack, the other in a small clearing adjacent to the bridge itself. Two more landed down the road from the bridge, with the remaining trio settling on the field directly across the Wabash.

The kids were in full panic now. They'd learned to fear any sudden appearance of the occupying fascist troops since some kind of violent bloodletting usually occurred soon afterward. This response, coupled with the roar of the chopper engines, was quickly turning the pleasant swim trip into a nightmare.

The first troops were now disgorging from the Blackhawks and running toward Fitz and his little group.

Please don't let them shoot me in front of the children, he prayed under his breath as the vanguard of NS reached his position.

There was a young captain leading the charge, and he ran right up to Fitz.

"You are the priest?" he asked, possibly thrown off because Fitz's starched collar was not fastened.

"I am," Fitz gulped, imagining his life was already passing before his eyes. "Please don't hurt the children."

The captain tried valiantly to ignore the statement, even as the rest of the troops from the nearby helicopters had surrounded the area and were bristling with weapons.

"You must come with me," he said. "Immediately."

Fitz habitually re-fastened his collar. He knew better than to ask where he was being taken.

"What about the children?" he asked the officer. "They can't be stranded out here."

"We will take care of the children," was the man's reply.

He snapped his fingers and two husky soldiers were soon standing at Fitz's side. Looking back at the kids, all huddled together and crying, he managed a brave half-smile and said: "Good-bye, children. I will see you all soon."

He turned and began walking with the two escorts, his gait slow and stooped, like a man walking to the gallows. Suddenly he felt a tugging at his pant leg and looking down saw one of the smallest children had run after him. The child was not crying as much as the others. Rather he was holding something up for Fitz to take.

One of the soldiers brusquely shooed the young boy away, but not before Fitz had taken his offering—it was a folded piece of paper—and stuffed it inside his shirt pocket.

It was only after he'd been put aboard the Blackhawk and it had taken off that he dared reach in and take out the folded paper.

It contained two crude yet decipherable drawings. One showed a man in a jet fighter—a rough but identifiable

F-16XL—and the other a man in priest's clothing. An arrow pointed to each, under which was printed in gigantic letters: "Heroes."

Chapter Fourteen

Football City

It was hot.

The two men, both bathed in dirty sweat, fastened the pull chain around the huge piece of granite and yanked it tight.

"Locked here," one said wearily.

"Here, too," the other replied, equally exhausted.

The other end of the chain was fastened to a long, heavy block of wood the length of a telephone pole. Twenty-two men were handcuffed to this pole and it was their job to push on it like an ox pushes on a yoke and thus drag the large block of granite from one end of the prison work yard to the other.

"Okay," the first man yelled, "Pull it!"

The gang of shackled laborers began struggling against the large, rotting, bloodstained wooden beam. Slowly the large block of granite behind them began to move.

It took twenty long minutes to drag the five-ton piece of rock two hundred feet across the crowded work yard. The effort was all but ignored by the five hundred or so other prisoners. They were busy with their own miserable tasks: most were chained to their own yokes, chipping away on similar blocks of granite or washing and polishing finished pieces of stone.

They were all unwashed, barely clothed, and malnourished. Many were sick. Many were dying. So many, in fact, that a small group of collaborative prisoners moved about the camp like sullen vultures, picking up the dead and the near-dead, haphazardly wrapping them in dirty white sheets and tossing them on to the back of a sputtering, rusted flatbed truck. On this, they would be transported to the huge burial ground several miles away from the prison, where they would be thrown into the day's mass grave and covered over, dead or not.

Watching over this little piece of Hell were fifty heavily armed men in black, Grim Reaper-style hooded robes and hobnail boots. These faceless soldiers were the omnipresent *Tod Schadel* — the Death Skulls. They were easily the most hated men in the prison camp.

Most of the five hundred prisoners were either Free Canadians, Native Americans and other foreign allies of pre-invasion America. A larger, even more hellish prison yard lay beyond the north wall. It held nearly two thousand two hundred former United American officers and soldiers.

The prison was known as *Drache Mund* — The Dragon Mouth. It was located on the western edge of the city once known as St. Louis, then as Football City, and now as *Fuhrerstadt,* City of The Leader. It was the capital of Fourth Reich America.

Waiting in one corner of the shadeless prison yard was a small, wiry man of sixty years named Dave Jones. He was dressed in the same drab and dirty prison clothes as all the other prisoners. His hands and feet were calloused and bleeding, his body showing the fallow signs of creeping malnutrition. He was like the prisoners in every respect but one — he had been an officer in the United American Armed Forces. In fact, he had once been the Supreme Military Commander of the brief entity called United America. He was, in effect, the last President of the United States.

Now he was a slave stonesman. A chipper. The man who made the final designated cuts on the huge pieces of stone before they moved on to the next station to be assembled and eventually erected.

Jones wiped the sticky, stone dust grime from his sweaty face and checked the position of the sun. It was slowly creeping toward midafternoon, a movement he welcomed for it meant that his long day which started at 5 AM was nearly half over.

"What is this one?" the man beside him asked. His weak and raspy voice barely audible above the nonstop racket of clinking chains, stone hammering, and despairing moans.

Jones checked the ragged set of plans in front of him. They detailed the enormous statue which was being constructed with the sculptured slabs of chiseled concrete. The monument, one hundred fifty feet tall when completed, was actually a wedding present. It was being given by the top Fourth Reich official in the occupied lands—the rarely seen *Amerikafuhrer*—to his bride on their wedding day which was just a few weeks off.

"If that is piece one-oh-four-east-seven," Jones answered, looking at the rectangular slab of stone and then referring to his plan, "then it is the mustache . . ."

The man beside him laughed derisively, the action quickly devolving into a hacking cough.

"You mean it's our privilege," he said, trying to catch his breath, "to chisel out the paperhanger's snot catcher?"

"God must be looking down on us today," Jones replied with equal bitterness and irony. The gigantic statue was indeed of Adolf Hitler and this piece was indeed his trademark mustache.

Jones's partner in hammer and chisel was his longtime friend and ally, Major Frost of the Free Canadian Armed Forces. Frost, like many of the United American's inner circle, had been captured soon after the Fourth Reich invaded America. Like them, he was still reeling from the devastating air strike against the bulk of the UA air force following their decisive victory against the bloodthirsty Norsemen on the beaches of northeast Florida. Like them, he didn't realize that the Norse raids had been little more than an elaborate feint to distract the United Americans while the Fourth Reich's huge landing fleet waited in mid-Atlantic.

Also like them, he'd lost his best friend when Hawk Hunter flew off to battle the fleet on his own and never came back.

The gang of handcuffed slave laborers finally deposited the chunk of stone in front of the chiseling station. As one, they collapsed to the ground from sheer exhaustion. Jones quickly lifted a makeshift ladle from his pail of dirty polishing water and splashed it onto the nearest of the twenty-two men. The warm dirty water brought a single moment of relief for the men it hit. Some even licked it from their dirty arms, though they tried not to make their actions show. They knew that had Jones been caught by the Death Skulls providing them with this drop of comfort then he would most likely have been shot on the spot. This made them appreciate the brave gesture even more.

The slave gang left the area, pronged and prodded by their Death Skull guards back to the far side of the yard where they would be chained to yet another slab of concrete.

Once he was certain that everyone else was out of earshot, Frost knelt down close to Jones.

"I think tonight is my night, General," he whispered hoarsely. "I think it's time."

Jones stopped chipping away on the piece of granite for a moment. "Are you certain?" he asked his old friend.

Frost fought off another coughing spell.

"Yes, I am, sir."

Jones resumed banging his chisel with the massive hammer again, reopening many of his hand blisters.

"No one can make the decision for you," he told Frost. "But . . ."

"My time is running out," Frost told him, splashing water on the stone where Jones was cutting. "Yours too."

The comment once again made Jones stop hammering for a moment.

"I can't take that step until that last possible moment," he told Frost. "I think the others here still need me."

Frost simply nodded in dejected agreement.

"With your permission then, General," he said slowly, watching as the vultures loaded another recent corpse onto their oily, sputtering truck. "Tonight, it will be my turn to die."

It was close to midnight when the last of the Death Skull guards left the prison yard.

They would return at the crack of dawn, roust the prisoners with whips and billy clubs, and direct the disposal of the ones who'd died during the night. But now, in these handful of hours, the prisoners were left alone, to sleep where they worked, to die where they lay.

To dream.

The dirty blankets were tossed about, and the wail of a particularly ailing prisoner echoed across the dusty yard. Most men were asleep quickly, their exhausted bodies knowing that the respite would be too brief. Others lay in a kind of limbo slumber, not conscious, yet not asleep; simply numb and reclining.

Jones and Frost, however, were wide awake.

On the opposite side of the courtyard, a man was slowly making his way toward Jones's darkened chiseling station. Sometimes crawling, sometimes walking in a crouch, he passed the main knot of sleeping prisoners, jumped over the pair of slit trench latrines, and made for the shadows of the far wall. All the while he clutched a small plastic bag to his chest. Inside this bag was possibly the most precious commodity in the entire city of *Fuhrerstadt.*

His name was Thorgils and he, like Jones, had once been a very powerful leader. Less than a year before, he'd been second-in-command of the entire Norse Legion, the brutally crude amphibious force which had wreaked so much havoc along the east coast of America. Now he was a prisoner too—a dupe of the Fourth Reich and the witch named Elizabeth Sandlake. It was she, he was convinced, that had murdered his father, the leader of all the Norse, and turned over their American conquests to the Fourth Reich in return for the promise of the largely ceremonial title of Queen of America.

Once the Nazis took over, Thorgils was hunted down and arrested as quickly as any United American soldier. As it turned out, his crimes were many, at least in the eyes of the Fourth Reich authorities. Not only was he part of the Norse First Family (and therefore very disposable), he'd also committed the most mortal of sins: disobeying an order passed to him by the Witch Elizabeth Sandlake.

Both were crimes punishable by death.

Now Thorgils, his formerly sturdy Viking frame reduced to skin and bones, crept along the wall, around the carcass of a recently butchered dog, and into the slight pit where Jones and Frost waited.

There were no exchanges of greetings, no handshakes or salutes. This was a business transaction.

"You have it?" Jones asked him.

"Do you have my payment?" Thorgils responded.

Jones looked at Frost who could only roll his eyes. This man, this Viking, who had been their archenemy less than a year before, was now more pathetic than dangerous. His eyes were perpetually glazed over, his ragged clothes permanently soiled. His hair was long and stringy and his beard bore the evidence of every meal he'd eaten in the past two weeks.

He was, in all senses of the term, an addict. It was his addiction that was very weird.

Jones pulled a dirty envelope from a secret compartment underneath his tool box. Sealed inside was a single photograph.

"Here is your payment," he told Thorgils. "Where is the merchandise?" Jones would not hand over the payment until the exchange was completed.

Thorgils slowly undid his fist to reveal the plastic bag of *myx*. Jones and Frost examined the golden, gooey contents for a moment.

"Are you sure it is enough?" Frost asked, his voice betraying a slight edge of nervousness. "Or could it even be too much?"

Thorgils cracked a broken tooth grin and looked at Frost.

"You must be the one who wants to die," he said.

Twenty minutes later, Frost was laid out in the middle of the chiseling station, next to the block of concrete which would be chipped down to form Adolf Hitler's mustache.

He was naked except for a pair of ripped shorts. His skin was smeared with oil and dirt. His eyes were open and thin tears of yellowish liquid were slowly rolling down his cheeks.

A slight white foam was running from his nose.

His lips were spread into a white, toothy grin.

"He went easy," Thorgils said, more to himself than Jones. "Obviously, this was the correct decision."

Jones looked down at his friend and couldn't help but feel a pang of sadness.

He's the last one left, he thought. *Now it's only me.*

Thorgils put his hand to Frost's throat and squeezed it.

"It's done," he said finally.

Then he turned to Jones. "My payment please?"

A pang of conscience hit Jones in the gut.

"You are a sick man in a world of sick men," he told Thorgils disgustedly as he handed over the envelope holding the photograph.

Thorgils took the envelope and held it to his chest even more securely than he'd held the ultra-precious *myx.*

"I've learned to live with that a long time ago," he told Jones in slurred broken English.

With that, he stole away into the darkness, leaving Jones alone with the rigid form of Major Frost.

The General would stay awake all that night and wait until the vulture wagon arrived at dawn to take Frost away.

Chapter Fifteen

It was only when Thorgils reached the far side of the prison yard that he relaxed slightly and took a deep breath.

"Made it," he whispered to himself. "Again . . ."

Unlike the other prisoners, Thorgils was not forced to sleep on cold concrete or filthy stone. He slept every night on a bed of hay. Nor did he have to fight for the cupful of soup which the Death Skulls spooned out once a day to the rest of the inmates. Thorgils ate some sort of meat — beef usually — nearly every day. And he had never resorted to putting stones in his mouth to relieve thirst and hunger. He didn't have to. He was always supplied with a cow or lamb bone to gnaw on, the rotting marrow and dried blood providing him with a veritable feast compared to the gruel the others lived on.

These luxuries did not come without a price, however. They were in fact part of his job.

Thorgils was not a stone cutter or a member of the block moving gangs. He was not a vulture, or a measurer, or a weigher.

He was the prison dog keeper.

It was an enviable job. The Death Skulls maintained a line of half mad German shepherds with which they walked the prison yard during the work hours. The dogs were all physically deformed in some way. Some had had their bones intentionally broken and then improperly set. Others were regularly fed small quantities of cement or clay. When it congealed in the guts, it cursed the canine with a nasty, permanent stomachache. A few had endured hours of shotguns being fired next to their ears while they were restrained. The result being that the dog, while being half deaf, would explode in anger at the slightest sound.

All this was done to make the Death Skulls' guard dogs wildly unpredictable and extremely vicious and the hooded Nazis had done their job well. On an average of once a day, a prisoner met his end by the teeth of these brutalized beasts. The infraction might be large or petty; it didn't make any difference. Once the Skull gave the order to *Angreifen!*—attack!—the targeted prisoner was doomed. Anywhere from five to fifteen minutes of horror ensued as the hapless victim was literally ripped to death and his corpse consumed by the attacking dog as a reward.

Thorgils was given the job as dog keeper by default. Simply put, none of the other prisoners wanted the duty; and several had chosen a bullet in the brain rather than pamper the Death Skulls' murderous pets. (Thorgils's predecessor had taken the job with the intent of killing all of the beasts via poison. He managed to put six of the twenty-four dogs out of their misery before he was caught and fed to the remaining shepherds literally one piece at a time.)

Thorgils had never entertained such thoughts. Rather he embraced his job, even though it meant lying in the same, dogshit hay as the individually caged beasts, eating out of the same filthy bowls that held their daily ration of usually uncooked cow or sheep entrails, and chewing on the bones they left behind. He had simply fallen back on the instincts of his distant relatives, the original Vikings who, during long trips in their raiding dragon boats, lived and flourished under nearly identical conditions.

So to Thorgils's unstable mind, he was simply communing with his ancient elders.

The job also allowed him to maintain his strange, unbalanced addiction. Now finally back at the dog pens, he crawled inside the large, smelly wooden structure and made for the far corner. Several of the shepherds stirred as he came in. They were, despite their various ailments, not light sleepers, and his scent was very familiar to them.

He scurried over to his own separate cage and hunkered

down in the cleanest corner, scattering several small rats in the process. Removing a carefully concealed floorboard, he reached down and retrieved a plastic bag of *myx,* similar in size and content to the one he'd given Jones. The only difference was this *myx* was much lighter in color. It was more yellow than golden, and therefore not as concentrated.

He studied the few drops of almost syrupy substance, making sure it had not become contaminated. It hadn't—not that it made any difference. He would have ingested it anyway.

It was a secret learned from his father that had gotten him in so much trouble. Back in their brief heyday, the Norse First Family had paid their looseknit alliance of warring clans with *myx.* By controlling the production and dispensing of the highly addictive, hallucinogenic drug, Thorgils and his father held sway over their frequently squabbling soldiers. It was a classic example of Pavlovian supply and demand.

What Thorgils and his father knew was a little *myx* went a long way. Just a single tiny drop in a tankard of lager was enough to send a man reeling for almost twelve hours. More drops—say, an eighth of a tablespoon—meant a longer experience. However, if a person drank or was given a larger amount, anything more than an eighth of a cup, then something very different happened. That person would go into a *myx*-induced coma so deep that they could literally pass for dead.

This was why the crazy United American officers were buying high-concentrated *myx* from him. Not to enjoy the drug and all the undeniable pleasure it brought to both body and mind. No. Twelve of them so far had used it to feign death itself, to get out of the Dragon's Mouth.

To get free.

Thorgils had no such bravado tendencies. He was happy where he was. With his dogs. With his *myx.*

There was only one more thing he needed . . .

He opened the plastic bag, stuck his finger inside and came out with the tips of two fingers stained with the sticky stuff. He immediately put the fingers under his tongue and closed his eyes.

The familiar sweet sensation ran through him immediately.

Suddenly the doghouse was a palace, its walls lined with gold, its floors sparkling like the finest jewels. The dark, humid night became cool and refreshing. The putrid water in the cracked cup next to him became a mug of the best ale. The rotting bone between his legs became the finest meal. The sleeping dogs were transformed into the truest thoroughbreds.

He was almost there.

With barely controlled emotion, he picked up the envelope. He'd been paid in various ways by the United Americans, but this is the first time he'd demanded what was inside the ripped and worn envelope. The foolish Americans had no other choice but to comply.

Now he carefully tore the envelope open. Then with a deep breath, he reached inside, drew out the photograph, and held it in the dazzling light sparkling before his eyes.

"Gods below," he whispered. His entire being vibrated with lust. "It's her . . ."

The submarine is rolling. Bells are ringing somewhere aft. He stands over the bed looking down at her. The gleaming knife is in his hand.

She is stunningly beautiful. As always.

His father is dead. Gone. Gone forever. Had he passed on to Valhalla? Did he die in battle? Did he die of a broken spirit? Was he murdered?

Would he ever know?

The last message from his father and king. Now it is in his ears and behis fore eyes. Do away with the Valkyrie. Kill her.

But why? Had she been disloyal? Did she break a sacred oath? Or did his father want her to join him in Valhalla? If so, did she not have to die in battle to ascend to that holy place?

He is mesmerized the lovely creature before him. Her hair is golden blonde. Her body is a vision; her face a masterpiece. He begins to cry.

He knows she was never a Valkyrie. Not really. She is not the type. She is a queen in her own kingdom. She would have to be. Of this he is certain.

How could he do it then? How could he defile one of the gods' most beautiful creations? Kill her? He couldn't kill her.

He loved her too much.

The solution may be then to turn this gleaming sword upon himself. To thrust it directly into his heart. To have her face the last to grace his pupils. To have her beauty be the last to race his heart.

To live or die? It is the choice of a lifetime.

But there is an answer. It is in the *myx*.

Reach down now and draw out too, too much. Put it on her lips. Feel your chest brush against her breasts. Touch the warmth of her breath. See her eyes close slowly. Behold her as she lies perfectly still.

Your lips to hers. Your hands on her bare shoulders.

Undo the top lace of her bodice.

Draw back the strings like petals of a flower.

See at last what you have been craving all this time.

There was a sudden damp explosion between Thorgils's legs.

Its intensity caused him to crack the back of his head against the dirty cement wall of his cage. The sound alone woke him from the orgasmic *myx*-induced dream.

He was getting good at this.

He opened his eyes and watched the world spin for the next half minute. Slowly, the golden walls and jewels and pearls evaporated in the darkening spiral. The dazzling lights were gone. So were the grand stallions. The palace was now the doghouse again. Smelly. Filthy. Dehumanizing.

He stared down at the photograph of the woman named Dominique; his hands still too weak to wipe away the accumulating drool. Her face was painted with alluring makeup. She was dressed in a low-cut black negligee, showing a substantial amount of her beautiful breasts. Her lovely legs were adorned in black silk. She wore a crown in the midst of the wildly erotic blonde hairdo.

He had been right all along, he thought. *She was a queen!* This picture proved it. She was a queen to soldiers of America. Nearly all of them still carried her photo with them.

Right over their hearts. They had told him so themselves.

And now like them, he had her picture. But the difference was, he had had her. Their queen.

And that made him their king.

He drew a dirty rag from the hay floor and stuffed it between his legs to sop up the consequences of the episode of blind, pure, self-indulgent lust.

Then he closed his eyes and heard the dogs begin to stir.

She is still sleeping somewhere, he thought.

Chapter Sixteen

The road leading into *Fuhrerstadt* airport was filled with hundreds of military vehicles.

The sun was just coming up and the legions of tanks, APCs, missile carriers, fuel trucks, self-propelled howitzers, Hummers, scout cars and troop trucks were causing a traffic jam of such massive proportions, a mushroom cloud of engine exhaust was nearly blotting out the first rays of the dawn.

The snarl of war machinery was not limited to the ground. Overhead, more than a hundred aircraft were circling in holding patterns perilously close to one another. Helicopters— Apaches, Blackhawks, Cobras, Hueys—were competing for the air space closest to the ground. While a wide range of state-of-the-art combat jets—Tornados and Jaguars mostly— sullied the sky between three and seven thousand feet. All of the aircraft were armed to the teeth, all of them wearing the distinctive blue-grey spot camouflage of the Fourth Reich Luftwaffe.

This was not a typical day, even for the city which housed the capital of the German occupying forces in America. The troops had been called out for an occasion—a ceremony to welcome the First Governor of *Bundeswehr* Four. It was protocol to pull out all the stops in welcoming one of the Fourth Reich's most powerful officers. It was also an excuse to lay on a giant helping of the lavish Prussian pageantry the Nazi soldiers loved so much.

The two-mile road leading to the airport was lined with thousands of spectators, though their enthusiasm was absolutely nil. These were Americans living under the occupation and forced to attend the impending parade. Most had lived in other parts of the country before the Fourth Reich's sudden and crushing invasion. They'd been deported to *Fuhrerstadt* as slave labor for the sprawling city's weapons factories and its perpetually busy river docks.

And there was plenty of work to go around. *Fuhrerstadt*, AKA Football City, AKA St. Louis, was not the capital of Nazi America due to some fancy. Rather it was its geographic location (on the Mississippi River and at near center of the occupied territory) and its accessibility from land, water and air that made it a natural for the seat of the fascist government. Therefore just about anything that was flown over from the European Fatherland to occupied America passed through *Fuhrerstadt* at some point, with much of the heavy lifting being done by once proud Americans who were now little more than human chattel.

On the main boulevard, heavily armed patrols of *Nicht Soldats* walked the gutters, using their AK-47 rifles to nudge any American who they felt was not waving their pre-supplied Fourth Reich flags with proper enthusiasm. Other NS stood watch on the rooftops of the buildings lining the route, their eyes painting the crowd from above, their orders to shoot anyone who might get out of line during the ceremony. At the same time, dozens of undercover police circulated inside the crowd itself, their ears perked for the slightest whisper of dissension.

At exactly 7 AM, hundreds of air raid sirens began to blare across the city. This was a signal. The airplane carrying the First Governor of *Bundeswehr* Four was now just five minutes from landing. It was time to sort out the traffic jam and rev up the false moxie of the very captive audience.

Four minutes and fifty-eight seconds later, the enormous C-5 carrying the First Governor and his entire entourage touched down at the end of *Fuhrerstadt* Airport's longest runway.

Screeching overhead was its ten-plane protection squadron, an elite unit made up of Tornados. They plowed a way through the spiral of *Fuhrerstadt*'s own circling jets, broke into pairs and came in for quick landings nearly on the tail of the big C-5.

The C-5 had slowed to the end of the runway by this time and had turned onto a taxiway which would bring it to the main terminal building. This taxiway was lined with 122-mm mobile artillery pieces, their long barrels cocked at 45-degree angles. Each gun fired off a single dummy round—long on noise and smoke but little else—just as soon as the tail of the Galaxy transport rolled by its position. This was an exercise performed with extreme precision and care. Woe to the gun commander whose crew shot too soon and impacted its powerbag onto the tail of the dignitary's airplane.

The huge jet transport made it through the gauntlet unscathed and turned toward the main terminal. There was no one there waiting for it. The governor of the *Bundeswehr* Four would be insulted by a simple airport greeting ceremony. Rather the big plane screeched to a halt about 200 feet from the terminal. Its crew quickly shut down its four massive engines.

Exactly one minute later, the front of the airplane lifted up like a gigantic mouth. Out of the maw came two VBL scout cars, a Bradley APC, a Hummer crammed with radio equipment, and a converted troop van which now served as an emergency ambulance. It came complete with an operating table and a six-man squad of the Fourth Reich's top surgeons.

Behind this vehicle came a long, pearl white, super-stretch Mercedes limousine. The front of this thirty-five-foot, sixteen-wheeled car was heavily reenforced, as were its many door panels and underbody. To the rear of the vehicle was a raised platform which featured a removable crystal clear bubble top. Underneath this bulletproof canopy were three chairs.

The one in the middle, slightly higher than the other two, was occupied by the resplendently dressed First Governor. In the seat to his left sat the young girl named Brigit, the former slave whose talents at artwork so enamored the Nazi high commander.

In the seat to the First Governor's right, wearing a tall white miter on his head and dressed in colorful satin vestments that rivaled those of Vaticans past, sat a very bewildered Mike Fitzgerald.

Exactly two minutes later, the small motorcade was roaring down the main boulevard toward the heart of *Fuhrerstadt*.

The thousands of slave laborers waved their small flags with less than controlled abandon as the visiting high officer's limo shot by. Many of the intersections were crowded with various NS ceremonial outfits, regimental bands, honor guards and such. These units would snap to action as quickly as the small parade of vehicles approached.

Those that could, caught a brief glimpse of the bemedaled and beaming visiting Governor, the young girl in the frilly white dress on his left who was waving somewhat stiffly, and the man in the religious robes, who was simply staring out at them, his face a bucket of confusion.

The motorcade passed the halfway mark and turned onto the main street which would bring it directly into downtown *Fuhrerstadt*. There, waiting at the main headquarters of the occupying German forces, was the *Amerikafuhrer* himself, the hermit Supreme Commander of Fourth Reich America. The plan called for him to greet the First Governor at the top step of the gigantic *Reichstag*, and then usher him and his entourage into the main dining hall for a four-hour, twelve-course state brunch.

But very soon, that plan would go awry.

The motorcade was about a half mile away from the *Reichstag* when the First Governor leapt to his feet and commanded the limo driver to stop the car. The man unquestioningly obeyed, screeching the vehicle to a halt so sharp, he was nearly ejected out the front window.

As the security people in the first two vehicles turned around in horror, they saw the First Governor's limo take a very unscheduled right turn off the main street and toward the largely abandoned west side of the city.

When the security chief radioed back to the limo to ask why it had veered off course, the First Governor himself took the call.

"This is where my work will begin," he told the security man calmly. "Perhaps you should all follow and learn something."

By the time the scout cars, the APC, and the ambulance turned off the main street, the First Governor's limo was roaring through the deserted streets. Its driver following directions personally called out by the top man via the car's radiophone. Two security helicopters had now joined the pursuit, alerted that something might be terribly wrong in the motorcade.

The choppers reached the limo's position roughly the same time the ground units did. They found the car had pulled over a dirty smoking truck, the First Governor apparently intent on questioning the driver.

Upon arriving, the security forces bounded from their vehicles and set up a hasty protective ring around their charge. They were horrified to see that the truck the First Governor had stopped was actually a morgue wagon, carrying the nightly fatalities from Dragon's Mouth prison to the mass grave on the other side of town. Even more amazing, the First Governor himself was out of his protective limo and was engaged in an animated conversation with the lowly vulture driving the sputtering hearse.

"How many of them are dead?" the First Governor asked the driver.

"All of them, I think," the totally stupefied man replied.

"Lay them out," the First Governor ordered the man. "Lay them right out on this street for all to see."

The confused, yet savvy, security men didn't have to be told to help. They practically knocked aside the driver and his goon assistant in their rush to take the two dozen bodies off the truck. Each corpse was wrapped in a dirty white sheet and sealed inside a reusable fiberboard box. These coffins had been recycled so often, however, that their lids barely stayed on.

Once the dead were arrayed in a long straight line down the middle of the road, the First Governor addressed the fifty or so people, security men and NS street troops from the parade route, in a loud, ringing voice.

"We are water," he declared definitively. "We come from the water, which in turn, comes from the stars. Just as water gives us life at birth, it can too give us life after death."

The security troops tried to remain looking grim, but it was hard to do when the First Governor's actions seemed so baffling. The six doctors who'd followed the scene in the rolling operating room had drawn out their own diagnosis of the First Governor's peculiar behavior days before. It was so apparent. He was displaying every single known symptom of acute *myx* poisoning, from giddy irrationality to tenth-degree megalomania.

"I have proof that this is true," the First Governor went on. "I have talked to people who have seen it, and now I believe. I want to prove it to you, so you will believe too."

He took the young girl in the white dress by the hand and together they walked down the row of shabby, corroding coffins. They stopped about two thirds of the way down the line. The girl, edged on by the First Governor's whispered instructions, pointed to a particular box.

"Open it!" the First Governor commanded. The truck driver and his assistant, at last realizing just who was giving the orders, jumped forward and began prying the nails out of the coffin lid. While they did this, the First Governor raised his hand and motioned back to the limo.

"Father!" he called to Fitzgerald. "Come forth and show us your secret of salvation!"

Mike Fitzgerald was just about frozen to the spot.

He'd been through many strange incidents in the past five years. Many strange incidents in his life, but this? This "Man of the Water" stuff? A messiah? *Him?*

He climbed out of the limousine, past the edgy security guards, and down the line of coffins. The two oily workmen had pried off the coffin lid by this time. As soon as Fitz reached the open box, the First Governor turned back to the crowd and resumed his pontification.

"This, my friends, is a true 'man of water,' " he told them, his hand resting on Fitz's shoulder. "Watch him. And believe . . ."

The First Governor turned to Fitz and smiled.

"Raise him," he said softly.

Fitz was almost paralyzed.

"Raise him," the First Governor repeated, pointing down at the sheet draped corpse. "Raise him, so they too will believe in you as I do."

Fitz had no choice. He knelt down and said a quick stalling prayer. He knew his masquerade would soon be over.

He pretended to finish with a whispered "Amen," Then he did a slow-motion sign of the cross.

"Prepare to believe!" the First Governor bellowed.

All eyes burning through him, Fitz reached into the box and placed his hand on the man's forehead.

Suddenly, the corpse moved.

It startled Fitz so he nearly fell over. The gasp from the crowd sounded like the crack of a gunshot.

"Believe!" the First Governor cried out. "Believe your eyes!"

Fitz was shaking visibly as he tapped the side of the figure's head. The body stirred again.

"No . . . it can't be," someone moaned in the crowd.

"Is this happening?" another whispered in a trembling, reverent voice.

Somewhere deep inside him, Fitz found the countenance to reach down and lift the sheet from the man's face.

"Oh, my God," he said as he stared down at the body.

The man's eyes blinked once and then popped open.

"Fitz? Is that you?"

Fitz couldn't speak.

It was Frost.

That was why he knew it had to be a setup. He knew it must be part of some grand plan, a plan hatched to regain control of the country or something equally heroic. It was the only explanation. The trouble was that only one man could have arranged it all.

And he was supposed to be dead.

Chapter Seventeen

Mass Grave Site No. 1

Lieutenant Donn Kurjan—code name "Lazarus"—checked his watch.

It was 1700 hours—5 PM. He slowly lifted a small set of binoculars to his eyes and scanned the road beyond the graveyard. Besides a pack of wild dogs and some crows, he saw nothing.

"What's gone wrong?" he whispered to himself. "Someone screwed up . . ."

Kurjan shifted uneasily in his heavy, branch draped uniform and continued to scan the long dusty road leading to the cemetery. In all the missions he'd been asked to perform in his three years in the Football City Special Forces, this one had to be the worst.

He was invisible. Of that he was certain. He was in a shallow trench selected carefully on the side of a small hill which looked out over the entrance to the graveyard. On top of him was a carefully constructed shield of dirt, branches, leaves, and grass, that he built himself following the rigorous standard as set out by a decades-old SAS manual.

This roof was indistinguishable from the topography around him. Indeed, more than once during this four-day, one-man mission, Death Skull guards had ventured very close to his hiding spot. One squad even took their lunch no more than ten feet away from him. Newly fluent in German, he had

97

little choice but eavesdrop on the Nazi soldiers' conversation which consisted almost entirely of past atrocities they'd committed as well as ones they were planning in the future.

He could have easily killed all seven of them. His M-16-1EG was not only silencer equipped, it also had laser designated sighting. But to have done so would have given away his position, and therefore terminate what had been, up to this time, a bold yet highly successful covert field operation.

Kurjan's mission was to raise people from the dead. *Literally.* As point man for the appropriately titled "Operation Lazarus," it was his job to station himself close to the Mass Grave #1. Once night had fallen, he would sneak down into the gravesites looking for the United American officers who had chosen to "die" that day via the controlled overdose of *myx.* Once found—and much talent lay in the finding—Kurjan would revive the escapee and spirit him away to a safe location, where he would be met by members of the local underground. These former militiamen would then escort the liberated man through a modern version of the Underground Railroad, a journey which culminated in the escapee reaching United Americans forces either in Free Canada or on the secluded islands in the Caribbean.

In the twenty days off and on that he'd been working the mission, Kurjan had succeeded in getting twelve officers out of their graves and into the escape system. Even the fruitless trips into the hellish pit proved educational. They served to hone his odd but useful skill of quickly determining who was dead and who was *myx*ed by jimmying the coffin lid, reaching inside, finding the candidate's nose through the death shroud and squeezing it. This temporary interruption of the already drastically slowed-down breathing process always proved just enough to wake the person out of their *myx*-induced stupor.

In other words, if the person didn't cough, he was dead.

Despite the perilous aspects of the mission—patience was the number one talent—he had managed to rescue that even dozen of officers without any problems at all.

Now, it appeared as if something had gone wrong with Escapee Number Thirteen.

He checked his watch again, the movement being painful as his shoulder muscles tended to cramp up after seven hours of studied nonmovement. 1710 hours. The stiff wagon supposedly carrying the "dead" officer was way overdue.

"Maybe thirteen *is* my unlucky number," he muttered.

Another tense hour passed. Still there was no sign of the death wagon.

The Death Skull detail had left twenty minutes before, leaving the cemetery unguarded against the looters who were known to sneak in at night and take the meager belongings of the prison camp fatalities. A thunderstorm had passed over and now the sun was dipping quickly in the west.

"No one's coming now," Kurjan thought. "Maybe no one will ever come again."

But then, just as he was preparing to make a quick, near silent radio call back to the underground's hideout, he saw a distant figure walking down the dusty road.

Kurjan now had his NightScope binoculars up to his eyes, their enhanced optics aiding his vision in the fading light of day. He'd never seen anyone actually walking on the grave road before simply because it was out in the middle of nowhere. The morgue trucks came and went, as did the guards' vehicles. But everyone rode to the cemetery—no one walked.

Yet here was a man, dressed in ragged shorts and wearing a part of a white sheet around his head like a turban, half-jogging, half-stumbling toward him.

He knew it could simply be another *sputnik*, wandering free on the edge of the glowing Nazi High City, simply biding his time until the security forces picked him up and turned him over to a slave farm.

Yet, upon closer inspection, this man just did not look like a refugee.

Kurjan watched and waited until the figure reached the crumbling wooden gate to the graveyard. At that point, he collapsed, first going to his knees and then flat-out, facedown.

Kurjan bit his lip. His first instinct was to slip out of his hiding place and go down and examine the man. But his training told him better.

Whoever the guy was, he would have to stay unattended. *Until dark.*

When Frost woke up, he found that he'd been lying in a putrid mudhole, one that was both oily and stagnant.

He rolled over, every bone, muscle and organ in his body, screaming out in pain, protesting that they had been assaulted.

He had nothing to calm them down; nothing to take away the ache that was pounding away at his cranium with the intensity of a fractured skull. Had he really died and this was Hell? For a few uncertain moments, he wasn't quite sure.

Then it started to come back to him. Ingesting the OD of *myx;* Jones helping him into his death shroud; the long, incredibly erotic and realistic dream he'd slipped into immediately after going under.

And then, just as he was about to ravage the most beautiful women he'd ever dreamed, the bubble burst. His shroud was lifted and he found himself looking up into the face of his old friend, Mike Fitzgerald.

It was at that point, Frost thought he was dead for sure.

First of all, he was certain that Fitz was dead. Secondly, his departed friend was wearing clothes stolen from the pope. Though the garb was ill-fitting, in that befuddled instant, it was definitely heavenly looking.

What happened next was equally otherworldly.

A top Nazi officer came forth and literally yanked him out of the coffin, admonishing him to stand up straight and be properly amazed that he'd just been raised from the dead. The crowd of troops gathered around him looked damned convinced. Some were simply pale with fear; others were openly weeping. Through it all, a teenage girl in a frilly white dress was using a thin piece of charcoal to draw his face on a large piece of yellow paper.

Frost endured bouts of tremors at that point—a side effect he'd been warned against should he be aroused from the *myx*-induced coma too soon. During this spell, he was led to a medical van to be pinched and probed by a squad of absolutely astounded Nazi doctors, one of whom was openly drinking a bottle of either gin or more likely vodka.

More NS officers arrived. It seemed like half of them wanted to touch or poke Frost in some way. The other half stayed as far away from him as possible. Through it all Frost simply kept his mouth shut.

He was finally rescued from the touchy-feely session by the top Nazi officer on the scene, the man who he'd gathered by now was none other than the high commander of Bummer Four, the huge occupied military district to the north.

Fitzgerald had been whisked away in another limo by this time, the security forces almost genuflecting to him as he walked past. Only a brief look back at Frost told him that his old friend appeared to be as astounded as he at what had just transpired.

The Bummer Four commander then did what might have been the oddest thing of all. After first declaring that Frost was "one of many," he laid his hand on Frost's head and pronounced him "a clean and free man."

Then he informed Frost that he was free to go. After a few moments of indecision, Frost decided that he'd best take advantage of the situation and started walking. Down the deserted street, and up and around the highway overpass, eyes straight ahead, never looking back.

It took him almost ten hours in the hot sun to find the place called Mass Grave #1.

Now as he lolled in the mud on his stomach. he felt a sudden nudge on his shoulder. He froze, his confused synapses telling him to play dead. Suddenly a hand was thrust up onto his face, and two fingers squeezed his nose like a vise.

He immediately half coughed, half sneezed and then jerked

the intruding hand away.

That was when he turned over and saw a man wearing a large bush and a black painted face smiling down at him.

"Don't worry," this man said. "You're back from the dead."

Chapter Eighteen

The air pirate named Itchy wasn't sure where he was.

Not exactly anyway.

The large body of water to his right was Lake Erie, the dozens of abandoned rusting buildings to his left probably the old Gary, Indiana USX steel works. Behind him were thirty or so miles of the railroad tracks he'd been walking alongside for what seemed to be forever. In front of him, many more miles of tracks before he reached his destination. Something from his childhood made him think that when lost following a railroad track was a good idea. Eventually you'll wind up somewhere.

Still he was uncomfortable not knowing his exact position. Spending the past few years in the cockpit of his long-gone fighter had spoiled him. He was no longer a land animal. If he'd been looking at this same piece of ground from the air, he was confident that he'd know exactly where he was.

Still, he knew that eventually he'd wind up in New Chicago, his ultimate destination. All rail beds in this area wound up in New Chicago eventually. All he had to do was keep walking west.

It had been six days since his frightening experience with the mysterious commandos, but the incident was still burning in his mind, especially the vision of the W's written across the sky. Itchy knew he was lucky. He just didn't know why. Who were those guys who captured him, drugged him, and then let him go? What kind of soldiers these days would do that? A bullet in the head was a much simpler solution, humane even, when compared to what he and his fellow air pirates had done to some of their unlucky victims in the past.

He had to laugh when he thought of those soldiers. They had no qualms about directing an air strike against some big city, but when it came to offing someone like him, they just wouldn't—or couldn't—do it. Did they really think that by sparing his life the world would be a little less evil? If so, the joke was on them. If anything, he knew his salvation would make the world that much worse.

What a bunch of saps, he thought.

It was getting dark, and he had to begin searching for a place to sleep. Preferring bugs to rats, he selected a small patch of still green weeds located near the edge of a filthy, rust water run-off stream, and laid out the remains of his parachute as a bedroll.

Once he was settled, he devoured two survival pack candy bars and one third of a canteen of water, Then he smoked half of his second-to-last cigarette, carefully extinguishing it after exactly six puffs. After another sip of water, he lay back and stared up at the imposing rusting hulk of a gigantic coal crane towering over him.

Should he or shouldn't he?

It was a question he'd been asking himself for the past six days. It would have been easier to decide if he knew exactly where he was. If this place was near the old city of Gary, Indiana, then it would only take a couple more days for him to reach New Chicago and rejoin his unit.

Go ahead. Do it. You deserve it.

It had been six long days of walking and eating candy bars. Maybe he deserved a little reward. If only for fighting off the temptation for so long.

Fuck it. Go ahead. What harm will it do?

He reached deep into the crotch of his flight suit pants and pulled out a small wax bag. Carefully pulling off the binding rubber bands, he wet the tips of two fingers and slowly dipped them into the bag.

He could feel the two fingers go pleasantly numb as he withdrew the few tiny drops of the sticky thick substance and studied it for a moment. It was just a little, stolen from the batch he'd given to the Nazis in Bummer Four. But it was more than enough for him. Closing his eyes, he dabbed his fingers on his tongue and then sucked off every last possible residue of the *myx*. When he opened his eyes ten seconds later, the dark rusting crane overhanging him was gleaming as if it was made of pure gold.

When Itchy came to two and a half hours later, his pants were sopping wet.

"Holy shit," he whispered, just then realizing that he was emerging from an incredible *myx*-intoxicated state.

"All those girls," he breathed. His body was weary as if he'd actually romped with a roomful of costumed nymphettes for two hours. "All those lovely fucking girls. . . ."

He immediately wrapped up his parachute bedding and prepared for a hasty leave. Just why he was doing this, he wasn't sure. It was still hours before dawn, and only a fool would walk this countryside at night. But his mind was telling him to get up and get going, and when one was under the influence of *myx*, they really had no other choice. Or so it seemed.

Still he couldn't help but wonder why. What was driving him at this point? Maybe it was his brain telling him that the sooner he got going, the sooner he'd reach New Chicago and the sooner he'd be able to cop some more *myx* and do the wet dream all over again. This time with some *real* nubile girls.

Or could it be that something else was calling him to walk the tracks?

He was moving west again within minutes. The last of the *myx* was still coursing its way through his system. He knew this because everything seemed to either be glowing like gold on its own or bright with illumination from nearby objects. He also felt the overwhelming conviction that he was damn near invulnerable. That was typical of most *myx* encounters.

If I'm lucky, this might last until noon, he mused.

His mind began to wander as he continued the rhythmical march of a railroad bed, alternately stepping on a tie, then gravel then another tie and so on. Back when he was still captured, when he'd seen all those *W*'s written across the sky, the incident had provided him with one clue as to who his captors were.

He'd never met up against the Wingman while flying with his air pirate gang. If he had, he would have been dust long ago. No, he knew only of the famous Hawk Hunter through the stories told by the older guys in the Cherrybusters. Itchy discounted ninety percent of their tales about the Wingman as being pure bullshit—supposedly he was in a dogfight alone against one hundred Soviet fighters and shot down every single one. Itchy was smart enough to know that the remaining ten percent probably had to be true, and that was a frightening thought.

How could a fighter pilot be *that* good?

But it made no difference now. The Wingman was dead. Everyone was damned sure of that, All those *W*'s were probably executed by the last of his buddies, running water hoses out the ass-end of their airplanes, just to get the big white spread.

Those guys could skywrite across the entire country, he thought with a laugh. *It still wouldn't bring their hero back.*

His thoughts drifted back to what he'd do when he finally reached New Chicago. He didn't have any money and he was sure his squadron commander would not loan him any. But this was not a problem. He would simply go downtown and rob someone, most likely killing the victim in the process. Then if it was enough money, he'd get some more *myx,* and probably some crack or heroin too. Once he started in on this combination, he knew he would feel a real spree coming on. Rape. Pillage. Mayhem. Maybe a thrill killing, if he was high enough.

The *myx*-induced thoughts of all this made him smile so hard he almost hurt his face.

Those saps should have killed me when they had a chance.

Suddenly he looked down and he saw his own shadow.

This was strange. Dawn was still at least two hours away. He blinked once, thinking it may be the *myx.* But it wasn't. Staring down at the tracks, he could definitely see his silhouette against the ties and rails.

He spun around and found himself staring full into the brightest light he'd ever seen.

It was hovering over him, no more than twenty feet above his head.

"Jesus!" he cried. "What the . . ."

He fell to his knees. The light was so bright. It was burning his corneas. But he could not look away.

"Please let this be the *myx!*" he screamed, terrified.

Then the sound came. It was an explosion of mechanical screaming. So loud, so sudden. he felt his eardrums pop like gunshots in a quick one-two succession.

Now he went down to all fours, his eyes burning, his ears stinging, his knees weak. The light moved directly over him and when it did, he could feel twin blasts of heat, so intense, they burned his hair. There was smoke too. Smelly, like exhaust, it was thick enough to blacken his teeth.

I'm dead. he thought. *And this is the beginning of Hell.*

Or maybe not.

After what seemed like an eternity, the airborne light slowly began to move away. With it went the ear-splitting thunder and the waves of smoke and heat.

Itchy watched, mesmerized, as the light suddenly turned to the east. Then in an explosion of flame and power, it rocketed away, passing over the dark horizon in a matter of seconds.

Itchy lay prone for the next hour. He was burned on his skin and head. His eyes ached, his ears were bleeding and his body was covered with oily exhaust soot.

But he was still alive.

And in that hour, only one question bounced around his mind: *Why?*

Chapter Nineteen

One week later

Frost picked up the bottle of champagne and checked the date. "Nineteen sixty-six," he said aloud, fingering the gold leaf raised Dom Perignon label. "A great year . . . I think."

He stared hard at the neck of the bottle. His eyes like lasers inspecting the neatly twisted wire assembly holding the cork in place. Suddenly the wire began to unravel on its own. Then the cork began to move. Slowly, but effortlessly, it raised itself out of the bottle stem, until it finally ejected with a loud *pop!*

Frost snatched the near ballistic cork right out of midair and handed it to the lovely, skimpily dressed redhead woman on his left.

"A souvenir for you, my darling . . ."

Never letting her dreamy eyes stray from his, the woman took the damp end of the cork, put it between her lips, and began sucking on it suggestively.

"It's so wet," she purred. "And so *hard* . . ."

Frost shuddered with an erotic rush. He turned to the equally delectable woman on his right.

"Champagne, my dear?"

This second woman lifted her glass for Frost to fill. She took a sip of the bubbly, giggled a bit, and then rose slightly to whisper something in his ear.

"I shaved for you today," she cooed, running her hand up her lovely, milk white thigh. "And not just my legs . . ."

Frost felt another tremor of lecherous delight. He poured himself a glass of champagne and turned his attention to the set of large jewel encrusted doors which dominated the far end of the spacious, harem-style room.

"Who are we expecting today, ladies?" he asked his playmates.

"Your all-time secret love," the brunette on his right told him. "The one you've been dreaming about having all these years?"

Now Frost was almost paralyzed with lust. He knew exactly who they were talking about.

"Really?" he asked in a gasp. "She is *really* here?"

"Yes, she is," the redhead told him, softly laying her hand mere inches away from his upper, inner thigh. "That is what you wanted, right?"

Frost could only nod his head by now. The hormones were flooding the glands in his body at such a rate, he thought he was going to explode.

"Call her in," he finally managed to say.

The brunette simply snapped her fingers and the two doors burst open. There was a puff of steam or smoke and somewhere in the background, violins began to play.

Frost saw the visitor's legs first. They were works of art, delicate slender ankles, perfectly curved thighs.

His eyes slowly moved up, following the contours of the lovely hourglass of hips, waist and chest. She was wearing a hockey shirt bearing the logo of the Montreal Canadians. It was ripped in strategically erotic places: He could just barely see the nipples of her lovely, small, pert breasts.

"My God," he whispered. All of his erogenous zones were pulsating madly, with no little help from the probing hands of his playmates. "Is . . . is it really her?"

At that moment the last of the smoke dissipated and he could now clearly see her face.

It was a vision of haunting beauty. Her long blonde hair was expertly tousled. Big blue eyes, classically structured nose, wide pouting lips, ears that begged to be nibbled.

Frost could barely catch his breath by this time.

"Mon Dieu!" he cried, reverting to his second language. "It is you. You are here. You *are* alive .

The woman was suddenly right in front of him, one hand

softly touching his trembling cheek, the other directing his fingers to her nearly naked breasts.

"Yes, Major," Dominique said. "I am really here."

"Major . . . Major Frost . . ."

Frost bolted up from the bunk like he'd been shot from a cannon.

The young Scandinavian sailor standing at his bedside caught him and steadied him.

"Sorry, Major," he said in slightly tinged English. "I apologize if I startled you . . ."

Frost struggled to get his bearings. He was inside a small stateroom. Just a bunk, a sink, a foot locker and a small desk and chair. The walls were painted gray upon gray and a myriad of pipework crisscrossed the ceiling.

It took a few moments more, but then he realized where he was: on board the battleship, USS *New Jersey.*

"Are you okay, Major?" the sailor asked him.

Frost wiped an embarrassing bit of drool from his mouth.

"I'm fine," he said quickly. "Just a dream, that's all."

The sailor handed him a note.

"It's from the captain," he told Frost. "The choppers are warming up right now, sir. You have to be up on the launch deck in ten minutes."

Frost took the note and read it quickly. It confirmed the sailor's verbal report.

The sailor saluted and left, after which Frost virtually collapsed back down on the bunk and took a deep breath.

It had happened again: another highly charged erotic dream, caused by the residue of his intentional *myx* overdose. He was experiencing them almost every night since being transferred to the *New Jersey.* Each time it took him a few minutes to settle back down.

He'd been on the battleship for a total of ten days now, having traveled through the escape network, first accompanied by the Football City Special Forces man who'd rescued him from the graveyard, and then by two members of the American underground movement. He'd spent much of that time on board recuperating mentally and physically from his escape ordeal.

Of late he'd been getting a crash course on the ship's wide array of offensive and defensive weapons. The enormous battlewagon was currently plying the waters off the east coast of Panama, its sophisticated early warning radars and artificial fog making mechanisms insuring that no enemy eyes could see it.

But this was no meaningless cruise, as Frost soon found out.

The battleship was under the command of the masked man known to all simply as Wolf. Frost had known of the mysterious Wolf before coming to the battlewagon. He'd been briefed on Wolf's brilliant naval action in support of the United American forces during the repelling of the Norse invasion of the Florida coast. The battleship and its massive 16-inch guns had destroyed no less than thirty of the Norse submarine troopships, damaging many, many more.

But now the *New Jersey* was serving as a flag ship for a very different kind of mission.

Despite his clouded mind and deteriorated physical condition, Frost had become aware of one indisputable fact during his first day on the ship. It had come in a personal message to him from Wolf which said, to wit, that despite small numbers, the forces of freedom were very quietly gathering on the periphery of the new, instant Nazi empire. Their intent was to strike a major blow against the occupying Fourth Reich fascists. One which would seriously disrupt, if not halt altogether, their rabid swallowing of America and its captive population.

But to do this correctly, Wolf had written, would mean a rallying of democracy s allies like never before. Covert actions had to be carried out. Weapons had to be purchased. Mercenaries had to be hired. And as many imprisoned UA officers had to be made free as humanly possible. This was why the elaborate and dangerous prisoner escape system had been set up. And this was why Frost had been brought to the *New Jersey*. He was to participate in nothing less than the first attempt to gain back a large piece of the imprisoned American continent from its treacherous Nazi overlords.

For a freedom loving individual like himself, it was like a dream come true.

But he also knew that it was an endeavor of monstrous propor-

111

tions. One that would have been handled by the late Hawk Hunter in past years. Now, it was apparently up to those who survived the initial onslaught of the Fourth Reich to carry the banner against their tyranny and imperialism. And try to do it in the way the late Wingman would have done.

Wolf frankly communicated to Frost that he would be expecting him to take on some very dangerous missions before the Grand Strike was launched, ones that would be plainly life threatening.

Frost was more than willing to risk his life for such a cause and he would have told Wolf personally if he'd had the chance.

But he didn't. Wolf wasn't talking to anyone.

In fact, none of the crew had seen Wolf or talked to him directly for a long time, even though he was aboard the ship.

Frost wasn't quite certain why Wolf had maintained this self-imposed isolation. He *did* know that the mysterious captain had been locked away inside his quarters for at least the last three months. Not seeing anyone, taking his monk's meals of bread, water and soup through an opening in his cabin door. Still the enigmatically reclusive Wolf had issued a steady stream of messages to his staff, instructing them on even the most minute details of the emerging liberation plan.

This strange behavior was not lost on anyone aboard. The rumors of what was going on behind Wolf's sealed door ranged from a near maniacal need to be alone to plot the crucial strategy to a kind of creeping insanity. The guards posted outside the door reported hearing Wolf banging away on his computer keyboard at times, and indeed the man had sent steering and course change commands directly to the ship's bridge via his computer.

Much of the time, though, there was dead silence behind the door, interrupted only by traces of hushed conversations. It was this last report, and the fact that the guards swore the conversations were absolutely one-sided that had given rise to the story among the highly superstitious, mostly Scandinavian crew that their captain was in fact communing with a ghost.

Frost didn't believe in ghosts. At least he didn't think he did. And he was certainly in no position to question Wolf's odd behavior. He was an officer and it was his job to carry out his orders, and that was what he was prepared to do.

One of them, carried down from Wolf himself the night before, involved the trip Frost was due to take that day. He was scheduled to chopper out with a squad of *New Jersey* commandos to a secret location, one known only to a handful of people in the world.

Wolf's message told Frost the trip was necessary for him to see for himself a crucial element in the emerging Big Strike plan. It would also allow the Free Canadian officer to see firsthand the clues in what Wolf described as a "mystery within a mystery."

It was with these enigmatic thoughts bouncing off his already *myx*-bruised thought processors that Frost hastily climbed into the dark blue utilities suit worn by the *New Jersey*'s newly-established, one-hundred-man commando unit, and checked his 9-mm Berretta pistol's ammo load.

At the same time he was trying with all his resolve not to think about why his most lustful *myx* dreams always seemed to involve the beautiful companion of his long-lost friend, Hawk Hunter.

Chapter Twenty

The two Westland Lynx helicopters lifted off from the USS *New Jersey* and quickly turned west.

Frost was squeezed in between two massive commandos, both of whom displayed classically chiseled Scandinavian features. Like the seven other troopers inside the cramped passenger bay, the commandos were armed with M60 7.62 AP machine guns, twin bandoleers of the appropriate ammunition and a sling full of hand grenades and flash bombs. Frost felt naked by comparison; his tiny automatic pistol looked puny when compared to the walking arsenal around him.

None of the commandos spoke fluent English. Norwegian seemed to be the language of choice. Not that it mattered. The combination of the Westland's powerful but noisy engines and the open bay doors made any kind of conversation impossible.

The pilot of the chopper was one man that did speak English. And as luck would have it, he was also an old friend. Bobby Crockett, one half of the famous Cobra Brothers attack helicopter team, had been flying helos for Wolf since the first days of the Fourth Reich invasion. His Cobra partner and brother-in-law, Jesse Tyler, had been missing since the first days of the German occupation.

Frost and Crockett had spoken many times since Frost's deployment to the battleship. They had gone through much together in the heyday of United America. Now both of them shared the grief of knowing that many of their close comrades in arms were either missing, imprisoned, or dead.

114

So it was with genuine appreciation and mystification that Crockett heard about Frost's incredibly bizarre encounter with another old mutual friend, Mike Fitzgerald. In fact, Crockett insisted that Frost tell him the story many times over, just to make sure he'd gotten all of the weird details straight. After imparting the story at least a half dozen times, Crockett admitted that he was as baffled as Frost as to what it all meant. A similar message to Wolf explaining the strange incident produced a similar reaction.

The pair of Lynx flew for about forty-five minutes over the clean green waters of the Caribbean. They passed over dozens of small islands, and intentionally flew around several more. Several times Frost spotted other aircraft, cargo planes mostly, flying off in the distance, heading west as he was heading east. As the Lynx pilots did nothing to avoid being spotted by these airplanes, Frost had to assume they were part of the growing anti-fascist coalition.

They'd just passed an hour in flight when Frost saw Crockett waving him into the Lynx's cockpit. It took the Free Canadian several minutes to unbuckle his safety straps and make his way over the mountain of commandos. But he finally reached the front part of the heavily armed, heavily loaded helo and crammed himself into the narrow space between the two pilots' seats.

"We're five minutes from touchdown," Crockett yelled to him. "I thought you'd want to see our destination from up front."

Frost immediately began scanning the far horizon, searching for some kind of landfall or an island on which he expected the Lynx to set down.

"Cuba?" he yelled up to Crockett, appreciative of the irony that would accompany his finding that a secret American base had been established on the island nation.

But it was not to be. The destination of the Lynx was not Cuba or any other island.

"There it is," Crockett yelled over the racket of the engine blades, pointing directly east. "See it?"

Frost strained his eyes to focus on the horizon, but saw nothing at first. But then, gradually, he began to make out something riding atop the green sea. It was just a speck, but it quickly grew large as the helicopter drew closer. Soon it began to take a definitive shape. It was a large black-gray rectangle, long and flat except for a brief interruption midway on its silhouette. It was definitely floating, and there seemed to be bits of air activity going on above and around it.

It finally dawned on Frost what he was looking at. He couldn't believe it.

"Is it?" he yelled into Crockett's earphone. "Is it really . . . ?"

The pilot nodded once. "It is," he confirmed.

Before them, riding still but proud in the calm tropic sea, was an enormous aircraft carrier.

Two minutes later, the pair of Westland Lynx were circling the ship.

Despite the immense majesty of its size, Frost could quickly tell that the aircraft carrier was far from operational. Its deck was bare of aircraft, save for two gray camouflaged Sea Hawk helos and a single all black Huey. None of its half dozen radar dishes were spinning, none of its navigation runners were lit. And, for want of a better description, the ship looked fairly beaten up. At the very least it needed a good cleaning and a fresh coat of paint.

"Which one is she?" Frost yelled to Crockett as they made their final circle before landing.

"It's the USS *Enterprise*," Crockett yelled back. "CVN-Sixty-Five. Last seen in the Indian Ocean the day World War Three ended."

Frost could not help but stare down at the massive ship in awe. Already he was rushing to some very likely conclusions. This was no doubt the aircraft carrier used by the Fourth Reich to launch their devastating sneak attack on the United American air forces right after the successful repelling of the vicious Norse assault on the Florida east coast. Yet it was obviously now in the hands of the Americans.

The big question was: *How?*

As it turned out, it was a query that had many different answers.

The two Lynx landed on the aft deck, right next to an up and operating Roland anti-aircraft missile battery.

Frost waited for the commandos to deploy before he finally crawled out of the back of the Lynx. He helped Crockett and his copilot secure the chopper to the deck bolts with ratch chains and then held the main rotor blade still while the two flyers tied it off by rope to the front of the aircraft.

His helicopter thus secured, Crockett led Frost to the ship's island and up toward its high tech Combat Information Center.

"You look over the evidence my friend," he told Frost. "Then you tell me what you think happened."

Ten minutes later, Frost and Crockett were sitting in a corner of the *Enterprise*'s CIC.

There were a few technicians from the *New Jersey* moving about, some off loading computer data to be used back on the battleship, others trying to activate a number of sophisticated communications and weapons systems which had not been turned on for at least a half year.

Before Frost and Crockett was a thirty-six-inch high-definition television screen, with a gaggle of attendant VCRs and remote controls. A cabinet containing hundreds of multi-hour video cassettes was close by.

"Somehow, Wolf's guys found this ship floating around the south end of the Grand Cayman Islands," Crockett explained as he lit up the big TV. "When they finally came aboard, they were very surprised to find that a lot of its critical stuff was still functioning. All in pre-set modes, all running on batteries.

"Now, as you probably know, the US Navy used to video record just about every operation on board its carriers. This ship was no different. What *is* different is that these cameras all around the ship stayed operating for quite some time after World War Three. Obviously the people who took over this bird farm wanted to continue this video history of its operation.

"But as you'll see, it didn't turn out the way they planned."

The screen burst to life and Frost found himself looking at a wide angle view encompassing about two-thirds of the carrier's deck. Unlike its barren and somewhat shabby present condition, the deck in the videotape was alive with men and machines, all of them obviously belonging to the US Navy.

"We've determined that this footage was shot on the last day of World War III," Crockett explained. "This is probably the last air strike launched."

Frost watched as airplane after airplane was hurled off the carrier via its three steam launch catapults. The airplanes—F-14s, F/A-18s, A-6s, S-3s—were all loaded to the max with ordnance, and it was obvious by watching the actions of the launch crews that this was a scene of desperation. The highly coordinated, yet chaotic looking dance of launching a carrier aircraft looked just chaotic.

"They knew the end was near," Frost confirmed.

The screen went blank for a few moments then came to life again.

This time the deck was covered with aircraft, so many in fact that it was too crowded to almost move about, never mind launch planes. Men in black coveralls were squeezing between planes or scampering beneath them, many carrying large black buckets of paint. Plainly these people were newcomers.

"What happened to the original Navy crew?" Frost wanted to know.

"No one has the slightest idea," Crockett replied. "They left the ship anchored a mile off Guam and then they just vanished. Maybe they got ashore, maybe they were boarded and all shot. We'll probably never know."

Frost felt a chill run through him. Five thousand brave Americans, gone just like that.

"This footage was shot the first or second day after the ship was reclaimed," Crockett went on. "We figure it was at least two years before anyone else came onboard."

"Who are these people?" Frost asked. "And what the hell are they doing?"

"Just who they are is still up in the air," Crockett told him. "But as you will soon see, they are painting over all the markings on the airplanes."

It was true. The men in black were systematically covering all insignia on the Navy planes, replacing the various numbers and symbols with two quick splashes of black paint in the form of an X.

"We figure that these guys might be part of a huge black market weapons gang," Crockett explained. "There are plenty of them in Asia these days. They apparently found the ship and salvaged it, not for their own use, but to sell to someone else."

He speeded up the video to another blank space. Slowing it

down to regular speed, the same camera angle showed the deck operating again, though on a much smaller scale than the hectic yet professional US Navy launches. As they watched in silence, barely two planes were launched in the span of five minutes, a speed that would be considered tortoiselike under normal Navy operating conditions.

"These are apparently the new owners," Crockett said, noting their light blue work uniforms. "They're slow, but they're getting planes off."

"And these people are?" Frost asked.

Crockett let out a long breath. "They've got to be closely connected to the Fourth Reich units who launched the big strike on Florida," he said. "This is obviously early in their operations. In later tapes, their 'efficiency' is very apparent, if you know what I mean."

Frost did.

Crockett pointed to the series of numbers rolling by in the lower right hand corner of the screen.

"Usually this is the setting for time and date," Crockett said, "but these bozos came up with their own time system. It's probably just a random thing, but after Wolf's crypto boys examined this tape they determined it was made fourteen months before the Florida sneak attack."

"So they'd been planning on attacking us all that time?"

Crockett shrugged. "Well, they were clearly planning on attacking somebody. But now, watch this . . ."

He ejected the videotape and quickly inserted another. It was the same angle, same view. But the activity on the deck was very different. Planes were being shot off the carrier at a much improved rate of two a minute.

It was obvious that the famous Prussian efficiency had kicked in.

"They must have trained their asses off to get that good, that quick," Crockett said. "It's an example of how dedicated, or should I say, *fanatical,* these guys were about this ship. About everything they do."

Frost shook his head in grudging agreement. "But what happened then?" he asked. "Why did they abandon this ship? It had to be their most formidable weapon."

119

Crockett inserted yet another tape and pushed the play button.

"The cryptos figured this is the tape that was shot during the launch of the Florida raid," he explained as the tape began playing. The launching of the carrier aircraft was now even more coordinated.

"Look at the underwing stores," Crockett suggested. "High explosives. Runway cratering stuff. Iron bombs."

"Everything they hit us with during the strike," Frost observed. "God, did they set us up!"

Crockett punched the tape to fast forward, stopping at the point where the carrier deck is finally cleared.

"This is where it gets interesting," he said, dead seriously. "Keep an eye on the timing numbers."

Frost watched as the numbers rolled by. Their infrequent changes and the sudden jump in the picture told him that what he was looking at was actually a time sequence.

"When there was no activity on the deck, they would set the camera to shoot only a few seconds of footage every minute," Crockett explained. "Then, when the air strike planes returned, they would switch it on full time."

But as Frost watched the numbers streak by, he realized something very strange was happening. The fateful air strike had taken place in the afternoon. The airplanes should have returned within a ninety minute time. Yet on the videotape, it was clear that night was falling. And there were no airplanes.

"They never came back?" he asked Crockett.

The Cobra Brother simply shook his head no. "Something—or someone—prevented them from doing so."

They passed the next few minutes of total silence as the time-lapsed videotape continued to roll. At times, figures could be seen moving about the deck, sometimes scanning the sky for the overdue airplanes. Night gradually turned into day.

Then it happened.

Suddenly the image began shaking violently. People could be seen scattering, smoke began blowing by the speeded-up camera's lens.

"Good God, they're under attack," Frost declared.

The fractured flickering style video continued. It was clear that a gunfight had erupted very quickly. Armed crewmen could be seen firing at something aft of the deck, something just out of the camera's range. But what was more, these men were unquestionably getting the worst of it. Burst upon burst of heavy cannon fire could be seen tracing across the deck and ricocheting into the waters below, frequently taking two or three of the armed men with it.

This weird fast-motion battle went on for a full half hour in real time, but finally, no more armed crewmen could be seen on the deck. Nothing happened for at least another two hours. At least not within view of the deck camera, and soon, it was apparent that night was once again falling.

At that point, Crockett reached over, ejected the tape and put in a final one.

"This is the last piece in this puzzle," he said.

The screen came to life once again. The scene had changed. Now the camera angle showed a long passageway somewhere in the heart of the ship. There was an incredibly vicious firefight in progress, the combatants appearing as so many shadows moving about, illuminated like ghosts in the glare of tracer bullets. The scene changed again; now the view was in a large hall that Frost recognized as one of the ship's below decks' airplane hangars. But the gun battle was no less intense. Nor was the casualty rate. It was very apparent that despite their overwhelming numbers, the armed crewmen were clearly getting the worst of the contest.

Then the scene changed for a third and, as it turned out, final time.

It looked as if this footage had been shot several days later. The camera angle showed one of the ship's mess halls. The place was filled with smoking clutter and wreckage. The remains of many armed crewmen were in evidence, as were casings of heavy caliber ammunition. There were many large gaping holes in the walls, floors and ceiling, most still sizzling with smoke and red glow, indications both that rocket propelled weapons had been used. There was no more shooting though, no more streaking tracer rounds. Just the wreckage, the smoke and the dead. The rampage was clearly over.

"He hunted down every single one of them," Crockett said, not daring to mention the name of the perpetrator of the vengeful destruction. "Wolf's guys found his shell casings in the vent system, in the crawl spaces, in closets, on the gang rail, up in the conning tower. Everywhere.

"More than twelve hundred men. The cryptos figure it took about a week. But he—whoever *he* was—got every last one of them."

"Damn," Frost breathed.

"After it was over, he rigged the ship's main computer to run on a makeshift autopilot system," Crockett continued. "It put the ship into a series of wide circles. Then he refueled the engines, disabled the catapult and disconnected the key components in the communications house. All that took about two weeks."

"And then?"

"And then," Crockett said with a deep breath, "he disappeared."

Chapter Twenty-one

Thirty minutes later, the pair of Lynx helicopters lifted off from the deck of the *Enterprise.*

Frost stared down at the bow of the ship as his helo ascended. At the very tip, near the end of the steam catapult channel, were two faint burn marks, distinct only because someone had painted two white circles around them, as if to preserve them. These were telltale marks of a VTOL (Vertical Take-off and Landing) aircraft, and further evidence that whoever attacked the *Enterprise* so many months ago had arrived and apparently departed in a jump jet.

Frost felt his mouth go dry. Strapped in next to the chopper's open bay for the return trip, he watched the carrier slowly fade from view. The evidence was certainly there: the jump jet burn marks, the relentless gun battle against astronomical odds, the selective destruction of some of the carrier's main systems and its eventual, pre-programmed autopilot circular course. It was obvious that there was only one person who could have waged the incredible single-handed campaign.

So then, why would no one say it? Why would no one breathe the name? Were they afraid that by speaking it, it wouldn't be true?

As the chopper climbed and the carrier finally disappeared into the haze, Frost wondered if they would ever really know.

Suddenly a warning buzzer reverberated throughout the cabin.

"Load weapons!" Came the call from Crockett to the nine commandos.

Frost was unstrapped and squeezing his way up toward the

123

cockpit in a flash. Load weapons? For what? They were out in the middle of the ocean.

Crockett was talking rapid-fire on his lip radio by the time Frost made it up into the cockpit.

"What the hell's going on?"

Crockett signed off the radio and put the helicopter into a long wide bank to the north.

"We just got a code two flash," he yelled back to Frost, as the copilot armed all of the copter's weapons. "We're going into action . . ."

Frost was astonished. "Action? Where?"

"Something big is going on," Crockett yelled back. "About forty clicks from here. They need all hands and all weapons there. Now!"

The nine Norwegian commandos were up and ready by the time the first smoke of the battle was spotted.

Frost was ready too. He was double strapped right at the edge of the open bay door, forming the bottom link in a human wall of machine guns and rifles. His own weapon was a .357 Magnum given to him by the chopper's copilot. Huge and bright silver, it had been adapted to fire enormous, high-impact cannon shells.

But just what would they be shooting at? It was a question running through the minds of everyone on board.

They had their answer just two minutes later.

From a height of four thousand feet and a distance of five miles, the enjoined battle looked like a swarm of bees pouncing on something hidden down below in an enormous cloud of fire and smoke. Struggling to keep his eyes focused and clear against the wind blowing directly into his face, Frost was able to pick out at least eight UA-marked Huey helicopter gunships flying in the midst of the battle. It seemed as if they were all firing their weapons at once: M-60 machine guns, TOW missiles, 2.75-inch rockets, 20-mm cannons, miniguns, 40mm grenade launchers. A virtual rain of steel and high explosives was falling on the still unseen target.

As fire packed as the venerable Hueys were, the pair of Westland Lynx were loaded with an even more overwhelming array of weapons. Each one had two Hellfire missiles strapped to its twin external pylon mounts. Each was also carrying a pair of computer-controlled torpedoes, and four small, air-launched depth-charges. Added to this the trio of 20mm cannons in each chopper's nose, plus a squad of commandos with their weapons poised and ready at the open door.

"Hang on, boys," Crockett yelled back to them through the crackling radio speaker. "We're going right in."

A second later the pair of Lynx began dropping out of the sky, their already loud engines roaring up to full attack power at a deafening pace. Frost rechecked his enormous hand cannon. It was secure and ready. The commandos all inched forward, their weapons up, their double-locked safety straps straining as they moved forward for the most optimum firing position. Still none of them knew what the target was.

One mile out, the two Lynx leveled off at five hundred feet, and at precisely the same moment, launched a computer-controlled torpedo into the billowing cloud of smoke and flame. Almost immediately, Frost could hear the nose cannons on each chopper open up. A Huey suddenly flashed by, its pilot turning it over so he could follow the Lynx in on their first bombing run. Another one was right on its tail. Now the sounds of the explosions hidden in the conflagration were rivaling the roar of the Westland's engines.

That was when the chopper finally broke through the shroud of flames and smoke and they all saw the target for the first time.

"Jesus!" Frost yelled over the engines and multitude of explosions. "I don't believe this . . ."

None of them could. They were so surprised, that no one fired a shot for a few seconds. What they saw before them was so astounding.

It was a submarine. Long, black, sleek, and shiny.

"Damn," Frost yelled above the wind and the noise of battle. "It's one of the *Fire Bats* . . ."

It *was* a *Fire Bats* and it was being absolutely pummeled from all sides with all kinds of weapons as it raced through the surface waters apparently too damaged to submerge. But still, it didn't look real somehow. It was more like something from a big-budget Hollywood movie of days gone by. He had heard of the *Fire Bats*—they all had. Four submarines had appeared at the same time as the Norse invaders, each one said to be carrying at least one nuclear missile. It was in their missile chambers that lay the nuclear terror which held all of the American continent in the grasp of two fascist fists. But they were as elusive as the Loch Ness monster.

Until now.

By some apparently incredible stroke of good fortune, the United Americans had found one of the mysterious, hated submarines on the surface. And they were not going to let it escape alive.

The two Lynx roared over the stricken submarine, their cannons firing nonstop. A second barrage was coming from the cargo bay itself as the jammed-in commandos let loose with all their weapons at once. It was evident from the maddeningly desperate fire power being unleashed onto the boat that every shot would count in preventing the *Fire Bats* from getting away. So, hanging on for dear life, and not quite believing what was happening, Frost added his large-caliber pistol fire to the fusillade.

Frost's Lynx roared up and over and swung back in for a second strafing pass. Two Hueys were lined up in front of it, all weapons blazing, their duo barrages of 2.75 missiles impacting all along the submarine's shiny black conning tower.

The Hueys cleared and the Lynx went in again. This time Crockett reduced the chopper's speed, giving his copilot and the men in back a longer opportunity to fire. Frost squeezed off two shots. The second shot might have shattered one of the sub's tower-attached antennae. Though in the storm of bullets, missiles, and bombs, it was truly impossible to determine who was hitting what. What *was* for certain was that the *Fire Bats*—flames and smoke pouring out of dozens of places—was mortally wounded.

"Pour it on!" Crockett was screaming over the intercom, as he turned the ship for its third pass. "Pour it on!"

The commandos and Frost obliged, emptying clip after clip at short range onto the sub's hull, even as the Lynx's second pair of torpedoes smashed into the rear of the vessel. The Lynx made another turn, lining up behind two more Hueys, and then flashed in for a third attack. And then a fourth. And then a fifth.

This aerial dance of death continued for ten long minutes, until finally, smoking heavily and aflame from its bow to its tower, the *Fire Bats* slowed and went dead in the water.

On a call from the flight leader of the Hueys, all of the gunships backed off and went into ragged orbits two hundred fifty feet above the sub. From these vantage points, all eyes watched with a mixture of awe and brazen satisfaction as the big sub shook with two explosions and broke in two.

Then, with one final mighty explosion, it slipped beneath the waves and went down for the last time.

Chapter Twenty-two

Lieutenant Stan Yastrewski, also known as "Yaz," woke up and found himself staring at two beautiful, naked breasts.

He instantly shut his eyes back tight and froze in position.

Where the hell am I?

His mind strained to recount what had happened in the past twelve hours. But it was all a big blur. Was he still aboard the so-called Great Ship? The former Royal Viking luxury liner was first converted into a command ship for the invading Norse armies and now served as a gigantic, bizarre reincarnation of Cleopatra's famous love barge. He thought so; he could feel the gentle rocking of the ship that had become so familiar.

But this was not his regular room. Through slits in his eyelids he could see that this cabin was easily a hundred times bigger. And this was definitely not his regular bed. His usual bunk was dirty, stained, and without a blanket. This bed—actually a water bed—was enormous and it was covered with satin sheets. Something else was different. Not a morning went by when he didn't wake up with his stomach screaming for food because he was only allowed one meal a day. Now, his belly was so full he would have let his belt out two notches. If he had a belt.

What happened to him?

He'd spent the last eleven months living in a cabin that was less than the size of a broom closet. Located deep within the bowels of the ship, it was not like one of the brig cells on the ship. They were much bigger. He was not a prisoner, not really anyway. He was, in fact, a "human resource," because of his knowledge of naval vessels. Since he was a commissioned US Navy submarine officer prior to World War III, the people who ran this ship had decided, as had his original captors, that he was better off alive than dead. Whenever a particularly sticky problem came up (with the engines, or the fueling system, or the navigation stuff) the ship's chief master would call him to "consult" on how to fix the malady. In return for this help, "Yaz" was allowed to live.

His somewhat helpless situation was a bit more tolerable for one reason only. Before his capture by the Norse invaders, he had been a ranking member of the United American Command Staff. The key factor of the United American past successes had been resourcefulness, doing the best one could with a bad situation. To this end, "Yaz" had spent much time gathering intelligence information about the Great Ship and its newest owners, telling himself it would be helpful to the United American cause someday.

He dared to open his eyes again in order to study the breasts. He did not recognize them. And the night before was still very hazy. He closed his eyes, knowing something had to be done. Still feigning sleep, he mustered up enough courage to turn over, and at least reconnoiter an escape route from the strange bed. To this end, he slowly rolled his body from his right shoulder to his left.

But when he opened his eyes, he found himself staring into *another* pair of equally lovely, if slightly smaller, breasts.

Oh, my God . . .

Now his mind was really racing, panicking in its amnesiac state. He sucked in a silent, deep breath and held it. Slowly things began coming back to him.

He had bedded down as usual the night before, on his little smelly bunk in his smelly little room. Of this, he was sure. Then the soldiers came. Not the usual ones who summoned him when repair work was needed. No, they had been the Queen's own personal bodyguards, distinct by the white naval uniforms.

They took him out of the room and forced him to drink something from an old wine bottle. As he recalled, it wasn't liquor exactly; rather it was sticky and sweet, with the consistency of maple syrup. He remembered being terrified, thinking it was poison. But then the guards led him onto an elevator that he knew was used only by the hierarchy of the Great Ship. They rode up to the fifth level in silence; the controlled breathing of his half dozen guards still ringing in his ears.

But then what had happened?

He slowly let the breath out and took in another.

The elevator door had opened and he was pushed inside a huge dining hall by the guards, who then disappeared. There were only two people inside this hall, but they were barely visible. Sitting at the end of a long table, their faces were obscured by a kind of golden fog.

After that, it got really sketchy.

He recalled walking toward them, compelled because they were calling his name. Their features still hidden, they gave him more of the sticky fluid to drink. After that they almost literally stuffed food down his throat.

He recalled their laughter. Good God—they were women! And they had . . . They had . . .

At that point it all came flooding back to him, The two women. The big water bed. The hours upon hours of sexual activity. Highly erotic. More talk and touching than actual penetration and fluid exchange. There were costumes and masks and strange music.

And the women had asked him if he knew Hawk Hunter. Over and over and over again.

Suddenly. he felt a soft hand slide down his back and begin probing his upper thighs.

"Don't pretend that you're asleep," the voice belonging to the owner of the hand said. "Do you really think you could fool me?"

"Yaz" felt a deep freeze run through him. He recognized *that* voice. It belonged to Elizabeth Sandlake, ruthless martinet, authentic witch, the virtually self-anointed "Queen of America."

He couldn't believe it. Like a strange wet dream, the hazy, druglike sex romp had involved the most powerful person on the ship—male or female. But this was not what had turned his spine to an icicle. No, rather it was the stories he'd heard about this woman Elizabeth in regards to her sexual habits. Quite frankly, she frequently murdered her lovers shortly after consummating, like a Black Widow devouring its partner once the heavy breathing had stopped.

"Don't worry," he heard her voice waft over his shoulder as she continued her light massage. "You're safe. I would never harm someone who was so close a friend to the late, great Hawk Hunter."

Her unseen reassurance did little to melt "Yaz" back to reality. He knew for a fact that it was a deceitful boast. Elizabeth Sandlake had been the one responsible for sending the person *closest* to Hawk Hunter—his girlfriend Dominique—off to her death. "Yaz" couldn't imagine why he'd be spared.

"It's because you are a man," came the answer to his unspoken dilemma. "You are the last man on this ship who can come anywhere near satisfying both of us."

That was when "Yaz" opened his eyes for real and found the beautiful face of Juanita Juaraez, Elizabeth's "companion," smiling sleepily at him.

"You are lucky," Elizabeth's voice told him as Juanita's hand joined hers. "For years, men have enslaved women. To feed them. To clothe them. To bear their heirs. To be their whores."

"Yaz's" eyes went wide as both women made a concerted effort to get him revved up again.

"But as of last night, *you* are now *our* whore."

It was almost thirty minutes later when the red phone on the table next to the huge water bed began buzzing.

"Yaz" was grateful for the break in the action. With his stamina just about peaking, he needed a few moments to catch his breath and coax some feeling back into his jaw.

Answering the phone with a cold, angry response, Elizabeth's attractive if deadly features drooped as she received the bad news from the unfortunate sort on the other end of the line. She hung up the phone while the caller was in midsentence, then slumped back to the water bed.

"Those heathens!" she cursed. "They've sunk one of the *Fire Bats* . . ."

"Oh no . . ." Juanita moaned. "How? When?"

131

Elizabeth ignored her questions. "They've obviously found out about my coronation." she said in a voice so low, that "Yaz," situated at the foot of the bed, barely heard her. "They want to spoil what is rightly mine."

Both women were totally ignoring "Yaz" by now. "Will we still go through with the ceremony?" Juanita asked.

"Yes! Of course!" Elizabeth bellowed. "We must go through with it. Now more than ever!"

Chapter Twenty-three

Dragon's Mouth Prison, Football City

General Dave Jones reached into the bucket of grimy water and splashed a few drops onto his dry, sunburned face.

It was closing in on noontime and this meant that his chiseling station, mercifully hidden in the shadows for most of the morning, would soon lose its shade and be subjected to the intense summer heat.

Jones gave his tired neck a crack and then picked up his tools and began chipping away at the massive block of stone in front of him. This was Piece 34-A Center, half of the buckle which centered on the uniform belt surrounding the massive stone impression of Hitler. He would have to chip away nearly half the two-ton block by sundown that day or face punishment. It was a daunting task made even more difficult by the fact that he no longer had an assistant. After Frost had "died," the prison camp administrators failed to assign him a new helper.

So now, besides the lonely fact that he was the only one left on the inside who knew that something was going on on the outside, his work load had doubled.

He chipped away for several minutes, working quickly as the last of the cooling shadows slipped away. Then, somewhere off in the distance, he heard a deep-throated whistle, like one from a steam pipe organ. Instinctively, many of the ragged men around him perked up. They had all learned that the sound of the strange whistle usually presaged the serving of their single daily meal.

Sure enough, a minute later the doors to the prison yard swung open and the mess truck rolled in followed by two jeeps filled with the hooded Death Skull soldiers.

The mess truck came to a slow stop in the center of the yard, and a line of hungry prisoners quickly formed. The meal was the same as always: a weak-tasting, foul smelling soup which only on the best of days featured a few raw vegetables swimming in it, plus a piece of stale black bread. Each man ladled out his own, one scoop per man, as the faceless, heavily armed Death Skulls stood by, whispering to each other through their black hoods. Once he'd drawn his meal, each prisoner was given five minutes to consume it before returning to work.

Jones wearily picked up his rusting meal can and made his way to the end of the food line. It was obvious that as the work progressed on the gigantic statue, the number of prisoners still available was dwindling. Deaths, real and otherwise, were gradually taking their toll on the officers' prison population.

He worked his way down the queue, finally scooping out a ladle of the bad stew and grabbing a piece of black bread. His usual procedure, acted out like a ritual when Frost was still around, was to head back to this station and eat in the last remaining bits of shade. But now, on this day, something attracted his attention to the far side of the prison yard.

A small group of inmates had gathered there and were in fact sitting and eating their meals together. This sudden show of solidarity mystified Jones. It was rare to see three or more prisoners sitting together in the work yard. To see as many as two dozen in one place was highly unusual.

He drifted over toward the group, dipping his bread into his soup and eating it as he walked. It wasn't until he was about fifty feet away that he realized the prisoners hadn't just spontaneously sat down in the rough semicircle. Rather they were listening to another prisoner, one who was sitting in the middle of the group.

The prisoner was Thorgils, keeper of the dogs and the dispenser of the somnambulistic doses of *myx*.

Jones instinctively slowed his stride, trying his best to catch wind of what the strange man was saying without having to join the group itself.

What he finally heard startled him.

"We will rise from here," Thorgils was saying, through bites of his own meal. "We will all ascend. Into the sky. We will be saved from this life. We will die and then be reborn. It's just a matter of time."

Suddenly Jones wasn't hungry anymore. There was an eerie feeling in the air as Thorgils's squeaky, broken English wafted over the crowd and bounced off the nearby walls.

"We will rise," he was saying again. "We will all be out of here soon."

Jones couldn't believe it. The man was preaching blasphemy as far as the prison authorities were concerned. Yet there were two hooded Death Skull soldiers standing nearby, if not directly listening to Thorgils's rambling. They probably didn't speak English, yet they were at the very least letting him continue.

"And once we arise," Thorgils went on, "I will be your King."

Jones now began working his way away from the gathering. Thorgils was obviously dipping heavily into his bag of *myx* and the last thing Jones wanted was to get caught along with that group once the Skulls realized what the fallen Norse leader was babbling about.

He returned to his station and cleaned out his soup can, watching as the Skulls finally began moving through the courtyard ordering prisoners back to work after the short five-minute break. He went back to chiseling the huge belt buckle, but the bizarre little scene began to gnaw at him. It was just a matter of time before someone in the prison administration realized what was going on with the unstable Thorgils and his stash of *myx*. When they did, they were likely to execute the Norseman on the spot. This would be a lucky turn of events, as far as Jones was concerned. The alternative would be if the Skulls decided to take Thorgils to their headquarters and interrogate him first before putting him to death.

And if that happened, Jones knew that he'd be in serious trouble. As the man who had given them the ODs of *myx*, Thorgils knew many secrets about him.

Jones felt the heat of the sun finally touch his forehead and bare chest. The last of the shadows were gone. He could now look forward to being baked by the brutal sun for the next five hours.

Sweat and grime returning with full intensity, he quickened the pace of his chiseling. At the same time, he tried to formulate a plan about what to do with Thorgils.

* * *

Mike Fitzgerald walked across his vast bedchamber and turned the air conditioner down to low power.

"The last thing I need now is to catch a chill," he thought aloud, walking back across the room and collapsing back onto his enormous satin pillow packed feather bed.

His head was aching, his stomach was grumbling, and he had developed a slight shaking of the hands. He wasn't surprised that he was in such a condition. To say that he had lived the last two weeks in a state of high anxiety was a gross understatement.

Sure, he'd been immersed in forced extravagance inside the *Reichstag*'s special guests' suite—eating the finest food, drinking the finest wines, wearing the finest silk clerical garb. But despite his opulent surroundings, he had endured nothing but a bad case of nerves in that time.

One big question had been answered: It was obvious to him now that all of the healing and raising from the dead stuff was actually part of some incredibly elaborate scheme concocted by the United Americans. The encounter with Frost had proven this point.

But why formulate such an ambitiously far-out ruse? This answer too came easily to Fitz. He was savvy enough to know that the whole scenario of providing him with a messianic image had obviously been constructed to get him here. Inside the supreme headquarters of the fascist occupying forces, he was close to the seat of Nazi power, close to the shadowy *Amerikafuhrer* himself. But what exactly *was* the next part for him to play? And who would tell him? And when? These questions were not so easily answered. But as a good officer and professional soldier, Fitz knew it was his duty to continue to go along with the charade and await further instructions.

Still it was this not knowing that had kept his psyche frayed for the past fourteen days.

About half that time, he'd spent at the side of the First Governor at a myriad of public displays. Sitting on the man's right, just as the fifteen-year-old girl prodigy was sitting on his left, it outwardly appeared that the First Governor immensely enjoyed soaking up the apparently never ending adulation heaped on him by the scores of occupying Fourth Reich soldiers.

Yet despite appearances, Fitz knew better. It was obvious to him that the First Governor was becoming more unbalanced as the days went by. They had appeared at more than two dozen official functions in the past fourteen days—state dinners, parades and nearly daily political rallies. But for the most part, the First Governor had simply sat and smiled. He quickly lost interest during the elaborate proceedings staged in his honor and spent most of the time staring off into space, trying to think the Big Thoughts.

On those occasions that he did speak, it was to ask Fitz about the moral implications of even his tiniest acts. By bathing every day, wasn't he wasting water needed by others? Wasn't it immoral to eat an egg because it meant taking an offspring away from its chicken mother? Was it not in opposition to Nature for men to fly in airplanes? After all, had he been meant to fly, man would have sprouted wings.

Fitz had learned quickly under fire to nod his head to each question and then give the First Governor a distinctly vague answer, which the Fourth Reich officer always seemed to enjoy interpreting. It was clear that he had come to regard Fitz not only as his personal resurrector, but also as his spiritual conscience, a bizarre concept for a man once known for his systematic brutality.

Through it all, Fitz silently prayed that they would not come upon a legitimately injured or dead person—an accident victim or a sudden heart attack, someone not in on the plan—which the First Governor would want him to cure.

It hadn't happened yet. But just how long could the balancing act go on?

A knock at the door brought a message from the First Governor's aide-de-camp.

Fitz was to suit up in his best priestly garments and be escorted to the front door of the *Reichstag*. He was to ride in yet another parade, this one to celebrate the halfway point being reached in the construction of the *Amerikafuhrer*'s one hundred fifty-foot wedding present statue of Adolph Hitler.

Once again, Fitz, the young girl, and the First Governor himself would be the guests of honor.

Chapter Twenty-four

Downtown Fuhrerstadt

It took only a half hour for the thousands of slave workers to file out of their factories and line up along the main parade route.

Many of the workers knew their assigned spots by heart. It had become a habit of their drudgery, this never ending cycle of orchestrated praise for those who kept them in chains. Walking to a particular place on a particular curb on the main avenue in slow, measured, sullen steps, they would stand silent and still until it was time to mechanically wave their small Nazi flags at the passing dignitaries. Then it would be the march back to the hellish factories again until it was time for the next parade.

Not everyone in the crowd were slave laborers. Hundreds of special riot-trained NS also lined the parade route, and a small army of undercover police always roamed the crowd. There was also a scattering of *sputniks*. Though mostly ill fed and ill clothed, the parade police would always yank one or two of these yet to be arrested people out of the crowd and place them in front of everyone at the curbside. This was by orders of the parade marshals who thought it wise that the parade honorees see more than just drab faces of the city's slave work force.

And this is what happened to the man named Itchy.

It had taken him nearly three weeks to walk to this place, the very heart of America's Nazi Empire. He'd arrived a changed man. Accustomed to being either stuffed inside a fighter jet killing innocents on behalf of his air pirate squadron or getting all drugged up and sexually assaulting young girls, Itchy's frightful encounter with the flying light on the tracks near Gary had altered his life forever. The intense beam had opened his eyes, both literally and figuratively. It had made him see not what he really was — he *knew* he was a murdering, sexually bent criminal who just happened to know how to fly a jet fighter — but what he could be. It told him he could change. It told him that he could make a difference. It told him to forget the old evil ways of New Chicago and divert instead to *Fuhrerstadt,* where perhaps he could change things.

And just as the beam of light had opened his eyes, the long journey through the countryside to *Fuhrerstadt* had opened his soul.

Lying in a field at night, he would stare up at the stars and weep openly at their beauty. In the day, he would frequently stop to admire a babbling brook or a bird's nest or a clutch of wild flowers and revel in their majestic simplicity. Far from being a wanton murderer now, he treated every person he met with the same reverential politeness. He had worked for his meals along the way, chopping wood, gathering food, even helping to paint a house for an elderly couple. With each act of his kindness, he was rewarded tenfold inside.

But his new life, and he truly did feel born again, had not blinded him to all the evil in the world. Rather it quite simply explained it to him: Men were the cause of all the misery and suffering on the planet. There is nothing inherently evil in any animal or plant or fish. It was the humans who caused it all. And some definitely more than others. Of this he was sure; simply because he used to be one of them.

With his rebirth came a new grasp of common sense. It was a smart man who realized the human world was inherently evil. It was an ignorant man who allowed himself to be victimized by it. For if one did, then it would prevent him from spreading the news of the enlightenment and joy he had received.

He had been inside the city only a few hours when he saw the parade route begin to form. (He took the fact that he was able to walk past the many checkpoints uninhibited as yet another instance of his newfound spiritual luck.) And now, he had been suddenly plucked from the crowd of thousands to be given this "place of honor," along the parade route.

It was yet another sign.

From his unobstructed vantage point he could see the first rows of the leadoff marching band coming his way through the canyon of skyscrapers which lined *Fuhrerstadt*'s main boulevard. The sounds of their blaring brass horns soon reached his ears. Within a minute they were upon him, trumpets, trombones and drums, all played by impeccably uniformed, goose-stepping soldiers.

Next came several units of NS scout cars, personnel carriers and main battle tanks, their crews looking all business in their highly starched combat fatigues. After the vehicles came at least a thousand NS infantrymen, marching with their bayonet equipped rifles held out in front of them in a display of choreographed hostility.

Finally came the vehicle bearing the guests of honor. Itchy thought it was an odd mix sitting in the back of this open-roofed car: on one side was a young girl in a white dress who seemed more intent on her drawing pad and crayons than the thousands of people rotely cheering her; on the other was a priest, splendidly dressed, yet looking oddly out-of-place.

Between them was a thin man in a white uniform covered with medals, ribbons, gold stars and swastikas. Quite unlike the other two, this man was beaming. He was waving, pointing, laughing at the crowds, almost as if he was convinced they were actually enjoying seeing him.

"Perfect," Itchy whispered to himself, reaching for his gun.

Fitz was never quite sure how it happened.

One moment he was riding along in the touring car, his rear end killing him from the hard seat, trying his best to avert the glazed-over eyes of the slave workers. In the next, all hell had broken loose.

He saw the flash from the gun barrel first. Once. Twice. Three times. The man behind the pistol was smiling oddly as he pumped three bullets into the chest of the First Governor. The next thing Fitz knew, the Fourth Reich officer was grabbing his throat and finding his hands covered in blood.

"What . . . what has happened?" he cried out.

The man with the gun was immediately shot. More than six members of the NS security forces emptied their guns into him, firing at the twitching body long after it was lifeless. The stunned factory workers nearby were frozen in place, not quite believing what they were seeing. Soon the street was mobbed with security people. So much so, the driver of the touring car had a hard time moving through the crowd and away from the shooting scene.

"Turn back!" someone was yelling "Go to the hospital!"

But it was too late. Even the two doctors who had jumped from their ever near surgical van onto the back of the car moments before it sped away knew that the First Governor was mortally wounded.

The young girl was in a state of shock, and Fitz was not much better. He found himself cradling the Nazi officer in his lap, his vestments quickly soaking in the man's blood.

Fitz couldn't help but look into the dying man's eyes. His lips were trembling as they went white.

"Please, Father . . ." the First Governor gasped, looking up at Fitz with teary, pleading eyes. "Please save me . . ."

Fitz turned to stone. His worst fear had come true, but not in any way he could have imagined it.

Now he could only stare back down at the dying man and say: "I can't . . ."

Chapter Twenty-five

Dragon's Mouth Prison

Thorgils picked a small piece of dirty straw from his beard and tossed it aside.

"Can you see the flames?" he asked the crowd of fifty inmates standing in front and slightly below him. "Did you hear the gunshots?"

"I can see the fire!" one prisoner yelled back. "Right over the top of the wall."

"I can too!" another cried. "Look — fire. *And* smoke. On the other side of the wall!"

Soon more than half the crowd was jabbering and pointing to the faint glow at the top of the prison east wall, many claiming that they could actually see flames and billowing smoke.

Thorgils smiled and took in a deep breath. For the first time in a long time the air did not smell of dirty hay and dog urine.

"I have told you, my friends," he continued, steadying himself on his creaky makeshift speaking platform. "I have told you that we will be plucked from here, haven't I? *We will all ascend.* We shall all rise up! If you see the fire, then you see light."

Hidden in the shadows about fifty feet away from the gathering, General Dave Jones was shaking his head in disbelief. "What a bunch of crap," he whispered.

Undeniably, he could see a slight glint of sparkling light just at the far edge of the east wall. But it certainly wasn't anything to get so excited about. And true, there had been the sounds of gunfire earlier in the day. But Jones was certain that it had to do with another big parade the Nazis had staged around noontime. An event he was sure had happened because the food truck was later than usual in arriving, and the stiff wagons were held up at the main gate by the Skulls presumably until the traffic out on the main boulevard was cleared.

Still Jones was very worried. The fact that the *myx*-addicted Thorgils could whip up the crowd of prisoners on such small pretenses and convince them that some kind of salvation was in the offing, was highly troubling. The dog man had been preaching nonstop now for several days, beginning with the short meetings at the noon meal, to long disconnected dissertations once the Skulls locked them all in at night.

And just as Thorgils's ramblings grew, so did his crowd. Jones was astonished how many people chose to sit and listen to his nonsense about "rising up" instead of getting as much sleep in the little time allotted to them.

All this meant trouble and as a military man, Jones knew he had to do something about it.

He'd been putting off any thoughts of escaping from the prison himself, not with nearly two thousand five hundred United American officers being held just beyond the next wall. Twelve, plus Frost, had escaped via Thorgils's *myx* potion, and he'd hoped until recently that more would be able to follow. For him to leave now seemed akin to a captain jumping from his sinking ship.

But on the other hand, when the Skulls finally decided to put an end to Thorgils's prophet fantasy—and it was just a matter of time—then the elaborate and dangerous escape system set up on the outside would most likely be compromised. He was sure that the Skulls could crack Thorgils like an egg. And when they did, he was just as sure that he would tell them everything. Then, the Skulls would come looking for him, and quite possibly begin reprisals against the rest of the prison's UA population.

So earlier that day, Jones had decided it was time to get out.

But he wasn't going alone.

It was close to 4 AM before Thorgils brought his revival meeting to a close.

As the crowd dispersed, he took offerings of extra bread and water from his congregation and made his way back to his cage inside the kennel.

Jones was waiting for him there.

"Were going on a trip," Jones told him. "You and me. We're eating the last of your stuff and getting out. Do you understand?"

Thorgils, his fragile psyche already battered and reeling, was speechless.

"But why?" was all he could offer.

Jones didn't answer him right away. Instead he pulled out the slim razor sharp sliver of metal he'd been fashioning into a knife for the past few weeks and pointed it at Thorgils's throat.

"Get your stuff," he ordered the man, keeping his voice low so as not to disturb the dogs. "One way or another, you re going out of here in a bag."

Mass graveyard No. 1, 24 hours later

It was raining.

The intense heat of the day had cooked the early evening clouds to a boil and a torrential thunder and lightning storm was the result.

The hard rain spattered across the Mass Grave No. 1, turning freshly dug individual graves into puddles, large mass graves into small ponds. If anything, the rain increased the smell of death which always permeated the place. Instead of washing it away, it simply reinforced it.

It was the dead of night, but there was a spark of activity in the burial ground. Two NS armored personnel carriers, both of them bristling with heavily armed, rain slickered troops, had their powerful searchlights concentrated on a single spot near the middle of the graveyard. Here it provided light for a smaller concentration of men—six soldiers, one officer and a civilian—who were down at the bottom of one of the larger mass graves.

All but one of them were poking at the bodies.

A major named Shiltz was in charge of this strange mission.

Even though he'd been a deep-dish Nazi for several years, at least one human element had yet to seep out of him: fear. Being in the graveyard this late at night, in the middle of a thunderstorm, was too close to a horror movie for him. Thus he was scared shitless.

"Check that one!" he ordered one of his Troops nervously. "And you, that one . . ."

The soldiers hopped instantly, slipping around the putrid mud, reaching up inside the death shrouds and checking for any indications of a pulse, however slow and faint they may be.

"Nothing, sir!" the first soldier called back to Shiltz, obviously relieved to withdraw his hand from the cold neck of an authentic corpse.

"Nothing here, either," the second soldier reported, equally relieved.

Shiltz was doing a slow burn. He'd been out in the graveyard for two hours, presiding over the morbid inspection of the dead. Now he was wondering if he was, in fact, on a ghoulish fool's errand.

He turned to the civilian. The man was soaked and ragged and dirty.

"Are you sure?" he asked him, his teutonic tone leaving no small impression that he was rapidly losing his patience.

The man stood almost motionless, head drooped, rainwater dripping from every part of him.

"I'm sure," he replied slowly.

The field was so green, it was sparkling.

There were flowers everywhere, and large graceful birds were flying overhead.

General Dave Jones was lying back in this field, soaking in a sun so bright, it almost hurt his eyes.

He'd been lying here for an entire day, and yet the sun had not yet moved. Every fiber of his being was singing with pleasure. Never in his life had he felt so good.

There were women all around him, of course. Beautiful women and girls. All in low-cut, flowing gowns, all plainly available to him whenever he wanted. He would partake—soon. But first, he was concentrating on a single figure walking toward him from about a mile away.

He didn't have to squint to make out the man's features, even at that distance. The man was small and wiry, just like him. He was his exact age. His craggy face was identical to his, as was his shock of white hair. He was wearing the blue dress uniform of a general in the United States Air Force, just as Jones was.

The man was, in fact, his twin brother, Seth.

Soon he was standing before him. They embraced warmly.

"I knew we would see each other again," Seth told him.

"It's been a long, long time," Jones replied. The warm summer breeze washed across his face, "We have much to talk about."

But then suddenly, the sunlight dimmed.

Jones looked up to see a massive dark cloud had drifted in front of the sun. Instantly the sparkling green fields began to turn brown and wither. The women all disappeared. The warm breeze turned into a cold wind. And it was raining.

Suddenly Seth's face looked old—very old—and the rain seemed to be collecting under his eyes like tears.

Without speaking, Seth reached across to Jones's face and began peeling away his shroud.

The next instant, Jones was looking up into the face of an NS soldier and the beams of two powerful searchlights. It was dark and rainy and miserable.

"It is him!" the soldier was yelping in thick German. "He is the one who is still alive!"

Jones blinked away some rainwater and stared hard at the two other men standing in back of the soldier. One was a Fourth Reich officer, his face pale with either fear or disbelief. The other man, ragged and weary-looking, was Thorgils.

It took Jones a few moments to realize what had happened. He and the dog man had taken their coma-inducing *myx* solutions just before dawn that day, Thorgils doing so only at the prompting of Jones's razor sharp knife. But it was apparent now that Thorgils—either by design or fate—had taken less than Jones, had come out of it earlier, and then turned him in.

146

Suddenly, the Fourth Reich officer was in his face.

"We know all about you," he told Jones in threatening German-tinged English. "And all you've accomplished in this death masquerade is that we will now have the opportunity to do it to you for real."

Less than one hundred fifty feet away, hidden on the side of a small rise, Lieutenant Donn Kurjan, code named "Lazarus," was watching the disturbing scene unfold before him through his crystal clear infra-red NightScope.

"This is not good" he whispered, carefully adjusting the NightScope goggles to his eyes. "Not good at all."

Chapter Twenty-six

New Orleans, six days later

The young Dominican priest walked slowly along the dock-way, saying his morning prayers and pacing every other step with the phrase *mea culpa*.

The piers had the same dreary look today as they did every day. Fog, a light drizzle, and various engine exhaust combined to blanket the place in a dirty cloud. As a boy, the priest used to come to this part of the New Orleans waterfront and spend hours watching the ships come and go. It all seemed so much brighter back then. The sun splashing on the harbor, seagoing vessels of all types moving in and out, some off to the world's most exotic locations.

No surprise then that the young priest originally aspired to be a tugboat captain.

But his mother convinced him that he was too sickly for such a demanding job (he'd had bronchitis as a kid) and steered him to the priesthood instead. It only took eighteen years of badgering—and another four in the seminary—for him to be allowed to take the final vows. His mother passed on soon afterward, and that's when he started questioning the authenticity of his vocation.

Simply put, he just didn't believe he was worthy enough to be a priest.

Just like every other morning, these were his thoughts as he paced along the rickety dockway. The harbor was just as busy, just as congested as the old days. And some big ships still came and went. But they were not filled with sugar, rice, or oil like they were back when he watched them as a child. No, these days they were more than likely filled with Fourth Reich weapons and soldiers coming in, and a galaxy of looted American treasures going out.

In and out. In and out. *In and out. . . .*

It was a slow rape, but a typically efficient one.

Among the smaller boats fighting for space were dozens of shrimp boats, oyster bedders and deep-sea fishing yachts. But even seeing these smaller vessels failed to fulfill his nostalgic desires. Each one of them was skippered by a Nazi thug. Each one carried slave workers. Each one turned over its catch to the brutal occupying government.

Still even in the oppressed atmosphere that had engulfed the formerly free-spirited New Orleans, the priest knew he was lucky. The threadbare tolerance the Fourth Reich had for Catholic priests allowed him to move somewhat freely about the city, working his myriad of jobs. One concerned collecting tax money from the poorest people in the city, the ones that lived in the shantytown just south of the main harbor. Another found him teaching basic education to children between the ages of four and eight. Still another had him operating a railroad switching station in the yards north of the city. And then, of course, he was the one who buried the dead.

Today was tax day. His prayers said, he picked up his pace and turned to the pierwalk which would lead him to the shantytown. The route was lined with knots of grimfaced NS who specialized in disdaining him and ignoring him at the same time. As always, a few civilians greeted him as he passed, some more openly than others. Occasionally, someone would press a few coins in his hand (low denomination real silver coins usually, give him a quick nod, and keep right on walking. Whenever this happened, he'd always use the money to help pay the chronically short shantytown tax bill. To do anything else with it, such as spend it on something for himself would be, to his mind, unforgivable.

He always knew he was coming to the halfway point in his trip to the shantytown when he saw Old Pegg, sitting as always on his battered wheelchair, with enormous wraparound sunglasses tight against the bridge of his nose, a frayed captain's hat for begging in his outstretched hand.

If there was one poor soul in all of occupied New Orleans that the young priest would have liked to have soothed, it was Old Pegg. The seventy-ish man had miseries beyond words. He was blind. He was mute. He was ninety-five percent deaf. He'd lost the use of both legs years before, and his left arm always hung limp at his side. He had no teeth.

The young priest always made it a point to stop and visit with Pegg whenever he passed his way. He would first make a slight sign of the cross on Pegg's forehead, just to let him know who he was. This action would inevitably result in a wide, toothless grin and a stately nod of the head. The young priest would then sit and talk to the man about the weather, the harbor, or old mutual friends. Pegg always seemed to enjoy the visits, nodding and bobbing back and forth as he listened with what was left of his hearing.

And always, he would dig deep down into his beggar's hat and come up with a coin to give the padre. This meager offering too would be added to the destitutes' tax fund.

"How are you today, Mister Pegg?" the young priest screamed into the old man's good ear after making the salutatory cross on his forehead.

Pegg nodded, *I'm okay.*

"Are you getting your food rations on time?"

Again Pegg nodded yes.

"Have you been able to locate any arthritis medicine?"

Pegg shrugged and shook his head no.

"I will try again to get it for you."

A big smile. No teeth.

The young priest took the next few minutes describing the nonmilitary boats passing them in the harbor.

"There are two big shrimpers out there today," he told Pegg. "I hear they're over from Shreveport. Saw an old-fashioned ferry earlier, too. I think it was bringing cars over from Galveston, just like the old days."

This brought an even wider smile and some merry rocking.

"Saw three more sludge barges today too . . ."

Suddenly Pegg stopped smiling.

"That makes about twenty in the past few days. They must be doing a very large dredging job further up the river. Way up I should say. The stuff they are hauling is awfully red in color, nothing like what they pull up around here."

Pegg's eyes narrowed behind the huge sunglasses. He held out two fingers on his good hand and put them together. This was his sign for twenty.

"Yes. Twenty or more," the priest replied to the silent question. "The largest barges I've ever seen."

Pegg nodded slowly and squeezed the priest's hand.

"You're welcome, Mister Pegg. I will see you next week."

The young priest walked away and found Pegg had pressed an old Kennedy half-dollar into his hand. He stared at that coin for a full minute, tears welling up in his eyes with the thought that a man so afflicted would choose to give money to others.

I am not worthy to be a priest, he prayed silently, *but I would move heaven and earth for that man to be somehow healed.*

Wiping the tears from his eyes, the young priest resumed walking toward shantytown.

Chapter Twenty-seven

Frost had never been to New Orleans.

In all the years before World War III, and in the turbulent years ever since. he'd never had occasion to venture down to what Americans used to call The Big Easy, and Canadians, the Big Sleazy.

But now here he was, dressed in the clothes of a fisherman, thinking the thoughts of a spy.

He'd received this mission after re-landing on the *New Jersey.* The entire ship was abuzz over the stunning victory the nascent United American forces had scored against the *Fire Bats* sub, though just how the vessel was found in such a vulnerable position was not entirely clear. However, with the action, the nuclear blackmail threat against the imprisoned American people had been reduced by a full twenty-five percent. And though brief, in the annals of American military history, the battle had to rank right up there with Midway and Kuwait in importance.

But Frost was only halfway into his first victory beer when one of the ship's intelligence officers tracked him down in the crew's mess. He was bearing another written message from the unseen Wolf, one which contained orders that appeared quite bizarre. Frost silently questioned whether Wolf might indeed have gone too far around the bend.

But after reassurances from the intelligence officer, Frost was given the set of fishy rags and put on a super quiet Seaspray helo for the three-and-a-hal- hour flight to a small island off the southern tip of New Orleans. From there, he was picked up by a fishing boat hired for that very purpose. Then, after working the boat for three full days, he was delivered ashore shortly after sunset this day.

Now he was making his way down the famous roadway once known as Bourbon Street, avoiding the gaze of the ever present NS troopers and doing his best to mix in with the assortment of rabble moving continuously up and down the damp and dirty thoroughfare.

He was astonished by what he saw. Gone were the barrooms, strip joints, jazz halls and Cajun restaurants that had once dominated the famous street. Now they were all replaced with the peculiar Nazi equivalent of decadence. Dozens of storefronts were covered with photographs of naked women, but all being offered in the guise of "scientific" paraphernalia. All kinds of people—young, old, male, female, and a few unidentifiables—were plying the street, offering their bodies to the hundreds of off-duty NS troops. The oddest of the odd might have been the bizarrely dressed characters who were walking the streets, each carrying a goose. Frost could not help but listen in on the conversation as one of these people propositioned an off-duty NS major.

"We both fuck the goose," the prostitute was telling him in broken English, their common language. "Then we cook it and eat it."

Frost hastened his step after that encounter. Moving down the street he came upon what might have been the strangest, most disturbing sight of all.

It was on the marquee of a dingy theater on one of Bourbon's many side streets. There was a crowd of about five hundred waiting outside. The number of Nazi soldiers and the absolute stoic air hanging over those gathered told Frost that this audience was about to view the coming feature under duress.

But it was the name of the movie, spelled out in cracked plastic letters on the marquee, that startled Frost the most.

153

The name of the movie was: "Hawk Hunter, Death of a Criminal."

He finally reached the spot indicated on the small but detailed map Wolf had provided for him through his staff intelligence people.

It was a deserted pier down to the south of Bourbon, a place so dilapidated it looked like even the rats avoided it. A low fog was rolling in as the tide was going out. Partially covering his nose with a fisherman's kerchief to ward off the thick odor of rotten fish, Frost stood in a nearby shadow and checked the time. His contact was due to appear in exactly five minutes.

Five minutes and six seconds later, he heard a clapping sound coming from the end of the pier. It was footsteps, one leg scraping along after the other. Frost reached for the 9mm Beretta in his boot pocket. He was sure the person coming from the other end was checking his weapon too.

A silhouette appeared in the fog and quickly took on a distinct shape. Short, husky, a wooden leg, dragging a wheelchair behind him.

He stepped out of the shadows just as the other man stepped out of the fog.

" 'Dolph is my driver,' " Frost said.

" 'I drive Leela's car,' " came the raspy reply.

Frost let out a quick breath of relief. With the correct sign and countersign given, he knew it was the man he was supposed to meet.

"Good to meet you, Captain Pegg," Frost said in a whisper.

"And to meet you, Major Frost . . ."

"Have there been any changes in the mission?"

"No, none," Pegg replied, slipping back into his wheelchair. "We are to proceed as planned . . ."

One hour later they were sitting beneath a dying willow

tree, their NightScope-aided eyes scanning the mouth of New Orleans harbor.

"Twenty just in the past few days, you say?" Frost whispered to the grizzled old sea captain.

"That's what I heard," Pegg replied, leaning against the folded-up wheelchair. "And I saw at least twelve myself the week before. How do you figure that?"

Frost shook his head. "Who knows? It could mean anything. That's what we're here to find out."

An hour passed. Frost constantly checked that their position was still secure, while Pegg kept an eye on the end of the harbor channel.

"It's too bad about our friend, Hawk," Pegg sadly said out of the blue. "You just think that people like him will never die. We're all a little bit lost without him I'm afraid . . ."

Frost almost bit his tongue, knowing Hunter was the common bond between him and Pegg. The old man had aided the Wingman in the opening phases of the campaign against the Panama-based, nuclear-armed, neo-Nazis of the long-gone Twisted Cross. He knew that Hunter and Pegg went way back. Still he hesitated a heartbeat. Should he tell the old man just what he'd seen on board the abandoned aircraft carrier?

Suddenly they heard the low moan of a tugboat whistle.

"Here they come," Pegg said excitedly.

Frost was already crawling out of his fisherman's disguise and into the wet suit he'd carried along in his duffle bag. Fate had provided a convenient interruption.

"I see two," Pegg reported. "Now three. Four. Five . . . There's ten—no, wait, eleven of them. Eleven and a heavy tug."

Frost was checking his utility belt and then his mask. He took one last look at the line of sludge barges and then passed his NightScope binoculars and his Beretta to Pegg.

"Time to go," he said, inching his way into the shallow water at the base of the willow.

"Good luck, boy!" Pegg crackled. "I'll be here when you get back."

Frost slipped into the water and immediately began swimming. It was about a mile out to the line of barges. And if he timed himself correctly, then his course would intersect with that of the center barge in the line of eleven with no problem at all.

The water was dirty, and not as warm as he would have thought. It made no difference. Ten years before, while attending university in Montreal, he was a champion swimmer, once winning the All-Canada Gold Leaf for freestyle. What was odd was that not many people these days knew of his athletic achievement of a decade before.

So as he methodically made his way out to the line of sludge barges, once again a nagging thought crossed his mind: How did the sequestered Wolf, a man he'd never met, know that he could make such a treacherous swim?

Twenty minutes later, Frost was climbing up the side of the sludge scow.

He'd made the swim with no problem, and had even landed on the barge of his choice, that being the middle in the set of eleven, equidistant from the heavily guarded lead barge and the similarly dangerous tug.

Once he was up and over the side, he would have to work quickly. Even as a champion swimmer, he knew the longer he took, the farther he'd be away from dry land.

He really only had to accomplish two tasks. One was to get a sample of dredged silt and sludge. He did this by simply taking a handful of the stuff and stuffing it inside a small but durable plastic bag he brought along. The sludge was reddish and with almost the consistency of clay. It also smelled awful.

His second task was to plant a location finder somewhere on the barge. This took a little more doing; finding the right spot was essential. Finally he decided to plant the device inside the gearbox for the scow's automatic lock/dislock mecha-

156

nism, figuring that it wouldn't likely be found there, plus it might continue to operate after the contents of the barge were off-loaded.

The LF in place, he tied the plastic bag to his utility belt and then slipped back over the side of the scow. The whole thing had taken only four minutes.

With the currents now working with him it was only a fifteen-minute swim back to land. Most of that time was spent wondering why in hell Wolf wanted a bag full of mud.

Within an hour, Frost and Pegg were back on the foggy pier, the Free Canadians arms aching not so much from the swim, as from having to push Pegg and his overloaded wheelchair.

He couldn't complain though. Both men knew that maintaining Pegg's cover as a see-nothing, hear-nothing, say-nothing old buck was just as important as the odd mission they'd just accomplished. He was a very valuable asset. In fact, he'd been gathering very useful information for the American Underground since shortly after the two-pronged Second Axis invasion.

But just as in life in general, things frequently go wrong.

Frost heard them first. Voices and the sounds of boots running, coming from the far end of the pier.

"Damn! It's the Brownshirts," Pegg hissed in an urgent whisper. "I'd know the sounds of their hobnails anywhere."

Frost had his Beretta up and armed in a flash. It was way too late for them to hide — not unless Pegg abandoned his well-cultivated cover as a cripple.

Yet in an instant Frost knew they had no other choice.

"Leave the wheelchair," Frost told him. "Maybe we'll get lucky."

Pegg scampered out of the wheelchair, knocking it over in his haste to get his partially concealed double-barreled shotgun from a rear compartment.

157

Thus armed, they both dove into the shadows. Not two seconds later, a band of six skinhead Brownshirts came running up the pier.

The Brownshirts were a quasi-military force trucked over from Europe by the Fourth Reich for the sole purpose of creating terror and havoc among the conquered American population. They weren't really soldiers. Sanctioned terrorists was a better description. They were the modern equivalent of the SA of Hitler's Germany. Back then, some SA units were so crudely brutal, they made the rival SS gangs look like Boy Scouts.

Even so, what Frost and Pegg next saw was incredibly repulsive.

The reason the Brownshirts were running was they had a prisoner with them. He was handcuffed and gagged and his face showed signs of a recent severe beating that rendered him unrecognizable. The Nazis had also tied a dog collar around his neck and were now forcing him to run behind them.

As it turned out, coming upon the overturned wheelchair caused the band of military sadists to stop for a moment. While their prisoner collapsed to the ground, the skinhead thugs had a quick discussion in German as to whom the wheelchair might belong. After all, their primary job in New Orleans, as in the rest of the major cities under Fourth Reich occupation, was to seize and punish curfew offenders.

The sight of the wheelchair gave them a small thrill. Perhaps they could brutalize a handicapped person tonight, too.

When the leader of the Brownshirts rapped off the order to three of his men to search the surrounding area for the owner of the wheelchair, Frost knew that action against the Nazi thugs was inevitable. He silently slipped the safety off his Beretta, at the same time watching Pegg as the man double-checked the load in his shotgun. They looked at each other and nodded. The gesture meant to do it as quickly as possible.

The first three Brownshirts fanned out and began scanning the area immediately to the right of the hiding spot, leaving the other three to turn their attention back to their leashed prisoner. They began kicking the man, who was now curled up tight on the pier deck, trying vainly to cover up the increasingly violent blows.

Frost tapped Pegg once and motioned first to his shotgun and then the trio of soldiers who were brutally stomping the man. Pegg got the message immediately. He was to take out the stompers while Frost would handle the other three.

Pegg made a fist, and then counted off with his stubby fingers: one . . . two . . . three. . .

Frost's first shot caught the Brownshirt closest to him square in the neck. His second bullet—fired at the thug about twenty feet to his right—pieced the man's jaw and exited out the base of his shoulder. The third Brownshirt had instinctively hit the pavement, but too late to avoid being hit by Frost's quick, three-shot barrage.

At the same moment, Pegg had leaped dramatically from the shadows and loosed a quick, one-two blast from his shotgun. The first load caught one of the skinheads square in the face, the deadly impact blowing him right off the pier. The second shot blew out his partner's stomach. The man clutched what was left of his guts and then crumpled to his knees.

Pegg himself went to all fours, and rolled to his left. Moving so slowly, it was as if he were caught in real-life slow motion. He managed to reload his shotgun during the tortoise-like maneuver, but not before the last remaining Brownshirt fired off a clip from his Mauser machine-pistol. Acting more, instinct than anything else. Frost leveled his pistol at this man and shot him through the heart.

It was all over in no more than ten seconds. But that was enough time to attract attention, especially the blasts from Pegg's shotgun.

"Time to make ourselves scarce," Frost was saying. At the

same moment, he knew it was too late. He saw headlights and then heard the sirens. The noise of the gunfight had been loud enough to bring an NS armored scout car onto the pier.

Now he saw a line of tracers coming right at them; typical of *Nicht Soldats* to shoot first and ask questions later. Pegg was helping the torture victim — his face a bloody wreck — to his feet. But the man was so badly beaten, he couldn't walk, never mind run.

Frost was forced to make a tough, but necessary, instantaneous decision.

Reaching into his boot pocket he came out with the sludge sample and thrust it into Pegg's hands.

"Take this and him and get the hell out of here!" he yelled at the old sea captain.

The old man began to protest, but he knew the only other choice was for all three of them to be caught.

Without a word, Pegg stuffed the sludge sample down his pants, yanked the victim to his feet and half dragged him away, off the pier, down the bank and into the shallow water.

Seconds later he heard a tremendous gunfight break out. Using the noise of the gunblasts as cover, Pegg noisily carried the bloodied man out from under the pier and to an alley a block away.

It was then he heard the gunfire from the pier come to a sudden halt.

He stopped for a moment, his ear cocked to the wind. But he could only hear the shouts of the NS as they swarmed over the docks. He was certain Frost had died, just so he and the beating victim could escape.

"Another friend gone," Pegg moaned.

He dragged the man up the alley, finally finding an open hallway. Only then was he able to wipe away some of the blood covering the man's face.

"I have to leave you here," Pegg told him, the sight of his battered face causing his already nervous stomach to knot up.

160

"Wait for a while and then try to make it to your home."

"You saved my life," the man gurgled, trying his best to clear the blood that was blinding him. "I was as good as dead."

Pegg didn't have time to accept compliments. He had to get out of the area as quickly as possible.

"Just return the favor some day," he said.

At that moment, the victim was able to clear most of the blood from his left eye, enough for him to see his rescuer for the first time.

"My God!" he screamed, his voice wild with astonishment. "Mister Pegg! It's you! You've been healed!"

Pegg lingered one last moment to look down at the man. In that time, he was able to ignore the many abrasions on the man's face and finally recognize him.

It was the young Dominican priest.

"Yes, Father," Pegg said hastily, not really knowing what else to say. "Thanks to you, I *have* been healed."

Chapter Twenty-eight

Dragon's Mouth Prison, two weeks later

The day dawned bright and hot over *Fuhrerstadt*.

The early morning heat had already dried what rainwater remained from a brief but violent thunderstorm the night before. Soon a steamy fog was rising from the dirty streets of the capital city of Fourth Reich America.

"A fine day," Mike Fitzgerald thought, watching the dawn from his small jail cell. "A fine day to die."

He knew he had less than an hour to live. He was anticipating the unlocking of his cell door at any minute. Then he'd be led out to a small courtyard located in the center of the prison, put up against a wall, and executed.

"Then at last, this madness will be over," he thought grimly.

He felt it was ironic that he would never know the exact details of the plan to make him out to be a messiah. The crucified mechanic, the old man and the young girl, the bombing victim from Gary, Indiana, and Frost—all of them operatives in some grand scheme that Fitz could only hope would be apparent to him once he passed into Eternity.

Even in these last hours, he hadn't come down with a bad case of religion. He was in the end just a soldier, and soldiers die. Still, he wondered what lay beyond. What would happen once the bullet pierced his heart? Would he see the brilliant and inviting white light at the end of the tunnel as reported by people who'd had near death experiences? Would he be reunited with his long dead parents in the afterlife? Would he see long deceased comrades like old "Bull" Dozer? Or other United Americans who'd died since the Fourth Reich invasion?

Would he meet up with Hawk again?

Somehow the thought of them all sitting around on clouds and playing harps didn't quite fit. Few fit the profile of authentic angels. Perhaps some of them were in a much "warmer" place.

I'll know soon enough, he thought, taking his eyes from the window.

He steeled himself when he finally heard the key turning in the jail cell lock. The door swung open to reveal an NS officer and two soldiers.

Nothing was spoken, nothing had to be. Fitz simply rose from his bunk, brushed some of the dirt from his ragged prison uniform and walked straight and proud out of the cell to a position between the two NS troopers.

"If this is their world now," he thought, eyeing the NS men with absolute contempt, "then dying will only be an improvement."

They walked him down the long, dank corridor, up a set of darkened stairs, and finally into the small courtyard.

Here he got the surprise of a lifetime.

He'd just assumed that his execution was the only one planned for this day. But he was wrong. Two other men were already lined up against the bullet marked wall. standing stiff but proud, braced for what was to come.

The surprise was that he knew both of them. One was General Dave Jones. The other was Frost.

Fitz felt an audible gasp spill from his lips. Jones was little more than a skeleton; Frost was bandaged from head to toe, as if he'd been in a shitkicker of a gunfight and somehow survived.

Their eyes all met, and there was the briefest of smiles all round. Fitz felt a simultaneous pang of relief and sadness. It *was* a comfort that they were all going together, but it was disturbing that two fine men would be put to death too.

The NS men marched Fitz over to the wall and stood him next to the right of Jones.

"Good to see you again, Mike," Jones whispered to him. "I thought they'd got you a long time ago."

"I'm proud to die with you, General," Fitz replied, the intensity of the moment finally breaking down his guard. "And you, Frost. What ever happened back there that day, I hope I find out."

"I wish I could tell you," Frost replied, in his sturdy clipped Canadian accent. "But . . ."

"No talking!" the NS officer screamed in broken English.

"Fuck you!" Fitz defiantly screamed back. "You're filth!"

The NS officer's face went beet red. He made a brief motion toward his sidearm, but thought better of it. In the obsessive-compulsive Fourth Reich mentality, prisoners had to be executed the correct way, not by a rash act.

The NS officer blew a whistle and the sullen Death Skull soldier who'd been waiting at the end of the execution yard stepped forward and cocked his AK-47 rifle. It was by perverse protocol that the Skulls served as executioners within the walls of Dragon's Mouth.

Once the hooded soldier was in place, the NS officer unfurled a scroll and began reading from it.

"You have all been charged with crimes against the Fourth Reich," he began. "Our tribunal has decided you are all guilty.

"For the man named Jones, you are charged with prison escape. For the man named Frost, you are charged with sabotage. For the man named Fitzgerald, you are charged with duplicity in the death of the exalted First Governor of *Bundeswehr* Four. The sentence for all three of you is death."

The NS officer paused to look up at the three of them. And then smiled cruelly.

"The sentence shall be carried out immediately!"

He turned to the Death Skull soldier and nodded. The Skull checked his rifle once again: adjusted his long Grim Reaper robe to give his arms free movement, then brought the weapon up to the aiming position.

"For America and Freedom!" Jones suddenly cried out.

"For Freedom!" Fitz and Frost defiantly replied.

The Skull turned the barrel of his weapon and .pointed it directly at Fitz's heart. He would be the first to die.

"I hope it wasn't all in vain," he whispered. Then he closed his eyes.

A second later, he heard the shot.

There was no pain. No feeling of impact at all. Instead, Fitz could hear himself breathing, and his teeth were chattering slightly.

This is what it's like? he thought.

But then, in a split second after hearing the shot, he opened his eyes to find that he was still in the courtyard. He looked down at his body and saw no blood, no wounds.

He lifted his head to see the NS officer sprawled on the ground next to the Skull executioner.

"What the hell?" Fitz blurted out.

Five seconds of absolute confusion began. Seeing their officer crumple to the ground, the pair of NS men hesitated a moment, not quite understanding what was happening. Then they raised their guns and pointed them at the Skull.

But the hooded executioner was much too quick for them. In a lightning flash move, he had his AK-47 up and firing before either Nazi could pull his trigger. Like their officer, both these men toppled over dead.

Fitz looked at Jones and Frost whose facial expressions matched his in astonishment. A loud mechanical noise suddenly filled the courtyard. In an instant, all three saw a pair of helicopters descending toward them.

"What is going on?" Fitz cried out.

That was when the Skull took two steps toward them and

165

said: "There's been a change in plans, gentlemen. And now it's time to leave . . ."

With that, he pulled back his hood. Fitz, Jones and Frost found themselves staring at the smiling face of Hawk Hunter.

Part Two

A Man of Air

Chapter Twenty-nine

Colorado

The pair of long-range NS mountain VBL patrol cars came to a halt on top of a snowy, wild blown rise.

The storm raging around them was now close to blizzard proportions. Indeed, it had been snowing heavily when they left their forward base early that morning and had only increased in intensity throughout the wearying ten-hour drive. Now, night was coming and the storm was growing fiercer. And they still had a long way to go.

Raising the turret lids against the blowing snow, the pair of vehicle commanders emerged halfway out of the vehicles and compared map coordinates.

"We have another ten kilometers before us," one officer yelled over the howling wind to the other. "And that's just to reach the bottom road."

"With this snow, it might take us two hours or more," the second officer shouted back. "And we are already hours behind schedule."

Both men turned and for a moment studied their intended destination, the snow-enshrouded eighty-seven-hundred-foot mountain that lay some fifteen miles away. Barely visible through the storm, it looked treacherous. Foreboding. Ghostly.

"We must press on," the first NS officer insisted. "We must at least reach the bottom road."

"Agreed," the second officer called back.

With that. they both climbed back down into their vehicles, locking their turret lids as they did so. Then, with a puff of smoke and a roar of engine noise. the armored cars lurched forward and continued their odd journey.

Their task was more then just a routine scouting mission. This desolate, rugged, mountainous stretch of Colorado was close to a very important boundary. For it was near here that a line began which split the American continent in two for the powers of the Second Axis.

Per their nefarious pre-invasion agreement. everything east of these mountains belonged to the Fourth Reich forces. Everything west provided the spoils for the Asian forces. It was hardly a fifty-fifty split. More than sixty-five percent of the American landmass was under Fourth Reich control. But this was not surprising. The Fourth Reich forces had spearheaded roughly two thirds of the invasion effort, not to mention its engineering of the successful pre-invasion feint by the Horse forces and the acquisition of the nuclear-armed *Fire Bats* submarines.

So the remaining third of the continent was actually a generous portion for the Asian Forces. In fact, many in the high command of the Fourth Reich considered it *too* generous. Though they would say so only under their breath or in the company of the most trustworthy compatriots.

That was a battle to be fought at another time.

The mountain before the NS troops was one of the highest sentinels of this border. And though the Asian forces had not yet reached the territories beyond the dividing boundary, they were certainly theirs for the taking.

That the new name of the mountain was Loki did not sit well with the highly superstitious Fourth Reich soldiers. In the old Norse myths, Loki was a trickster god, and the series of brutal summer snowstorms that had been blanketing the region for the past few weeks seemed to indicate that he was in high form. Just about anything could happen if one fell under Loki's spell. To this end, both officers. as well as their

170

separate crews of three, were carrying a small twig of mistletoe in their uniform pocket. The famous kissing plant was also rumored to carry powers strong enough to pacify Loki's supernatural mischief.

The officers knew they might need it. A similar two-vehicle patrol had been dispatched to the area the previous week with orders to survey the top of the mountain as a possible site for one of the enormous *Schrecklichkeit Kanones,* the "frightfulness cannon." This patrol had reached the top of the mountain, and per its orders, reported back to the Fourth Reich forward base inside the old city of Denver, some thirty miles to the southeast. Then they vanished. All attempts to contact the two armored cars were unsuccessful. An aerial recon of the area around Loki also turned up nothing. It was as if the men and their vehicle had simply disappeared.

The two cars of this latest patrol were sent out to look for their lost comrades.

They knew that the missing patrol reached the summit of Loki using a rough but usable supply road that had been built years before. Their last report was made from the peak near the abandoned ski lodge which guarded the top. Nothing seemed out of the ordinary during this last radio transmission, though the reporting officer did mention that several of the troopers thought they'd heard the sounds of machinery churning away somewhere in the distance. Contact was broken soon after that and the patrol was never heard from again.

The search patrol had no idea what awaited them atop Loki. The very least they could expect was to find the missing armored cars, their engines empty of fuel, their crews frozen to death. Or perhaps the patrol became separated and spent valuable time and fuel looking for one another. There was even a remote possibility that the lost patrol might have encountered a hostile force. Scattered bands of United American guerrillas operated in the general area, plus Free Canadian Special Forces units had been known to sneak across the border and travel undercover for days just to launch lightning raids against either Fourth Reich or Asian installations. These symbolic actions were designed to inform the Second Axis that they would always have an angry neighbor to their north.

Then there was always the possibility that the missing soldiers had fallen prey to the mean-spirited Loki. According to his myth, the gods once punished Loki by binding him with the entrails of his own son. This did not bestow an aura of benevolence upon the god. Quite the opposite. It made him even more ruthless. His victims had been paying for the ghastly bondage ever since.

The search patrol reached the bottom road of the mountain two and a half hours later.

The commanders conferred again and it was decided that with barely an hour of daylight left, they should attempt to gain the summit as quickly as possible. This would mean lightening their cars as much as possible to make the trek up the mountain easier and faster. They ordered their crews to off-load any weighty, unneeded items—food packs, spare radios, half their ammunition, and any equipment that was redundant between the two vehicles.

When this was done, they restarted their engines and began the long climb up.

The road was potholed and dangerously narrow in some places. But thanks to the velocity of the storm which tended to deposit most of its precipitation in huge drifts parallel to the roadway, it was barely covered with snow. Still the journey up the mountain was as treacherous as it was slippery. The heavy tires of the VBL armored cars were just not made for climbing such an icy surface.

In the end, the cold, cautious climb would take nearly three hours.

The storm had subsided somewhat when the two cars reached the top of Loki.

The place looked like something out of a fantasy book. Everything at the summit—the old ski lodge, the rusting remains of the ski lift machinery, the rows of power poles, the strings of snow fences—was encased in a thick covering of ice. The roadway itself, now leveled out and straight at the summit, was actually underneath a long ribbon of ice. This forced both car commanders to stop, and order two crewmen to get out and let air out of their patrol car's rear tires, a somewhat desperate attempt to get more traction from the power wheels.

After much skidding and sliding, the armored cars reached the entranceway to the lodge and turned up toward the huge, dilapidated building.

They were amazed to see a light burning inside.

Deploying about fifty feet from the entrance, the commanders left one man apiece with the patrol cars, and then ventured up to the front door of the place. They hardly had the propensity to knock. Instead they violently kicked down the large oak door.

They found themselves stumbling into a main hallway which was set up as a workshop. Carved wooden figures—toys, statues, puppets—were hanging everywhere. Two large logs were burning away in a fireplace at the end of the hall. The smell of sawdust and burnt wood was in the air.

And sitting before a work table not too far from the roaring fire was a man.

He looked elderly, and was portly, balding, and sporting a great white beard. He was dressed all in red, except for black boots and a short, green work apron. A long cornpipe was stuck between his teeth, a thin wisp of smoke escaping from its bowl.

The man barely looked up as the soldiers burst in.

"More visitors?" he chuckled, his substantial belly jiggling as he did so.

"What nonsense is this?!" one of the NS officers demanded. "Who are you and what are you doing up here?"

173

"I live here," the old man replied innocently, getting up from his workbench and carefully approaching the heavily armed troops. "I've lived up here for years."

"Do you realize that you are in violation of the rules as set down by the military commander of this territory?" the officer asked harshly. "Do you realize we could shoot you right now?"

"That's what the other soldiers told me," the old man replied evenly.

"You saw the others?" the first officer asked, taking two belligerent steps toward the man. "When?"

"A week ago," the man replied, his voice soft and cheery despite the circumstances. "I fed them. They stayed with me for hours. We got along wonderfully."

"Where are they now, old man?" the second officer demanded.

The man in red just shrugged. "They left," he said. "They told me they had to return to their base. But they promised to come back. I thought you were them at first."

The two officers were infuriated that the man would talk to them with so little respect. For the next five minutes they barraged him with questions pertaining to the missing patrol, sometimes screaming at him from less than a foot away. But through it all, the man in red never lost his composure. He simply repeated over and over that the patrol had come to the lodge, had questioned him, had taken a meal with him and then left on apparently friendly terms.

At the end of the badgering session, the officers could only glare at the man and then at each other. Neither knew what to do.

"Please, gentlemen," the man told them. "Come in and sit down. I have stew. I have hot coffee. Surely you can abide my hospitality."

"Shut up!" the first officer bellowed at the man. "We don't need your hospitality. We will take what we want without it."

With a single movement of his hand. he ordered his troopers into the area near the fire where they could get warm. The second officer returned to the front door and called for the two soldiers watching the cars to come inside. Soon all eight soldiers were gathered near the fireplace, warming their cold and tired bones.

"We must arrest this man and bring him with us," the first NS officer told the second.

"But how?" the second officer replied. "We cannot fit him into either car. Not down the mountain. Not for the long ride back."

"That's exactly what the others said," the old man called across the hall to them. He was busily stirring a large pot of stew which was cooking over a smaller hearth fire. "I would have gone peacefully with them. I don't want to be an outlaw. But there was no room."

"Why didn't they shoot you then?" the first officer asked him suspiciously. "That is the only alternative . . ."

The man with the white beard shuddered for a moment.

"You can eat a hot meal first," he said, his voice barely a whisper.

Reluctantly, the two officers agreed to have a meal of stew and coffee brought on. They carefully inspected the well-stocked soup and had a lowest ranking man taste it before allowing the rest of the troop to dig in. The old man played the perfect host, refilling any wooden stew bowls that were in any danger of being emptied as well as keeping a top on each man's coffee mug. He worked so hard he didn't eat any of the meal himself. When the main meal was finished, he surprised them with several loaves of fresh, sugared bread and a jar of jam as dessert.

The supper took an hour, followed by another thirty minutes of more benign questioning of the old man. But by this time the officers had convinced themselves that he knew nothing about their missing comrades. They were also reluctant to shoot him outright. They agreed instead to place him under house arrest with a promise that another patrol would return and bring him into custody.

The troop made a call back to their forward base and received orders to recon the summit and then proceed back down the mountain. On their way out, the old man approached the officers with a tray containing eight small glasses.

"Cherry brandy," he explained. "It will help against the cold."

A curt nod from the officers allowed each man to swig his portion and the officers took theirs as well.

Then with little more than a grunt, they left the lodge, rudely leaving the door open behind them. The old man used all his strength to force it closed against the strong winds.

Then from a tiny, misted window he watched the two VBL armored cars roar to life and drive back down the lodge's entranceway.

The two armored cars circled the darkened ski area for the next 30 minutes looking for any sigh of their missing comrades.

But it proved to be a fruitless search, Eventually they found themselves coming up on the ski lodge again; this time approaching it from the south side via the carved out supply path. At the end of this path they turned onto a small ski road which would eventually lead them to the main road and back down the mountain.

It was on this ski road that they found the missing patrol.

The ice encased vehicles were right in the middle of the road, one in front of the other, almost as if they were intentionally parked there. The road was lined on both sides with two rows of pine trees, each one also surreally encased in ice. The small grove represented the only substantial number of fully grown trees at the summit of the mountain.

The search cars pulled up next to the two vehicles, and their crews slowly emerged to study the situation. It took several minutes of hacking through the ice of the first vehicle before the soldiers were able to free the turret hatch. When they did, one of the two commanders crawled into the first frozen vehicle.

The missing crew was still inside the car, all four of them at their posts. They were long dead, of course. Their hands frozen in midair, their faces stretched and white, their eyes wide open, their mouths freeze-dried into grotesque grins. Each one had a bullet in the head.

"Ambushed . . ." he whispered, instantly knowing the ramifications of his theory.

The NS officer scrambled up out of the scout car, unfastening his side arm as he did so. But it was much too late for him and his men.

He saw the first muzzle flash come from the iced over tree directly above him, then another from the tree next to it. Suddenly the cold night air was thundering with the sound of gunfire, the loud reports echoing across the frozen mountaintop. Horrified, the NS officer realized at once that his patrol had fallen into the same trap as had the first two scout cars. Now they were also paying the ultimate price.

He watched stunned as his men were chopped to pieces by the concentrated gunfire from the trees. A fusillade of bullets ripped across his chest. In his last moment of life he thought it peculiar that they felt so terribly cold.

Another burst ripped across his neck, this one stinging hot. He immediately slumped over and felt the life ooze out of him.

He managed to gasp out one last word: "Loki . . ." Then he fell forward, cracking his head on the vehicle turret and opening a wide bloody wound.

It didn't matter—he was already dead.

The shooting stopped less than a minute later. Then one by one, men in black uniforms jumped down from the trees, crunching the ice encrusted snow below.

"We've got them all," one man said to the commander of

177

the ambush team. "Just like last time."

Captain "Crunch" took the empty magazine from his M-16 and replaced it with another full one.

"Yeah, but there will be more," he said, surveying the top of the mountain which was now eerily silent. "We can be damn sure of that . . ."

Fuhrerstadt

The heavily armed NS sergeant quietly slipped inside the ornate bedroom and slowly closed the huge steel doors behind him.

At the far end of the room, sitting in a shaft of sunlight, was the young girl in the white frilly dress. In front of her was a large easel and canvas. A tray containing dozens of oil paints and brushes was at her side as was a small official photograph of the assassinated First Governor of *Bundeswehr* Four.

The NS man approached her slowly, bearing a small jar of paint thinner in hand.

"You requested this, Miss?" he asked her in heavily accented English.

She looked up at him for the first time, her eyes sad and teary, her young face seeming drawn and pale.

"Thank you," she replied softly. taking the jar from him and immediately dipping several of her brushes into it. "I'd run out."

The NS man shifted uneasily. His guard unit had been assigned to watch over the young girl right after the assassination of the First Governor. Unlike the priest who was imprisoned for complicity in the shooting of the high Fourth Reich official, the young girl had become a protected ward of the American Nazi government. On orders from the *Amerikafuhrer* himself, she'd been installed in one of the most luxurious top-floor suites inside the rambling *Reichstag*. She was watched over by no less than ten NS troopers at all times, plus a gaggle of nannies, including a nurse and a palmreader. She also had her own chef, her own butler, her own dresser and even a squad of "house mistresses" who bathed and oiled her every day.

Yet it was clear that the young girl was not doing too well psychologically. Witnessing the assassination of the strange man who had quite literally saved her from a life of slavery and degradation had taken a quick and brutal toll. She barely spoke to anyone, and many of her meals went untouched. She never left her quarters, and refused most visitors, perhaps knowing that they were sent by the *Amerikafuhrer*'s staff people in an effort to lift her spirits.

In fact, since the shooting, she had done little else but paint and stare out the window of her suite, as if these two things alone would somehow restore her to the normal life that she should be leading as a mere sixteen-year-old.

The NS man could not help but glance at her most recent work. One quarter of her canvas was covered with dark blue, indicating a night scene was evolving. In mid center, the rudimentary lines of a snow-covered mountain were taking shape and light sketchings of buildings were emerging from the background. But all in all, even the luggish NS man knew the painting was still in its very beginning stages.

"I keep having this dream," the young girl suddenly confessed as she added another dark blue wash to the canvas. "I don't know what it is, or where it is. But I thought it was best to paint it."

"That seems like a good idea," the NS man replied nervously. "It looks fine so far."

The young girl began to say something else, but quickly stopped herself. She sighed instead, her shoulders slumping appreciably. Then she brushed back her long brown hair with one unintentionally suggestive movement.

The NS man was really tense now. This was not a comfortable situation for him. He'd participated in many raping

179

sprees during the *blitzkrieg* of America, claiming girls such as her among his victims. Now to be head of the unit protecting such a delectable item was ironic, to say the least.

"Will there be anything else, Miss?" he finally managed to blurt out.

She simply stared at her painting for a moment, working some of the dark paint to form one of many trees on the side of the mountain form.

Then she turned and looked back at him.

"Is it true the priest escaped?" she asked him point-blank.

The NS man could only nod. "Yes, Miss, I'm afraid he did," he replied. "He and two other dangerous criminals."

"Do you think he'll ever come back here?" she asked, demurely dipping her brush into a small puddle of white paint.

"I would doubt that, Miss," the sergeant answered confidently. "If he did, he would be captured and shot immediately."

She gave a slight, sad shrug. "But then he would just raise himself from the dead," she said, her voice an offhand whisper. "Wouldn't he?"

Now the NS man stiffened completely.

"I really don't know," he finally replied.

Chapter Thirty

He was a ghost.

He felt like the sun's rays could go right through him. He felt like he cast no shadow. If he were to look in a mirror, he wondered if he'd see any reflection.

Probably not.

He'd accomplished what every great military commander had sought to do at least once in their careers: he'd become invisible. He'd gone on the offensive against overwhelming odds on many fronts, day or night, for nearly a year and had won every engagement simply because he'd mastered this science of transparency. It really wasn't that difficult—and this was not surprising. All great things were essentially simple. So too the secret to being invisible. It actually turned on one simple rule: make sure the enemy is not looking for you.

And how best to do that?

Make them think that you are dead.

But there were definitely drawbacks to being invisible. Much had to be given up. Much had to be surrendered. All of it with little chance of being recovered. He didn't look any different. There was the sturdy, slender frame. The powerful shoulders. The lightning quick hands. The steel blue eyes. The handsome face. The hair too long.

Yet he *was* different. And he knew why. The problem with being a spirit was that you were always in danger of being empty—inside as well as out. You tried to feel it, but sometimes there was nothing deep anymore. As a phantom, noth-

181

ing real remained of his life. No home. No roots. No friends. No loves. No real future. If anything, he become just a name now. Someone spoken about between breaths, or between beers, if at all.

Yes, the sentence he'd given himself was the worst kind of self-inflicted wound. The Native Americans knew it best.

How does a man feel when he's lost his soul?

He feels like a ghost.

The mountain looked out over miles of rolling flatlands of what was once upstate New York.

This territory was all but deserted now. No civilian in his right mind would live in such an absolutely lawless region when Free Canada, with its liberty, its laws, its high regard for human life, was barely a hundred miles to the north. It was much simpler to just walk across the border and leave all the fear and oppression behind.

Yet it was here that The Wingman had chosen to stay. Why? It had fit his needs. He'd found jet fuel here. He'd hidden stores of ammunition here. Trusted allies were stationed nearby. It was an unlikely hiding place, yet a good location from which to project the beginnings of the intricately far-reaching plan he conjured up over the last dozen months.

It was also a good place to think.

He'd lost count of the number of times he'd flown down near Football City, keeping the jump jet low and evading the Fourth Reich's rinky-dink radar nets, landing and hiding whenever he got too close and resuming his mission on foot.

It was on his last mission to the Fourth Reich capital, when under the new disguise as a Death Skull, he'd got wind that his three friends, General Jones, Major Frost and Mike Fitzgerald were still alive, but due to be executed.

His rescue of the trio resulted—and it too fit neatly into his plan. If the situation hadn't been so desperate, he might have enjoyed the astonishment of his friends longer when they first saw him. It was so obvious that all three had believed he was dead. After all that *was* the impression he'd been working hard to preserve for nearly the past year.

As it turned out though, their reunion was painfully brief and utterly silent. He'd arranged for three separate helicopters piloted by Free Canadian volunteers and expertly disguised as Fourth Reich aircraft to swoop down and immediately take each of his friends away to three very different locations. Each one thus began their own very secret yet very crucial mission as explained to them by the crew members of their individual rescue choppers.

Meanwhile, he had stayed on the ground. Hidden in his Death Skull robes, he was able to gather more information on the UA officer compound within the prison before returning to the Harrier which he'd hidden on the east side of the Mississippi.

Oddly enough, if everything went well, he would not see Jones or Frost or Fitzie until the last stage of his grand plan. He'd mused more than once about what this longer reunion would be like. His three friends bugging him for details on how he was able to pull off the daring rescue. Meanwhile he held off divulging any more information until he'd secured promises of the many rounds of drinks due him in return for saving their necks.

It would be just like the old days, he thought.

But he always caught himself laughing at this last notion. *The old days*. They seemed like a million years ago.

As a ghost, he'd been many other things over the past few months besides a Death Skull. It was easy for a spirit to step into many disguises. He'd posed as a slave, working in a granite quarry in old Indiana, carving out huge pieces of stone. He'd walked the dusty roads of the American Midwest in the rags of a *sputnik*, working for food and spreading rumors of his own death. He'd donned the garb of a lowly NS sub-private and had driven a garbage truck back and forth through dozens of cities and towns located on both banks of the southern Mississippi. He'd constructed a raft of driftwood and had sailed up and down the Big Muddy.

He had done all this for one reason: *To spy.*

And what had he found?

That in many ways the Fourth Reich was no ordinary enemy. That they were not the usual gang of criminals and thieves elevated to a higher status simply by possession of military equipment and control over thousands of soldiers who would use it.

No, the Fourth Reich was more than that. It was in fact a movement. A state of mind. Not some Johnny-Come-Lately post-World War III crackpot brigade. The beliefs espoused by the Fourth Reich had been ingrained in world history for decades. It was an unholy religion, one that preached that a single race of people was somehow superior to another, not simply because of skin color or ethnic origins, but because of their *beliefs.* This was the worst kind of arrogance, and it produced the worst kind of enemy, one that apparently could not die. World War II had been fought to put an end to it. But despite the sacrifices, it did not kill it completely. Many battles big and small had been fought since, yet it was still here. How would it be possible to kill it now in a wildly anarchic world, when five years of war and one hundred million dead back in the Forties couldn't do it?

It was a problem for the ages.

Yet in years past, Hunter would have attacked this menace head-on. Full steam ahead. All-out. No questions asked. This was because he'd believed back then that he had one key advantage over his enemy. He believed that he was in the right. That he was fighting for Truth, for Freedom, for the universal Good. The right side of people, of nature, of the Universe.

But, yes, he'd changed.

The sometimes barely visible, yet seemingly unextinguishable, flame of optimism which had burned in his heart for all his life was now out cold. It was dead. Snuffed by his realization that, in the end, there was no even struggle between Good and Evil as he had always believed. It was never a fair fight. Evil was always prevalent. Sure, the forces of Good could deflect it every once and a while, and give the appearance of triumph. But it was simply an illusion of victory. Evil *always* returned. Why? He didn't know. But he had come to the conclusion that the Universe had been set up this way.

So why fight this time? Why become a ghost? What was the point? What was the sense in battling time and time again when the enemy always reappeared? He and his comrades in arms had fought hard to reunite America again and won more than a handful of times. But still *nothing had changed*. America was still not free. The people were still enslaved. Why? Again, the only possible explanation to his mind was that it was meant to be that way.

So it was all these gloomy thoughts that had brought him to this place, to look out over the grand landscape, to dream about what it looked like before the world flipped upside down.

The place afforded such a view that he imagined it to be an ideal location for a vision.

Sometimes he became filled with rage. Sometimes he would shake his fist at the sun and wish that a bolt from Heaven would hit him. *Damn!* He needed a big bright fucking bolt of lightning to hit him on the head and reveal something—*anything*—to him.

But always, in almost the same moment, he felt foolish for thinking the thought. Miracles, like Truth and Love, could not be manufactured.

Or could they?

He ran his hands over his tired face and then back through his long hair.

He'd lost so much over the years. Friends, now dead or missing. His country, divided up between those who in the end were simply jealous of it all.

The one true comfort of his life; his friend, his lover, his soul mate, Dominique. Probably gone . . .

But he knew he had to fight. He'd know it for months. But what he didn't know was why. Until just lately. What motivation could he summon up this time? There was really only one left and it was not the most admirable of human traits.

But it would have to do. It was appropriate in its way.

So this time, he would not make war for Truth, or for Freedom, on for the preservation of America's heritage.

No, this time he would do it for the most base of reasons. This time, he'd do it purely for revenge.

His plan was actually a plan within a plan.

It was based on several indisputable facts that he'd discovered during his time as a ghost. One was, when confronted with a threat, the Fourth Reich always reacted the same way: with something he could only label as "aggressive caution."

They unwittingly proved it time and time again. Despite their overwhelming strength in men and armor, they weren't really military men. They didn't have the slightest idea as to the difference between strategy and tactics. When posed with a threat, they rarely counterattacked. Instead they simply bolstered their defenses and hoped whatever happened wouldn't occur again.

A prime example was the so-called "Noninterference Decree." He'd learned of the unusual semi-secret Fourth Reich field order while ransacking a small NS outpost in Louisiana. Simply put, the Noninterference Decree forbade Fourth Reich officers from ordering their troops to fire on Free Canadian cargo aircraft, even though they might encounter them in Fourth Reich airspace. The reason behind the order was to prevent an incident—mistakenly shooting down an off-course FC airplane filled with nonmilitary goods, for instance— which might provoke a war with the large democratic neighbor to the north.

On closer examination, the rule was pure insanity on a military level. It allowed Free Canadian cargo planes to routinely violate Fourth Reich skies on intelligence gathering missions, guerrilla supply drops and so on. From a military commander's point of view, this should be an intolerable situation. But the Fourth Reich was not made up of military commanders. They were not warriors. They were occupiers. And when they became afraid to provoke an action they could not handle, they'd simply legislate the problem away.

But on the other hand, they were so arrogant that they believed anything positive that happened to them was simply the result of destiny. They believed good fortune was their fate, and any evidence presented to them under this wrapping they took as gospel, no matter how foolish or unlikely it seemed. Just like a follower of the zodiac who cannot believe the stars could be wrong becomes a slave to their alignments, so too the Fourth Reich found their paths laid in superstitions and rituals. Their never ending stage managing of "official state ceremonies" was a good example of their misguided self-fulfilling prophesies. In stirring up all the pomp and circumstance, they hoped to find some end result. More knowledgeable conquerors of the past knew that just the opposite was true.

It was with these typical Fourth Reich blunders and many more that Hunter had so carefully constructed his plan within a plan.

Chapter Thirty-one

Off the coast of Mar del Plata, Argentina

The trio of technicians inside Argentinian Imperial Air Corps Radar Post Number 6 didn't notice the blip on their radar screens at first because all three were fast asleep.

Their dereliction of duty was partially understandable. It was two in the morning, and their fourteen-hour shift was drawing to a close. Few airplanes flew at night anymore. And if they did, it was only under escortany and with permission from whatever governments were in power along their air route. Not to do so might result in either a confrontation with jet interceptors or a nasty meeting with a barrage of surface-to-air missiles.

So the Argentinian Imperial Air Corps technicians had no reason to expect to see anything on their radar scopes, never mind an airplane as large as a Hercules C-130. But when the warning buzzers suddenly came alive and the rows of trip wire red light indicators began flashing, the cacophony of noise was enough to instantly knock all three techs out of their insubordinate slumbers. A rush of sleepy button pushing and triangulation ensued, and gradually the three men determined that a big Herc had wandered into their airspace.

But there was more: by calculating its gradually sloping flight path, the techs realized that the airplane had not only violated Imperial Argentina's airspace, but that it was in serious trouble.

Calls went out to the local interceptor base as well as the

nearest pair of SAM sites. But it was already too late. The C-130—its unmistakable radar profile well known to the Argie radar men—was losing altitude very quickly. They watched with a mixture of astonishment and horror as the blip fell off their radar screens less than a minute after it had lit up the fort.

By another round of quick calculations, they determined the airplane had crashed about a mile offshore from the small fishing village of Tia Tipuncio into a coastal area called Mar del Plata. It was an area pockmarked with hazardous reefs and jetties.

They passed this information on to the local militia commander and continued to monitor the situation by radio for the next half hour. But gradually it became apparent that their role in the unfolding drama was over. The plane was down and that was it.

Less than a hour later, all three were back asleep again.

It was dawn before the 25-man Imperial Argentinian militia unit reached the wreckage of the HC-130.

The commander of the unit had secured five fishing boats from Tia Tipuncio, but with the tides running in, his men found it tough going just to travel the mile and a quarter out to the wrecked and burning airplane.

They finally made landfall on a small jetty close to where the plane had come to its end. From here they could see up close how the big cargo craft's wings were practically twisted off and that its fuselage was almost neatly severed in two. Several small fires were still raging toward the rear of the airplane and the stink of aviation fuel filled the early morning sea air.

Leaving five men to stay with the boats, the militia commander set out over the eighth of a mile of seaweed covered rocks with nineteen men, intent on inspecting the wreck and determining the fate of its crew.

The airplane was painted all black and had no insignia, but this was not unusual. Few airplanes flying the wild, pirate filled South American skies these days wore their colors proudly. Still fewer went about unarmed. Yet this airplane was definitely not

189

a gunship. It appeared to carry no weapons, offensive or defensive. Instead, its ripped wings and cracked fuselage bore the evidence of many extra fuel tanks having been carried in lieu of armament. From this, the militia commander could only draw one supposition. The Hercules had been on a very long flight, perhaps one that originated from North America.

After much slipping and sliding, the militiamen finally reached the wreck. The airplane's nose was facedown on the jetty and torrents of seawater were rushing through the cracked cockpit windows. It was apparent immediately that any crew members stationed on the flight deck—either alive or dead—had been swept away by the raging sea long ago.

Instructing his men to be wary of the same fate, they carefully inspected what was left of the airplane, inside and out. But there was little to be found at first. There were no bodies and the commander's initial suspicion proved correct. The airplane was carrying little else but fuel. Several large inflatable rubber bladders had been stuffed inside the cargo compartment, two of which still contained full loads of fuel.

With the threat of an explosion imminent, the commander ordered his men back to a safe distance. But then he crawled up as far as he could get to the shattered, deluged cockpit, just on the outside chance that the airplane was carrying money or gold. He did find a small safe that had been broken open, presumably by the crash, but there was no money or gold inside. Instead, it contained a packet of documents loosely wrapped in black cloth. Grabbing the papers, he beat a hasty retreat as the big plane began shifting again, slave now to the raging waves and fast flowing incoming tides.

Once back to safer ground, the commander did a quick check of the documents, and was at once astounded. Even though his grasp of English was rudimentary at best, he still could read enough to know that the documents were the equivalent of a ticking time bomb.

First off, they told him that this plane *had* originated up in the northern hemisphere, specifically from an island in the Caribbean and that the only two people aboard—a pilot named Jones and his navigator Frost—were North Americans.

Secondly, it was apparent by the flight plan that the airplane was on its way to East Falkland Island, where a small outpost of British military entrepreneurs ran a quasi-secret air base. The militia commander knew there was only one reason why an American airplane would make such a long-range treacherous flight. As unlikely as it seemed, East Falkland Island, with its natural isolation, had become a go-between point for many secret yet major arms deals in the post-World War III world. Obviously the two Americans had been making the journey to buy weapons.

But the real bombshell was yet to come. Opening up a separate black folder sealed in Jones's name, the militia commander discovered documents that he knew would make him rich or famous or both.

What he found inside the folder was a blueprint for a secret United Americans' counterstrike against the Fourth Reich.

Chapter Thirty-two

Fuhrerstadt

It was the only triangular shaped room in the *Reichstag*.

The unusual design had more to do with the egos of the three men who occupied the large office than any kind of design element. All three were Fourth Reich Field Marshalls of absolutely equal rank. As such they were the highest officials in Occupied America next to the *Amerikafuhrer* himself. The Marshalls were so far up the Fourth Reich's organizational ladder that they were nearly as insulated from their troops and staff as was the Top Nazi. They were so removed that even their names and identities were state secrets.

They were known then as Erste, Zweite and Dritte, literally "first," "second" and "third" — top secret codenames that were derived for operational purposes from the men's ages and not their rank. Still even this was a sore spot among them. The boisterous, aggressive Zweite felt in all ways superior to the mild-mannered intellectual Erste and he didn't think he should be labeled with the less than grandiose code name of "second," just because he was two weeks and a day younger than his rival. By the same token, Dritte, the youngest, was a very accomplished, though slightly paranoid, ass kisser. He believed that his "interaction skills" with the *Amerikafuhrer* were so high, that Erste and Zweite were pretty much superfluous. Though he would never dare to tell them so to their faces. No surprise then that Erste thought the other two were dull and boorish.

There was one thing the three men agreed on. They believed they, and not the *Amerikafuhrer*, should be the ruling force in Fourth Reich America. After all, they were military men. The *Amerikafuhrer* had his position simply by quirk of birth, a curse of nepotism that went back decades. They had experienced combat, paying their dues in the blood of their men. The *Amerikafuhrer* had never even fired a gun. They knew how best to exploit the conquered lands. Their Leader was frankly more concerned with the direction of his sexual compass.

So as distrustful and mean spirited as they were to each other, they had in concert been plotting against the *Amerikafuhrer* for some time. It was they who had arranged to have the First Governor of *Bundeswehr* Four brought to *Fuhrerstadt*. Believing that if they succeeded in poisoning or shooting the *Amerikafuhrer*, then the ruthless man from the Fourth Military District would make the ideal replacement puppet with which they could truly gain ultimate power. But then the First Governor went insane and was shot, *kiboshing* that intrigue. Now the trio of high Nazi officers was forced to their back-up plan, dealing with a person so notorious, even they, with all their power, feared her.

The person was the Witch Elizabeth Sandlake. And it was they who had arranged her marriage to the *Amerikafuhrer*.

Like the Norse before them, the three Marshalls knew that the real power in this new world lay in control of the nuclear-armed *Fire Bats* submarines. Whoever had their finger on the mysterious subs' buttons could threaten anyone, friend or foe, with nearly instant nuclear annihilation.

At the moment, the Witch held that power. But they knew she wanted something more: to be crowned "Queen of America." As silly and preposterous as it sounded, the trio of Reich Marshalls was certain that if they satiated her insane megalomaniacal desires by getting her married to the *Amerikafuhrer*, then they could slowly wrest control of the *Fire Bats* from her.

And then they could kill her and her new husband.

Arranging the unholy matrimony had been no problem. Through smooth, secret-pouch diplomacy, they'd convinced Elizabeth long before that the closest she would ever come to being "Queen of America" was to marry the *Amerikafuhrer*. For his part, the *Amerikafuhrer* sanctioned the bonding as a cover for his actual sexual orientation. While being far from unique among the Fourth Reich hierarchy, it nevertheless always posed a threat of deep embarrassment — especially back in the European Fatherland where such things simply weren't tolerated anymore.

So it would be a marriage of convenience all around: the Witch would get what she wanted, the *Amerikafuhrer* would get what he wanted, and, after the newlyweds were done away with, Erste, Zweite and Dritte would get what they wanted.

There was only one factor standing in the way: what was left of the damnable United Americans.

The three Reich Marshalls had no illusions about the potential of the United Americans. All three had fought against them with Viktor in the first Circle War, and later with the neo-Nazi Twisted Cross in Panama. They'd seen time and time again what the American "comic book" heroes could do. They knew that if anything, the Americans were even more dangerous when faced with depleted resources or impossible odds. They were also troubled by persistent, if secondhand, reports that small elements of the United American forces were gathering somewhere in the Caribbean.

The recent rescue of the three United American officers right out of Dragon Mouth's execution yard was just one more very dangerous example of the Americans' boldness. Especially, since the dramatic rescue had all the dark elements that The Wingman himself was behind it.

No wonder then that the three Marshalls had quickly put a clamp on the whole affair. They'd ordered swift and secret executions for just about anyone at Dragon's Mouth who knew of the incident, forty-four people in all. They had even kept the truth from the *Amerikafuhrer* himself, deciding to tell him only when it suited their purposes, and certainly not before.

They were wise to be so cautious. They knew if the whispers began inside the High Command, or among their troops, or even throughout the captive American population that the United Americans were still a force to be reckoned with, then it would be enough to throw their more long-range plans into disarray. It would be even worse if the rumor that the famous Wingman was still alive spread throughout the captive lands. If that happened, then the situation would most likely tumble completely out of control. The three Marshalls realized that dead or alive the name of Hawk Hunter alone was enough to incite rebellion and renewed patriotism in even the most dominated of souls.

In this case, both the man and the legend were equally powerful.

But now, all that could very well have changed. They felt that today might actually hail the end of the United Americans' well-cultivated myth.

For today, they'd learned of their enemy's most secret plans.

This valuable information had come to them via the fascist and friendly government of Imperial Argentina. An airplane hired by the United Americans had crashed in bad weather off the coast of that country. A plane that may have been carrying two of the officers who'd been plucked from the executioner's gun earlier. Found inside the airplane was nothing less than a secret strategy of how the UA planned to disrupt the strong-arm rule of the Fourth Reich in America.

Even in their glowing hatred for the Americans, the three Marshalls had to admire the pluckiness of the recovered secret plans. In them, the UA revealed what every good military command should know. They recognized their limitations. Knowing that it would be impossible to defeat the enormous resources of the Fourth Reich, the UA was going to go for a small but highly symbolic action, one that quite literally could bring them back from the dead.

The plans spelled out, step by step, how the UA was to first purchase some heavy weapons, tanks mostly. Next they would purchase air transport, mostly in the form of helicopters. Then they would raise a small but competent army, probably through recruiting mercenaries. Then, they would attack, occupy and hold a section of the Fourth Reich's conquered territory. The would declare this spit of land "New America" and then hang on in hopes of inciting the general population to rise up and throw off the yoke of their Nazi masters.

Even in a bitter har- fought defeat, the United Americans would be considered the winners, and the population would be left smoldering, ready to flame up again at any time in the future. Worse too, an all-out massacre of the Americans by the Fourth Reich might prompt Free Canada to step into the fray. This was a troublesome aspect for the Fourth Reich as it would take major resources to battle the large army of the unfriendly neighbor to the north.

So the Americans had come up with an ingenious plan—but its best points were now moot. Because all good military operations needed one thing—*surprise*.

And that was now lost.

Chapter Thirty-three

New Chicago

The short, bald, weary man wiped the last of the grease from his hands and slumped into the hard folding chair in the corner of the oil caked workshop.

"What I'd give for a taste of beer," he wondered, smacking his dry lips. "Or even a sip of wine."

He studied the disassembled airplane engine before him. It was an ancient Cyclone, a too big power plant that he was trying to convert for use in a Cessna Special Edition AE. It was proving an impossible task.

"Idiots," he muttered, turning a worn and cracked rubber gasket over in his hands. "Where is their efficiency these days?"

His name was Roy From Troy, and not many years before, he'd been one of the richest men in post-World War III America. Roy was a salesman. Before the war, he'd sold everything from aluminum siding to indoor/outdoor carpeting to Tupperware. After the war, and the wild days of the disputed armistice that followed, Roy From Troy began selling airplanes.

His timing had been perfect. The former-United States had just been carved up into a mishmash of territories, fiefdoms and so-called Free States. Each one quickly realized the need for defense, especially in the air. But under the harsh New Order "peace" terms, the majority of the world's military aircraft had been scrapped.

That was where Roy came in. Armed with a bag full of real silver and gold coins, and a loophole in the armistice agreement that you could fly a Boeing 747 through, he'd bought a large, abandoned tract of land in what was once known as Ohio. The land, sold as ten square miles of concrete, just happened to contain one of the US Air Force's "airplane graveyards." Instead of dismantling the four hundred near antique military airplanes that came along with the property, Roy hired mechanics to make them flyable.

In a world starved for aircraft, Roy From Troy was suddenly the man with the Midas touch. Almost single-handedly, he outfitted every burgeoning air force in the eastern part of fractioned America. In the process, he became one of the richest men on the continent.

But all of that was long gone now—the money, the babes, the fine booze. Now he was reduced to a lowly grease monkey, a salesman trying to fit a massive airplane engine into a small airframe. The trouble was he didn't have the faintest idea what he was doing. The NS had just assumed that because he once sold airplanes that he knew how to fix them. They couldn't have been more wrong. When they found out that he'd avoided work in the granite quarry by misleading them about his knowledge of aeronautical mechanics, they would surely execute him.

"Fucking Nazis," he murmured for the hundredth time that day. "They always ruin everything!"

Roy checked the time. It was almost midnight. He'd been ripping apart the engine for more than twenty-four hours now, and he was sure the ruse could not go on much longer.

It was enough to tempt him to crank up what was left of the sputtering engine and suck on the exhaust pipe until dead.

Just then he realized the dim light in the workshop got a little bit dimmer. He looked up to see a shadow course its way across the far wall.

"Who's there?" he called out, shakily reaching for his only weapon, a large monkey wrench.

Suddenly the shadow took on a more definite form—tall, black, almost ghostly. It was barely ten feet away from him now.

"What is this?" Roy cried out, not really wanting to know the answer. "Who the hell are you?"

He heard a slight mechanical sound as the figure walked forward.

"Is that a way to greet an old friend?" said the barely recognizable voice.

Roy felt his eyes go wide and his jaw suddenly drop.

"Hunter?" he gasped. "It can't be . . . you're supposed to be dead."

Hunter stepped forward into the light for the first time.

"Then maybe I'm just a ghost," he told Roy.

Chapter Thirty-four

Aboard the Great Ship

"Yaz" was seasick.

He couldn't believe it. In the past ten years, he'd spent more time aboard ships than on land—US Navy submarines, Norse troop-ships and, for the past year, this converted cruiseliner. He had never gotten sick before.

Until today.

Now lying spread-eagled across the huge waterbed in the center of Elizabeth Sandlake's boudoir, he knew the cause of his nausea. It was all the intoxicants he'd ingested the night before. Elizabeth and Juanita had really gone off the beam in the past few days, using him as their nonstop sex toy. Plying him with liquor and *myx*, they demanded that he perform for them *and* with them for incredibly long periods of time.

These marathon sessions had left "Yaz" a rather reluctant stud. He felt so used, that he swore if he ever got back to civilization—or whatever passed for civilization these days—he would never treat a woman like a sex object again.

Not unless she wanted to be.

So it was a hangover combined with the more than gentle rocking of the grand cruiseliner that had set his stomach gurgling into a seasickness which left him feeling one step from Death itself.

Juanita was sitting across from the huge bed, doing her nails. Although they had both explored each other's most intimate parts many times, they rarely talked whenever they were not thrashing about.

But today, as "Yaz" would learn, it would be different.

"When she comes back, you'd better show some enthusiasm," the dark Spanish beauty told him, barely looking up from her industrial strength nail filing. "This is a special day for her. You'd be wise to take notice."

"What's so special about today?" "Yaz" asked her, his words slow and measured so as not to upset the delicate balance of his grumbling stomach. "Other than the fact that this ship is rocking . . . and rocking . . ."

Juanita shot a glance at him that would have frozen a blowtorch.

"You are not here to ask questions," she zapped. "Just do as you are told."

"Yaz" tried to steady himself on the waterbed, closing his eyes and trying to imagine his stomach settling down. But it was impossible.

Suddenly he heard the door to the large love nest open, and felt a perceptible change come over the room.

Without even opening his eyes, he knew that Elizabeth Sandlake had just made her entrance.

"My Lady!" he heard Juanita cry out. "You look . . . absolutely stunning!"

" 'Stunning'?" Came Elizabeth's caustic reply. "Don't you really mean, 'beautiful'?"

"Yes, certainly, My Lady. I meant 'beautiful.' "

"Yaz" couldn't imagine what all the gushing was about. He knew less about the goings-on around the ship since he'd become the resident human blow-up doll than he did when he was relegated to the hole down at the very bottom of the ship.

But he also had learned that the beautiful but very unbalanced Sandlake needed a healthy dose of adulation every day to keep her raging megalomania stoked. And woe to the person who failed to feed this addiction.

So it was with much discomfort that he managed to turn over on his queasy stomach and check out the fuss.

What he saw was almost enough to make him heave, not from repulsion, but from laughter.

Elizabeth was standing before him in a full-length pearl white wedding dress.

"White?" "Yaz" said too late to stop the word from escaping his lips.

Elizabeth glared at him. "You dare . . ."

"It's very, very beautiful, My Lady," "Yaz" quickly recovered. "The color white becomes you . . ."

Elizabeth straightened up a bit and turned to examine herself in the room's huge full-length mirror.

"It's our own design," she told her image. "It's the dress I've wanted ever since I was a little girl."

Now "Yaz's" eyes were rolling as much as his stomach. The self-proclaimed "Queen of America" had come up with many different costumes for their enforced lovemaking sessions. She'd dressed up as a cowgirl, a belly dancer, a man, a priest, a nun and on and on.

But dressing as a bride as a prelude to another lust fest was a bit too much, even for her.

But that was when "Yaz" got his second surprise of the early day.

"You can have your gown made as soon as we get to the ceremony," Elizabeth told Juanita who had jumped up to help her mistress out of the flowing dress. "We used all of the material on board for this one."

The two women then began an extended conversation, that if "Yaz" didn't know better might have concerned a real wedding.

Ten minutes into this talk of floral arrangements, band numbers and whether a waltz was proper as the first dance at a formal reception, "Yaz" began to think that he was missing something here.

He swallowed hard and opened his eyes again. The only thing that had kept him sane during his long months on the Great Ship was that he'd strive to convince himself that he was on an unexpected, yet valuable, intelligence mission. This meant getting important information, hopefully for use in the United American cause later on. This crazy conversation about the wedding sounded important.

But before he could open his mouth, Elizabeth had spun around and was glaring at him again.

"What are you thinking, knave?"

"I am thinking that you might actually be getting married, My Lady."

She took off her flower and lace wristlet and slapped him twice across the top of the head with it.

"You are not here to think!" she screamed at him. "You are here to *fuck!*"

She'd stepped out of the dress by this time and was now naked except for the long white veil. "Yaz" felt his stomach turn a complete triple somersault as he was confronted with her lovely, heaving body once again.

"Now turn over," she ordered him. "And get to work."

Chapter Thirty-five

Fuhrerstadt

The young man known as the *Amerikafuhrer* tugged at the highly starched collar of his white NS dress uniform jacket and spit.

"It's too tight!" he said, stamping his foot once. "It has to be looser . . ."

One of the three tailors kneeling at his feet stood up and made yet another measurement of the young man's neck size.

"And what happened to the rows of little flowers you promised on the lapels?" the *Amerikafuhrer* asked him.

"You never told us what kind of flowers, Your Excellency," the tailor dared to reply.

The young man, barely eighteen, closed his eyes in an attempt to hold in his anger. "I told you roses," he said through gritted teeth. "Roses were my great, great, grand-uncle's favorite flower. Or have you never read your history book?"

The tailor gulped audily. "I have, Your Excellency," he stuttered. "And I will personally sew the roses on your lapel for you."

The young man habitually brushed back his blond hair and closed his eyes once again.

"I'm tired of this," he said, effectively ending the fitting session. "Finish tomorrow . . ."

The three tailors quickly retrieved the jacket and their sewing boxes and hastily left the room.

"And make sure no Jew, no colored person, nor any American savage touches that garment!" he called after them.

As the three tailors departed, they were replaced by a very concerned-looking NS colonel. The officer stood briefly at attention and saluted.

The *Amerikafuhrer* was clearly uncomfortable with the man's sudden arrival. He recognized him as being from the office of his three Reich Marshalls: Erste, Zweite, and Dritte.

"Isn't it much too early for my daily briefing?" he asked the officer.

"I am here at the request of the Reich office, sir," the colonel told him. "And I'm afraid I have bad news."

The *Amerikafuhrer* collapsed onto his purple velvet couch.

"Bad news?" he groaned, somewhat sarcastically. "Why didn't your superiors come and tell me themselves?"

The NS colonel wisely chose to ignore the question. He knew that the three Reich Marshalls had been keeping a very dirty secret from just about everybody until this day. And it was the misfortune of lower rank that led to his selection as the person to pass on the troubling news to the high-strung Nazi Leader.

"Several days ago, sir," he began nervously, "there was an incident at the *Drache Mund* Prison. Three men escaped."

The young Nazi leader's face screwed up into an angry frown.

"Escaped?" he hissed incredulously. "Two days ago? Why wasn't I told earlier?"

"We didn't want to bother you, sir, until we finished our investigation," the colonel lied.

The *Amerikafuhrer* narrowed his eyes and stared long and hard at the officer.

"I thought escape from Dragon's Mouth was impossible, Colonel," he said finally.

The colonel gulped. "Apparently not, sir . . ."

"Well, who the hell were they?" the young man fumed, working his way into a full-fledged snit.

The colonel hesitated for a few heartbeats. "One was the false priest who we believe was part of the conspiracy to murder the First Governor of *Bundeswehr* Four," he replied slowly. "Another was a man previously caught escaping while pretending to be dead. The third was a United American saboteur caught down in New Orleans and transferred up here for interrogation. All were about to be executed."

"You mean they were three *condemned* men?" the *Amerika-*

fuhrer asked, plainly astonished. "How did they possibly get out?"

"We are not sure," the colonel answered. "They were led into the execution yard and their sentences were about to be carried out. Shots were heard, but everyone in the immediate area just assumed they were caused by the gunfire of the Skull executioner."

"Well — what does *he* say of it?" the teenaged leader asked.

The colonel looked blankly at the ceiling for a moment.

"He's dead, sir," he finally replied. "As are the officer of the day and two guards."

"Were they all shot by the prisoners?"

"We are still investigating that aspect," the officer said quickly.

The *Amerikafuhrer* stood up and began pacing nervously.

"Well, these prisoners didn't just disappear into thin air," he said. "Or did they?"

"There is some evidence that the prisoners escaped in helicopters painted in our colors," the colonel replied.

The *Amerikafuhrer* slammed his fist twice against his forehead. "And these are dangerous men, I suppose?"

"The assassin's cohort certainly is," the colonel told him bluntly. "As you know, he had constructed a very elaborate ruse to get close to the First Governor. His duplicity in the assassination has never been questioned. We have already flooded the city with wanted posters bearing his likeness."

"Is that really necessary?" the young leader asked worriedly. "All that clutter. All that potential litter?"

"This man might still be in the city," the colonel replied. "And he might be intent on shooting you, Your Excellency."

The young *Amerikafuhrer* felt a lump form in his throat, He felt a veil of paranoia descend upon him. Was this a legitimate threat? Or yet another case of his Reich Marshalls subtly torturing him again?

"Do Erste, Zweite or Dritte think I should postpone my ceremony because of all this?" he asked the colonel.

"No, sir," he replied firmly. "All three are confident that the ceremony can go on as planned. Security will be tripled. There should be no problems."

The *Amerikafuhrer* stopped pacing in mid step.

"I want you and them to make sure there are no problems," he said to the officer. "I want you to tell them that from now on there will be no more citizens allowed anywhere near our state functions.

No more crowds at the parades. No more crowds at the rallies. And definitely no crowds at my ceremony. Is that understood?"

The officer stood motionless for a few long moments, then he performed a shallow bow. "Perfectly, sir . . ."

"Now get out of here," the *Amerikafuhrer* ordered him.

With that, the officer quickly walked out of the room confident that he'd made it through the difficult duty relatively unscathed. Something that would undoubtedly bode well for him with the Reich Marshalls.

After the officer departed, the *Amerikafuhrer* spent the next few minutes fighting back an unmanly tear. He knew that other men in his high position would have simply ordered the officer bearing that kind of bad news to be shot. But he could not bring himself to do it. He had ordered civilians to death of course, and indirectly caused the deaths of many others, simply by signing off on the most oppressive occupation decrees. These deaths never bothered him.

But he could not find the courage to purge his own commanders, whether they be lowly colonels or the Marshalls Erste, Zweite and Dritte. He was certainly entitled to dispose of them. He knew they all lied to him on a regular basis. Even now, he wasn't quite sure whether they were telling the truth about beefing up security for his ceremony, or how the prison break was executed, or whether it had even happened at all.

Now the tears came for real. It was by an accident of birth that he was in this position. And though he was the highest official in this occupied land, he believed at that moment he was also the most lonely and isolated.

His glum thoughts were relieved somewhat when a smiling face walked through the door. It was his personal dresser, a young Swede named Lance. He was carrying a large, gift wrapped box with him.

"It is time to prepare our lunch," Lance whispered to him.

Both men grinned as he set down the box, opened it, and lifted out a small, squawking goose.

Chapter Thirty-six

East Falkland Island

The long range HC-130 Hercules gunship went into a tight circle over the bare, windswept air base and then came in for a reasonably smooth landing.

The blowing snow picked up as the big Herk taxied up to the base's single operating hangar. Two men were waiting for the plane, both wearing faded but cleanly pressed pre-war Royal Air Force uniforms.

The HC-130 reached its parking station and its pilots began shutting down the plane's major systems. The side door opened quickly enough and three people emerged. Two were members of the Football City Rangers Protection unit.

The third was Mike Fitzgerald.

The pair of RAF officers walked forward and met Fitz with two handshakes.

He introduced himself to the RAF men. and they to him. The senior officer was Major Sandhurst Jerrold. His aide was Lieutenant Patrick Sally.

"Sorry, we couldn't arrange for better weather," Jerrold told Fitz. "But I trust you had a good flight?"

"Problem free," Fitz replied.

He looked around the air base. The wind was up to fifty knots at least, its moaning provided the soundtrack for the bleak desolate spot of land that Britain and Argentina once fought over in the first, real high tech war. Now the base, like the rest of the island, appeared virtually deserted.

"Has the other side shown up?" Fitz asked the Brits.

"See for yourself," Sandhurst said with a nod.

He showed Fitz to the door of the base's main hangar. Using a battered remote control device, the RAF officer opened the airplane barn's creaking doors to reveal an all black Boeing 707.

"They flew back in late last night," Sandhurst told Fitz. "They went to their quarters and we haven't seen them since."

Fitz couldn't take his eyes off the big black converted airliner. He'd seen it before. It had once belonged to the Canal Nazis of the Panama-based Twisted Cross. Once that admittedly amateurish fascist group was defeated via a United American invasion, the 707 had bounced around the world's arms markets, being bought and sold on the whim or fortune of its owners.

Now it belonged to a very shadowy North African weapons trading firm named Big Blast Incorporated or BBI.

It was representatives of BBI that Fitz had flown down to this cold end of the world to meet. It was well known that the RAF Reserves ran the East Falkland Island base as a kind of neutral ground. It had hosted several peace conferences in recent years, mostly among the gaggle of militaristic cults who were constantly battling each other for control of the South American continent. It was also the quietest, most secure place in the world to make major arms deals.

And that was why Fitz was here. It had been a long trip but a necessary one, a crucial part of the plan.

"Can we begin right away?" he asked Sandhurst. "We're up against a very tight deadline."

Sandhurst pointed to the base's operations building and nodded.

"Grab yourself a cup of tea and sandwich in there," he suggested. "I'll round up our other guests."

One hour and ten minutes later, Sandhurst ushered Fitz into a small room just off the operations building's main hallway.

The BBI men were already there. It appeared that everything Fitz had heard about them was true—and then some.

Both men were wearing the garb of Bedouin Arabs. Both had hair that reached to their waists and was elaborately braided.

Each also wore a long thin beard held in place by shiny hair grease. They would hold hands through the entire meeting.

"Our deepest regrets to your comrades lost in the unfortunate plane crash a few days ago," one of the BBI men said in cracked English and without an ounce of sincerity.

Fitz quickly eyed Sandhurst, who barely nodded back.

"I thank you for your concern," Fitz replied. "I lost two good friends on that flight."

"Was it a bomb on board or simply mechanical difficulties?" the second BBI man asked with a twisted grin.

Fitz stared hard at the two strange men.

"We'll never know," was all he said.

An uncomfortable silence descended on the room. Finally it was up to Sandhurst to break it.

"Well, then," he said in a perfect stiff upper lip accent. "Shall we begin?"

Fitz cleared his throat for effect and pulled his chair closer to the table.

"I have no time for formalities, gentlemen," he said soberly. "We need weapons and we need them quickly. The plane crash has set our schedule back by some very critical days. So now our needs increase by the hour."

"How will you pay for these weapons?" one BBI man asked.

"Gold," Fitz replied firmly.

Both BBI men smiled stained gaping grins.

"We can appreciate your timetable," the man on the right said. "So let us get our manifest."

He passed a thick document to Fitz, with an exact copy to Sandhurst. Fitz turned to the first page which was headed: "Heavy Weapons—Mobile."

What followed were ten pages of descriptions of wholesale lots of main battle tanks, armored personnel carriers, Multiple Rocket Launch Systems, and mobile howitzers. Beside each lot was an ID number and a price.

Fitz studied each page carefully, jotting down notes as he went along. Then he went back to the first page and looked up at the dark arms dealers. It was against his better judgement to deal with such men. He knew they would have no compunction about dealing with the Fourth Reich or any one of a number of other enemies of America.

But these were desperate times. And he had to stick to the plan.

"I will take six squadrons of Chieftains," he began again, referring to the British Army's main battle tank. "I will take the two squadrons of M-1A Abrams only if they are NightScope fitted."

On and on it went, for the next half hour, Fitz reading out the weapons he wanted to purchase, with the BBI men gladly punching in the corresponding prices. At the end, he had more than four hundred pieces of heavy battle equipment, including two hundred main battle tanks, plus service equipment and ammunition.

The price: twelve hundred pounds of real gold and four thousand pounds of real silver.

"And where is the money, my friend?" the BBI man on the left asked.

"When can I inspect the merchandise?" Fitz responded.

The BBI man began to say something, but Major Sandhurst interrupted him.

"I am holding Mister Fitzgerald's money," he said in his precise, clipped British accent. "It is aboard his airplane under tight guard. And I am assured you can deliver the hardware for inspection within twenty-four hours. Is that correct?"

The men from BBI nodded happily.

Sandhurst clapped his hands with delight. "Perfect," he declared. "Then let us have a spot of gin to celebrate, and we will consummate this agreement tomorrow morning. Is that acceptable?"

The BBI men were nodding giddily now. They had just made a fortune.

"Sure," Fitz replied, reaching to tug at his priest's collar which was no longer there. "Tomorrow, it is . . ."

East Falkland

The next morning dawned cold and blustery.

Fitz and Major Sandhurst made their way through the deserted streets of Port Stanley, moving down the narrow main boulevard and to a predesignated spot on the ice encrusted east beach.

The two arms traders from BBI were already there, displaying their gold plated AK-47s as prominently as their personal computers.

"God be praised for this morning," one said, as they both bowed deep at the waist. "And for the life he gives us every day to . . ."

"Yeah, sure," Fitz huffed in reply, his disdain for the shady weapons merchants not dimming a bit. "Let's just get on with this."

The men bowed again. They were used to being insulted.

One produced a small portable radio and made a quick call: "Please flash ID lights! Yes, flash ID lights!"

The perpetually falling snow almost completely obscured the far horizon of the cold South Atlantic. But no sooner had the man made the radio call when Fitz could see a trio of red lights begin blinking way out to sea. Soon there were three more, and three more and three more.

"We picked them up on the Air-Sea radar last night," Sandhurst whispered to Fitz. "They were eighty miles out at midnight and pushing full steam toward here."

By this time there were more than forty red lights blinking across the entire snowy horizon. Fitz knew each of these lights was attached to a container ship carrying the weapons he'd ordered just the day before.

"We at BBI pride ourselves in prompt delivery and service . . ." one of the arms dealers said.

"Yeah, great," Fitz said, once again cutting short the BBI man's bullshit. The quick service was crucial, but he knew it was not entirely due to the BBI's good business practices. The arms cartel had had an enormous fleet of supply ships cruising the west coast of Africa on a selling voyage when the first UA-BBI meeting was arranged. Those ships immediately diverted to the Falklands and had been a day away when the first Herk crashed in Argentina. They'd been waiting just over the horizon ever since.

"The use of the ships comes with the price, of course," one of the BBI men explained to Fitz for the fifth time. "We will transport your weapons to one port of call, or help you with one amphibious landing. Then, for extra considerations, we can . . ."

Fitz waved away the man's overkill pitch.

"I insist on inspecting each ship cargo myself," he told him. "And I want a squad of my own men on each ship that passes inspection and heads north."

The BBI men wrapped their robes around them in the suddenly cold wind.

"This is highly unusual," one lied. "Our business is based on trust and . . ."

Fitz held up his hand, cutting the man off at the quick. There were too many stories about arms dealers selling good stuff "on the front end," only to load up the back end with junk. With the UA's precarious position, such a rip-off would mean disaster.

"I know all about your business," Fitz told them. "That's why I insist that my men accompany every load."

"But it could take some time to get your men here and on board the ships, my friend," the second BBI man whined. "And as a high official of your army, shouldn't your place be up north, with them?"

Now it was Fitz's turn to shiver. Suddenly his thoughts flashed back to that sunny bucolic day he'd spent with his kids swimming in the Wabash. It seemed like a hundred years ago.

"My place is here," he replied soberly. "For however long it takes."

They spent the next six hours moving from ship to ship in Sandhurst's Lynx helicopter, checking lot numbers and inspecting tanks.

Despite his obvious dislike for the BBI men, Fitz silently gave them credit. The first four ships he inspected held more than seventy-two tanks in both their holds and in containers lashed to the deck. Random checks proved that the tanks—huge British-made Chieftains mostly—were in top working condition from greased barrels to the latest in fire control computer software. Despite their smarmy ways, it was obvious that the BBI men kept the wares in good shape.

The long day came to an end in Sandhurst's small dining area. He and Fitz were splitting a bottle of no name Chilean wine while the two men from BBI were noisily slurping from the same bowl of soup.

"You were pleased today by what you saw?" one of the arms dealers asked Fitz, his question seeking nothing more than another begged compliment.

"So far, so good," Fitz replied crisply.

"You know, for large purchasers such as yourself, we usually offer a very nice *personal* item," the second BBI man said. "Something in normal times you might consider too extravagant, yet now, you might consider a good buy."

Fitz looked at Sandhurst for help in figuring out exactly what the weapons merchant was talking about. But the stately British officer could only shrug. He had no idea either.

"It's an airplane, sir," the first BBI man said, reading Fitz's thoughts exactly. "One of only a few left on this planet. We know you Americans are fond of high tech aircraft. This might be something for you to treasure, once the infidel has been expunged from your lands."

Fitz was curious. "What kind of airplane?"

The two BBI men stopped eating immediately. One reached into his pocket, produced a small brown envelope, and passed it to Sandhurst. He opened it and a single photograph fell out. He glanced at the photo, and Fitz saw the officer was suitably impressed.

"I'll say it's a rare bugger," he said, passing the photo to Fitz.

Fitz took one look at the picture and felt his jaw drop.

It was a photo of an F-117 Stealth.

Fuhrerstadt

The young officer in charge of the Fourth Reich's central communications unit knocked once on the huge oak door, then entered the strange triangular shaped room.

Walking to the center of the three-cornered rug, he turned and bowed separately to the three Reich Marshalls, each of whom was

213

sitting behind a massive mahogany desk in his own corner of the room.

"An important communique has just arrived from one of the southern tier agents," he told them. "I believe it requires your immediate attention."

"Has it been properly decoded?" Erste asked him.

"I have to assume so, sir," the officer said, turning in Erste's direction.

"And how was it transmitted?" Dritte wanted to know.

"Via the CommStar satellite," the officer replied, spinning around toward Dritte.

"Who else has seen it?" Zweite asked.

"Only myself, Herr Marshall," the CCU officer answered, turning to the third corner.

"Very well," Zweite boomed. "Read it to us."

The young communications officer took a deep, but nervous, breath. This was a big moment in his career. He knew the message had been sent by one of the Fourth Reich's many undercover agents working inside the BBI weapons cartel. If the news contained within it pleased the trio of high Nazi officers, he might be the recipient of some kind of commendation, or possibly even a promotion.

"The message reads as follows," he began. " 'United Americans have made large military hardware purchases this date, East Falkland air station. Mobile armor, ammunition and parts. No airplanes. Paid in gold. Delivery starts immediately and will be ongoing as trusted transport crews can be put in place. UA agent now in residence at RAF officers' quarters, indicating long stay.' "

Instantly all three Reich Marshalls gave out a whoop of joy.

"It fits the Argentine plans perfectly!" Dritte exclaimed, pounding his fist triumphantly. "At last, our serendipitous find is confirmed."

"It is so intriguing," Erste declared, smugly fingering his completely cosmetic monocle. "They've gone ahead and bought their armor and not airplanes. Just as the plan stated."

Even Zweite was happy. "Now we know the 'how,' " he said. "What is left is the 'when' and 'where.' "

The three men gathered near the center of the room where a

214

large war table containing an elaborate laser generated topographical map of the North American continent was set up. Having not been officially dismissed, the CCU man remained hovering a respectful distance from the planning table.

"We know they'll stage a seaborne landing somewhere on the East Coast," Dritte said; pulling out his telescoping map pointer. "I would guess it will come anywhere from the mid-Atlantic region up to the old New England area. The tides are better, they have a wider range of landing sites, plus our population control is lacking a bit in some of those areas."

"We can be certain it will be some relatively unprotected piece of shoreline," Erste said, pulling out his own, slightly larger map pointer. "I would guess somewhere in the middle. The Chesapeake Bay area would work to their advantage. That way they would have access to sea supply, plus they'll have a large river system to work with."

"I agree," Zweite continued, "and as the plans said they will try to establish a protectorate of their own, and set up a provisional governmen,. that area is certainly suited for it."

He let out a long cruel laugh. "In fact, they can set their government either on the beach or in the swamps."

"They can go sunbathing while they appeal for their precious civil uprising!" Dritte joined in, with an uncharacteristically boisterous laugh.

"Yes. they'll be the sunburned warriors," Erste added with an appropriately evil chuckle.

"And we will crush them!" the lowly communications officer shouted from behind them. He'd become totally caught up in the high-level discussion.

In an instant, three sets of high-official eyes were burning a hole right through him.

On cue, all three Reich Marshalls bellowed at the lowly CCU officer: "You are dismissed!"

Chapter Thirty-seven

The name of the place was Grand Royal Island, but despite the moniker, it was little more than a dot of land practically lost in the middle of Lake Erie.

The highest point on the four-square mile, pine tree covered, crescent shaped island was a fifteen-hundred-foot hill which looked out onto a small settlement and an even tinier airfield. It was from this vantage point that Hunter and Roy From Troy studied the terrain below through NightScope glasses.

Even through the pre-dawn darkness, it was obvious that at one time the place had served as a vacation resort. But now it looked practically deserted. Of particular interest, however, were the dozens of grassy mounds which dominated the area surrounding the small airfield. To the casual observer, these mounds would have appeared innocuous enough, especially from the air.

But Hunter knew better.

"How long have you known about this place?" he asked the airplane salesman, who was still pale and queasy from his first flight in a Harrier jet.

"Years," Roy burped back. "We used to stash planes up here during the New Order years, whenever things got real hot. I don't think anyone's ever bothered to figure out whether it's inside Free Canada or not. But it was close enough for us, especially back then, when no one knew what was what. After the Circle Wars, and things eased up, we used it for awhile as a stopover point. But I'm surprised it's all still here. It's amazing no one has found it and plundered it."

Hunter had to agree. "Not many places like this left anywhere," he said packing up the NightScope. "Too bad we've got to blow the lid off this one."

Captain Ryan St. Marie, a retired fifty-year veteran of the Canadian Armed Forces, was the tiny island's only resident. Basically a caretaker with little to do, he spent his time holed up inside the small building which had served as its police station many years before.

He was reading an ancient copy of *Playboy* when Hunter and Roy From Troy walked into his office.

St. Marie immediately reached for his handgun. He hadn't had a visitor in years. But no sooner had he found the handle to his pistol when he found himself staring down the barrel of Hunter's M-16.

"What is this? A hold-up?" he asked, stunned by the quickness of Hunter's rifle.

"No," Roy told him. "We are here to talk business."

"Business?" St. Marie asked incredulously. "No one's been here for business in years."

"Then we should get some real bargains," Hunter told him.

"Maybe," St. Marie admitted. "But what do you have as payment? We don't take silver, real or otherwise. Never did. And you wouldn't insult me by offering cash . . ."

Hunter and Roy heaved a heavy money chest up onto St. Marie's desk.

"Open it," Roy said.

St. Marie complied and found himself staring at about fifty heavy gold bars.

Roy took out one of the bars and tossed it to the old man. St. Marie studied it and then a wide smile spread across his craggy features.

"Well, gentlemen," he said. "I think we can do some business . . ."

Ten minutes later, Hunter, Roy and St. Marie were walking out to the fringe of the air field.

St. Marie was still glowing from the sight of the huge chest of gold bars. It was more money than he'd ever seen in one place in his life.

"We aim to please here, you understand." he told them over and over. "We don't have the customers we used to. You know, things are so much different since the mainland was overrun."

"To say the least," Hunter muttered.

He reached the first "grassy mound" and studied it for a moment. It was actually a large piece of camouflage netting with a multitude of fake plant stems weaved in. The netting had been in place for so long that real plants and trees had grown up and over it, adding immensely to its innocent appearance.

"Good 'rug' job," Hunter admitted. "Take nothing less than a high-power infra-red scan to find them, and maybe even not then."

St. Marie was anxious to accept the compliment. "We try our best," he said, the wide grin never quite leaving his face.

Hunter poked the snout of his M-16 under the netting and gently lifted it, dislodging a number of the plants, both real and fake.

Underneath was a near antique CH-47 Chinook troop helicopter.

Roy From Troy nearly knocked Hunter aside in order to get a good look at the aircraft. His ingrained salesmanship was now kicking at full throttle.

"This one is cherry, Hawk," he told Hunter. "It's old, but look at the finish. Not a pockmark anywhere."

Hunter knew Roy's enthusiasm was justified. He could even smell the fresh oil coming from the chopper's engine bay, a good indication that the Chinook had been well maintained during its long dormancy.

They inspected the chopper for five more minutes, but Hunter had been convinced from the start.

"I'm sold," he told Roy. "It's probably older than we are, but we won't find anything even close as good anywhere else."

St. Marie was positively bursting with happiness now. He would be due a nice ten percent commission for selling the helicopter, with the balance going to his boss in Brazil.

But the caretaker had a surprise coming.

Roy quickly counted out roughly fifty mounds. "Are they all like this?" he asked St. Marie.

"They are, my friend," the caretaker replied, his smile getting even broader. "You were thinking of buying more than one, perhaps?"

"We want all of them," Hunter told him point-blank.

St. Marie almost swallowed his tongue.

"All of them?" he gasped. "Do you realize, kind sir, there are fifty-three in all?"

"You said they are all in as good a shape as this one, correct?" Hunter asked.

"They are . . ."

"Well, then," Hunter said, "Let's talk price . . ."

Fuhrerstadt, two hours later

The young communications officer studied the most recent communique even as it was being printed out by his laser-fax machine.

It had just flashed in from Brazil, sent by a paid informant who worked for that country's royal family.

The message read: "Unconfirmed but reliable report that two UA operatives have purchased fifty heavy-lift helicopters from unknown source. Delivery immediate. Paid in gold."

The CCU officer studied the message a second time. He knew the trio of Reich Marshalls would be pleased. The chopper purchase fit squarely into the strategy that the Fourth Reich was expecting from the United Americans. That was, a seaborne landing somewhere on the upper east coast. Such an operation would be obviously enhanced by fifty heavy-lift helicopters, especially in getting crucial weapons and supplies on the beach in a hurry.

But the CCU officer knew better than to deliver this message to the *troika* of Marshalls himself. After his previous faux pas, he was lucky he was still alive, never mind in uniform.

So he copied the communique twice, keeping a copy for his own files. Then he called in his assistant and ordered him to deliver it unopened to the three Marshalls immediately. Let them eat a mouse for a change.

Once outside the CCU, however, this young officer skillfully opened the sealed pouch to read the message. After doing so, he could barely contain himself. He'd been working the CCU long enough to know that the news would please the Reich Marshalls to no end.

So with a spring in his step, he headed for the triangular office, convinced that good things frequently came to the man bearing good news.

Chapter Thirty-eight

Near Old Johnstown, Free Territory of New York, three days later

It was a calm, clear night above the rugged mountains of the central Adirondacks, the sky moonless and starfilled.

The peaceful setting was misleading. Hidden below, among the vast forests of these mountains, were bands of highwaymen, cutthroats and other assorted human vermin. Hideouts were everywhere. Here and there, evidence of temporary air pirate bases could be found, scorch marks on the miles of abandoned highways being the most obvious clue. There were even stories that these mountains had become haunted in the post–World War III era. Tales abounded of the spirits of risen Native Americans patrolling their old hunting grounds, trying to find final peace.

This area, once known as upstate New York, was unique in Second Axis America for one reason. After the Fourth Reich invaded America, it chose to leave this territory virtually unoccupied. Save for an occasional long-range ground patrol or irregular aerial recon missions, the Nazis had conceded the Adirondacks to the outlaws and the ghosts.

Falling somewhere in between those two definitions were the men who ran the small paramilitary facility known as Jack Base. And it was over this small, nondescript, heavily camouflaged air field that the clear mountain skies suddenly became very crowded.

First there were six of them, flying without running lights, their enormous twin rotors carving up the still night air. Then came six more. Then six more.

Painted all black with no markings, some of the helicopters had guns protruding from various portholes, but the majority were virtually unarmed. Once they arrived above the small air base, they would split up. Following landing lights no brighter than flashlights, each would set down to a quick landing. Seconds later it would be rolled into a revampment specially built under the thick canopy of trees. Once six were down and hidden, another half dozen would come in. Then another. And another.

In less than twenty minutes, all fifty-four Chinooks had been landed and concealed. Only then did the all black Harrier jump jet touch down.

"Coffee or whiskey. Hawk?"

"Both," Hunter replied. "And keep it coming."

He was sitting in an overstuffed chair in one corner of a room that was a cross between a military bunker and a particularly randy officers' club. This was the headquarters of Jack Base.

Sitting across the huge oak desk from him was the commander of the base, a former chief of police named Captain Jim Cook. He and Hunter had become friends years before when the small base served as a refueling station in the relatively brief post-war time when the American continent was both united *and* free.

Jack One had been virtually ignored when the Fourth Reich's invasion forces swept through. It was abandoned when they arrived; they searched it thoroughly, found nothing of value and moved on. That the fascists had not chosen to destroy the base or at least post a small garrison there had been a big mistake because the place had been slowly and quietly coming back to life ever since.

The base itself was nondescript. It was little more than a two-mile strip of asphalt and a handful of small white hangars. The people who ran it were far from bland. They called themselves JAWs as short for "Jacks Are Wild." Their nucleus was made up of former members of Cook's police department which had protected the small nearby city of Johnstown back in more peaceful times.

As the world changed and became more violent, the twenty-man JAWs unit had evolved from a local police force into a crack commando outfit. Unlike other post-war militia units who tended to specialize in one thing (mountain fighting, urban warfare, coastal patrol) the men in JAWs became experts in many things.

So it was to Hunter's great benefit that he could call on them now.

Cook poured out two strong black coffees and then added a healthy splash of no-name bourbon to each.

"We're refueling all the birds right now," Cook said, passing the steaming mug of laced coffee over to Hunter. "We should be done installing all the little lightbulbs by midnight and ready to go by 0300."

Hunter took a long swig of the hot java. "That's great," he said. "The sooner the better."

"Looks like you've got a hold of a good crop of pilots," Cook told him, consulting a photocopy of the chopper force's roster list.

"Every one of them is a Free Canadian," Hunter replied. "Every one of them a volunteer. Not one of them wanted a penny."

Cook took a sip of his own spiked coffee and then took a long, slow look at his friend.

"When was the last time you got some sleep?"

Hunter stared at the ceiling of the office and pretended to be contemplating the question.

"I don't know," he finally replied with a straight face. "I think it was back in grade school."

"Well, you look it," Cook told him.

Hunter couldn't argue. He really couldn't remember the last time he'd caught some substantial winks. It wasn't that he wouldn't welcome a good night's slumber. The trouble was that whenever he found a few minutes to conk out, he couldn't. There was too much going through his mind. The plan. It had to be carried out in precise time and precise order. One little deviation and the whole ball game would be over.

And still, there was much to do.

"You didn't have to do everything yourself," Cook told him. "You know my guys could have taken those recon missions up around the Lakes off your hands."

Hunter could only offer a weary shrug. He knew Cook was right, but he also knew there was another deeper, more personal reason he'd undertaken the near crippling work load.

It was so he wouldn't have time to think. Think about those few precious months when he'd retired from active duty. Think about the farm he'd tilled over on Cape Cod, the place called Skyfire. Think about the days he'd spent living there with Dominique.

Those were the days of Heaven, he thought. Now these were the days of Hell.

"You and your guys will be in the thick of it soon enough," Hunter finally replied, swigging his coffee and bourbon and trying to deflect the heart of Cook's question. "And I hope each one of you knows you don't have to go just because I asked you."

"Are you kidding?" Cook replied, freshening both their mugs with another shot of bourbon. "They were in here beating down my door to volunteer. They wouldn't miss this for the world."

Hunter held his mug up high in a toast to Cook and his men. By then he became very somber.

"How many of them have wives or families?"

Cook frowned. "You know who they are," he replied. "Warren Maas. Mark Snyder. Sean Higgens. Clancy Miller. They're all attached in some way or other."

"And they're willing to give it all up—for this?"

224

Cook began shaking his head slowly. "You know better than to ask that," he told Hunter.

Hunter nodded and rubbed his tired eyes.

"You're right," he said, draining his mug. "I guess I just don't want them to go through what I've been through."

Cook shook his head once again.

"Hey, Hawk," he said. "That's exactly *why* they want to do it."

Chapter Thirty-nine

Fuhrerstadt

It was almost midnight, yet the young girl named Brigit was still wide awake.

She was sitting at her window, staring out onto the bustling city of *Fuhrerstadt*. There was much activity on the streets tonight. Soldiers were everywhere, some speeding up and down the main boulevard in tanks or other armored vehicles. Others slowly walking the streets in heavily armed patrols of six or eight.

But despite the huge military presence, there was an undeniably festive aura around the city. The big wedding celebration would be held soon. The exact date was a top secret, and preparations for the event were moving ahead at a feverish pace. Grandstands were being built, flower beds and trees were being planted; everything was getting a good wash. It also appeared as if the entire city had been strung with lights — miles of bright whites, reds and yellows. These long colorful strings ran like spiderwebs up and down buildings; across street corners and main thoroughfares; and up one side of the old Gateway Arch and down the other. All the bridges were blanketed with them, as were the docks and pierworks on either side of the Mississippi. Even the helicopters that constantly droned in and out of the city were wrapped in tiny multicolored lights.

It made for a magnificent, if bizarre, sight. Yet the young girl was not too interested in the illuminated pageantry at the moment.

Instead, she was trying to remember her dreams.

The painting on the canvas before her was nearly finished. The snow covered mountain was all but complete, as were the intricately painted snow-tipped pine trees. She'd included a gloomy gray cloud bank on the left hand corner—it had been there the first night she had had the dream. In the background she'd put a large modern city; tall buildings mostly, near a waterfront. They were all in flames, yet the streetlights of the city were still on, as if nothing unusual was happening at all.

It seemed odd, but that was how it appeared in her dream.

The very top of the mountain was bare though and this was troubling her. Why would she feel compelled to go through all the psychic effort to paint her recurring dream if it simply depicted a snow peaked mountain in front of a burning city? There had to be something more to it than that. Her intuition was telling her so.

But now, as she stared out on the brightly lit city of *Fuhrerstadt,* she simply didn't have an idea what that something might be.

Dragon's Mouth Prison, five miles away

Thorgils, Prince of the Norse, bit down on the rancid piece of beef bone and tore off a mouthful of gristle.

One of the German shepherds nearby snapped at his greasy hands in an effort to dislodge the bone from them, but Thorgil quickly punched the dog on the snout.

"Get your own," he growled.

Despite everything that had happened in the past few days, Thorgils was once again a happy man. He was back inside his doghouse, back at his old job of tending the vicious Death Skull guard dogs. In return for his help in catching the United American officer named Jones, he'd been spared from a firing squad for his own escape attempt. Thorgils thought it a fair exchange. He was sure that Jones was dead by now, and hence not a threat to retaliate.

More importantly, Thorgils had been able to resume his preaching to the inmates. His epistles had become a regular staple now as soon as the Skulls closed the prison for the night and he counted many of the two hundred fifty prisoners among his flock. Each evening they listened to his oft repeated passages about how they would all be carried up and away from the prison someday. And when they were, Thorgils would be their king.

He finished his disgusting, yet filling, meal with a slurp of dirty water from the dogs' large tin trough. A moment later he heard the distinctive clinking sound of the gates of the prison being locked by the Skulls on their leaving.

"Once again, my work begins," he said to the ten canines nearby.

He crawled out of the doghouse to find that an extra large crowd of inmates had gathered to wait for him. Several broke out into applause as soon as he appeared.

"Brothers," he said, making his way through the hundred or so men. "It is time for us to begin."

Thorgils was escorted to the small wooden box which served as his pulpit and he waited as the sixty or so bedraggled prisoners settled down in front of him.

"Our time is coming," he began as always. "Our time to ascend. To leave this place. Our time to fly. We should be . . ."

"When?" one man at the back of the crowd interrupted him. "I don't know how much longer I can take this place."

"Soon," Thorgils assured him. "I have seen it, brothers. I have seen it sure as I see the moon and the sun. Soon. This I promise you."

"But this is what we've heard now for a long time," another voice spoke up. "We've heard your promises, but nothing ever happens."

Thorgils stiffened for a moment. This was the first sign of dissension he'd heard from his flock.

"Patience, brothers," he told them. "Our fate is dictated by the stars. By the sun. By the gods!"

228

"But you left us once," a third voice up front said. "How do we know you won't leave again for good?"

"I was *forced* to leave," Thorgils replied. His tone getting less beatific. "And I came back for you, didn't I?"

"Only because the Skulls *made* you come back," a new voice called out. "You tried to escape."

"No!" Thorgils cried. He could feel he was losing the crowd. "I came back for you."

"Bullshit!" someone yelled. "We're sick of your promises. We want action! We want to get the hell out of here!"

The crowd's anger began rising to a fever pitch. Some men were standing and shaking their fists at the Norse prince. Others were throwing rocks. Thorgils began trembling. He wished he had some *myx*.

"It will be soon," he shouted over the cries.

"When?" came the angry chorus.

But suddenly Thorgils wasn't listening to them anymore. Instead, his ears were cocked toward a deep rumbling sound far off in the distance.

Within seconds, everyone inside the prison yard heard it too. Mechanical. Frightening. Growing in intensity. It was getting so loud, so quickly; all of the dogs began barking at once.

"They are coming to kill us!" someone yelled in full panic. "Because of you!"

But again, Thorgils was not paying attention. His eyes were squinting, trying to make out something coming from the south. Trying to identify the source of the spine-tingling roar.

Then he saw them.

At first they looked like a galaxy of stars moving as one across the sky above the wall. But then, he connected the noise with the lights.

No more than a half mile away and five hundred feet high was a formation of at least fifty huge helicopters, all of them wrapped in hundreds of blinking white lights.

Less than a minute later, the Chinooks were dropping out of

229

the sky and landing in groups of twos and threes in the middle of the prison yard.

Black-uniformed men in dark Kevlar helmets were scampering out of the copters. Some waving guns, others large flashlights. In addition to the strings of white lights wrapped around its fuselage, each helicopter had a large American flag painted on its side.

"We're Americans!" the airborne soldiers were yelling over the Chinooks' shrieking engines and the howling, rotor-whipped winds. "We're here to rescue you!"

With that they began herding the stunned prisoners into their open cargo bays.

"C'mon, move!" the soldiers were yelling. "Move!"

As luck would have it, those prisoners not gathered before Thorgils's pulpit were the first to be loaded onto the big Chinooks. As soon as a helicopter was full with forty or fifty men, it would quickly ascend into the night sky. Then another would descend and take its place.

There were a few moments of confused astonishment before many of Thorgils's faithful realized what was happening. Then it hit them. This wasn't just a prison break. It was an *airborne* prison break. *They were ascending!*

"It's true!" many were now yelling at once, tearing their vocal cords to be heard over the scream of the engines. "It is our time to go!"

Some of the more lucid prisoners could see that an even larger operation was under way on the other side of the wall, in the prison yard where the hundreds of United American officers were being held. Chinooks were descending in packs of six and eights over there, picking up loads of skeletonlike prisoners and then taking off again like clockwork. All the while a second protective ring of Chinooks converted into gunships was circling around the daring nighttime operation. Some firing could be heard in the distance, and explosions were going on just outside the prison. But it was apparent that the Fourth Reich defenses had been caught completely off-guard by the raid.

Amidst the noise, confusion and blowing dust and smoke, Thorgils found himself walking through the prison yard, watching with absolute shock as his prophesy came true.

"Go, brothers!" he was calling to the men who were rushing past him now, ignoring him in their haste to climb aboard one of the big airships. "Go! *Ascend in the night!*"

Suddenly a bright stream of gunfire ripped across the prison yard. Hitting the ground and looking up, Thorgils saw a squad of Death Skulls had gained the far wall and were raking the work yard with heavy automatic weapons fire. One of the Chinooks dedicated to fire suppression swooped low over these men and began returning the fire three-fold courtesy of their converted M-163 Vulcan cannons. From another wall, a Death Skulls squad had activated several flamethrowing devices. With one huge whoosh! the center of the work yard was awash in bright orange flame. Another Chinook gunship arrived and began pounding away at the Skull fire team with their rapid-fire cannons. Several waist gunners in the ascending rescue choppers also joined in.

Still above it all, Thorgils could hear yet another strange sound. It came in the form of a loud screeching, much more intense than the combined symphony of helicopter engines, the rapid-fire cannons, and the clattering of automatic weapons. He looked up; and through the whirring copter blades, exhaust, smoke, flame and clouds, he saw a Harrier jump jet coming down almost right on top of him.

"No . . ." Thorgils whispered. "This is impossible . . ."

The jump jet came out of the sky with a deathlike scream—through the flames and streaking tracers from the Death Skulls, kicking up the dust and dried blood shed from so many hours of slave labor.

The Norse prince watched in horror as the strange jet came down with a bump, no more than twenty-five feet away from him. Its canopy was opened even before the plane had touched the ground. Through the cloud of dust and exhaust, he saw a man emerge from the airplane, climb out on the wing, and jump to the ground.

The pilot was dressed in an all black flight suit and wearing a bizarre black helmet. He was carrying an M-16.

"The gods, no!" Thorgils cried out full-throated this time. "It can't be!"

At that moment the Norseman realized he was looking at a ghost.

Hunter scanned the fiery confusion of the prison yard and quickly spotted Thorgils, dressed in his filthy long white gown.

The Norseman seemed paralyzed as Hunter ran toward him. That was fine with Hunter. It would make it all the easier to subdue the whacked out Viking, haul him back into the Harrier, and carry him out of there. For capturing Thorgils had been a small, but important, part of this bigger plan all along.

But just as Hunter was about to reach out and grab the man by his scrawny neck, Thorgils suddenly sprang to life.

"You are not real!" he screamed at Hunter before turning and dashing away from the rescue helicopters. "You were supposed to be dead!"

Hunter had little choice but to pursue the crazed man. Shooting him was out of the question. He had to take him alive.

With his M-16 up and firing streams of tracer bullets at the Death Skulls up on the prison walls, Hunter chased the wildly screaming Thorgils across the fire scorched work yard; over the face and hands of the nearly completed Hitler statue, around the two slit trench latrines, and back toward the doghouse. Bullets were flying all around him. as was the occasional terrifying burst of flame from the Skull fire teams. All the while, Chinooks were coming and going amidst the harrowing confusion. Their crews were picking up prisoners and firing at the Skulls at the same time.

But above it all Hunter could hear the bone chilling yelps of

Thorgils, screaming nonsense as he fled in panic.

He finally ran up the side of a carved piece of stone that looked like a mustache and launched himself feet first at the fleeing Norseman. He landed square on Thorgils's shoulders, knocking him head over heels into the brittle wooden stage he'd once used as a pulpit. Rolling out of the way of a Skull generated tongue of flame, Hunter yanked Thorgils into the temporary cover of a huge piece of stone which had been carved into the shape of Hitler's nose.

"Where is she!" he growled at the emaciated Norseman. "Where did you leave her?"

Thorgils stared up at him, his eyes wide and bulging with terror.

"You are not alive!" he spit out, blood inexplicably running from his nose and mouth. "You are from Hell!"

Hunter slammed the man's head twice against Hitler's left nostril.

"You crazy son of a bitch!" he screamed directly into Thorgils's ear. *"Where the hell is she?"*

At that moment, a particularly vivid explosion of streaming fire shot across the work yard. Instinctively, Hunter rolled once and put a barrage of tracers right into the source of the flame, knowing that a Skull fire team lurked behind it. The accurate fusillade eliminated the Skulls operating the flamethrower, but it was a split second too late. For no sooner had Hunter pulled his trigger when he realized that instead of getting away, Thorgils had jumped up and dashed right into the heart of the spewing fire. His garment instantly ablaze, it seemed like the man's body exploded with a flash. A second later he was totally engulfed in flame.

Shielding his eyes from the glare and horror not ten feet away, Hunter was startled to see Thorgils was gesturing to him through the flames. Time suddenly stood still. It seemed like the Horseman was laughing and crying and shouting something, all in the same horrible moment.

But what was the dying man trying to say?

Hunter jumped up and moved as close as he could to the burning man. Then he heard the words. Screamed above the crackling of the death flames and the clattering of gunfire, they were the last words Thorgils ever spoke.

"We brought her home . . ."

Chapter Forty

Several hours later

The first rays of dawn found a long column of NS troop trucks, APCs, scout cars and tanks moving swiftly south along the highway known as the *Sieger Bahn* — the Victory Road.

The former US interstate highway cut through the heart of central Illinois and ran the most direct route from *Bundeswehr* Four to *Fuhrerstadt*. At this moment, ninety percent of the *Bundeswehr* Four Home Garrison — nearly an entire mechanized division — was rushing down the roadway toward the capital of Fourth Reich America. Though not officially briefed on the situation, most of the troops in the column had heard rumors that several hours before *Fuhrerstadt* had been the scene of a shocking raid by the United Americans. Official reports were sketchy though and even the division's top officers were still in the dark. All they really knew was that the Home Garrison was being called on to bolster up the already formidable defense forces around the Nazi capital.

As they sped past the halfway point in their journey, the Home Garrison troops began to see some disturbing signs of serious trouble. The main air defense radar system hub, located at a place called *Goebbelstadt*, was in smoking ruins. Its trio of large tracking and communication dishes reduced to three smoldering masses. The destruction of this key facility meant the entire heart of the Fourth Reich's air defense system was now blind. Observing the damage from their speeding troop trucks, the soldiers knew that such accurate hits could only have come from a barrage of smart bombs, specifically anti-radiation missiles designed to home in on radar signals. But such sophisticated items were rare in Fourth Reich America. Until today.

Farther down the highway they passed by two power stations that had been recently destroyed and a small oil cracking plant that was still ablaze. Several times they saw contrails passing high overhead, moving west to east, not north to south, indicating that they might not be Fourth Reich aircraft. And more than once many of the troops thought they'd spotted large helicopters way off in the distance, heading north.

Obviously, something big was afoot and the closer the Home Garrison got to their destination, the more incidence of recent bombings they saw. A small airfield destroyed. A military police barracks demolished. A truck staging area flattened and burning. But oddly none of the bridges between the *Bundeswehr* Four troops and their destination had been bombed.

This served only to further convince the NS troopers that whatever was going on, they were probably headed in the wrong direction.

Hunter checked his Harrier's weapons available read-out screen and found he had one HARM smart bomb, one two-hundred-fifty-pound fragmentation bomb and six hundred fifty rounds of cannon ammo remaining.

"I hope it is enough," he thought.

The handful of hours since the prison break had been among the most hectic of his lifetime. An ultimate, high-speed roller coaster ride of air strikes, strafing runs and AAA suppression. From several high altitude aerial refuelings courtesy of Free Canadian KC-135 tankers to the just completed, dirt scraping, below-radar cannon attack on the Fourth Reich truck farm. Hunter had called on all of his expertise as a pilot to get him through in one piece. He'd already expended three HARM anti-radiation missiles, two frags, a five-hundred-pound iron bomb and two hundred cannon shells in blasting selected sites along the highway leading from *Bundeswehr* Four to *Fuhrerstadt*. And yet the most difficult part of the mission still lay ahead.

But through it all, his mind kept drifting back to the horror in the prison courtyard. He could not erase the image from his mind of the burning figure of Thorgils, beckoning him from the inferno, calling out to him, mouthing words that were not yet clear in Hunter's mind.

The difference between ghosts and men, he'd mused grimly, was that men still had to think.

He checked his fuel and then his operations clock. A very crucial milestone lay ahead, and he was encouraged that he was still on schedule.

Despite his foot travels deep inside Fourth Reich America over the past few months, Hunter had never been to the city which served as the capital for the Bummer Four.

But now, flying low over the absolutely flat, dry fields of what used to be called Indiana, he at last could see the faint outline of the strategically significant city on his northern horizon.

He took a deep gulp of oxygen and tapped the American flag he always kept in the breast pocket of his flight suit.

With all the luck it had brought him before, he hoped it would not fail him now.

It was Assistant Chief Medical officer of *Bundeswehr* Four Aerodrome who heard the strange airplane first.

He was walking toward the control tower at the huge air base when he detected a sound that seemed oddly dissonant to him. A trained violinist back in Europe, the doctor prided himself on his excellent sense of hearing. What he was picking up now was not at all like the throaty roars of Tornados and Viggens that he was used to hearing at the base. This one was more high-pitched and thin, almost eerily resonant above the normal racket of the air base.

He looked around in all directions for the source of the unfamiliar noise, but could find nothing out of the ordinary. Not untypically for so early in the morning, things seemed to be moving half speed around the sprawling air base. As usual, there were several dozen Fourth Reich *Luftwaffe* jets lined up on the tarmac with a small army of mechanics servicing them. As usual, some of these airplanes were in various stage of pre-flight. Four were taxiing out toward the main runways, in anticipation of take-off; four were rolling to their hardstands after having just landed from local patrol.

But something was wrong. The doctor could not only feel it, he could hear it.

He knew of the massive and unexpected movement of most of *Bundeswehr*'s Home Garrison toward *Fuhrerstadt* earlier that morning. But not being in the official high command loop, he had no idea why the division was suddenly rushed south. Like many people at the base, he just assumed it was a readiness exercise, or perhaps a maneuver called in anticipation of the *Amerikafuhrer*'s upcoming wedding ceremony. Whatever the reason, the base was now running on a skeleton crew, which made him one of its senior officers. Accordingly, he was on his way to the control tower to start his tour as that facility's officer of the watch.

But now the strange noise was growing louder, and competing with the roaring engines of the eight *Luftwaffe* planes in transit. Within seconds, the whine was so high-pitched, it began to buzz like an electric drill inside his ultrasensitive eardrums.

That was when he saw it.

It was coming in so low that he thought it was going to crash. He didn't think it was a *Luftwaffe* airplane—he knew the profiles of the Tornados and Viggens and Jaguars. No, this was a much smaller plane, painted all black and flying no more than twenty-five feet off the ground. It was coming right at him, out of the cornfields to the east, heading for the main airplane parking area.

Suddenly the airplane's nose erupted in flame and smoke. In an instant, the four Viggens preparing to take off on patrol were ripped apart with an incredibly accurate burst of cannon fire.

As the medical officer stared with mouth ajar, the airplane banked hard to the left. It was at this moment that the Nazi physician realized it was actually an AV-8F Harrier jump jet. That accounted for the strange high-pitched whine his ears had detected moments earlier. Now he watched in horror as the airplane's pilot released a large white missile from underneath his right wing. The missile shot forward at tremendous speed and less than two seconds later slammed into the Aerodrome's massive air control radar complex. The Harrier flew right through the resulting explosion, pulling straight up on its tail and looping high and around again.

This maneuver gave the medical officer enough time to snap out of it and get his feet moving. He ran up the control tower's external stairway, screaming at the top of his lungs for the base to go on red alert. But it was too late. The jump jet had already banked around to the right and was riddling the top of the control tower with a ferocious cannon barrage.

The medical officer soon found his feet acting on their own, turning him around and forcing him to run back down the stairway, a rain of broken glass and hot metal chasing him as he retreated.

He stumbled to the bottom of the steps to see the rampaging jump jet had turned again and was headed straight for the base's communications building. Just like in slow motion, the medical officer watched as the large black bomb dropped from the airplane's left wing and slammed into the comm shack no more than fifty feet away.

The explosion was so loud and powerfully concussive that it lifted the medical officer up off his feet and slammed him against the wall of a hangar twenty feet away. He crumpled instantly, feeling like he'd just taken a five-hundred-pound punch in stomach. When he caught his breath, he was able to focus his eyes enough to see the Harrier flash over the air base once again and then quickly depart to the east from where it came.

In all, the devastating attack had lasted less than a minute.

Biting his tongue so he wouldn't go into a state of shock, the medical officer checked himself for any serious injuries. He had multiple cuts on his arms and legs, and a large contusion on his back. Nothing seemed life threatening.

However, there *was* something seriously wrong with him.

Just as the silhouette of the jet passed over the eastern horizon, the man knew what had happened. The base was in flames, and secondary explosions were going off everywhere. Soldiers and mechanics were running about, shouting at each other. Several jets not caught in the barrage were gunning their engines, not to take off but to taxi to their concrete emplacements in anticipation of another attack.

But despite this cacophony of sounds, the medical officer could hear nothing but the last of that low, squeaky whine.

He began to panic as it dawned on him what was wrong. As a result of the last explosion, he had become suddenly and totally deaf.

Crouched and crying in a doorway of the partially destroyed hangar, the Nazi medical officer watched the *Bundeswehr* Four Aerodrome dissolve into a state of silent, utter chaos.

He knew the base had little in the way of anti-aircraft defenses. The appropriations people in *Fuhrerstadt* had decided long before that a facility so close to the center of the Fourth Reich's American empire wouldn't need many SAM batteries or AAA guns simply because they felt there was no way a potential enemy could get past the Reich's supposedly solid wall of AA defenses lining its ill-gotten borders.

Now tortured by the endless whistling in his ears, the medical officer realized the enormous blunder in that decision. For off in the distance, coming in over the same flat cornfields, he saw a sight that needed no accompanying noise to strike fear into his heart. The sky, from horizon to horizon, was filled with helicopters.

In his disoriented state, he strangely began to count them. First he saw a dozen. Then twenty. Then thirty. Then even more. They were large, two rotor machines, painted all black and wearing no markings.

"Where in hell did they come from?" he asked aloud.

Off to his right he saw several more helicopters enter the field of view. He felt a momentary pang of hope as he realized that these choppers—six Blackhawks and about ten Hueys—belonged to the *Bundeswehr* Four defense force. Immediately the copters turned toward the oncoming flying army, nose guns blazing. Suddenly, the air over the far runway was abuzz with twisting, turning helicopters.

But then the accursed jump jet reappeared, its cannons firing ferociously. As a strange, whirring blade dogfight was joined, the majority of the other enemy helicopters neatly flew around the air battle and continued on toward the base. Within a half minute, the first of these helicopters began landing, and disgorging black uniformed soldiers in Kevlar helmets, the distinctive garb of the United Americans. These airborne soldiers quickly fanned out and engaged the pitifully small groups of defending Fourth Reich troops.

What the hell was going on here? the medical officer asked himself. Had the Americans actually pulled a feint of some kind down in *Fuhrerstadt,* causing the Fourth Reich high command to panic and send the *Bundeswehr* Four Home Garrison to reinforce the Nazi capital? If so, then the Americans were now attacking the Fourth Reich in their most weakened spot—Bummer Four.

"The fools," the doctor cursed at his own superiors. His

panic rising when he was unable to hear his own voice, "The bloody fools . . ."

He watched with growing despair as more of the big American helicopters landed, dropping off more troops. There were several firefights going on around him. The multitude of muzzle flashes was almost blinding, but he knew it was a hopeless cause. The copter vs. jump jet dogfight had been painfully brief. He could see four Fourth Reich aircraft were down and burning out on the far runways, with a handful of survivors turning to the south in retreat.

And now a new element. High above the base, he saw four enormous C-5 cargo jets circling, gradually getting lower, obviously preparing to land.

About twenty NS defenders were making their way back toward the medical officer, their puny resistance quickly falling apart in light of the sudden, overwhelming American attack.

"What shall we do?" one of these soldiers asked the doctor.

But the medical officer could only shrug and desperately point to his injured, bleeding ears. By this time some of the Americans were peppering the hangar with small arms fire while others were dashing about, securing key positions around the huge air base. And all the while, more helicopters were landing all over the tarmac.

The medical officer cursed that this would be the day that he was the officer in charge of the air base. In past wars, a German officer in his situation would simply take out his pistol, put it to his head and pull the trigger. The medical officer would have done just that, but he didn't have a pistol.

"Ubergabe!" he finally called out to the retreating NS troops, once again, unable to hear his own voice. "It is time to surrender . . ."

It took only another ten minutes for all the shooting to stop around the *Bundeswehr* Four Aerodrome.

The medical officer was now one of forty Fourth Reich soldiers bound by his hands and feet and placed in a long line parallel to the base's main taxiway, prisoners under the watchful eyes of two dozen heavily armed United American troops.

From this vantage point, the doctor could see just how dicey an operation the sudden UA assault had been. Many of the helicopters that arrived at the tail end of the strike literally came crashing down to the tarmac, their blades barely turning, obviously out of fuel. The holds of these choppers, as well as most of the other aircraft, were not filled entirely with UA soldiers either. Rather, they were carrying ragged, incredibly thin men who the doctor knew must have been POWs from somewhere.

Why would the Americans bring along so many obvious noncombatants? It was a question the medical officer would not soon find an answer to.

The quartet of enormous C-5 cargo planes had come in for a landing, followed by the Harrier jump jet. No sooner had the four unmarked C-5s rolled to a stop when their huge hinged doors opened and a small army of soldiers came charging out. The medical officer glumly recognized their uniforms right away. Blue with red piping, the soldiers were units of the super elite Free Canadians' Special Forces.

Just as soon as these troops disgorged, the emaciated POWs were directed to the big C-5s, many of them having to be carried by stretcher into the maw of the gigantic airplanes. As soon as one of the C-5s was filled, its pilots turned the huge airplane back out to the main runway and took off, rising slowly and heading to the north. All four were gone within twenty minutes.

Throughout it all, the doctor was simply amazed at the gall and cunning of his enemy. Once the POWs were gone, he could almost count the number of UA soldiers walking about. They had in fact taken over the Aerodrome on as much bluff and bluster as manpower.

And, of course, they had the help of the man flying the Harrier jump jet.

The medical officer had kept his eye on this pilot ever since he'd landed in the Harrier. He'd directed the loading of the UA POWs and the deployment of the Free Canadian troops. He'd conferred at length with the pilots of the UA helicopters, some of which had taken fuel off one of the C-5's and were now airborne again flying protective orbits around the air base. He'd also helped locate and comfort the handful of UA troopers who were wounded in the initial, lightning assault.

Now this man was walking right toward him, accompanying several UA officers. He was tall, dressed in an all black flight suit, carrying a laser-sighted M-16 and wearing a black futuristic crash helmet.

Flipping up the visor on this helmet, the pilot made his way down the line of Fourth Reich prisoners, studying each one. When he reached the spot in front of the medical officer, he stopped and leaned over him.

"Doktor?" he asked.

But the medical officer could not hear him. Instead he pointed to his injured ears and shrugged.

The pilot asked again. *"Sind ihr Doktor?"*

Again, all the medical officer could do was shrug.

It was obvious that the pilot was growing more angry with him by the second.

"Are you a doctor?" the pilot demanded. "We have injured men out here . . ."

The medical officer was getting the gist of the message, but far be it from him to volunteer his services to the enemy—especially in his hearing-impaired condition. So he simply shrugged again.

Suddenly the pilot leaned over, grabbed him by his tunic collar and gave him a hard slap on the side of his head.

"Are you a Goddamn doctor or not?"

Suddenly the German felt the buzz leave his head. His eyes

went wide, and so did his mouth. The sharp, hard slap had had an instant miraculous effect.

"Danke! Danke!" he began screaming with joy.

He could hear again.

Chapter Forty-one

Fuhrerstadt

The trio of Fourth Reich Field Marshall's paused for a moment before entering the *Amerikafuhrer*'s chambers.

"What if he doesn't agree with our assessments?" Dritte asked, nervously fingering the silver-plated Iron Cross hanging around his neck. "He may choose to see it all in a much different way. And then . . ."

"He can be dealt with," the aggressive Zweite declared, harshly cutting him off.

"Perhaps." said Erste. "But then again maybe not. Then what?"

Zweite sniffed at the concerns of his compatriots.

"Then we just kill him," he said, lowering his voice a notch. "Right here and now."

Erste and Dritte gulped audibly as Zweite knocked once and entered the huge ornate room. The *Amerikafuhrer* was lounging on a long couch located at the far end of the pinkish room. He was wearing a long satin dressing gown, tackily decorated with gold-leaf swastikas and many items of jewelry.

"Your Excellency, may we talk with you?" Erste said. "It's very important."

The young, rather girlish blond-haired man motioned the three officers to come forward.

"You all look worried," he said in his singsong voice. "I think I can tell when you are worried."

"We are definitely *not* worried, sir," Zweite countered.

"Just the opposite, sir. We are supremely confident."

"But something *has* happened," the *Amerikafuhrer* said. "All that shooting last night. What was it all about? I've been trying to get a straight answer all day."

The three Nazi officers hesitated for a moment.

"The United Americans attempted a prison break last night, sir," Erste finally said. "At the Dragon's Mouth. Using helicopters and deception."

The *Amerikafuhrer* was clearly stunned. "Another one?"

Zweite quickly stepped forward. "Yes, but our *Tod Schadel* troops killed most of them," he lied. "Many of the prisoners died too. Killed by the guns of their own countrymen."

"They killed their own people?"

"Yes, sir," Zweite replied. "In fact, we believe this was the point of the whole operation."

The *Amerikafuhrer* tugged nervously at his frilly Nazi gown.

"But why would they do that? What was the point?"

"Propaganda," came Zweite's quick reply. "As you know, sir, these Americans crave the martyr image."

The *Amerikafuhrer* turned to Erste, the man he trusted the most.

"How many American helicopters were involved in this operation? One? Two?"

Erste gulped. "Several dozen . . ."

"Several *dozen?*" the top Nazi leader asked, incredulously. "How could several dozen helicopters get through our air defenses?"

"They destroyed a key radar station," Erste admitted. "One still under construction about thirty miles down the river. They were able to fly low after that, and gain entrance to the city's airspace. They were covered with strings of ceremony lights, just like our other aircraft. This way they came in . . . well, unnoticed, sir."

The *Amerikafuhrer*'s face turned pale then red.

"Just like that?" he demanded.

Once again the Marshalls chose not to speak.

"There must be someone held accountable for this," the *Amerikafuhrer* declared. "The officers at the radar station. Or their superiors. Someone."

Zweite stepped forward again and clicked his heels. "I will order a round of executions in the morning," he declared. "And that will be the end of it."

The *Amerikafuhrer* sighed heavily and reached for a banana from his overflowing fruit bowl. Dritte stepped forward and toadily peeled the banana for his high commander.

"What else?" the young man asked his officers, his tone indicating that he really didn't want to hear the answer.

"We have had more enemy activity, sir," Erste told him frankly. "Up north. In *Bundeswehr* Four . . ."

The *Amerikafuhrer* stopped eating the banana in mid bite. "What kind of activity?" he demanded of the three.

"The kind which plays right into our hands," Zweite piped up. "You see, the United Americans have made their move, Your Excellency. Just as dictated on the plans we secured."

"Explain that," the young man said. "And do so quickly."

Zweite took a deep breath. "We know from the secret documents recovered in the Argentine air crash that the United Americans were planning on attacking and holding a section of our territory. The idea behind this rather desperate strategy was to incite a public uprising.

"Now, it is obvious that the Americans covet the territory around *Bundeswehr* Four."

"That's insane!" the young leader erupted. "Even I know it would be foolish for them to try and carve out a piece of territory in the middle of our empire."

Zweite began sweating profusely He had a loaded derringer in his uniform pocket and at the moment it felt like it weighed a ton.

"Sir, this is obviously their way of trying to *surprise* us," he stammered. "Instead of going for a piece of coastal territory, they've gone for something, well, *unpredictable*. Something reached by helicopters and not amphibious craft. They've always been known for their unpredictability. The captured plans are rife with it."

"It's true, sir," Erste interjected. "During the Circle Wars, the Americans wore their unpredictability like a badge of honor. In fact, they're so damn unpredictable, that they are now very *predictable*."

The *Amerikafuhrer* let out a long sigh. "But these captured plans you so religiously adhere to," he said. "Do they not also contain references to purchasing tanks and other heavy equipment?"

"Yes, sir," Erste replied quietly. "And we believe the Free Canadians might be aiding them on just that aspect. In fact, Free Canadian cargo planes were seen above *Bundeswehr* Four district earlier today."

The *Amerikafuhrer* raised his hand. "Were they fired upon?" he asked urgently.

"No sir," Erste replied just as quickly. "They were quickly identified by our troops as cargo planes and therefore, they held their fire, per the "Noninterference" decree. Besides, we know what firing upon the Canadians would involve and we have come to expect some minor Canadian involvement. They have traditionally given aid to the Americans, but we believe it is simply to mollify their own people, many of which yearn for the old, rather democratic days."

"The Canadians do not want an all-out war with us," Dritte dared to say. "They have too many people to protect. And they know that is a path we do not want to walk either."

"And what path do we want to walk?" the *Amerikafuhrer* asked wearily.

Zweite spoke up once again.

"We know what the Americans' plans are, sir," he reiterated. the small gun seemingly burning a hole in his uniform pocket. "We are now prepared to match them step for step."

"How so?"

Zweite calmly cleared his throat.

249

"By sending a very strong force against them, now!" he declared. "We can send five divisions against *Bundeswehr* Four immediately and surround them. It will take much less time than if we had to battle them on the beaches of the East Coast. Once they are encircled. we will blast away with these rebels. We can use our superior artillery, our superior tank strength. We can even use the *Schrecklichkeit Kanone* at Indianapolis. We will strangle them. *We will crush them.* And believe me, news of our victory will carry far and wide. Every *sputnik* in the territory will know the story. We will broadcast it, day by day, on the *Volksradio*. It will be both a stunning propaganda victory as well as a military one."

The *Amerikafuhrer* looked to the other two officers.

"Do you both agree with this strategy?" he asked them.

Both men hesitated for a heartbeat or two. Then they nodded.

"It is a sound plan," Erste said.

"Very sound," parroted Dritte.

The *Amerikafuhrer* sighed heavily once again.

"Then do it," he hissed at them. "And do it before my wedding. Do you understand?"

All three officers clicked their heels in agreement and then turned to leave.

"But there's one more thing," The *Amerikafuhrer* said, reaching for another banana.

The three Reich Marshalls stopped in their tracks.

"I was under the impression that the United Americans were leaderless," the *Amerikafuhrer* began, sucking on the unpeeled piece of fruit. "Despite their elaborate secret plans, you still consider them a 'rag tag army.' However, now with their two raids on our prison and their activity up in *Bundeswehr* Four, doesn't it indicate some rather complicated military coordination?"

"They have been through several major wars sir," Erste offered by way of explanation. "They have been known to take rather desperate risks in the past."

"But who is leading them?" the *Amerikafuhrer* asked bluntly. "Who could it possibly be? Hawk Hunter?"

The trio of officers stood stone silent for a long moment. Each one knew that a Harrier jump jet had been spotted both over Dragon's Mouth the night before as well as at *Bundeswehr* Four earlier that day.

But they weren't about to tell that to the *Amerikafuhrer*.

"It is impossible, sir, that the outlaw Hunter is involved," Zweite declared finally. "He is long dead."

Chapter Forty-two

Aboard the Great Ship, somewhere in the Atlantic

"Yaz" tried his best to pull the fighter pilot helmet down over his head, but the damned thing was just too small.

He'd already attempted to widen the hard plastic material by hand and even considered heating it, but it was still useless. The crash helmet was just not his size and no amount of poking and pulling was ever going to make it so.

By comparison, his flight boots were two sizes too big. So was his flight suit itself. The multitude of safety straps and belts were enough to heft the garment up on his small frame, and wearing three pairs of socks did away with the sloshing sensation in walking in the oversized boots. But the helmet was going to be a problem.

He felt like a fool wearing the costume. But like everything in the past few weeks of his life, he knew it was necessary for his own survival. Though never totally comfortable in his new role of Elizabeth Sandlake's boy toy, he was wise enough to know that being a sex slave was better than being just a plain old slave. And though he was getting tired of eating oysters three meals a day and concerned that all the Vitamin E was turning his skin a little too pinkish, it was better than cleaning up fish guts, or regreasing toilet mechanisms, or ripping apart the Great Ship's massive sewage ejection pump.

He just wished he didn't have to dress up like his old friend Hawk Hunter all the time.

He took a deep breath, let it out, and then with a lot of effort finally forced the helmet down over his ears and into place. Instantly he felt like his head was in an ever tightening vise and that his teeth were slowly going to grind together until they popped out.

With little more to do to alter his strange wardrobe, he waddled out of his dressing room and down to Elizabeth's love chamber. Slipping inside, he saw both Sandlake and her companion, Juanita, lounging on the massive waterbed, blithely fondling each other's breasts. He heard them both gasp when he walked in. An instant later the unmistakable scent of *myx* reached his nose.

"You tease us," Elizabeth cooed to him. "We've been waiting too, *too* long."

"I'm sorry," "Yaz" croaked, feeling a pain equivalent to several impacted molars. "This uniform, this helmet, it's just not my size."

Both women giggled, not from amusement but from the *myx*. Their eyes were watery and dreamy. Their bare chests were heaving. Their legs were twitching spasmodically.

Another day at work, "Yaz" thought.

Elizabeth leaned over and kissed Juanita full on the lips.

"What shall we play today?" she asked the dark Spanish beauty.

"Let's chain him up again," Juanita gushed.

Elizabeth climbed off the waterbed and retrieved a set of fur-lined chains from her closet. "A capital idea!" she declared.

She strutted across the room and grabbed "Yaz" by the crotch. "I hope you've taken your vitamins today," she told him mockingly.

"Yaz" gulped audibly as she attached one end of the chains to his wrists and then fastened the other end to a pair of eye-hooks high over her waterbed.

"Our captive audience," Juanita laughed, as she put a hammerlock on "Yaz's" rear end. "Once again, we'll see how tough these fighter pilots really are . . ."

As they took turns undoing the myriad of zippers on his flight suit, "Yaz" was unable to do anything but stand by helplessly and let them have their way with him. Once the majority of his body was exposed, the two women began to fondle him in earnest.

Then came a sudden knock on the cabin door.

"Who is it?" Elizabeth singsonged, the *myx* absolutely roaring through her system.

The door opened, and the Captain of the Great Ship himself took one step in.

"A very important message for you, your majesty . . ."

Elizabeth stopped in midstroke. Suddenly she was up off her knees and back into her witching mode.

"Important enough to interrupt me!" she screamed at the man.

The captain quickly nodded. "I believe so, My Lady," he said nervously. "It is direct from Zweite."

Elizabeth grabbed a blanket from the bed and covered her naked breasts. Then she ripped the message from the man's hand and dismissed him with nothing more than a cold, hard stare.

"This is a conspiracy!" she belleven bowed once the captain had departed. "Every time I want to have some privacy, something like this happens!"

She tore open the sealed envelope and quickly read the message. Suddenly the blanket dropped from her grip.

"At last!" she declared. Her face filling with intoxicated euphoria once again.

"Good news, My Lady?" Juanita asked expectantly.

"Yes, my dear," Elizabeth said softly. "Everything is finally in readiness for our ceremony. We have been cleared to proceed."

Juanita instantly perked up too. "That is wonderful!"

"It gets even better," Elizabeth went on. "As a wedding present from Zweite, the Fourth Reich has surrounded a large

254

force of United American rebels and are in the process of annihilating them."

"Again, very welcome news, My Lady," Juanita chimed. "The perfect gift."

"Get dressed," Elizabeth ordered Juanita, happily crumpling the message and tossing it against the wall. "We must go to the communications room at once and send our reply."

With that the two women climbed into their dressing gowns and hastily left the room, leaving a very confused "Yaz" helplessly hanging by the fur lined chains, his helmet feeling tighter than ever.

Somewhere over the Atlantic, one hour later

Major Frost was alive and well and dreaming about rolling around in a room filled with shaving cream when he was roused awake by one of the crewmen aboard the long-range P-3 Orion airplane.

"Sir, we're getting a new transmission. You'd better hear it."

Frost rolled out of the incredibly tiny fold-away bunk and sleepily bounced his way tip to the airplane's communication station. He'd never flown in an Orion before, and up to this time, he considered himself blessed. The durable, anti-submarine aircraft was cramped, noisy, smelled of engine exhaust, and bathroom disinfectant. It was also the roughest riding airplane he'd ever been in. He'd been aboard the damn thing for fourteen hours straight, and this flight was his ninth mission in as many days.

Now he hoped this aerial marathon was about to pay some dividends.

He finally reached the communications shack to find the pair of radio specialists excitedly pushing buttons and taking notes.

One of them handed him a pair of headphones.

"They've been broadcasting on an irregular sequence for the

past ten minutes," the radioman told him. "It's going out on both UHF and VHF. Primary code, under a secondary scramble signal which we've sorted out."

"Is it in English or German?" Frost asked, putting on the headphones.

"Both," the radioman replied.

Frost had to wait a moment, but soon the broadcast in question came screeching through the headphones. It was undeniably a woman's voice.

"Daylight . . . daylight. Sunrise has been scheduled. High tide. Ocean storm. Return. Return. Storm Birds. No lightning. No thunder. No clouds . . ."

Frost listened as the message repeated twice more, and then went into the German translation.

"What's the decode?" he asked the radioman.

The officer had already scribbled out the decoded message. Frost read it over and felt his jaw drop. Suddenly he knew that the long trips in the cramped, smelly Orion *had* proved worthwhile.

"We've got to get this to the *New Jersey* at once, he said.

Chapter Forty-three

48 hours later

The roads leading to the out skirts of *Bundeswehr* Four were so clogged with Fourth Reich military equipment that dozens of vehicle radiators were bursting like small bombs, due to engine overheating.

Five divisions of the Fourth Reich's best troops had the small city surrounded, nearly fifty thousand heavily armed soldiers in all. An infantry division from New Chicago had sealed off the city from the north, with another from the Illinois-based *Bundeswehr* Five taking up positions to the west. A reinforced mechanized division of the *Amerikafuhrer*'s own personal NS Guards had established a line ten miles to the east of the city, and another *Fuhrerstadt* division was stationed just to the south of them.

It would be the *Bundeswehr* Four Home Garrison who would spearhead the operation. They were presently jammed up on the Victory Road fifteen miles due south of the city.

That the impending action had been planned and implemented so quickly was a tribute to the famous Fourth Reich efficiency, or so it seemed. Their propensity for creating monstrous traffic jams notwithstanding, the gathering of so many forces on such short notice had convinced the NS commanders that they'd pulled off some kind of logistical miracle, like corraling hundreds of actors for a grand Wagnerian epic performance on just two days notice. In doing so, the stage was now set for the annihilation of the fledgling United Americans, and, it was hoped, an end to their brief but stinging resurgence.

The element of surprise was essential to the upcoming NS operation so no aerial reconnaissance had been done of the target city. As it turned out, none was really needed. The NS Signals Intelligence units had been monitoring radio traffic coming from *Bundeswehr* Four since the United American occupation began. Much of it involved calls back and forth to stations just over the border into Free Canada and contained mundane military matters such as ammunition stockpiling, fuel reserves, and food distribution. The NS had happily learned from these radio transmissions that much of the UA's large helicopter force was inoperable due to lack of fuel and parts. It was also apparent that an agreement to supply these much needed items via an arms dealer in Nova Scotia had fallen through, further isolating the occupying force.

The most recent intercepts were even more advantageous to the Fourth Reich. The night before the Signit units reported a stinging radio exchange between the leader of the UA occupying forces and the commander of the Free Canadian border units which had flown into the small city shortly after the Americans' airborne assault. The argument was over money. The Free Canadian commander complained that he had not been paid in advance for the services of his troops. The Americans countered that the FC troops had yet to see action, therefore no payment was yet required.

In a stunning blow to the UA cause, four C-5s had set down at the Aerodrome earlier that day and had apparently withdrawn to Canadians. (Intelligence officers, attached to the New Chicago NS divisions holding the ground north of the city, confirmed seeing the C-5 cargo planes pass overhead.) It was this last piece of information which had gathered much anticipation of success in the hearts and minds of the NS High Command.

With the troublesome Free Canadians out of the way, the

quick, clean, *efficient* destruction of the UA occupying forces was now assured.

It was now noontime.

The plan called for the opening shots of the campaign to be fired by the *Schrecklichkeit Kanone* at Indianapolis. The target was centered on the western outskirts of the *Bundeswehr* Four capital, an area that was known to house many civilians, yet was far enough away from any quality NS military installations that could be reoccupied once the UA force was wiped out.

After a barrage from the "Frightfulness Cannon," the *Bundeswehr* Four Home Garrison would move in, the Aerodrome being their first objective. Any path of retreat by the UA forces would be cut off by one of the surrounding NS divisions. Though, according to the captured UA plans, the struggle for this "New America" was to continue to the last man.

Once the fighting had ceased, however, any surviving UA troops would be massed at the airport, along with any civilians who might have collaborated with them. A mass execution would then ensue. The whole operation would be videotaped by special communications units for viewing by the Fourth Reich high command and later for editing into a propaganda film.

In all, the retaking of the *Bundeswehr* Four capital was expected to take ten hours at the most.

The five-minute barrage from the Indianapolis *Schrecklichkeit Kanone* began precisely at 12:05. Even though they were a full fifteen miles from the impact points, many troopers in the Home Garrison suffered bleeding ears during the twenty-shot fusillade, such was the power and the concussion from the large Frightfulness Cannon's shells. Once the barrage was lifted, advanced units of the Home Garrison moved out, cutting off feeder roads from Victory Road and heading hellbent for the Aerodrome.

The retaking of Bummer Four had begun.

Oberlieutenant Karl Fuchs was in the lead VBL scout car of the first unit to reach the perimeter of the *Bundeswehr* Four Aerodrome.

In the vehicle with him was his driver, a gunner, a radioman and a video camera operator whose equipment was attached to the car's turret. Scanning the airfield through high-powered field glasses, Fuchs was not surprised to see a lack of enemy activity. He was certain that the Americans knew the NS was coming now, especially after the massive artillery barrage. Before jump-off his commanders had predicted that the Americans would probably hunker down inside the airfield's many hangars, put up initial stiff resistance, and then fight their way back into the city itself once the shooting began in earnest.

It was however to the NS's advantage that the fighting be confined to the open spaces of the airport, thus preventing collateral damage to their many facilities inside the city itself. Therefore it was up to advance units like Fuchs's to engage the Americans quickly, pinning them down and then gradually overwhelming them with superior numbers.

"Is the camera rolling?" he asked the communications officer.

The man replied in the affirmative.

Fuchs instructed his radioman to call back to command and inform them that they were moving on the Aerodrome's main hangar area. Then with his unit of twenty-two patrol cars and APCs checked and ready, Fuchs gave the order to prepare to move out.

The plan called for a quick dash across the open tarmac to the massive repair barn which sat on the far eastern edge of the airfield. Should Fuchs's men be able to make the cover of this hangar, then the first and most crucial step in reclaiming the Aerodrome would be accomplished.

On his call, and with his VBL in the lead, Fuchs's unit began their mad rush across the two thousand feet of open tarmac. Pistol up, his face pulled back into a mad Grim Reaper grin, Fuchs was gurgling with the nervous excitement which always arose in the opening moments of battle. He knew that the first shots from any enemy were rarely accurate. and this increased his chances of surviving the mini *blitzkrieg*. All the while he promised himself that he would shoot dead the first enemy soldier of the assault, thus insuring himself a commendation from his superiors and possibly a meeting with the *Amerikafuhrer* himself. It was for this reason that Fuchs made sure that some part of him was always within range of the video camera's lens.

The VBL reached the halfway point in the charge and still a shot had not been fired.

"They are hiding already!" Fuchs screamed wildly into the wind as his VBLs and APCs fanned out on the open concrete space.

Seven hundred feet to their objective, and still there were no shots.

"They are paralyzed!" Fuchs screamed, making sure his words and actions were being picked up by the turret-mounted video camera.

Five hundred feet to that hangar and still no shooting.

"They have no ammunition to spare!" Fuchs yelled, with just a smidgen less enthusiasm. "Perhaps they will use it on themselves!"

Two hundred feet to go and still nothing. Fuchs found himself at a loss for words so he simply screamed: "*Amerikafuhrer siegreich!*—the *Amerikafuhrer* victorious!" All the while he was waiting for the first bullet to hit him square in the eyes.

But it was not to be.

The hell-bent charge petered out at the entrance to the hangar. It was quickly apparent that it was empty, as was the one next to it and the one beyond that. More NS units entered the Aerodrome's vast space and found all of the buildings unoccupied. It took less than twenty minutes for the lead NS units to determine that although there were fifty idle Chinook helicopters scattered out on the tarmac, and that many of the base's fighter aircraft had been destroyed, the Aerodrome was absolutely deserted.

Within a half hour, the city itself was searched with the same results. The Fourth Reich units could find nothing. No enemy soldiers, no civilians, no NS POWs.

The only clue came when NS troops stormed the *Reich Palast,* the seat of the *Bundeswehr* Four military government.

Set up inside the building's elaborate communications center were six interconnected reel-to-tape recorders. By using a simple looping mechanism, these recorders were blaring false radio messages into four open microphones.

Checking the footage counters on these tape recorders the Fourth Reich Signals Intelligence men made a startling but no longer surprising discovery. Bummer Four had been empty for at least twenty-four hours.

Chapter Forty-four

The line of eleven barges was one hour from New Orleans harbor.

Their crews were shackled Native Americans working under the gun of low-level NS officers. This was just one of many trips they'd made in the past several weeks, voyages so fraught with unsafe working conditions that it wasn't unusual for one or two men to be lost to accidents or a drowning somewhere along the way.

The procedure was to reach a spot about twenty-two miles out of New Orleans and one by one dump the contents of each barge. Two hours' worth of slavish clean-down followed, then the tiring task of erecting each barge's protective canvas canopy. Then came the return trip back through New Orleans harbor, up the Mississippi to wherever the huge dredging boats were working. At this point, the barges would be re-loaded and the whole process would start all over again.

It was midnight when the dumping spot was reached. A bleat of the klaxon from the huge tug pushing the eleven barges signaled that the dumping procedure was to commence. The tug killed its mighty engines and soon the line of barges slowed to a stop.

The first barge was disconnected and its pair of piston-driven blades were activated. These huge slow-moving metal plows shoveled most of the sludge out of the barge's lowered front end, an operation which took about five minutes to accomplish. Following behind the sweeps, six chained Native

Americans used brooms, sticks and bare hands to dislodge the remainder of the putrid muck.

Once the first barge was emptied, it was steered around to the end of the line, using a thick wire and winch system. But when it reached its new positioning point, the NS tug master was startled to find that the barge's crew of six were nowhere to be seen.

By this time the second barge had been emptied, and when it was pulled around in line, he found its crew was gone too. The NS officer in charge of the operation immediately stopped the third barge from off-loading and sent his four armed guards leap-frogging up to it. They radioed back that there was no crew on either barge three or four.

The NS tug commander was absolutely baffled. They were out in the middle of nowhere—the nearest dry land was twenty miles to the north. Where the hell could twenty-four shackled crewmen go? Had they all fallen over the side? Had they jumped?

Had they . . .

Suddenly the tug commander heard gunshots. He reached for his own sidearm, but as he did, he felt a warm, stinging sensation in his rib cage. He looked down and was astonished to see a bright red stain quickly spreading on the front of his shirt.

"Have . . . I been . . . shot?" he gasped.

A barrage of tracer fire slammed into the wheelhouse an instant later, shattering the tug's windshield and demolishing its radio. The NS officer staggered back against the wheelhouse wall and tried to catch his breath. But it was impossible. Looking out on the barges, he saw that streams of tracers were now lighting up the dark night. In their illumination he could see his broad, flat-bottomed boats were swarming with armed men, some in black uniforms, others in skindiving suits. Among these men, he saw the missing Native American crew members. All were unchained.

As a kind of red mist began to cloud his eyes, one last

question came to his mind: *Why would anyone want to take over a bunch of barges?*

Roy From Troy loved boats.

He'd always loved them. They were predictable, yet at the mercy of the elements. He'd spent much time in all kinds of boats as a young man. That was why, despite his trade of buying and selling aircraft, he never really understood pilots. If he'd had *his* choice, he would have been sailing on the ocean, not flying forty thousand feet above it.

But at that moment, he'd wished he'd never mentioned to Hunter his love for all things nautical, during their time together doing the big Chinook deal. And he agreed that these were strange times.

So strange that he was now the captain of a huge tugboat pushing eleven captured barges.

The takeover of the scows had gone off like clockwork. No casualties on their side, no survivors on the other. Plus, he was certain that the NS men didn't have time to get off an SOS. That, too, was crucial to the overall plan.

Now, as Roy consulted with his navigator, a Football City Ranger who'd run a fishing boat in more peaceful times, he was certain he was on the right course. In front of him, no less than fifty United American specialists were furiously working over the barges, cleaning them, oiling them, laying down protective matting, installing portable electrical generators and setting up separate radio linkups. The newly liberated Native Americans were working to erect the crucial canvas tops which capped the barges whenever they weren't full.

"The weather looks good for the next twelve hours, General," the navigator told him. "After that, it could get a little windy."

Roy could only shrug once and shake his head. "If we don't have this show on the road within twelve hours, it won't make any difference how windy it gets."

265

At that moment, the portable radio inside the wheelhouse crackled to life.

"We've got contact," was the staticky message from the radar team located on the first barge. "Twenty-eight miles from our position. Correct number of blips. Correct heading."

Roy nervously bit his lip. A belt of scotch would go good right now.

"If those blips aren't who we are expecting, this could be a very brief party," he said to the navigator.

"It will certainly be a wet one," the navigator replied.

Twenty minutes later, a small motorboat pulled up alongside the tug.

Under the watchful eyes of the fifty heavily armed UA troops, two men climbed out of the boat and up to the deck of the tug. Roy met them with a curt nod and nothing else. He was embarrassed at times that his business dealings years before had put him in the same league as these men. Now he couldn't bear to shake hands with them.

"Glad you made it," he said, keeping his tone all business. "We're running very tight on time here."

The two BBI men in long Bedoiun gowns bowed deeply, their heavily greased beards nearly touching the deck of the huge tug.

"Our aim is to please you," they said in unison.

Chapter Forty-five

New Orleans

It was a clean-shaven, walking, talking, seeing, hearing Captain Pegg who found himself standing atop the stone wall which at one time formed part of the defenceworks of the old Civil War fort, a camera he had no idea how to operate dangling around his neck.

By no longer feigning handicap status, he had in fact created a new disguise from himself: that of a somewhat respectable-looking, elderly gentleman who happened to be a photographer who happened to specialize in big events, like pre-war football games, political rallies, Hollywood extravaganzas. He couldn't really say that he liked his "new look"—he'd been "grizzled" for so long, imagining life being any other way was almost impossible. Plus he knew next to nothing about taking pictures.

But the change had to be done at this critical juncture. Plus he definitely had more mobility.

Now with two impressive-looking suitcases of recently stolen photo equipment at his side, he looked out over the long wall and estimated that there were at least 5000 NS troopers strung out along the mile-long battlement. It was slightly unnerving to be the only civilian in sight—he was, in fact, one of the last civilians left in New Orleans. Two nights before, the NS, suddenly begun evacuating the city, trucking tens of thousands of its citizens to relocation camps in Florida and Alabama. The reason given was that a major state

267

event was been planned for the city, one that was so high up on the Nazi gush scale, that the *Amerikafuhrer* didn't want any of the lowly American citizenry mucking it up.

It was only because Pegg was able to convince the local NS commander that his photographic skills were needed to record such an event that he was allowed to stay, along with all the city's doctors, cooks and, of course, hookers.

It had been quite evident for some time that the event being planned was going to be enormous even by Fourth Reich standards. The entire city was now lit up day and night, and long strings of white lights had been plugged in absolutely everywhere. Pegg had detected a sudden influx of Fourth Reich men and materiel to New Orleans several days before. These units were from bases as far east as the Florida Panhandle and as far west as Central Texas. That they were mostly ceremonial in nature—marching bands, honor guards, and the like—provided another clue that a major Nazi lovefest was in the offing. But it also told an old veteran like Pegg something else: Although the city was now crawling with NS men, very few were actually from combat units. This could mean that the real soldiers were urgently needed elsewhere.

He'd been in secret radio contact with other UA groups continuously over the past few days, feeding them information about what was going on inside the city. And he knew this intelligence was going right to the top of United American command structure.

In fact he was certain that at the moment, he was probably the most important intelligence source the UA had on the ground. It was a big responsibility—and he loved it.

The sun was climbing higher in the sky now and the thousands of troops lining the walls more or less at attention were becoming uncomfortable in their heavy wool uniforms. Pegg deliberately took a long time pretending to set up his equipment—all the better for him to eavesdrop on the soldiers and officers nearby. The gist of their conversations was that while they weren't exactly sure what was about to happen, they were sure that it was about to happen soon.

This meant Pegg had to start acting like a real photographer of grand events. But first, he had to figure out how to operate his cache of stolen cameras.

The sun was half wayup the sky when they saw it.

It was like a mini-sunrise, popping up from the far southeastern horizon, a gleaming speck of gold and light.

Bands who'd been sweating out the early-morning heat were finally cued to begin playing. Dozens of ceremonial flags were unfurled and ran up dozens of newly-installed flag poles. Cannons positioned on both sides of the hazy, steamy harbor began firing the opening rounds of what would eventually be no less than a 1001-gun salute. NS officers walked behind their lined-up troops urging them along in a series of rehearsed cheers just like a cheerleader would incite a football crowd.

This pre-programmed cheering grew in volume and intensity as the speck on the horizon grew in size. It was soon apparent to Pegg that it was indeed a ship out there, shimmering in the mid-morning sun. But it was not like any ship he had ever seen. It was enormous, painted pearl white with multiple trims of gold. Its masts were festooned with thousands of small twinkling gold lights—it was these that gave the vessel its intense sparkling quality even in the brightest sun of the day. Flying from the rear of the ship was a huge flag, one that had equal elements of Fourth Reich emblems and obscure Norse runes. Attached to the bow was an enormous Dragon's Head similar in design to those that once graced the Viking raiding ships of old.

Pegg knew it was the Great Ship, the vessel which had once served as the floating command post for the Norse invaders. Now it had been turned into something from a *myx* dream, gold, audacious, somehow not real-looking.

"So that is the witch's ship," he murmured under his breath as the vessel drew closer to the entrance of the harbor.

So many things fell into place now, that Pegg almost let out a whoop. He knew that this was why the Nazis had been dredging for miles up and down the Mississippi, providing a trench that would allow this ship's enormous draught to pass through all the way up to *Fuhrerstadt*.

But he also knew that this massive dredging enterprise would also wind up adding to the Fourth Reich's undoing.

It was almost noontime before the huge ship had disappeared up the muddy river.

Finally the bands stopped playing and the flags stopped waving. The 1001 gun salute fired its last blast. The thousands of NS troopers were now off the wall and clustering in groups for the march back to the city.

And Pegg had yet to take a real picture.

It didn't really matter. He'd relocated to a tall hill about a mile away from the old fort, and dearly hoped that he would be safe here. Now using the long-range zoom lens on one of the cameras, he was scanning the horizon. Looking for . . .

Suddenly he heard it. That high unmistakable scream in the still air. It was not an airplane, or a helicopter or even a missile.

It was in fact, a 2200-pound shell, fired from one of the largest naval guns ever built.

Just hearing that whistle was enough for Pegg. He was halfway down the other side of the hill when the projectile hit more than a mile away from him. Still he was knocked to the ground.

Rolling down the rest of the hill and recovering quickly he couldn't resist peeking through some trees and back to the harbor fort. Where one minute before several hundred NS band troops were lined up to walk back to the city, now was

270

nothing more than an enormous, smoking crater, at least an eighth of a mile across.

Pegg let out an authentic whoop this time, and then quickly began moving as fast as he could away from the harbor area.

He knew the *real* fight for the American continent had just begun.

The destruction of all the Fourth Reich military installations in both New Orleans and along its harbor took less than ten minutes.

No more than 200 NS soldiers who'd taken part in the Great Ship ceremony survived the monstrous barrage of 16-inch shells, and many of them were in a state of shock. The harbor was absolutely devastated, the city itself engulfed in flames. But through the fire and smoke resulting from the massive surprise attack, those could still see beheld a sight that dwarfed the passing of the Great Ship from the Gulf to the Mississippi.

For entering the harbor and bound for the exact same course the Great Ship was following up the river was the enormous battleship USS *New Jersey.*

Roy From Troy gazed out on the square miles of burning rubble that was once New Orleans and shook his head in amazement.

He'd seen many things in post-World War III America, but never anything close to the frightening bombardment that the Big Easy had just suffered at the hands of the *New Jersey.*

"What a waste." he sighed, gripping the handrail at the bow of the battleship just a little tighter. "All those restaurants . . ."

He'd wound up on board the battleship a week before, after Hunter arranged for him to catch a UA flight down from Montreal to a small uncharted island not too far east of Puerto Rico. The *New Jersey* was anchored offshore, its manmade fog banks shielding its identity from unlikely eyes. Also close by was the aircraft carrier, the USS *Enterprise*—or what was left of it. It had been stripped of much of its electronic and weapons gear, with the remainder intentionally disabled just in case the bird farm fell back into the wrong hands.

The *Jersey* set sail the following day, and Roy spent the next few days studying all aspects of his part in the great barge takeover. Now, with that little adventure behind him, he was back on board the *Jersey,* strictly as a "weapons appraiser."

Alongside him on the rail were several Football City Rangers. Like him, they were watching the pall of smoke and flames from the devastated city of New Orleans fade in the distance as the *New Jersey* made its way further up the Mississippi.

"I wonder if someone will ever rebuild it," one asked.

"It would be nice to get the air delivery rights if they do," Roy replied.

All of them were both carrying M-16s and wearing flak jackets and helmets. But at the moment the threat of any hostile gunfire coming from either bank was low. Anyone foolish enough to fire at the ship would receive a return shot a hundred times more deadly. The battleship was literally a floating arsenal. Its three enormous turrets were slowly sweeping from side to side, their 16-inch gun barrels pointing menacingly in all directions. Many of its dozens of smaller 5-inch guns were doing the same thing. Its six cruise missile batteries were primed and ready, and two Lynx helicopters flew its aerial escort, their underwing carrying a frightening array of air-deliverable weapons.

But actually, this was just the beginning of the *New Jersey*'s combined offensive weaponry.

Being towed behind the battlewagon were the eleven barges commandeered by Roy and the UA troopers earlier. It was these unglamorous vessels which had held the key in many ways to the United Americans' bold plan. For it was these barges that had tipped the UA that a major dredging operation was under way up the Mississippi. That dredging turned out to be in preparation for the grand entrance of the Great Ship, bearing Elizabeth Sandlake for her unlikely wedding to the *Amerikafuhrer.* By studying the sludge samples retrieved by Frost, the UA was able to determine that the trench being dug to allow the Great Ship to pass was also deep enough to handle the draught of the *New Jersey.* The strike plan virtually wrote itself from there.

But the barges proved themselves twice valuable. Not only did they tip the Fourth Reich's hand on the river dredging, they also made the ideal platforms for the other half of the UA's offensive punch. For crammed into each of the first seven flatboats now were twenty Chieftain tanks, their turrets poking out over the side of barges, their guns armed and ready. On barges Eight and Nine were some NightScope-equipped M-1 Abrams tanks. Barges Ten and Eleven were each carrying four fearsome Multiple Rocket Launch Systems—or MRLS—apiece. Each barge was also big enough to carry the weapons crews and plenty of spare ammunition.

All in all it made for one very impressive, and deadly floating display.

"Tell me something," one of the Rangers said to Roy. "I know that our ultimate strategy is to chase the Great Ship up the river and break up a big ceremony the Nazis are planning. But, whose idea was it to watch the barges in the first place? I mean, it was so, what's the word? Is it 'innocuous?' "

Roy actually smiled, a rare occurrence for him these days.

"It was the same guy who scouted this entire river for us a half dozen times. The same guy who came up with the Bummer Four deception. The same guy who saved some very important people who were about a half second away from being target practice for the Nazis . . ."

273

"Yeah, it figures," the Ranger said, still gazing admiringly on the small but awesomely power-packed fleet being towed behind the battleship. "Only the Wingman could pull off something like this."

"That's true," Roy replied. "But we all still have a long way to go."

Chapter Forty-six

Fuhrerstadt

The three Reich Marshalls were sharing a bottle of sherry when the communications officer walked into the triangular office.

The young officer was shaking in his boots — literally. He'd read the communique sealed inside the envelope he was carrying and knew that it contained devastating news.

And it was his sad duty to deliver it to the Reich Marshalls.

"This is urgent," the officer announced simply, his body too numb to salute.

Erste, Zweite and Dritte looked up from the war table and stared at the man.

"Well, read it," Zweite ordered him, pouring himself another glass of pink sherry.

The communications officer gulped loudly and opened the envelope. His mouth was so dry, he knew he would have a hard time talking.

"It comes from the Eighth Auxiliary Communications unit stationed fifteen miles outside New Orleans," he began with a croak. " 'Be advised, heavy attack on New Orleans city and harbor fifteen minutes after this noontime. Heavy damage. Heavy casualties. Please advise.' "

All three Reich Marshalls smiled upon hearing the report.

"This is the worst screw-up I've ever encountered," Zweite said with a tipsy laugh. "These people obviously heard the thousand and one gun salute for the Great Ship and interpreted it as an attack on the city."

Erste and Dritte joined in the laughter. It *did* seem to be a typically military mix-up.

But the young communications officer wasn't through.

"Excuse me, sir, but there's more . . ." he said, his voice getting weaker by the syllable. "The same unit sent a second message a half minute after the first."

"So read *it!*" Zweite ordered him.

" 'Be advised. New Orleans and harbor area has been attacked from the sea, Enemy vessels are now making their way up the Mississippi. They continue to attack targets of opportunity. Estimate enemy vessels are approximately thirty minutes behind the Great Ship.' "

Only now did the Reich Marshalls begin to take notice.

"This has got to be a ruse. A practical joke . . ." Dritte said.

"A bad one," Erste declared. "And a dangerous one."

"This is one more transmission," the communications officer told them, his voice regaining some of its pitch. "It was sent exactly a minute later: 'Be advised. We are under attack. Enemy vessels are shelling us with very large guns. Helicopters also. Return fire is non-effective. Please advise.' "

Zweite stepped forward and ripped the communique out from the officer's hands.

"Whoever is responsible for this will die!" the Marshal declared. "It is simply impossible for this to be happening. The Great Ship has just passed through New Orleans no less than two hours ago."

"We tried to confirm the report," the communications officer said. "But every station between New Orleans and Ba-

276

ton Rouge is off the air. Ten stations in total."

"Have you tried raising the station that sent these messages?" Zweite asked, waving the yellow fax paper in the man's face.

The communications officer nodded slowly. "There was no reply, *Herr* Marshal," he said slowly. "They too have gone off the air."

Zweite turned to look at his counterparts. Both were nearly trembling next to the war table; Dritte's hands were shaking so much, he was spilling his sherry.

"It can't be happening," Zweite yelled back at them. "It's impossible. The Americans are obviously sabotaging our communication lines."

The communications officer picked this inopportune moment to interrupt. "Sir, if I could just suggest that . . ."

Zweite spun around and nearly punched him.

"You are dismissed!" he screeched at him. "And not a word about this to anybody."

The young officer quickly left the room, instinctively knowing that he had heard too much.

"This could be serious," Dritte began whining as soon as the man had left. "We *have* to inform the *Amerikafuhrer* and the rest of Command . . ."

Zweite's face turned beet red. "Are you insane?" he spit at Dritte. "If this is true, the last thing we want to do is let him in on it. He'll be peeing his dress in a second."

Erste was tense and yanking on his chin. "He *will* panic," he said. "He *will* want to call off the wedding."

"He has to be informed!" Dritte insisted. "He is *our* leader."

"We can take care of this our way!" Zweite screamed back. "We can destroy these boats—*if* they exist. How big can they be?"

"We don't have the troops *or* the weapons to do any such thing," Dritte shouted back. "The only units down there are the ceremonial battalions. If there are any left. Most of our best units are still up at *Bundeswehr* Four, looking for the Americans. We could never get them to the area in time."

Erste was now literally pulling the hair out of his chin. "We might be able to stop them from the air."

"How?" Dritte cried. "A major portion of our fixed-wing air force was lost at *Bundeswehr* Four. We have but two squadrons here at *Fuhrerstadt* and some helicopters, but it will not be enough if this force is as large as those people reported."

A dead silence fell over the triangle room for what seemed like an eternity.

"Can't you see what has happened?" Dritte finally whined. "They've tricked us. They've forced us to move our best troops north and now they attack us from the south. They've destroyed most of our area air force and it will take time for any reinforcements to arrive. We've got nothing but a bunch of horn blowers and drummer boys between us and them!"

"You're panicking!" Zweite yelled at him. "They're still seven hundred miles down the river."

Erste downed another quick glass of sherry. "But what if they catch up with the Great Ship and . . ."

Now it was Zweite's turn to panic. He began to say something, but caught himself at the last moment. Dritte stepped forward and grabbed the communiques out of his hands.

"I am taking these to our Leader," he declared. "It is his decision on what should be done. We have to consider that . . ."

Dritte never finished his sentence. Zweite had his derringer out and had fired a shot to the man's temple at such close range, Dritte was dead before he hit the floor.

Zweite then turned to Erste. "Do you agree with my decision?" he asked his remaining other partner. "And that we can handle this our own way?"

Erste nodded, with the tremors spreading throughout his body.

"First thing we do is liquidate the communications officer," he replied.

Chapter Forty-seven

Outside Baton Rouge

It was nightfall by the time the 800 men of the 3rd Battalion of the NS *Strom Wacht*—River Guard—were allowed back to their barracks.

It had been a long, hot day for the crack unit. They'd been forced to stand along a two-mile stretch of the Mississippi's west bank since noon, waiting far the Great Ship to appear. But several tricky turns just west of New Orleans harbor had slowed the huge ship's journey considerably. So instead of passing through Baton Rouge shortly after 1200 hours, the vessel didn't appear until well past 4 PM.

The eventual four-hour delay was not an excuse to let down any of the pageantry planned for the grand occasion, and this was why the troops had spent the hot afternoon standing in the sun at parade rest, their heavy wool, dark-blue ceremonial dress uniforms seemingly gaining more weight by the hour. On the other bank of the Mississippi, were several thousand additional NS troops. band units and ceremonial flag squads mostly. They too had suffered the long afternoon standing with their instruments ready in the hot sun. But unlike other huge Nazi occasions, there were no American citizens about. Instead of being pressed into service by the thousands to wave flags and cheer at whatever Fourth Reich dignitary was passing at the moment. The citizens of Baton Rouge had been trucked out of the city the day before, evacuated to points unknown.

When the ship finally did sail up the river and past the city, the reception it received while not spontaneous, was nevertheless very tumultuous. The crowds of NS ceremonial soldiers cheered on cue and the dozens of gun salutes went off like clockwork. As the only real combat troops involved, the members of the *Strom Wacht* snapped to crisp attention and stayed that way. The military bands played, military choruses sang, and dozens of lowly transportation troops dropped rose petals on the ship as it passed below the specially constructed draw bridge just north of the city. All the while, a trio of Fourth Reich Blackhawk gunships circled overhead continuously, showering those below with tons of confetti on each piece of which was printed a microscopic recreation of the Fourth Reich's swastika logo.

It was a long, tortuous affair. And while the troops of the 3rd *Strom Wacht* liked a good *Zeremonie* as much as anyone, they were just as glad to see the damn ship pass safely under the new bridge and continue on its slow northwesterly direction up the river, trailed by a wake of muddy wash, drowning rose petals and soaked confetti.

As a reward for their long day's work, the commandant of the River Guard Battalion officially ordered ten kegs of Austrian lager delivered to the 3rd's barracks. At the same time, the top officer unofficially ordered that 100 young girls left behind in the evacuation of the city be shuttled to the 3rd's camp by midnight, this to provide his men with additional carnal pleasure.

With the ceremony finally done and the Great Ship safely continuing up river, a sense of relief and accomplishment settled over the Baton Rouge headquarters of the Fourth Reich. So much so that it went widely unnoticed by the city's NS commanders that the official radio message sent up to *Fuhrerstadt* reporting on the ship's safe passage went totally unacknowledged.

* * *

The beer arrived at the camp of the 3rd *Strom Wacht* shortly after sundown.

The troops had gathered in their camp's main recreation hall where the lager flew and plans were made to stage an elaborate auction as a way of parceling out the soon-to-be-arriving young girls. Only those *Strom Wacht* posted for guard duty on the new bridge span nearby and at the front gate of the camp would miss out on the night of drinking and wanton debauchery.

It was one of the camp's main gate guards who saw it first.

Initially, it was just a slight movement, about 100 feet into the thick willow-tree forest which collared the 3rd's camp on all four sides. The sullen guard, his mouth dry from want of lager, thought at first that he was seeing things. It looked like a long, dark, slender tube moving slowly past the tree branches off to his right. He heard no noise—not at first anyway. Just the slightest reflection of the full moon's light off this strange. slow-moving cylindrical object.

There were many swamps in the area, and the guard had seen firsthand what swamp gas could do. Lights sometimes bounced crazily off the ever-present methane mixture, while at other times it would accumulate so tightly in a small area as to suggest something solid in nature.

But the guard knew this was not swamp gas. This thing was dark and moving slowly but steadily toward him. More out of curiosity than a sense of duty. the soldier left his post, went out the side gate and walked to the top of a grassy knoll which looked down into the woods. Raising his NightScope binoculars to his eyes and punching them up to full power, he was absolutely astonished to find himself looking down the turret barrel of a heavily-camouflaged Chieftain main battle tank.

The curious guard was dead an instant later, his body literally blown apart by the opening volley of the impending night battle. The shell which took him smashed into the main guardhouse at the entrance to the *Strom Wacht* camp, vaporizing it along with three other guards. A second shot, fired by another Chieftain lurking nearby, slammed into the camp's communication hut, instantly demolishing it and the gaggle of long range antennas and satellite dishes which had decorated its roof. A third shell fired an instant later landed squarely on the camp's tiny fuel depot, causing an explosion so violent it broke nearly every window for two miles around.

The succession of three quick accurate shots startled the drunken troops inside the rec hall, some of whom yelled at first that the noise was simply from leftover celebratory fireworks. Sober heads knew better, and within seconds. the camp's klaxon was blaring everyone to battle quarters. The first soldiers to run outside the hall were astonished to see no fewer than five enormous Chieftains in the process of busting down the camp's surrounding wire. Machinegun fire was washing all over the campground. The power blinked once then went out. Caught in the powerful beams of searchlights attached to the Chieftains' turrets, the drunken, unarmed Nazi soldiers began falling by the dozens to the brutally accurate cannon fire.

Within a minute's time. more than half the battalion's 800 men were dead.

The sounds of the sudden explosions alerted the 25-man unit charged with guarding the new bridge about two kilometers away.

Repeated calls over to the 3rd's encampment found no reply, and the ever-increasing glow from the general direction of the camp gave rise to fears that some terrible accident had taken place, possibly involving the battalion's weapons magazine.

A 12-man squad was immediately dispatched to the scene, while calls went across the river to the Fourth Reich's General Command HQ located in the middle of Baton Rouge itself.

But when the dozen men arrived ten minutes later at the camp, they were confronted with a very perplexing, bizarre scene. The 3rd Battalion's camp was simply no more. Every building was either destroyed or still burning. Not a man was left standing. Fires were raging out of control in every quarter and indeed the camp's weapons storage bunker was in the midst of self-immolation.

But these men also saw evidence of tank tracks and destruction that could only have come from heavy weapons. Yet there were no enemy tanks about. But even more mysterious, they found that the trees ringing the outside of the perimeter had been splashed with gallons of green luminescent paint forming a huge, glow-in-the-dark circle around the camp.

Radioing this perplexing news back to their commanders, the entire military district around Baton Rouge went on a high state of alert. The ceremonial troops in the city for the passing of the Great Ship were now issued weapons and assigned to positions around the new bridge. Helicopters with powerful searchlights were sent aloft to patrol overhead. Searchs of houses left empty by the mass evacuation were conducted.

Yet nothing was found.

Confused and in need of advice, the Fourth Reich Baton Rouge commander made an urgent call to *Fuhrerstadt* to report the situation. But while the message was received by the communications unit in the *Reichstag* itself, there was no immediate reply.

Perplexed, the commander then radioed the headquarters of the huge New Orleans NS garrison, only to find that there was no communications link to that city at all.

It was the members of the 465th *Musik Korps* who saw it first.

Stationed on the approaches to the large, brand new drawbridge built specially for the Great Ship's passage, they saw the red lights first, moving slowly toward them from downriver. Gradually the pinpricks of light grew in size and brightness and it was soon obvious they were attached to some kind of vessel.

Normally the 3rd Battalion of *Strom Wacht* would have been charged with defense of the bridge, but with them completely destroyed, the task fell to these unprepared ceremonial troops.

Predictably, their commanders immediately panicked. Radio calls went back and forth to Baton Rouge headquarters, and more semi-combat troops were dispatched. But by this time, the vessel was in full view of the musician-soldiers, many of which couldn't believe their eyes. Bathed in intense searchlights from the bridge and the surrounding banks, the NS troops were astonished to see the enormous menacing outline of the battleship *New Jersey*.

Armed with no more than AK-41 rifles and mortars, the woefully unprepared troops nevertheless opened fire on the looming battlewagon.

But it was hopeless from the start. The ship was moving at 30 knots: was firing all of its five-inch guns at once, ripping up the *Musik Korps* positions with deadly efficiency. Tank shells being lobbed by Chieftains installed on Barges #1 and #2 came down like rain on the hapless NS troops. The city's solitary Blackhawk made the mistake of coming in low over the *New Jersey*, its pilots attempting to shoot out the battleship's communications antenna array—it was quickly dispatched by two, well-placed SA-2 anti-aircraft missiles, the midair explosion lighting up the river battle even further.

By this time, most of the *Musik Korps* troops had fled in panic, their officers not bothering to stop their flight.

Less than five minutes after it first appeared around the bend in the river, the *New Jersey* with its line of heavily armed barges in tow passed underneath the new bridge and continued on up the Mississippi.

Chapter Forty-eight

Laurelsburg, Mississippi

The men of the 71st NS *Hubschrauber* squadron awoke to find their large air base had been put on alert.

An unusual pre-breakfast unit briefing was called, much to the whispered grumbling of the pilots who had worked long shifts the day before providing airborne escort for the Great Ship as it passed by their sector.

The briefing began with a terse announcement by the base commander. He informed the 60 pilots of the helicopter gunship squadron that an entire *Strom Wacht* battalion had been wiped out the night before down in Baton Rouge, fifty-eight miles to the south. The cause of this catastrophe was under investigation.

The reason the alert was called for the 71st base was twofold. First, the usual chopper patrols would be doubled all day, with special emphasis on looking for any evidence that might be deemed "terrorist actions." The second reason: the 71st's base commander was anticipating an order direct from *Fuhrerstadt* to conduct a surprise retaliatory strike against the civilians around Boca Raton. When that mission came down, he wanted his men to be ready.

The pilots finally got their morning chow late, and then began the daily routine of getting their helicopters—*Luftwaffe* Blackhawks mostly—ready for the day. Although the base had 36 such choppers in all, the 71st utilized only about a quarter of the large airfield as its four long runways were more suited to landing large fixed-wing aircraft.

The first two-ship mission lifted off twenty minutes after mess, and immediately turned toward the Mississippi River, just a mile to the east. Two more copters took off five minutes later, turning for their patrol sector north of the base; a third pair left shortly afterward to patrol the skies west of the base.

No surprise then that the nightmare came out of the south.

It began as a high-whistling whine which quickly turned into a low rumbling. The first thought of many at the base was that one of their copters was returning with mechanical trouble. But as soon as they got a clear sighting on the machine hurtling toward them from the treeline to the south, they knew they could not have been more mistaken.

The Harrier came in over the base at high speed, just barely 50 feet off the ground. Attached to its underbelly was a JP233 bomblet cannister. No sooner had the jump jet appeared when this cannister began dispensing dozens of parachute-laden bomblets all over the Fourth Reich helicopter base.

The first wave came floating down on a line of sixteen Blackhawks that were fueling up when the attack began. The combination of the deadly sub-munitions hitting the exposed fuel trucks created a series of massive explosions which incinerated everything within 200-foot radius. As the stunned mechanics and pilots who survived the sudden Hell scattered for cover, the Harrier banked sharply and came back over the huge airfield. sowing more bomblets along another string of idle choppers, systematically destroying every one of them.

This done, the jump jet came to a screeching halt in mid-air. Lining up its nose with the base's operations tower, it let loose with a direct, accurate barrage of cannon fire. The furious, unwavering fusillade literally decapitated the tower in a matter of seconds, shearing it off in one whole piece and sending it crashing in flames to the ground. The hovering

288

Harrier then suddenly bolted forward and disappeared over the eastern treeline.

At this point, two of the patroling Blackhawks returned to the base to find it in flames. Not quite knowing what they should do, they attempted to land near a line of burning repair hangars.

Neither of them made it.

The Harrier reappeared right over them, and in a stunning maneuver, first went into a hover and then into a lightning quick 180-degree turn, its underwing pod cannons spraying both copters with withering fire. One pilot tried to pull up and out of the deadly barrage, but in doing so, collided with the second copter whose pilot was heading in the opposite direction. The two aircraft exploded in midair, scattering pieces of flaming wreckage and deadly twirling blades all over the base

It was only now that the base's anti-aircraft units were roused to action, many of them ordered at gunpoint by their officers to get out of their hiding places and do something. The base's air defense system consisted of four Gepard *Flakpanzers,* each which boasted twin 35-mm gun turrets on top of a converted Leopard tank chassis. Deadly against conventional aircraft, these AA guns were laughably ineffective against the hummingbird-like jump jet. No sooner were they manned and operating when the Harrier attacked one after another with its now-you-see-it, now-you-don't, hover-move-hover tactic. Even those Nazis cowering in their hiding places were amazed at the skill and speed with which the enemy pilot dispatched the four AA wagons and their crews. All four were destroyed inside a minute.

By now the raging attack was just three minutes old. Yet all of the NS's main structures were in flames, as were all of its helicopters and air defenses. Its control tower was destroyed and most of its fuel supply had gone up in smoke.

Even those surviving Fourth Reich soldiers guessed that the

air base's runways would be next. But it was here that the Harrier pilot did a curious thing.

Banking around once again, the jump jet came in low over the base's longest runway. But instead of dropping another runway cratering device, it unleashed four small white wingborne cannisters in a precise, yet staggered fashion. These cannisters smashed into the runway one after another with enviably precision, but they did not explode. They couldn't—they contained no explosives. They were filled instead with green luminescent paint.

Once the Harrier had finally left and the handful of survivors emerged to inspect the wholesale damage, they discovered that the four paint cannisters had splattered their contents onto the runway in the form of a huge, rough, but recognizable "W."

Chapter Forty-nine

Redwood, Arkansas

The nickname for the place was *Riesespeisenhaus*—roughly, "the giant food house."

The huge, year-old facility built by the NS engineering corps on the west bank of the Mississippi was a combination food storage bank, weapons depot and railroad center. Rows of long, slender warehouses dominated the place—their rough unpainted wooden exteriors being very reminiscent of the death houses at Dachau and Buchenwald. Bordering the warehouses on three sides were hundreds of railroad tracklines, spokes and turnarounds. Located at the far western edge of the installation were hundreds of concrete bunkers which contained either weapons or ammunition. Surrounding the entire complex were dozens of heavily fortified guard towers.

In addition to weapons dispersal, the place was the major food storage facility for the Fourth Reich's southern tier of military districts. Some of the long warehouses were refrigerated and it was here that meat and dairy products were stored. Others featured glass roofs and sides and these served as climate-controlled vegetable greenhouses. Still others held hundreds of large wooden casks which contained roughly half the beer consumed by Fourth Reich troops in occupied America.

The enormous facility operated with typical fascistic efficiency: full trains were leaving every minute of every hour of every day, lugging food, drink and weapons to Nazi troops both in the largest military concentrations in the middle of the conquered continent to the smallest, most remote outposts way out in the Colorado territory. Passing them were the empty trains returning to be loaded and sent out again.

But no matter where the subsistence was going, it all had one thing in common: it was to be consumed only by Fourth Reich troops. By decree, the captive American population was denied any food not grown by other Americans, and less than one percent of Americans were allowed to be farmers.

In this simple, efficient way, the conquerors were able to keep the vanquished continually on the brink of starvation.

Five miles to the north of the *Riesespeisenhaus* was a long winding curve where the eastern most tier of track paralleled a bend in the Mississippi. Any trains using this route naturally had to slow down making the curve, so close it was to the bank of the Big Muddy.

So it was with the 11:47 night express coming down from *Fuhrerstadt*. Approaching this last bend before reaching the straightaway on the outskirts of *Riesespeisenhaus,* the engineer of the 45-car train routinely slowed down to 20 mph.

Feeling the attendant clanking and swaying, the engineer rounded the curve to find a Chieftain battle tank waiting right in the middle of the tracks for him.

The engineer immediately yanked on his brake bar, pulling the empty set of cars to screeching, noisy halt. At first he thought the tank belonged to the local NS unit. But no sooner had the train come to a halt when the engineer and his assistant found themselves surrounded by two dozen heavily armed, black-uniformed soldiers. The only distinguishing mark on each man's uniform was a patch over their left breast pocket that read: "JAWs."

"Get out," one of these men ordered the train crew. *"Schnell!"*

The two men complied and they were quickly bound and

gagged. After they were set down next to the track bed, they watched with muffled amazement as the small army of men began quickly loading crates onto the empty box cars. It was obviously heavy work, but the 24 men accomplished the task in less than five minutes, loading a total of 300 crates onto the locomotive and the first six box cars.

The train crew's worst suspicions were confirmed when they saw one of the men gingerly set a fusing device onto the bottom crate of the ten piled aboard the locomotive. Then with one last check of their handiwork, the majority of the men climbed on board the tank. Three lingered behind long enough to release the locomotive's main brakes and set its throttle to high. Then they too jumped aboard the tank, clinging to its rear end as it rumbled back up the tracks and around the bend.

Horrified but helpless, the train crew watched as the 45 cars rolled by them, picking up more speed and momentum with every second. They tried fiercely to free themselves but it was no use—their plastic binds were just too tight. Knowing there was little else they could do, both men rolled over and tumbled down the bank and into the shallow waters of the Mississippi.

The train full of explosives roared into the main spoke of the *Riesespeisenhaus* less than five minutes later.

Chapter Fifty

Fuhrerstadt

The Reich Marshall code-named Zweite gazed out his office window at the activity near the old Gateway Arch, just two miles to his east.

The huge, riverside statue of Adolph Hitler was nearly complete. Heavy-lift helicopters were shuttling pieces from the Dragon's Mouth stone yard to the erection site with clockwork frequency. Hundreds of workmen—NS engineering corps troops mostly—were moving about to the tall, covered scaffolding surrounding the 150-foot statue at a feverish pace, attaching the necessary pieces as soon as they were lifted in place by the hovering copters.

Two miles to the west were the walls of Dragon's Mouth prison. He knew those statue pieces not completed at the time of the big prisoner breakout were now being worked on by other NS troops inside the prison work yard. In fact an entire division of combat-ready troops now occupied the *Drache Mund*. Instead of carrying rifles and other weapons, they were armed with hammers and chisels, doing the back-breaking labor that was once the life of the skeletonish, yet free POWs.

"How things change," Zweite sighed.

He and Erste had just completed supervising the redecorating of their office. It was no longer triangular—rather the walls had been expanded to make it a perfect circle. Zweite's desk now sat at the north end of this circle, Erste's at the southern end. Nearly all evidence of their late, third partner, Dritte, was gone, including the bloodstains on the marble floor where he'd fallen.

The only items remaining that had once belonged to Dritte were his chair and his antique but working 9-mm Mauser machine pistol. After much discussion, Zweite successfully claimed the chair. Erste got the gun.

He'd been reading the latest communique from their agents in BBI when his attention was distracted to the statue's construction. The message had been simple enough: "UA agent still in residence in East Falkland. Long stay virtually certain. More weapons purchases likely."

What the communique told Zweite was that the UA were the most confident bunch of SOBs on Earth. They had already pulled off the large prison break, had occupied a major Fourth Reich district capital, had destroyed or disabled nine-tenths of the *Luftwaffe* assigned to the combined *Fuhrerstadt Bundeswehr* Four area, had somehow melted into the surrounding territory, had started another even stranger action way to the south, and *they were still buying weapons?* Zweite almost felt a tinge of admiration for the Americans—almost, but not quite. Because of who he was, and what he believed, he would never be able to distinguish the difference between arrogance and confidence.

To him, they were one and the same.

He turned away from the window and walked back to the war table where Erste was sitting, slumped over like a drunk in a bar.

"This waiting is killing me," Erste admitted. "Why did those American bastards have to complicate things so much?"

"You worry too much, my friend," Zweite told him without an ounce of sincerity. "Time is on our side. It's a simple matter of calculations: the Great Ship is faster than this American battleship—much faster. It will arrive here long before the Americans do—*if* they do. And the wedding is scheduled to take place a mere hour later. We will hold the celebration, convince her to give us the *Fire Bats* launch code, and then we kill them both."

Erste's spirits picked up, but only slightly. "It will be a classic *putsch*—one studied and admired for generations of NS men to come . . ."

Zweite gave the man a rare slap on the back. "You see," he laughed. "It's all in the timing. If there was any real threat to us, do you think I'd be foolish enough to have an entire division of combat troops working in the stone yards? *No.* Or have our best helicopter units moving the stones to the erection site? *No.* Timing, Herr Erste. Timing is everything."

A knock on the door brought a fresh-faced communications officer. He was holding a handful of dispatches.

"Excuse the interruption, *Herr* Reich Marshalls," the young man said with surprising confidence. "We are becoming overloaded with messages from command centers to the south. They are all reporting enemy action along the river and are requesting advice or some kind of response. Shall I read these to you?"

Zweite looked at Erste, made a face, then walked over to the young communications officer.

"Are you new to this duty, Lieutenant?"

The young officer nodded confidently.

"And what happened to your former superior?"

The officer's facial features sagged just a bit.

"He was killed, sir. In an accident with a machine gun, sir . . ."

"That is too bad," Zweite said. "He was a good man. I hope you remember him well."

"I will, sir . . ."

With that Zweite took the handful of dispatches from the young officer and calmly dropped them into his wastebasket.

"Is there anything else, Lieutenant?"

The communications officer tensed noticeably. He wasn't so wet behind the *Ahres* that he didn't appreciate the little piece of theater acted out by Zweite. Still he had a job to do.

"We are also receiving inquiries from the other military districts," he forged ahead. "The First Governors of *Bundeswehrs* Five and Six have been especially inquisitive. They have been hearing reports of . . . well, *some* kind of activity down south and they want any information we can provide them."

Zweite turned back to Erste, who was smiling—just a little.

"It warms my heart that our brothers are so concerned about us," Zweite said, his voice dripping with sarcasm.

"How shall I respond, sir?" the communications officer asked. "Or should I respond at all?"

Zweite spun around back toward the man. "Of course we will respond! What questions are they asking?"

The communications officer was totally confused by now—and he was certain that was the point.

"The first major question seems to be about the reports of a major catastrophe down in New Orleans harbor," the officer said.

Zweite clicked his heels together twice and then began pacing.

"Take notes," he commanded the young officer. "Respond to all parties asking that question in the following way:

" 'Shortly after the Great Ship began its voyage up the Mississippi, a tanker carrying natural gas exploded at the mouth of the New Orleans harbor. It was only through the valiant efforts of our frontline troops that this catastrophe did not affect the passage of the Great Ship.' "

The young officer diligently wrote down every word, though his face was a mask of consternation.

"And, sir," he managed to say, "we've had inquiries about an incident in Baton Rouge . . ."

"A terrorist act," Zweite said. "A crazed individual with ill-gotten explosives taped to his chest, gained entry to one of our camps posing as a man in need of food. Taking pity on the man, our guards let him pass through in order to secure a meal. Somehow this terrorist gained access to a large ammu-

297

nition storage bunker near the mess hall and detonated his bomb. Many of our brave soldiers were killed in the incident."

Once again, the communications officer wrote down every word.

"And another incident at a helicopter base in Mississippi?" he asked. "Three squadrons of helicopters rumored to be destroyed . . ."

"One of the pilots went berserk," Zweite said, not missing a beat or a step. "We have discovered since that he was addicted to the *myx*. When he couldn't get any . . . well, he went insane. Shot up the place. Killed many of his comrades before killing himself. A shocking incident which if anything should serve as an example to our troopers that they should not use drugs—or *myx*, anyway."

"A third inquiry, sir," the young officer pressed on. "A report that the railroad yards near our large food and weapons distributions center was somehow destroyed?"

"Improperly stored munitions," Zweite declared. "A railroad car was improperly loaded with tanks of HE. It was a hot day down there. There was a spark . . . and well, you can fill in the rest."

"Are there any more, Lieutenant?" Erste asked the man, actually giving him his cue to leave.

"Just one, *Herr* Marshalls," the man naively went on, once again reading from his notes. "It was from the First Governor of *Bundeswehr* One, I believe. He had heard a rumor that a large United American warship is making its way up the Mississippi, towing almost a dozen barges which are filled with battle tanks and other military equipment, and that it is expected to arrive here, in *Fuhrerstadt*, shortly after the Great Ship does . . ."

Zweite's eyes went wide with astonishment and anger. Erste almost fainted dead away.

"That is the most reprehensible piece of *stier dungen* I have ever heard from a Fourth Reich official!" he exploded. "Please communique to that man that he is hereby under investigation by this office for spreading false rumors which might have an adverse effect on our brave fighting men. I will personally bring this matter to the attention of the *Amerikafuhrer* who, I know, will recommend the harshest penalty possible for such an insidious crime . . ."

The young communications officer was trembling as he wrote down the words.

"Now is there anything else, Lieutenant?" Erste repeated stonily.

The young officer quickly shook his head. "No, *Herr* Reich Marshall," he said, with a salute and then a deep bow. "I assure you, that is all."

Chapter Fifty-one

The river bends at Memphis.

It becomes wide and shallow in spots, and is guarded by a picket line of trees and bulrushes. The bridges become more numerous now too, and not so easy to pass under. It is like this all the way up to the city they once called St. Louis.

A small mountain overlooks the bend from the east, its flattened, hard summit perfect for landing a jump jet. Its top was scorched with dozens of exhaust and soot marks, indications like rings on a tree of the many times the jump jet has rested here.

Despite the damage, somehow, the Earth doesn't seem to mind.

Hunter was sitting on the left wing of the Harrier, looking out on the sunset. He had a clear view of the river for some thirty miles to the south and at least that far to the north. To his left, the gathering darkness was spotted with the glow of a dozen major fires—these were Fourth Reich installations destroyed by the guns of the *New Jersey* and the tanks on the weapons barges. In its narrow yet utterly fierce path of destruction, the mini-armada had laid waste to bridges, dockways, gun emplacements and especially communication facilities. (It had also left some burning but intact, crucial pieces needed by the UA for later in the game.)

The resistance so far was akin to the Iraqi strategy in leaving Kuwait years before. Basically fire one shot and then try to get the hell out of there. It was cowardly, Hunter knew, but then Nazis were all basically cowards at heart.

So the feeble resistance so far was not surprisingly.

Plus, he knew it was to end soon. Three heavily guarded bridges lay ahead, veritable fortresses that spanned the waterway. He'd already done some high-altitude recon on them and returned with proof that the troops manning these bridges were not marching bands or trained flag spinners. They were skilled, frontline units, alerted, though not officially, that something was coming up the river toward them and that it was up to them to stop it. Because beyond them was the prize: *Fuhrerstadt*.

As he looked down on the river now, the *New Jersey* was passing directly in front of him. Its massive outline looked surreal moving through the gathering mists of the dusk. Despite his overloaded processing capacities, he was heartened to find that he could still appreciate the irony of the moment. The massive battlewagon, mostly staffed by a Scandinavian crew improbably sailing up the Big Muddy, its passage courtesy of the same trench gutted out for the Great Ship. Behind it, the string of giant barges, carrying British-made tanks, bought from crooked North African arms dealers and manned mostly by Free Canadian chopper pilots who'd undergone quick transformations to tank commanders and men who were until recently near-dead POWs.

And they've been running from us, he thought.

For the most part his plan within a plan was working. Everyone—from the guys on the barges to Fitz in the Falklands—was still playing his part. And that was exactly what they were doing. Playing a part. Moving like actors in tragic play. Because, from a strictly military point of view, there was no way one big warship and eleven barges stuffed with tanks could beat the Occupying Forces of the Fourth Reich. But that was the beauty of his plan within a plan. The United Americans didn't have to defeat the Fourth Reich. All they had to do was set the stage.

From there, the Fourth Reich was more than capable of beating themselves.

* * *

He remained on the mountaintop until the sun had finally set.

Breathing in the heavy air of Memphis, he vowed to come back in a more peaceful time. Who would be with him? Would he be by himself? Probably. Because the only person he'd want to be with was . . .

Where was she?

He shuddered when he thought of the possibilities. The first bolt of cosmic good luck on this mission happened when those Hueys found one of the *Fire Bats* riding on the surface. It was a totally unplanned piece of the puzzle, a favor from the gods. The super-sub's subsequent destruction and sinking served to loosen the noose around the continent's collective neck by one of four notches.

But ever since he had heard of the incident, Hunter had been plagued with one gruesome thought: *Had Dominique been on board?*

His almost-otherworldly talents of extrasensory perception told him no. But how could he be sure? There was no way.

Another group of neurons suggested that she might even be on the Great Ship itself. But again, that extra-activated part of his brain was flashing in the negative. The Great Ship was only about a hundred miles up the river. If Dominique was aboard he would have *felt* it by now. But again, how could he be sure? He couldn't.

What had Thorgils meant when he screamed to him from the inferno? *He brought her home.* But where was *home?* It had to be Thorgils's definition of "home," and knowing the crazy Norseman, that could mean anywhere from Scandinavia, to a literal Norse Heaven or Asgard or Valhalla, or the center of the Earth. In other words, it could have meant that Dominique was already dead. Again his extra-senses were saying no.

But could they guarantee that feeling?

302

No way.

So he knew he had to do what he always did in this situation. He had to fight. He had to fight and win and fight and win again. He had to press home the battle. He had to utterly defeat what was slowly killing his country, because if he allowed it to succeed, then it would slowly start to kill him too.

So he had to fight to live. To save what so many held dear. And in doing so, he could ask the cosmos for a favor. And leave the rest up to them.

Chapter Fifty-two

East Falkland Island

Fitz was slowly sinking in the cool water, the bubbles and turbulence of life on the surface rushing over his head.

He breathed in deep and the water flowed into his lungs. But he couldn't feel it. It didn't hurt. There was no suffocation. No blotting out of the brain processes. Just the calming influence of water, surrounding him, flowing through him.

He was flying, not through air, but through the Earth's liquid. It was a totally different sensation. He was, at last, invisible. Invisible to everything. He could see out—no one could see in. It was a power he had to exercise.

He sank deeper into the cooling water. He knew swimming would be useless now.

He was much too deep for that.

So dive down, his mind tells him. See what's at the other end of the sea . . .

Fitz woke up with a start.

He was suddenly very cold, not very wet. Outside the wind was howling and the snow was blowing fiercely, the combined result of a typical South Atlantic winter storm.

He sat up on the small bed, looking around the RAF guest residence room, getting his bearings. He'd gone through many things in his life—a stint with the Thunderbirds, a successful swipe at business empire building in the post-World War III days, a return to the role as a soldier in the many battles that followed to keep America free.

But in all that time, he'd never had a dream like that one.

Despite his Irish heritage, he was not a particularly mystical man—not even after the strange events occurred during his days as the fake priest. Those false healings were all staged by Hunter—he was certain of this—as small but obvious parts of the grander scheme.

But in all his experiences, from fighter pilot to priest, he'd never had a vision that carried so much psychic information. One that was so open and clear to interpretation—at least to him.

He fought back a shiver and listened to the wind howl for a long time.

Then he knew what the dream was telling him to do.

He knew that with his country in turmoil again—and with his friends fighting to save it at the opposite end of the globe—then this miserable speck of land in the raging South Atlantic was no place for a warrior like him to be.

And that was about to change.

Chapter Fifty-three

Near Old Toledo

Nicht Soldats Major Tomas Glanz stared up at the star-filled sky and wondered why some stars were moving.

He was perched on the tiny porch attached to the large igloo-like building which housed the Oerlikon-Buhrle SAM launch systems. Inside, in the system's launch control room, the threat-warning indicators were buzzing off the consoles. His three crew members, their noses pressed to the trio of radar screens, were excited beyond their profession at the number of large blips coming out of the north from Free Canada.

They'd been manning this SAM site for nearly four months now, and had never seen so much activity as they had in the past five minutes. There were two dozen airplanes flying long elliptical orbits just inside Free Canadian airspace, over the city of Windsor and no more than 20 kilometers north of the SAM's location. What it all meant—and exactly what kinds of airplanes they were—was beyond the rather limited acumen of Glanz.

So like all underachieving NS officers, he'd been on the horn to his superiors since the time the first blip hit the screen.

The trouble was, his superiors were not responding, not even to tell him that it was unbecoming of a Fourth Reich officer to wet his pants just because the FC was up and flying a few extra planes.

This lack of response bothered Glanz. His superiors rarely missed a chance to blast their subordinates, and this seemed like too good an opportunity for them *all* to pass on. It could only mean one thing: They knew what was happening and were concentrating instead on saving their own *Esels*. In such dire instances, Glanz knew that underlings like him were usually hung out to dry.

When the blips on the screen suddenly turned south, Glanz began working the radio phone even harder. He called his unit commander, his brigade commander, even the division commander—all to no response. With the 24 Free Canadian aircraft now but five minutes away from entering Fourth Reich airspace and coming on strong, Glanz decided to call directly down to *Fuhrerstadt*.

He was astonished that someone acknowledged his radiophone call right away. The man on the other end identified himself as the officer in charge of *Fuhrerstadt* central communications unit, a job he added that he'd been working only a few days now.

Glanz excitedly told him of the vast fleet of Free Canadians airplanes that were less than three minutes from flying right over his position. His standing orders were to shoot down any Free Canadian aircraft that appeared to be showing "hostile intent." Glanz wanted to know if 24 massive airplanes grouped together and pouring on the coals toward occupied America's airspace constituted a "hostile threat."

The CCU officer listened politely and then asked if Glanz thought the FC aircraft were cargo planes. By this time, Glanz could see the vanguard of the aerial stampede, and yes, these planes *did* look like massive C-5 Galaxys, the largest cargo plane left in the world.

The CCU officer then read to Glanz, word-for-word, the *Amerikafuhrer*'s "Noninterference Decree," as it pertained to Free Canadian cargo planes. Glanz would have taken notes but he knew the rule by heart.

But now there was another problem: As these Galaxys passed directly overhead, Glanz saw that they were carrying what looked to be many, many missiles or bombs of some kind under their massive wings. He reported this, as it was happening, to the CCU man in *Fuhrerstadt*. Immediately this man's attitude changed. He became as jittery as Glanz.

"There is only one person who can authorize firing on Free Canadian cargo planes," the CCU told him coldly. "And that is the *Amerikafuhrer* himself."

"Can you ask him?" Glanz blithely asked the officer.

"He is asleep," was the CCU man's reply. "And he cannot be awakened. Even for this . . ."

Glanz was shaking now. If he fired a missile at the C-5s, he could be responsible for starting the incident which led to the war with Free Canada. If he didn't fire, and the C-5s were out for a night of "hostile intent," then it would befall him the curse of being the man who'd left the door open.

What should he do? he asked the CCU man.

Call back in five minutes, he was told.

But when Glanz did—exactly 300 seconds later—the CCU man wouldn't take the call.

Chapter Fifty-four

Loki Mountain, Colorado

The *Aerospatiale* Super Puma helicopter circled the top of the snow-capped mountain once before landing 100 feet in front of the iced-over, seemingly-abandoned ski lodge.

No sooner had the large assault chopper set down when its doors opened and a 25-man unit of the Fourth Reich Alpine Guards poured out of its passenger bay, followed by two officers. The heavily armed soldiers, dressed in the warmest of arctic combat gear, quickly took up positions around the chopper, with the majority of their firepower facing toward the dilapidated lodge itself.

The soldiers were on an armed search-and-rescue mission. Two ground patrols had been dispatched to Loki over the past two weeks and both had vanished. The contingent of Alpine Guards had been sent out to look for them.

It would turn out to be a relatively easy, if grisly task.

Not 50 feet away from where the Super Puma had set down were the four VBL scout cars, each one underneath a thick transparent sheet of ice. While the main force consolidated its defensive positions, one of the unit's two officers took a five-man squad to investigate the abandoned vehicles.

It didn't take long after cutting through the thick ice covering the vehicles to find the bodies of their missing comrades. Each scout car contained five corpses. All had been killed by gunfire. All were now frozen in surreally grotesque positions.

Now the five-man squad's task became even more gruesome.

They would have to thaw out each dead soldier to the point that the body was pliable enough to be pulled up and out of each scout car's narrow turret.

With portable heaters retrieved from the Puma, this ghastly procedure began. Meanwhile. the Alpine Guards' officers in charge then turned their attention to the mysterious ski lodge.

A contingent of ten Guards had already surrounded the lodge. Using rifle butts and fire axes, the remaining ten easily busted down the building's main door.

It looked like the lodge had been empty for some time. The wood stove was stone cold, and there was no evidence of food or cooking about. There were bits of cut wood and metal filings in one corner, however, and the floor was covered with about an inch of sawdust.

The search became more intriguing as the troops broke into the lodge's enormous cellar. Here they found elaborate power tools, pneumatic drills, blowtorches, plus discarded and destroyed computer software. In a garage attached to the cellar, they found the remains of a tractor trailer truck, its sides battered in, its tires flattened, so it could fit inside the garage and thus be out of sight from the air.

The officers were baffled by these odd discoveries. It was obvious that something was or had been under construction inside the lodge cellar. But just what that was, seemed to be an unsolvable mystery.

Except for one clue.

There was a distinct odor of paint in the air. One of the officers discovered a large but faint outline had been left on the floor of cellar: the result of an overspray of white and red paint. He ordered his men to locate an outer point on the outline and stand there, in an effort to get an idea of what shape it was that was painted.

When all ten men were in place, the officers were astonished to find the outline was obviously that of a large, delta-winged jet aircraft.

"Someone was building a jet airplane? *Up here?*" one of the officers asked the other.

The second officer couldn't believe it either.

"They were assembling one at least," he replied.

Leaving their 20 men behind to search the cellar more thoroughly, the two officers returned to the grisly scene outside.

Not seeing any of their troopers about, they climbed up onto the last ice-encased VBL and made a frightening discovery. Stuffed inside the small patrol car were the five fresh bodies of the men they'd just left to thaw out their dead comrades. They'd all been quietly stabbed to death.

Instantly, the two officers ran to the huge Puma helicopter, only to discover its pilot and copilot slumped over the control, also dead of stab wounds.

Their panic rising by the second, the officers retreated to the lodge, yelling for their troopers to come up out of the cellar.

But there was no response.

With the last bit of courage they could muster, the two officers descended the steps to the dark basement and were horrified to find all 20 of their troops had been quickly and quietly killed.

The two officers were trembling now—from the bitter cold *and* from shock. They both had feared coming to Loki Mountain—obviously the place was extremely haunted. Now as they rushed back up the stairs, intent on getting to the Puma and making an emergency radio call back to their base in Denver, they were faced with the most bizarre sight of all.

Standing in the middle of the large kitchen area was a stout elderly-appearing man wearing a red costume, a long white beard and smoking a long corncob pipe. He was holding a huge pot of steaming soup in one hand, a ladle and two bowls in the other.

"You gentlemen look cold and in need of a hot meal," this ethereal apparition told them. "Please, let me serve you."

Neither Nazi officer could even raise his gun to shoot at the ghost. They were just too numb with fear and confusion. Their hesitation proved fatal. Two Pacific American militiamen appeared from nowhere and took them down quickly and quietly via their razor-sharp bayonets.

More PA men appeared and carried the bodies outside. Captain "Crunch" was there and he went through the officers' pockets, searching for ID and personal weapons. Meanwhile, the stout, middle-aged militiaman named Nick was struggling to get out of his red-on-red costume.

"I can't do this another time, Captain." Nick told "Crunch" as he removed his false gray beard and white wig. "It's really getting to me."

"You won't have to," "Crunch" replied, grimly. "They'll be up here with four choppers soon enough."

Nick hastily lit a nerve-calming cigarette. exhaling the smoke into the frigid morning air.

"Will we be finished by that time, sir?" he asked "Crunch."

"Possibly," "Crunch" replied. "But whether it will do any good or not, I just don't know."

Chapter Fifty-five

Fuhrerstadt

The burly NS sergeant peeked inside the open door leading to the young girl's quarters before entering.

She was at her window as usual, staring out at the lit-up city below. Her work-in-progress was still on its easel, the snow-capped mountain scene looking bizarrely tranquil with the city raging in flames in the background. He checked his watch. It was nearly two in the morning.

Someone her age should be in bed, he thought.

He walked over to her as quietly as possible, passing three trays of lavish but uneaten meals on the way.

"The watch is changing," the NS trooper told her in a subdued voice. "Is there anything I can get for you before I leave?"

She looked up at him, her eyes as sad and teary as usual. She'd removed her white frilly dress and was clothed only in a T-shirt and jeans—the clothes she'd worn when she was a slave.

"What is going on outside?" she asked him. "There's so many lights. So much activity for the past few days."

The NS sergeant didn't know how to answer her. All the preparations were for the upcoming wedding of the *Amerikafuhrer* and the Witch Elizabeth. It was hardly a state secret, yet the NS man knew he would feel awkward trying to explain it all to her.

"There is a big ceremony coming up," he said simply. "Your maids or your dresser will tell you all about it."

She just shrugged and then stared at her painting for a long few moments.

"I just can't seem to finish it," she said, more to herself than to the NS sergeant. "Yet, I can't go to sleep."

She nonchalantly ran her hands over her tight little body and stretched. As always, the NS man grew fidgety.

"I will leave you now," he said, stumbling over each word. "Try to have a good night."

The soldier beat a hasty retreat, leaving the girl alone once again. She was tired, but the many times she'd lain down to sleep, nothing happened. It was like she'd forgotten how to sleep.

And she was worried that when she *did* fall asleep, that she'd forget how to wake up.

Something had to change. Inside and outside. She got up and walked to her dresser drawer. One of her maids had slipped her a small plastic bag earlier in the day, knowing that she needed to sleep. Now the young girl retrieved the bag, wet her finger and stuck it inside the bag. She came out with a slight amount of the sticky golden substance on her fingernail.

What would happen if she took it?

What difference did it make if she did?

She took one long look back at her painting and then put the *myx* to her lips.

Chapter Fifty-six

The Bridge at Myersburg

Its official name was the "Captain John Henry Long Memorial Bridge."

Named after a Confederate war veteran who also fathered no fewer than 19 children, the 475-foot suspension bridge joined the town of Myersburg, Tennessee on the east bank of the Mississippi with the small city of Sunshine, Missouri on the west.

The underbridge clearance was 97 feet, leaving plenty of room for even the largest ships to pass underneath. Even though the huge celebration planned to mark its passage was cancelled at the last minute, The Great Ship had passed underneath the span around dawn that morning, quietly and with no problems.

It was now close to noontime.

The Long Memorial Bridge was now covered with Fourth Reich troops. Two full battalions—1800 men—of the elite *Strom Wacht* were stationed on the bridge and on its supports alone. Another reenforced battalion had been split into two and entrenched on the banks fanning out about 200 feet from the bottom of the bridge.

Many of these soldiers were armed with Soltam 160-mm heavy mortars, a monster of a weapon which could accurately hurl a large HE shell more than 8500 meters. Others were manning anti-tank weapons, small portable rocket launchers and even long-range grenade throwers. In all, more than 800 heavy weapons were armed and ready. All were aiming south.

The River Guards weren't exactly sure what was coming toward them—only that it was big, packing a lot of firepower, and was literally just around the bend. Whatever it was, the *Strom Wacht* were confident they could stop it with their "superior" firepower, although that was an adjective used exclusively by their officers.

Still, not a man among them was not astonished when the massive battleship appeared around the bend about two miles away, its stacks belching black smoke nonstop from engines going at top speed, its decks bristling with men, its turrets swinging nine enormous gun barrels.

Almost lost in the spectacle were the eleven gun barges following dutifully behind the battlewagon. Their crews too were at battle stations, the tank turrets turned out at 45-degrees, their MLRS tubes lowered to the most extreme firing angle.

It was not shaping up to be a typical, quantity-vs-quality miliary engagement. It was more like "quantity-vs-*quantity*." The NS troops were capable of launching almost 125 tons of ordnance at the battleship once it came into range; the ship and the gun barges could hurl nearly 95 tons back. The NS troops had the advantage of fighting from fixed as opposed to floating positions, and they had command of terrain on both sides of the river.

The Nazi troops on the bridge were mystified then when they saw the battleship seemingly come to a dead stop about a mile and a half away. They had been prepared to stop the ship from running under the bridge, setting up such a gauntlet of weapons that the ship would be a battered hulk before it even reached the bridge. Now, by stopping dead in the water, it seemed as if the ship was committing one of the world's worst nautical errors: losing momentum.

But as the NS troops prepared their weapons to fire on signal from their commanders, they saw the massive warship begin to turn slowly to the right, its turrets turning one way as its hull turned the other.

Thirty long seconds went by.

Then the *New Jersey* fired its guns.

All nine of them went off at once — nine massive, sixteen-inch guns, each hurling a high-explosive shell weighing more than a ton at a fixed target a little over a mile away.

The old John Henry Long Memorial Bridge never had a chance. Neither did the men on top of it.

The massive broadside didn't so much drop the center span of the bridge as it did vaporize it. Mere seconds after the nine, one-ton shells exploded on impact with the center girders, the middle 200 feet of the steel bridge simply vanished in a cloud of flame, metallic dust and a billion bits of flaming shrapnel. The concussion alone killed more *Strom Wacht* on the bridge than the actual explosions. Many more on the banks died as a result of the storm of white-hot debris that pelted them for more than two horrible minutes.

Even before the smoke and flame had cleared, the battleship had pointed its bow north again. Its engines cranked back up to two thirds speed, it passed underneath the demolished bridge a minute later without another shot being fired.

Its relentless journey north had been delayed by a mere five minutes.

The Bridge at Cairo

The large drawbridge located one mile south of Cairo, Missouri had been built primarily for railroad traffic.

It was a relatively new construction, stacked steel girders held in place by massive concrete supports. It was nearly three times as wide as the John Henry Long Bridge, twice as long and a full twenty feet higher.

Thousands of NS troops had been gathering in the area since early that morning. Their commanders had already heard what had happened down at the Myersburg bridge; they were determined not to let it happen at Cairo. So no troops were actually stationed on the bridge itself. Rather they were dug in deep on the east bank of the Mississippi, their lines stretching two full miles down from the span.

These NS units—actually a light division consisting at approximately 4200 troops—were not infantrymen. Rather they were in the artillery business. Specifically they were the 11th Heavy Field Gun Division.

Their main weapon was the S-23 180-mm heavy artillery piece, an enormous cannon capable of firing a 40-pound, rocket-assisted shell more than 30 miles at velocities approaching half the speed of sound.

Common sense seemed to dictate that a shell fired from this gun with its barrel depressed all the way could inflict damage on the heavy-plated battleship which would be passing a mere quarter mile away.

This assumption became mind-boggling when multiplied by the two hundred guns in the 11th Heavy Field Gun Division, and downright astronomical when the element that the guns could fire three times in thirty seconds was factored in.

And once again, the plan was to stop the warship and its barges before they even reached the bridge.

It was growing dark when word reached the 11th Division's commanders that the warship was now a mere 12 miles away and steaming at 15 knots.

Word was passed down the line to prepare the massive 180-mm guns for immediate firing. A blanket of silence descended on the two-mile line of Nazi cannoneers, broken only by the sharp clanks of gun breeches being locked into position. The artillery pieces were arrayed in such a way as to create a massive field of fire that would pin in on the ship. Each gun crew was told to prepare to fire three shells within the advertised half minute time frame, and an additional three only on orders from the individual gun captains.

Privately the top officers in the 11th NS were confident that two shots from each gun would prove plenty in sinking the battleship.

* * *

Like most low-level fighter attacks, the troops near the target never heard the jet coming.

One moment the only noise rustling through the 11th NS positions was the gurgling of the river running on by; in the next, the air was filled with a horrible mechanical scream.

The Harrier flashed by their positions at top speed, the exhaust from its engine actually creating a steamy turbulence on the river's surface. It was flying that low.

It was by them before any of the soldiers could react, sweeping from side to side before it streaked underneath the bridge and up into a ass-end climb.

Coming back around, the Harrier actually slowed its speed down to 300 mph, flying at a louder, slightly higher altitude. The NS troops were ready for it this time, and they took the only action afforded to them: they blocked their ears. The 11th was not outfitted with any kind of anti-aircraft weapons, and by being thrown into action without its usual support units, it was now absolutely defenseless from the air.

And that's exactly what the pilot in the Harrier wanted to know.

Hunter checked his clock and his fuel load and then put the Harrier into a second, straight-up climb.

His dangerous yet essential tactic had worked; he was certain that the entrenched heavy gun unit was not equipped with AA guns. If they had been, one or two of them surely would have taken a shot at him by now.

He pulled out of the climb at 7500 feet and turned north. Timing had been the key so far to his plan within a plan. He hoped it would not fail him now.

A few seconds later, he had his answer.

Off in the darkened horizon, he saw first one, then two sets of red blinking lights.

A moment later, his radio crackled to life.

"This is Maple Leaf Flight . . . do you read me? Over."

Hunter recognized the voice right away. It was General Jones.

"Ten by ten, General," Hunter replied. "You're right on time."

Hunter had closed to within two miles of the red lights by now, close enough to see the outlines of the enormous C-5 Galaxy cargo planes coming toward him.

"Everything is set on this end, General," he called over to Jones who was piloting the lead C-5. "There's a slight east to west gusting down there, but I think it's too low to be concerned with . . ."

"Roger, Hawk," Jones came back. "This thing wouldn't sway in a hurricane."

Hunter swooped down and under the C-5s, lining up about 500 feet below the second Galaxys right wing. With the precision of an air demonstration team, the three planes—the two flying behemoths and the small VTOL attack jet—turned as one, gliding into a 180-degree, slow descent. At the end of the maneuver, they leveled off at 1200 feet, just four miles down from the 11th Field Gun Divisions positions.

Even though it had been his idea, Hunter wasn't 100-percent sure that his arming of the huge C-5s was feasible. But because the airplane was the only one in the FC arsenal that could fly over Fourth Reich territory unopposed, he knew he would have to work with it within the parameters of his overall plan.

The key was the gigantic cargo jet's enormous wing span. Designed for heavy lift—the plane could carry more than 260,000 pounds of anything—the wings were both long, wide and durable. They weren't adaptable for carrying heavy iron-bomb payload. They proved very adaptable, however, to carrying bomb dispenser canisters, similar to the one attached to the bottom of Hunter's jump jet.

But while the Harrier carried that single canister—capable of dropping more than 120 parachuted bomblets—the Galaxys had been adapted to carry 20 dispensers, each. That produced a staggering drop potential of 2400 bomblets, per airplane.

The implications were very frightening.

But Necessity was a mother after all, and desperate times usually spawn some pretty sound ideas. So Hunter had drawn up the plans months ago while sitting on his upstate mountain retreat and passed them on to the FC Air Force Special Operations Unit. A newly sprung Jones joined them soon afterward, and working together, they completed the adaptation just twenty four hours ago.

The problem was, it had never been tested.

Hunter went in first, sowing half of his 120 bomblets on the first half mile of NS cannons, the combined flare from the dozens of separate explosions giving Jones and the pilot of the other C-5 a bright visual target to key in on.

Hunter's parachuted barrage caused quick, extensive damage to the first two dozen heavy enemy guns. No sooner had he dropped them, when he gunned the Harrier for all it was worth in order to get the hell out of Jones' barreling-in C-5. He saw the stream of bomblets spewing out from the first C-5's wings and the only way to accurately describe it was as a blizzard. A blizzard of slowly descending HE bomblets, originally intended for hard duty like cracking runway asphalt, or denting some tanks.

By the time the blizzard hit the ground, Jones had already pulled the big C-5 up and away to the west. What followed in its awesome wake was an almost indescribable storm of fire, smoke, destruction, death. Ordered to stay at their guns no matter what, hundreds of Nazi troops were slaughtered within mere seconds. Not only that, the two thousand sown bomblets created such a combined explosive impact, that a huge trench was instantly formed along the first mile of the 11th NS positions. Within seconds it cratered off and a mighty rush of water came flowing in from the temporarily diverted river.

The second C-5 mimicked Jones's run perfectly—with almost the identically horrible results. The second mile of huge guns and the hapless soldiers who manned them to the end was simply bombed into the earth. There was no reason for Hunter to swoop down and add what was left of his canister onto the target. There wasn't even a reason for him to go down and take a closer look. It was quite clear from even 5000 feet that nothing was left of the 11th Heavy Field Gun Division.

Its engines slipped from idle to the one half speed, the *New Jersey* and its grateful crew steamed past the site of the carnage and continued on under the tall railroad bridge, its eleven gun barges lined up perfectly in tow.

Chapter Fifty-seven

The Bridge at Cape Giraud

It was midnight when the officers in charge of the defense of the Cape Giraud Highway bridge got word about the massive United American carpet bombing down at Cairo.

Though appalled at the carnage, and by the equally devastating defeat at Myersburg, the NS officers made a grim decision that they would not be caught in any hellish maelstrom delivered by either the UA's naval fire or its air power.

Theirs was a combined force—the first to meet the floating American fortress that was, at that minute, just 20 miles down river. It totaled 14,000 men. Half were hard-nosed *Fuhrerstadt* Home Guards, infantrymen who specialized in terrorizing the occupied countryside. The other half consisted of what was known as a *Verbindung Kommando*—a Combined Command. Its troops were equally adept at operating SAM systems to anti-tank weapons to river coastal defense. It was this last talent that set them apart from the rest of the Nazi troops trying to stop the *New Jersey*.

For the first time, the warship would be faced with soldiers who were used to fighting on the water.

The *Kommando's* coastal defense teams used a simple weapon against large floating targets.

They would load up rubber boats with as much high explosive as they could carry and by using wire-guided control for

323

power and steering, would direct these floating bombs into their target.

The added twist for the CD teams this night was their loading up of rubber boats filled not only with HE but also napalm cannisters specially triggered to explode up and out on contact with their target.

The idea was that if the HE boats weren't able to rip a hole in the side of the battleship, then the napalm boats would at least set the ship on fire.

It was 0130 hours when the battlewagon was spotted, steaming at one-third speed up toward the Cape Giraud bridge.

While the bridge itself was brightly lit and obviously bristling with troops of the *Fuhrerstadt* Home Guard, the Coastal *Kommando* units were hidden in the high weeds and bulrushes on the west side of the river. A total of 50 rubber boats were set to launch, half with HE, half with napalm exploders.

As the huge silhouette of the battleship loomed toward them, the *Kommandos* started their small motors and got set to fuze their explosives.

But immediately, it was apparent something was very wrong. The *Kommando* officers using NightScope glasses could clearly see the battleship, barely a mile and a half down the river. But it was alone. There were no barges in tow.

It took a few moments for the implications of this discovery to sink in. If they didn't know where the hell the barges where, then they didn't know were all the tanks were either.

They found out though, less than a minute later.

The first squadron of Chieftain tanks hit the left flank of the *Fuhrerstadt* Home Guard so quickly, many of the NS troopers simply threw up their hands and surrendered.

On the right flank, the second squad of Chieftains attacked the bridge defense command post and battled the hard-core but improperly armed *Fuhrerstadt* Home Guardsmen. It took fifteen minutes of intense fighting to subdue the more fanatical defenders, but the combined weight of the two-pronged tank attack was too much for them. Fighting toward the middle of the bridge, more than a few of the Nazi soldiers shot themselves rather than be taken prisoner or fall in battle. Many more simply took a death drop off the side of the tall bridge.

Once the bridge was taken over by the UA tank crews, the battleship moved to within a mile of the span. Then with a deadly accurate combination of five-inch naval gun and tank fire, the slow, systematic decimation of the Coastal *Kommando* began. Ten shots would come from the tanks on the bridge, ten would come from the battleship. Just about every shell hit its mark—not by luck, guided there by Hunter, who was hovering a half mile directly above the *Kommando* positions, directly fire via his pod-adapted LANTIRN device the acronym standing for "low altitude navigation targeting infrared, night."

It didn't take long to wipe out the *Kommando* unit simply because they were caught up to their waists in dark muddy water, and surrounded by many pounds of HE and many gallons of napalm. Each shell that landed anywhere near them would set off at least two secondary explosions, and in some cases as many as eight or nine.

Many of their charred bodies would wind up floating downstream for several hundred miles.

Chapter Fifty-eight

Fuhrerstadt

"Yaz" rolled over on his dirty, oily bunk and let out a long, tired breath.

This is not the kind of life my parents wanted me to lead, he thought. *This is not the kind of life anyone's parents would want their kid to lead . . .*

In a word, he'd been demoted. He was no longer a nonstop, living, walking, breathing sex object for the eternally demented desires of the unstable Elizabeth Sandlake and her equally screwy companion, Juanita. He was now back where he'd come from—in the tiny broom-closet-size room, located at the bottom ass-end of the Great Ship, cold, dirty, hungry and just waiting for some shit pipe to burst so he could slosh around in smelly waste water for a few hours.

He tried to tell himself that it had been good while it lasted—how else to describe more sex in a matter of weeks than most people experience in a lifetime? But that was just the point—it had been strictly sex. No love. No caring. No sharing. Just raw, uninhibited, no-holds-barred intoxicated lust.

God, how he missed it!

The Great Ship had arrived in *Fuhrerstadt* earlier that morning. He didn't have a porthole through which to view the grand entrance—but then he didn't need one. Just by listening to the ships engines, to the scrambled Scandinavian PA announcements on-board, to the endless renditions of "Wedding in White," as oompah-ed by the Great Ship's pathetic little band—

he could tell what was going on.

Today the Witch was getting married.

The last time he'd seen her was when her royal guards were hauling him out of the waterbed-equipped love chamber for the last time. Like any good bride-to-be, she'd insisted that they have sex while she was wearing her flowing white wedding gown, an oyster-induced performance which Juanita recorded via an ancient video camera.

Once the pre-nuptial *bonk!* was completed, Elizabeth calmly rang for her guards and "Yaz" was unceremoniously dragged away. Down the elevator, through to the bowels of the ship, and thrown back in his little hole where she apparently thought he belonged.

Thus ended his life as a stud.

He tried to sleep, alone for a change, but found it impossible.

The general hubbub of the ship, and the endless playing of band music—at least three were competing for attention somewhere on board—the crackling of fireworks and endless cannon salutes, all conspired against his even closing his eyes.

But it was also a troubling thought which kept him awake: What would happen once the Witch and Little Hitler the Third, Once Removed, were married? Who would kill whom first? Did it make any difference? Either the Nazis would complete the rape of America, or Elizabeth and her wacky ideas of a new American Aristocracy would do the job for them.

Whatever the outcome, he knew that the American people would be the ones to suffer. And there was little he could do about that.

He'd finally closed his eyes and felt himself drifting off, when the noise of heavy footfalls on the slimy metal deck snapped him awake again.

His tiny door was flung open and he found himself staring up into the unsmiling faces of two soldiers. Judging by the gaudy medal-happy black uniforms and the presence of a swastika on every button, he guessed correctly that they belonged to the Fourth Reich Armed Forces.

"You are wanted on deck," one said in a voice so bereft of human emotion, it chilled "Yaz" instantly to the bone.

He felt tired, out of breath, out of energy, out of respect.

"Who wants me on deck," he challenged the soldiers. "And what the hell for?"

The second soldier revealed a small bag he was carrying. He emptied its contents over "Yaz's" head. It was a dress suit: a jacket, pants, shirt, tie and cummerbund.

"What the hell is all this for?" he exclaimed.

"Put it on," the first soldier droned. "You are giving the bride away . . ."

Ten minutes later, "Yaz" was escorted up to the main deck, and out to the area at the rear of the ship where the wedding was due to be held.

It was the first time he'd been out in the fresh air in a while so he couldn't help but take a few deep breaths and look around. The Great Ship was moored along the west side of the river, no more than a half mile from the famous though fading Gateway Arch. The crowds stretched from the dock all the way back into the city itself, but they appeared to be made up entirely of soldiers. There were no civilians to be seen and this surprised him. He knew the Nazis never missed a chance to manufacture a cheering crowd. But everyone he saw, with the exception of himself and the bride's entourage, was wearing a military uniform.

This was his first clue that everything was not right with this picture. Despite the band-playing and the proliferation of streamers and confetti, many of the soldiers on board and in the crowd nearby were obviously on duty. "Yaz" could see them grimly scanning the crowds, the nearby bridges and even the skies.

He knew they just weren't being cautious. He could tell they were expecting trouble. Soon. And this told him that all was not right in the bizarre goose-stepping fantasy world.

"Yaz" straightened out his too-tight cummerbund and walked down the steps to where the wedding party had gathered. Elizabeth was there, looking undeniably beautiful in the long white gown he'd screwed her in just hours before. Juanita, wearing an off-pink gown which showed just about all of her expansive breasts, was standing next to her mistress, blubbering just like a good maid of honor should. The Captain of the Great Ship—a man "Yaz" came to think was as much a captive as he—was nervously tugging at his dress white uniform and fingering what looked to be a Bible with a broad swastika on its cover.

Everyone else crowded onto the deck looked worried, miserable, definitely on edge—and "Yaz" loved it. After all the time and effort and fascist hoopla of dredging the Mississippi—digging up the Mississippi, for God's sake!—it was quite obvious that the enormous Nazi love fest was not turning out as everyone had planned.

An English-speaking Nazi officer yanked "Yaz" over to the center of the wedding party and told him in an urgent whisper that all he had to do was stand there, next to Elizabeth and nod anytime the Captain asked him a question. If he screwed up, or tried to disrupt the ceremony in any way, he'd be shot. It was as simple as that.

"Yaz" gave the man a sullen nod and then took his place next to and slightly behind Elizabeth, who was totally ignoring him.

Now looking off to the south for the first time, "Yaz" was startled to see that a tall, covered object of some kind had been built about 500 feet from the dock. There were even more troops surrounding this thing, which "Yaz" guessed was at least 150-feet tall. It was wrapped in white cloth which was whipping in the breeze and making everyone jump when it crackled a little too loudly. A long series of ropes were attached to the top of the structure and it was obvious that it was about to be unveiled.

Suddenly a PA system sprang to life, and the crowd of 10,000 or so was subjected to a loud blaring of staticky, feed-back-plagued German. At the end of the long rambling announcement—little of which "Yaz" understood—the voice on the PA induced the crowd into a countdown.

"Funf . . . vier . . . drei . . . zwei . . . eins . . . null!"

The ropes surrounding the object were yanked and the white sheeting covering unraveled to reveal the enormous, incredibly tacky statue of Adolf Hitler.

"Yaz" almost laughed out loud—an indiscretion that he was sure would have meant a bullet in his head. But he almost couldn't help it. Far from being an *objet d'art,* the statue looked like something an eight-year-old kid had thrown it together during a slow afternoon. The head was much too small in proportion to the body; one side of the famous mustache was much too long for the other. The eyes were crossed, the nose looked like it was running, and the mouth was lop-sided in such a way it looked like the *Fuhrer* was wearing a clown's frown.

The uniform was carved into the stone like a bad suit, and the bottom of the statue, where the *Fuhrer*'s feet should have been wasn't even completed. Instead, the steel reinforcement rods were wrapped in pinkish cloth, giving the impression that Adolf was wearing a pair of woman's house slippers.

The thing was so ghastly that the crowd barely cheered its unveiling, much to the embarrassment of the gathered Nazi officers.

This is fucking great, "Yaz" thought, his long-tortured mind finally succumbing to some authentic glee. *I just wish Hawk and the guys could have seen this . . .*

Two men in Fourth Reich uniforms appeared at the door leading out onto the bow, and suddenly everyone—including Elizabeth—snapped to attention. These two men—one small and professorial-looking, the other wide, red-faced and thuggish—were wearing the braids of Reich Marshalls. They appeared to be the ones responsible for running the wedding ceremony.

With everyone snapped to on the deck, a third person walked out of the doorway. He was small, young, with girlishly blond hair. He was wearing a suit that was halfway between a dress uniform and a tuxedo. This was the *Amerikafuhrer*, and he was looking for all the world like he would rather be any other place but on the ship at the moment. Behind him, another young man was primping his master's suit, brushing away the lint and dust, straightening out the shoulder pads, more like a mother-in-law-to-be would be doing to a bride. This was Lance, the official "dreser," and the *Amerikafuhrer's* best man.

One of the Reich Marshals read yet another proclamation in German, rushing through it so quickly, even the people who understood the language couldn't understand it. "Yaz" saw this as yet another clue that the Nazis were expecting the sky to fall in on them at any moment.

Finally, there was a flourish of bad horn playing, and the *Amerikafuhrer* was ushered down the short aisle and placed next to Elizabeth. She was smiling, and gushing and so much playing the part of a blushing bride that "Yaz" was newly appreciative of just how deep her insanity ran.

Finally everything seemed set. The Captain indicated that the two ideological lovebirds should hold hands. Then he read a passage from his "Good" book that was as hasty and incomprehensible as the Reich Marshall's earlier speech. This done, the Captain spewed some Scandinavian at "Yaz" and he dutifully nodded back. Juanita burst out into tears again as did Lance, the best man. Several *Luftwaffe* helicopters flew over in a pathetic attempt at a ceremonial aerial flyby and at last, the rings were called for.

But then, just as the *Amerikafuhrer* was placing a large gold band around Elizabeth's trembling ring finger, the crowd was subjected to a painfully-sharp screeching noise. The ceremony stopped dead in its tracks. Everyone was looking around for the source of the screeching, but nothing could be found—at first.

Then "Yaz" noticed that many of the soldiers in the crowd surrounding the Great Ship were instinctively hitting the dirt.

They knew the sound of incoming fire when they heard it.

331

* * *

The first shell hit the top of the Hitler statue square on its runny nose.

The impact of the one-ton HE shell completely blew away the *Fuhrer*'s head, creating an instant cumulus-type cloud of white smoke and dust.

There was a stunned moment of silence as everyone in attendance tried to comprehend what had happened.

Then a second screeching was heard—this one louder and coming in faster. This shell impacted at the base of the huge statue, blowing out the pink-slipper supports and instantly bringing the huge sculpture crashing to the ground. Hundreds of Fourth Reich soldiers were immediately crushed in the rain of tons of stone, and the Great Ship was rocking violently from side to side reacting to the concussion of the two quick massive explosions.

That was all it took. A second later what was left of the crowd of 10,000 went into an immediate hysterical panic.

Not two seconds later, "Yaz" was up and over the side of the Great Ship and swimming like mad for the far shore.

Chapter Fifty-nine

The battle for *Fuhrerstadt* lasted less than three hours.

Not unexpectedly, many of the Fourth Reich troops surrendered as soon as the main assault force of Chieftain tanks rumbled up to the southern edge of the city. The *New Jersey,* having anchored itself ten miles down river to disgorge the gun barges, was now systematically pounding the city's major military installations with its monstrous guns, laying waste to the heart of the Fourth Reich's murderous empire. Dozens of the city's command officers — including Zweite and Erste — took the coward's way out by delivering bullets to their own heads, rather than risk capture by the small but advancing United American Army. Hundreds of foot soldiers followed suit, exposing one more symptom of the rotten system collapsing from within.

Hunter was all over the skies for the final battle, sighting targets for the *New Jersey*'s big guns, positioning the squadrons of Chieftain tanks rumbling through the broken, burning city, and carrying out several attacks whenever any of the UA forces met up against some particularly fanatical resistance.

All the while huge Free Canadian C-5s were landing at the *Fuhrerstadt* airport — many, like Jones's converted gunship — had been roaming the skies for the past handful of hours, hitting targets of opportunity with their multi-canister weapons dispensers. Guided by the bright luminescent *"W"* painted across its main runway, the C-5s had originally refueled at the former NS helicopter base down near Laurelsburg, Mississippi which Hunter had so expertly attacked earlier in the lightning-quick river campaign. Now their cargo bays were filled with troops—many of them United American officers and men formerly held at Dragon's Mouth who had ridden out of *Bundeswehr* Four with everyone else on board the big cargo planes a full day before the Nazis knew what was going on. Now many had regained their strength to the point that they came back to take part in the liberation of the city. It was befitting then that many of these men were charged with escorting the thousands of surrendering Nazi troops back to the hated *Drache Mund* prison, where they would now have the chance to switch the roles of prisoner and jailkeeper.

Hunter had landed quickly at the airport, speaking briefly with Jones while his jump jet was getting refueled. There was one surprise that both were glad did not happen. They had not expected much in the way of Fourth Reich air opposition simply because the majority of the *Luftwaffe* planes had been disabled up at *Bundeswehr* Four. The others—those stationed at *Fuhrerstadt* and smaller bases surrounding the city—had simply vanished. Their pilots wanted no part of the battle once word had spread that the United America—and Hawk Hunter himself—were alive and kicking.

The unpleasant surprise that never came was an air attack by the missing US Navy air wing that had so devastated the United Americans a year ago near the beaches of northern Florida. When Hunter originally attacked the aircraft carrier, the airplanes were not there. In fact, they never returned to the carrier after the Florida air raid—and no one knew where they were. Not even he.

But he and Jones agreed that it was a problem to deal with later.

For the moment, the battle for the capital of Nazi America had to finished.

It was three in the afternoon by the time the UA forces had completely surrounded the *Reichstag*.

The fighting had raged house-to-house for the past hour, determined UA troops battling the last of the ultra-fanatical *Furherstadt* Home Guards. The outcome was never really in question though, and as the sun began to dip in the sky, the last remaining Nazi soldiers holed-up inside the *Reichstag* found themselves looking out on hundreds of UA tanks and thousands of UA soldiers. So many of the Nazi troopers were shooting themselves and each other, it sounded like a gun battle within a gun battle.

Hunter had set the Harrier down in a field two blocks from the *Reichstag*, and now, crouched in a bomb crater with Captain Jim Cook and the men from JAWs, he prepared for the final assault on the last Nazi stronghold.

Coordinating their actions with the local UA commanders, Hunter, Cook and six other troopers quietly went through a small fence just east of the *Reichstags* main gate, and soon gained the side of the huge building itself. They were all but certain that the *Amerikafuhrer* himself was hiding inside. It was essential that he be taken alive, for only he could order all of his troops to surrender and thus end further bloodshed.

Checking the ammo on their identical M-16s, Hunter and Cook went through a ground-floor window of the *Reichstag* and found themselves in the *Amerikafuhrer's* personal kitchen. It was filled not with the finest cuisine, but with cases of old, but apparently well-preserved junk food of every imaginable type.

"The kid must have quite a sweet tooth," Hunter said, surveying the hundreds of boxes of cupcakes, cookies and candy. "His dentist could have been a millionaire."

"What dentist isn't?" Cook replied.

They moved slowly out of the kitchen and into a hallway. The place was absolutely silent—it was as if no one was home. Occasionally an explosion off in the distance would rattle the place, and inevitably it would be followed by a series of single gunshots—more Nazis taking the easy way out.

They made their way to the front hallway of the place, and

after meeting no opposition, simply unlocked the massive steel front doors and opened them. An advance unit of Football City Rangers was waiting outside. Hunter gave them the thumbs-up signal and the troopers began pouring into the place. It was quite a sight to see, and Hunter felt a tinge of pride in his chest. One last proviso in his plan within a plan was that the *Reichstag* be retaken by men from Football City. It seemed very appropriate in a way.

Now that had been done. All that was left was to find the *Amerikafuhrer*.

The young girl named Brigit had painted throughout the battle.

Her ears were oblivious to all the noise outside the *Reichstag*, and she hadn't bothered to look out the window since emerging from the extended *myx* dream hours before.

Now her painting was very close to completion. She had seen it all in the strange, intoxicated dream—the missing pieces had come to her like some great religious revelation.

It was an experience she would never forget.

Dabbing her brush into a last puddle of blue, she made three quick strokes and then stood back from the easel.

"My God," she said. "I think it's finally done."

It *was* done. As before, the painting showed the snowy mountaintop, the masses of angry gray clouds and the modern city near the lake burning in the background. But the last element she had added—the one that had come to her in the *myx*-induced dream—had turned the rather unusual scene into one fraught with mystery, at least for her.

What she had added was the form of a jet fighter. It was delta-shaped, painted mostly in white with red tips on the wings and a blue streak down the center of the fuselage. She had no idea where the image of the futuristic airplane had come from—she'd never seen one like it before. But to her mind, it fit, teetering on the peak of the snowy mountain though it was.

336

"I shall call it 'A Future Discovery,' " she declared. "Do you like it?"

She turned toward the young blond man cowering in the corner.

"It's very good," the *Amerikafuhrer* said, his thin lips trembling. "I think my great, great, grand-uncle was a painter once . . ."

A minute later, the door to the girl's chamber exploded inward, courtesy of Hunter's well-placed boot. He and Cook led a squad of seven Football City Rangers into the huge room.

Everyone had their rifle up and ready, but there really was no cause to start shooting. The young girl had hidden away her painting, and now simply sat passively before her empty easel. The *Amerikafuhrer* was still cringing in the near corner.

"Please don't kill us," the young man pleaded. "We're just kids . . ."

Hunter walked over to the Nazi leader and yanked him to his feet. He looked deep into his eyes, trying to find the reason behind the hate that this punk stood for. What came back surprised him: the *Amerikafuhrer* was right. He *was* just a kid. Barely old enough to drink, never mind control an empire.

But age was no excuse. There were millions of kids younger than he who had more guts, more smarts, more human character than this poor excuse for a human being.

"You better start growing up right now," Hunter growled at him. "Because like it or not, you've just become a man."

Ten minutes later, all fighting in and around the *Reichstag* had stopped.

The last of the defending Fourth Reich troops either surrendered or shot themselves. In the end it really didn't make much difference anyway.

Hunter, Jones, Cook and the rest of the UA and FC commanders had gathered in the *Reichstag's* huge communications room. The other guys from JAWs had erected a temporary but powerful antenna on the roof of the Nazi headquarters, replacing the one that had been blown off in the early fighting. Now the *Amerikafuhrer* was sitting at the microphone, broadcasting out to All Fourth Reich installations on the American continent via the one-channel propaganda station known as *Volksradio*.

His message was clear: all Fourth Reich troops were to lay down their arms and destroy them immediately. Then they were to wait until local American forces—be they militiamen, regular UA units, or even armed citizens—arrived to take control. The attack on the place called *Riesespeisenhaus*—"the giant food house"—insured that much of the southern-tier states would soon be under control of American citizens who would be able to get arms and much-needed food from the warehouses there. In the north, the Free Canadian army was moving in to take temporary control of the major cities. The transfer of power out in the isolated western states would take longer.

As soon as the *Amerikafuhrer* was finished repeating the broadcast a tenth time, he was yanked out of his chair, shackled and led away. Plans called for him to be thrown in with the thousands of other Fourth Reich prisoners at the *Drache Mund* to await trial.

Once the *Amerikafuhrer* was gone, the radio was used to broadcast news of the Fourth Reich's defeat up to Free Canada and other outlying UA units.

Old pros at reclaiming their oft-embattled city, the Football City Rangers immediately established some sense of normalcy and calm after the stunning American victory. Their leader, a man named Louie St. Louie, was reported already on his way out of hiding to retake the reins of the city which he had built up into a highly successful if notorious postwar gambling mecca.

338

"They'll be filling the casinos in two month's time, Hunter said to Jones after hearing that St. Louie was on his way home.

That was when the bad news arrived.

It came in the form of an urgent radio message from Cook's guys. They'd broken into a secret room located in an isolated wing of the *Reichstag*. They'd found two people inside. One of them was demanding to talk to Hunter.

He and Cook ran out of the communications office and reached the area in question within a minute. Cook's main guys—Maas, Snyder, Higgens and Clancy—had sealed off the entire corridor, and were now in their flak jackets and heavy helmets.

"There's a dame in there who's claiming she's got her finger on a pretty big button," Maas told Hunter. "She says she wants to talk to you or she'll blow us all to Kingdom Come."

"And you believe her?" Hunter asked the JAWs commando.

"Just take a look, Hawk," Maas replied.

Hunter walked slowly over to the room and carefully took a look inside.

Stretched out on a long sofa, completely naked, was Elizabeth Sandlake. At her feet was a very unconscious Juanita Juarez, deep into a *myx*-coma.

Elizabeth was fondling a small radiophone which Hunter immediately recognized as a CommStar sender/receiver. Proper use of this high-tech device meant instantaneous communication with just about any spot in the world, via a CommStar satellite.

After taking quick note of radiophone, Hunter lowered his gun and took two steps inside.

"We meet again," he said to her.

She looked up and saw him for the first time.

"Good God," she exclaimed. "You really *are* alive."

She insanely began fondling her own breasts. "And you came to see me," she cooed.

"Where's Dominique?" he demanded of her.

339

The strange, sex-starved smile immediately left Elizabeth's face.

"I am here, waiting for you ... *wanting* you," she cried. "And you ask me about her?"

Hunter took two more steps toward her. She was nuts— dangerously nuts. And one burst from his M-16 would have saved a lot of people a lot of grief.

But he never for a moment considered killing her.

"I figure you are the only one left who would know," he said, his voice reflecting his growing anger.

"If I tell you, will you make love to me?" Elizabeth asked, returning to her coquettish mode.

Hunter just shook his head. She was once one of the most talented archaeologists in the world. Her madness was born when the Nazis of the Twisted Cross kept her inside the dark caves of Central America for many weeks at a time, forcing her to help them find hidden Inca gold. So twisted had her mind become that here she was, not three years later, working *with* another gang of fascist super-thugs.

"You need help," he said, his eyes wandering slightly up and down her admittedly beautiful body. "Just tell me where Dominique is . . ."

Elizabeth shrugged her lovely, naked shoulders and began seductively stroking her inner thighs.

"That fool Thorgils is the only one who knows where your precious girlfriend wound up," she said almost nonchalantly.

"Thorgils is dead," Hunter told her.

She smiled at him, absolutely devilishly. "So you *are* out of luck, Mister Big American Hero," she mocked him. "But it really doesn't make any difference. You'll be dead within a half hour. We all will be."

Hunter felt like an icicle had just been run through him. Both his mind and his gut were telling him that Elizabeth wasn't bluffing.

"You know why they all wanted me, don't you?" she began again, calmly checking her nails. "Because I know the codes."

Hunter was tensed to the max. "What codes?"

"Four words, spoken into this radiophone," she went on, the tone of her voice bouncing from sultry to suicidal and back again. "And the last Atlantic *Fire Bats* launches its missile right at us. That's an eighteen-megaton warhead, Mister Bigshot. Or is it twenty-eight megatons? I'm not sure. Suffice to say it will be enough to kill everyone — and everything — for about fifteen miles around, wouldn't you say?"

"You're crazy," Hunter told her. "But you're not *that* crazy . . ."

"I know," she said, the insane smile never leaving her lips. "And that's exactly why I am doing it."

Before Hunter could move, she had clicked on the radio phone and had screamed four words into its mouthpiece: "Return From The Inferno!"

He lunged at her, struggling to get the radiophone out of her hands, at the same time trying to deflect her naked breasts which she was intentionally thrashing in his face.

He finally managed to pull the radiophone from her grasp, but he knew it was already too late.

She laughed in his face and then stretched back out on the couch.

You're a fool, Mister Wingman," she said running her hands over her naked form. "You should have taken me when you had the chance."

Somewhere over the Gulf of Mexico

Frost was up and out of his bunk at the first blare of the warning buzzer.

Running down the narrow cabin of the P-3 Orion, he reached the communications deck in record time. Just about the entire crew had already gathered there, each one wearing an expression of shock.

"We've got confirmation of a launch," the man behind the

341

master communication panel told him. "Flashed from a CommStar device up near Football City right to the *Fire Bats*. We got the infra-red indication ten seconds later. Here's the confirmation read-out."

The man was pointing to an auxiliary computer screen which was filled with numbers Frost didn't have time to understand. All that was important was the dire message flashing at the bottom of the screen: "Launch Confirmed."

"Where's the damn thing heading?" he asked the man.

"That the weird part, sir," the man answered. "It was called in by someone up at Football City to *hit* Football City."

Frost felt all of the energy suddenly drain out of him. Had they really gone through all this — just to have Football City nuked?

"How long to impact?" he asked gravely.

The man simply pointed to the auxiliary read-out screen. "There's the countdown, sir," he said. "Just below twenty minutes. Now at nineteen minutes and fifty seconds . . ."

Frost was trying his best to think straight. "Can we divert it in any way? Screw up its guidance systems or something?"

Just about everyone on the P-3's communications deck just shook their heads.

"There's nothing we can do," the communications man finally said. "There's nothing *anyone* can do."

Hunter had the Harrier's engine screaming at full speed as he rocketed nearly straight up into the sky south of Football City.

He knew it was hopeless. Checking his situation clock he saw it was just barely eight minutes before the missile's impact. Just spotting the incoming nuclear weapon would be close to impossible, even for someone with his keen eyesight. It would have to be a million-to-one-shot of being in the right place at the right time.

And even if he *did* spot the missile, then what?

342

He had about 80 rounds left in his cannon pod, but what good would shooting it do at this low altitude? It was probably an airburst warhead anyway, timed to go off at 10,000 feet and blow downward for maximum destruction. Even if he was able to intercept it at say, 20,000 feet, *and* get an accurate shot off, the warhead would probably still detonate. In fact, he would probably succeed only in allowing the blast and the deadly radioactive aftereffects to disperse over a wider area.

No—he knew the only way he could have averted a catastrophe was to intercept the missile way up near 50,000 feet, just as it was on its final re-entry path. Then, what he would have to do was get an exact shot, right on the warhead, and hope it wasn't completely fused yet. If all these things happened, then he might be able to prevent the warhead from going completely nuclear.

But there was a grave price to pay for this: If he got close enough to shoot at the warhead and it did break apart, then he'd be exposing himself to an invisible but instantaneous blast of radiation, one that would spread out in the upper atmosphere for miles in less than a second. It would only last a few seconds, but it would be enough to give him a quick, but very high dose.

Pushing the Harrier's throttle to the max, he continued his desperate climb, prepared as always to make the ultimate sacrifice.

Back at the recently rechristened Football City Airport, Jones, Cook and the other UA commanders were watching the grim drama unfold before their eyes on a huge tracking radar screen. The only major player not there was the mysterious Wolf. Apprised of the situation, he'd chosen to stay with his ship and crew.

"There's the missile!" one of the UA radar technicians declared, pointing to the small white blip that had just entered the green, oval screen. "It's sixty klicks out, eighteen high and coming on like crazy."

Jones did some quick calculations and then looked a Cook. "We've got less than three minutes."

The feeling of helplessness was hanging over the airpor control room like a lead cloud—indeed, it hung over the en tire city. After one of the most brilliant campaigns eve fought had regained freedom for a large portion of America it was now all going to go for naught, just because a crazy person had her finger on the button.

Jones turned away from the screen and stared out the hug window overlooking the airport. Hundreds of UA trooper were just standing around—more or less in a state of shock knowing what was about to happen, but simply not having enough time to do anything about it.

In the midst of these stunned soldiers, he saw one grimly amusing sight. Down on the tarmac, moving about the hand ful of captured Fourth Reich aircraft, was Roy From Troy notebook in hand, taking down the vital statistics of speci mens which in less than four minutes would be vaporized int little more than radioactive dust, along with everything else within twenty miles.

"A businessman to the end," Jones said, shaking his head. "Now *that* was America . . ."

Suddenly he heard a great *whoop!* come from the men gathered around the radar screen.

"I don't believe it!" Cook was yelling. "He did it. Hawk did it!"

Jones was back at the screen in a second. "What's happened?"

"The blip looks like its breaking up, sir," the radar tech said, trying his best to keep his cool.

Jones followed the man's finger; he saw that indeed, the white blip representing the missile had busted down into at least six little blips, and even they were fading from the screen.

344

"How can we be sure?" Jones asked.

"Just wait about fifteen seconds," the tech replied.

They all stood there, staring at the screen and at each other. Would the missile hit? Or had Hunter saved them all again—to the detriment of his own well-being.

Time crawled. Everyone had their watches up and their eyes glued on the seconds indicators.

"Five . . . four . . . three . . . two . . . one . . ."

Nothing happened.

Ten minutes later, the Harrier came in for a noisy, yet soft landing.

A crowd of troopers and technicians formed a wide circle around the jet, being careful not to get too close, as they assumed it had been irradiated. Pieces of the now harmless missile had fallen about twenty miles west of the city in a totally unoccupied area. But they were sure Hunter had flown through the resulting "hot" cloud.

The canopy popped and a weary Hunter climbed out. Somewhere, someone had dug out a radiation protection suit, and it was elected that Jones don it and go out and talk to the Wingman.

But no sooner had he climbed down from the wing when he was telling Jones that it was OK. Neither he nor the Harrier were hit by the radiation.

"You mean you didn't stop the missile?" Jones asked him incredulously as he removed the anti-radiation helmet.

Hunter was sadly shaking his head. "No, I never got high enough and I never saw it coming."

Jones was totally confused. Happy to see that Hunter was safe, but baffled about just how the nuclear disaster had been avoided.

"But Hawk," he finally managed to say. "If you didn't stop the missile, who did?"

Hunter turned to the north and pointed to the black air-

345

plane that was just lining up for a landing.

"He did . . ."

The specially adapted, long-range F-117G Stealth fighter bounced in for a less-than-perfect landing and taxied all the way to the far end of the base.

It sat there, its engines white-hot and smoking, its pilots not able to even pull the canopy release lever.

Now wearing the anti-radiation suit, Hunter walked slowly out to the airplane alone. He pushed a ladder up against the jet's cockpit and climbed up three steps, using the emergency release lever to pop the canopy.

Fitz was inside, his face pale and drawn, his eyes and nose running uncontrollably.

Hunter stuck his head inside the cockpit and grasped his old friend's hand.

"I was in the right place at the right time," Fitz explained, with a halting, weakened voice. "I'd been following Frost's radio communications the whole way up."

"You saved us all," Hunter told him, never letting go of his friend's hand. "We were as good as dead, and you saved us."

Fitz coughed once, hard, and then had trouble catching his breath.

"It's eating me up inside," he said, his voice fading. "I can feel it . . ."

Hunter squeezed his friend's hand. He tried to speak, but couldn't.

"Did you find Dominique, Hawk?" Fitz asked him out of the blue. "Is she . . . alive?"

Hunter just nodded. "I think so, Mike," he managed to say.

"And we beat the bastards, didn't we?" Fitz said, his voice getting weaker with every word.

"*You* beat them," Hunter replied.

Fitz managed one last laugh. "You're the one who came up with the grand scheme," he said, each word coming harder

346

than the one before it. "Making me out to be some kind of miracle worker. How were you able to do it, Hawk? How did you arrange for it to look like I actually saved those people from drowning in the river? Or brought that guy back who'd been nailed to the cross? Or the guy from Gary, who'd been cut up so badly in the big gun blast? It must have taken some doing . . ."

Hunter stared in at his friend. He knew he was fading fast, but . . .

"Hey, Fitz," he said, squeezing his hand for a final time. "I don't know what the hell you're talking about."

Fitz looked up at him, his eyes widened to twice their normal size. He tried to say something but he no longer could speak. He gripped Hunter's hand, the look on his face being one of total bafflement and then, maybe finally, some kind of understanding.

Then he leaned back and smiled.

And then Fitz died.

Epilogue

Loki Mountain

"Crunch" had his troopers arrayed in the best possible defensive positions, but he knew it was probably hopeless.

Far below, but getting closer, he and the remaining Pacific American militiamen could see no less than six Puma helicopters ascending toward them. If each Puma had twenty five Nazi soldiers onboard, then the odds would be one hundred and fifty to twenty five, or six to one.

It was one bad bet.

"Crunch" was angry—at himself as much as the approaching Nazis. Maybe he'd screwed up a long time ago by bringing this little unit up to Loki. What had he been thinking of? What drove him to do it? They had been carrying one of the most important items in postwar America all around the Rockies with them, and if he'd been smart, he would have just hid it away someplace and waited for a better time.

But no, something had compelled him to put it all together again, and to display it, in hopes that someone would see it and know that at least one great American was not dead.

Looking back toward the very top of the summit of Loki, he suddenly felt very foolish. It had taken them almost two months to put it back together, even still he doubted if it actually worked. But every piece was in its proper place—if that counted for anything.

At that moment a streak of sunlight broke through the perpetually cloudy overcast, and fell on the F-16XL jet fighter that seemed teetering on the peak of the mountain.

"What the hell *was* I thinking of?" he asked himself one more time.

The Pumas were overhead now and circling. "Crunch" and his men had no anti-aircraft weapons, in fact they were armed with little else than rifles and machineguns. He'd told them earlier not to waste precious bullets shooting at the helicopters before they landed. Every shot would have to count when the Nazis hit the ground and came out attacking.

But then a very strange thing happened.

One of the doors on the nearest hovering Puma opened and a white sheet was draped out. Suddenly the same thing happened to a second chopper. Then another, and another.

Within a half minute, all six choppers were displaying large white flags.

"What the hell is going on, sir?" Nick, the grizzled old militiaman yelled back to "Crunch." "These guys look like they're surrendering . . . to us!"

"Crunch" had no reply. Nothing fit. But then the choppers descended and sure enough, the Nazi troopers began piling out, the hands raised over their heads and screaming: *"Ubergabe!"* over the combined roar of the six chopper engines.

"Goddamn, they are giving up," "Crunch" whispered to himself, not quite believing what he was seeing. "What the hell has happened?"

Suddenly, one of the young militiamen was standing at his side. It was the same man who'd spoken to him so gravely the night they'd miraculously escaped the pursuing Asian armored column.

"I don't know what's going on, sir," the young man said. "But I feel like I've just come back from the dead."